PENGUIN BOOKS

THIEF OF LIGHT

David Ramus is a former art dealer, who lives with his wife and three daughters in Atlanta, Georgia. *Thief of Light* is his first novel.

DAVID RAMUS

THIEF OF LIGHT

PENGUIN BOOKS

SIGNET

Published by the Penguin Group
Penguin Books Ltd, 27 Wrights Lane, London w8 5tz, England
Penguin Books USA Inc., 375 Hudson Street, New York, New York 10014, USA
Penguin Books Australia Ltd, Ringwood, Victoria, Australia
Penguin Books Canada Ltd, 10 Alcorn Avenue, Toronto, Ontario, Canada m4v 3b2
Penguin Books (NZ) Ltd, 182–190 Wairau Road, Auckland 10, New Zealand

Penguin Books Ltd, Registered Offices: Harmondsworth, Middlesex, England

First published in the United States of America by HarperCollins 1995
First published in Great Britain by Hamish Hamilton Ltd 1995
Published in Signet 1996
Reprinted in Penguin Books 1997
1 3 5 7 9 10 8 6 4 2

Set in 9.5/12pt Monotype Plantin
Typeset by Datix International Limited, Bungay, Suffolk
Printed in England by Clays Ltd, St Ives plc

For Cathryn

With special thanks to Larry Ashmead and Jason Kaufman, for their efforts at making this novel a success, to Molly Friedrich and Sherri Holman, both of whom are formidable allies, to Mary Fowler, whose sharp criticism and intelligent advice were invaluable, Charles McNair, Madison Prickett, Jane Griffin, Cheryl McEwin, and my mother, Connie Kaufman, who believed fairy tales can come true.

PROLOGUE

The artist chewed the end of his brush, oblivious to the thick white paint spotting his lips, and glared at the unfinished canvas. To hell with this, he thought, standing back from the painting, gnawing harder on the brush. It had been this way for weeks. He had never experienced painter's block before, but he sure as hell had run into a stone wall now. Thoroughly disgusted with his lack of progress, he squeezed his eyes shut and tried to think it through. Instead, he imagined himself casting for bonefish in the skinny waters off Cat Cay. Doing something real. Something tangible. You either caught one, and held on for all you were worth, the fly-rod alive in your hands as the fish split the shallow salt water, or you didn't. He shook himself out of his daydream and opened his eyes. The painting hadn't changed.

He thought about putting down his brushes and leaving it the way it was. It looked okay. Most would think it beautiful. But it was still wrong. He wasn't sure why – but it didn't sing. And more than anything, fishing included, Paul McHenry wanted his work to sing.

Struggling to correct the problem, he pressed harder, but the more he pressed, the more elusive the late afternoon light became. He laid a stroke of lead white across the reflection of a cloud, then changed brushes and pushed more viridian onto the surface of the water, moving back and forth, stalking the canvas like a hunter. But still the light defied him. He advanced, then retreated, squinting to observe the effects of his efforts.

Finally he put down his brushes and palette, wiped his thin fingers on a rag, and stood back.

How the hell had Monet looked at a lily-covered pond and seen the light so clearly? He pressed the heels of his hands into his eyes, then up through his thinning brown hair, smearing a long streak of pale green paint across his high forehead.

McHenry leaned back against a long oak table. It sagged under the weight of paint tubes and jars of pigments, cans of mineral spirits and turpentine, old rags, and hundreds of brushes standing in coffee cans. He glanced at the drink he'd poured over an hour ago, then reached down and picked up a large jar of powdered lapis lazuli and held it up, the blue mineral vivid in the studio lights. It reminded him of the Gulf Stream.

Putting the jar down in its exact spot, he took up his brushes and palette, then turned back to the painting. The light. Concentrate on how Monet had seen the light. He lifted the brush. Damn, Monet hadn't had to deal with a partner like Adrian Sellars. He hesitated, then backed away.

Strands of his long sparse hair were plastered to his pink scalp in some places, standing out wildly in others. He hadn't shaved in days, and his stubble, as patchy as his hair, formed odd bristly continents on his flushed cheeks.

He could hear his partner's voice, 'You're overworking it. Just finish it. Finish. Finish . . .'

Why doesn't he understand, McHenry wondered. It's not just a forgery. Then he added out loud, as if addressing both Adrian and the gods of painting, 'It's alive, damn you. I've put life into it. One brushstroke at a time. It'll be finished when I say it's finished. Not before.' He pointed at the canvas with a sharp jab of the brush. 'Tanaka will have to wait, and so will you, Adrian Sellars.'

His words ricocheted off the walls of the loft. If the gods of painting were listening, they remained silent, unimpressed.

McHenry lifted his brush again, Adrian's words echoing in his mind. There was a fortune at stake – $650,000 – once he completed the canvas. But he was beginning to doubt he'd ever finish. He hesitated and lowered the brush again. His head was spinning. 'Tanaka . . . Finish . . . You're overworking it . . . Finish.' He felt dizzy, light-headed. There wasn't enough air in the loft. He wanted to scream.

Instead, he paced the open area between his studio and the back door, thinking about the money. Soon there would be enough to start painting his own creations, whether they sold or not. He walked back over to the table, picked up his glass, drained the inch or so of vodka that remained, and took up his position. Leaning against the table, he looked at the canvas for a long time. He sucked on the ice cubes, scrutinizing his work, trying to figure out what was missing.

Then, on the verge of giving up and going out for air and a bite to eat, he saw it. Adrian had been right: the painting didn't need more work, it needed less.

Fatigue and hunger forgotten, he picked up a dry brush and scrubbed most of the cloud reflections on the surface of the water, lifting off the feathered strokes of white paint that suddenly looked so wrong. Then he reworked the reflections, using a much subtler touch, slightly altering his palette, lightening the grays and blues, standing back occasionally to admire his work. Finally satisfied, he took up a fresh brush and carefully applied the signature of Claude Monet. Then he added his own hidden cipher, exactly five centimeters in from the center of the left edge, completing a forgery he knew would stand up to the closest scrutiny.

He was reaching for the phone when a sharp cracking noise jolted him. The door to the back stairwell splintered and crashed open. Two teenagers burst in.

'Down motherfucker! Get your ass on the floor. Now!' the larger of the two shouted. He was massive, with a shaved head gleaming in the harsh glare of the studio lights. Breathing hard, he gestured vehemently toward the floor with a crowbar clamped in his fist.

McHenry froze. His mouth suddenly felt like it was full of wet sand, and although he meant to obey, he just stood there, gaping.

The smaller one giggled and chanted a rap. 'I am a stone killer . . . A nightmare walkin' . . .'

'Fuck you, man, I said down,' the tall one cursed, raising the crowbar and smashing it down on McHenry's left shoulder. The iron bar made a sickening crunch as it hit him.

The rap penetrated the gauzy haze that enveloped McHenry. The hardwood floor felt cool against his cheek. Opening his eyes, he eased onto his back. His shoulder was burning. When he reached across his body to touch it, white hot blossoms exploded behind his eyes, and squeezed the breath from his chest. Overcome by a wave of dizziness, he retched and tried not to vomit. Then he was floating in a white silence.

A loud thump brought him up from the depths. His eyes flicked open. McHenry couldn't see the two intruders, but he could hear them moving around the loft. He didn't want to see them again, he wanted out. He tried to get up, pushing against the floor with his good arm, but his sight blurred around the edges. This time

4

he fought it. Goddamn, his neck and shoulder were on fire.

He managed to turn around by pushing against the floor an inch at a time with his legs, while he cradled his arm. With each push his shoulder made an ominous grinding noise, cold sweat ran down the back of his neck, and pulsating shadows hovered at the edge of his vision. But he kept on. Eventually, he faced the back corner of his loft. The door was now on his left, the studio to his right. He swallowed hard, and tried to lever himself up so that he could gauge the distance to the stairs. If he could make it down to the second floor, he might find Don or Marty; they would help him. He noticed his stereo and VCR, now stacked by the shattered door. Something in his shoulder gave, and he fell back.

When he opened his eyes again the smaller of the two was standing over him.

'Go. Just take what you want and go.' His own voice sounded weak, like it was coming from a distance.

'Shut the fuck up,' the kid replied, prodding Mc-Henry with a Nike-clad foot. He turned and looked at his friend. 'I'm tellin' you man, when I was up to her crib movin' boxes, I heard her on the phone. Bitch didn't even know I was listenin' in on her shit – told someone this dickhead is rich.'

The kid's eyes were dilated, they seemed to spin like pinwheels as he pulled a straight razor from the pocket of his jeans and flicked it open. He began chanting his sick bit about a nightmare. McHenry looked up at him, the coppery taste of fear coating his tongue.

'Maybe something wrong with your ears,' the tall one called out, bending over the stereo equipment by the door. 'Don't see no fuckin' fortune – what you say we call and ask her where it's stashed?'

5

'Fuck that – the bitch go nuts she find out we here.'

'Hey, nigger, you sound scared a' her – goddamned peewee.'

'Peewee?'

McHenry felt the kid tense. His own breath caught in his throat.

'That's right. Peewee. You a fuckin' peewee, till I say different.' The tall one drew himself up to his full height and stared down at the kid. 'Ain't nothin' look like no fortune here. You done fucked up, as usual. Screw up again and you ain't even a peewee, you clean outta my crew. Understand? Now let's get this shit and jet.'

The kid flinched. Then he averted his eyes. 'What about this motherfucker, R.J.?'

'He all fucked up, Peewee, leave him be.' R.J. waved dismissively. 'Come on and help me, we gonna see what the rockman think a' this shit,' he ordered, examining McHenry's CD changer.

'I ain't no fuckin' peewee,' the kid muttered under his breath. Waving his razor, eyes spinning, he turned toward McHenry and added, 'I'll show you who's a fuckin' peewee 'round here. I'll cut your fuckin' ears off you keep lookin' at me that way.'

McHenry immediately dropped his gaze down to Peewee's unlaced shoes. Every muscle in his body went rigid as Peewee straddled him and planted one foot on his stomach. McHenry held his breath and risked looking up. Peewee's eyes were closed, his young face slack. His body jerked, and his head moved to the beat of his rap. McHenry stared into that empty vessel of a face and heard himself whispering a childhood prayer he thought long forgotten. 'Now I lay me down to sleep . . .' Peewee stepped over him into the studio. McHenry closed his eyes, and exhaled.

'R.J., check this, I'm an arteest. What you think, man?'

McHenry looked up and cried 'No!' – but it just seemed to egg him on. Peewee picked up McHenry's brush and palette and tagged the still wet painting with a large red *X* underlined by two squiggles.

'Stop it. Please stop,' McHenry begged. 'I'll get you money. I've got money in the bank.' He pushed with his legs until he was facing the two of them.

'Goddamn, Peewee, you a sight. Let me try that.' R.J. took the brush from him and added his own tag.

'Please. You don't know what you're doing,' Mc-Henry pleaded, slapping weakly on the floor with his right hand. 'Take what you want and go, but leave the painting alone.'

R.J. and Peewee took turns embellishing their graffiti.

Peewee looked over the table of brushes and paints. 'How much rock you think we get for this shit?'

'Not much,' R.J. answered.

'Well, fuck it then,' Peewee said, picking up jars of pigments and hurling them against the wall beyond the painting. R.J. joined him. By the time they were through, McHenry's brushes had been reduced to kindling, and every jar and tube of paint lay crushed and broken. Peewee surveyed the wreckage, then took out his razor and sliced his graffiti tag from the center of the 'Monet.'

Tears of rage and pain slid down McHenry's unshaved cheeks. 'You didn't have to do that,' he whispered. 'You're animals. Fucking animals.'

'You talkin' to me?' Peewee asked, stepping toward McHenry, the razor in his right hand, the fragment of canvas trailing in his left.

Peewee dropped the canvas and grabbed a handful of

McHenry's hair, pulling him up to a sitting position. His shoulder popped and crunched, a blinding flash of pain shot up his neck, and he was floating again. When he opened his eyes, the two of them were nose to nose. The kid's breath was hot against his cheek. He inhaled its sour odor as he struggled to breathe, and was surprised by the softness of his skin. Peewee jabbed his crushed shoulder with the razor, and the blossoms burst bright white behind his eyes again.

When his vision cleared he was looking into Peewee's glazed eyes. Instantly, a leaden ball of ice formed in his gut. There wasn't any hatred burning in those shuttered windows. They were absolutely blank. There was nothing behind those spinning eyes, and that terrified McHenry more than anything he'd ever imagined. As the cold blade pressed against his face, his bladder let go.

The first slash went all the way through his cheek, the razor scraping against his teeth. A low guttural groan forced its way up from his chest and lodged in his throat. He gagged on the blood, choking, unable to spit it out. A silent shriek tore at the roots of his consciousness. And the razor was coming down again, glittering in the light. Everything was happening too fast. He flinched, but Peewee's grip on his hair was too firm. A stinging blow hit his neck. He hovered on the edge of a precipice, wrapped in white cotton. As the razor dug in again, the scrape of sharpened steel against bone penetrated his haze only dimly. His head jerked as the blade pulled free.

He began to drift, to float away, connected to the madness only by the thrumming beat of his heart. And when that faded and eventually stopped, he floated higher. Freed from the tethers of his life, he floated higher still, up into a bright effervescence, understanding for the first time the true nature of light.

Outside Peewee continued chanting his rap:

> ORIGINAL GANGSTA, MONSTER TALKIN' . . .
> A STONE KILLER, A NIGHTMARE WALKIN' . . .

He stopped for a moment, shifted the VCR he was carrying, and felt in the pocket of his starter jacket, just to be sure. Then he smiled to himself and continued down the street. He hadn't forgotten to take McHenry's ears.

CHAPTER ONE

Ten thousand dollars in used hundreds makes a stack between one and two inches thick. Worn from countless fingers that at one time or another had caressed them, the bills were soft, limp in my hands as I counted them out. They didn't make much of a bulge as I slid them into the inside pocket of my suit coat. Still, the weight of them lying against my chest sent a little shiver, a thrill dancing up my spine.

The empty safe deposit box made a hollow thump as I slid it into its slot. I shook the box once to make sure that it was all the way in, then I rang for the guard to relock the little door that secured it.

'All finished, Mr Sellars?'

'Yes,' I told him. That was it. The last of my cash until I closed the deal with Tanaka.

'Very good, sir. We'll see you in a few weeks, as usual?' he asked.

I nodded. Maybe. Damn, McHenry had better finish soon.

The main floor of the bank looked more like a train station than a financial institution, with its vaulted ceilings, hard surfaces and gilt, heavy mahogany furniture. Looking around, I half expected to hear announcements of arrivals and departures, but there were no trains, no loudspeakers, only the quiet murmur of discreet business, and the tap-tap of well-heeled customers striding across an enormous expanse of shiny black Italian marble.

On my way out the head teller, Nancy Grinnell, called

out, 'Adrian!' and waved from her window. My partner, Steven Ballard, called her 'the Grinder.'

He and Nancy had dated for a few months, but recently Steven had rather abruptly ended their affair. I never asked why he called her 'the Grinder'; it seemed obvious enough. You could always tell when Steven had spent the night with Nancy. The next day he seemed to move in slow motion, walking with an exaggerated, bowlegged gait, as though each step were a painful reminder of some poorly considered but interesting conjugal exercise. I smiled at her and waved.

'Come here,' she mouthed.

She was attractive, in a platinum-blond kind of way. Just a kid, but sexy as hell, even in her banker clothes. I liked her.

'Come over here,' she repeated in her thick Brooklyn accent. I looked at my watch.

'I'm late,' I mouthed, pointing at my wrist.

Her face fell. She turned back to her cash drawer.

I took another couple of steps, but something in her wilted expression tugged at me. I hesitated, then walked over to her window and waited for her to finish counting.

'You doing all right, Nancy?'

She looked up. 'I thought you were late.' Her voice was pouty, a good trick with her accent.

'I am. What's up?'

'I haven't heard from Steven. Why hasn't he returned my calls?'

'Well . . . it's a busy time for us, the auctions, out-of-town clients –'

'He could have called.'

A line was forming behind me.

I shifted my weight and looked at my watch. 'Listen, I

really am late. You want me to tell him I ran into you – that you asked about him?'

She nodded. 'Would you? That would be good.' A hint of a smile returned to her face.

Outside I buttoned my coat and leaned into the wind. Fall had started out mildly enough, but for the past couple of days the temperature had hovered around the freezing mark. With the wind, it felt more like February than the week before Thanksgiving. Oscar Fedder was expecting me at three forty-five. If I hurried, I might get there by four o'clock, but my mind wasn't on the art world. I tapped the money in my pocket, and my pulse quickened. I wondered what Marta was wearing.

The Hampton-Smith Galleries occupy a four-story brownstone on East Sixty-fourth, between Fifth and Madison. The place reeked of money and power. I stopped and looked at the small display window set in the limestone exterior. The Matisse that had been hanging there was gone. Damn, I should have found a way to buy it. My fingers had itched from the moment I first saw it. A line drawing, no larger than a cereal box, of a woman with swept-back hair and almond eyes. Something in her smiling face was beguiling. She was seductive and challenging at the same time. With barely a handful of strokes, Matisse had captured her essence. And what an essence she must have had; even on paper she looked wild. Matisse had been a laser with a pencil. Maybe it wasn't sold. I wondered if I could talk Fedder into letting me take it on the arm; I didn't owe him that much.

Inside the gallery was hushed, intimidating. The first two floors were display space devoted to changing exhibitions. The third floor was set aside for offices and a private viewing room, where the big fish were treated like royalty. I had never been in the basement. It was rumored to hold more than five hundred million dollars in inventory on any given day. Oscar Fedder, His Highness, kept watch on his domain from the fourth floor, which housed his inner sanctum. A lavish suite of offices, an exercise room with Nautilus training equipment, a sauna, a whirlpool, a private dining room complete with kitchen and French chef, took up half the floor. The other half housed Fedder's research library, one of the best in the world. Oscar Fedder was the Hampton-Smith Galleries. There never was a Hampton, or a Smith. They were just a couple of WASP names Fedder had picked out of the phone book.

After I stood at the front desk for a moment, my eyes watering, happy to be out of the wind, the girl manning the telephone looked up and smiled. She rolled her azure eyes, trying to explain to someone on the phone how to get from the Empire State Building to the Hampton-Smith Galleries. After a lengthy explanation of which way Fifth Avenue ran, she put down the phone. She was all black curls and blue-eyed innocence, twenty-two, twenty-three at the oldest.

'Can I help you?' she asked in a soft New England accent.

She had the longest eyelashes I had ever seen. Probably just graduated from Bryn Mawr or Sarah Lawrence, and now she was spending a year or two in New York to round out her education. A gallery girl. There must have been a thousand like her in New York. Living off their trust funds, working for peanuts just to be part of the art scene. This one was prettier than most. I was wondering if she was as innocent as she looked when a booming voice behind me interrupted my fantasies.

'Adrian Sellars, leave Sandra alone. She's new here, and I haven't had a chance to warn her about you.'

I didn't need to see Shelby Lewis to know it was her.

'Jesus, Shelby, I haven't even said a word.' I was still making eye contact with Sandra.

Sandra's smile grew a little vague as her eyes flicked from me to Shelby, then back again. Not sure what to make of it all, she looked relieved when the phone rang. As she answered it, I reluctantly turned and faced Shelby.

'What am I going to have to do to protect my girls? Put a written memo on the time clock about you?' All three of her chins jiggled as she wagged an index finger the size of a sausage under my nose. 'Warning! Adrian Sellars could be dangerous to your sanity and well-being. Stay clear at all costs.' She laughed, a low series of barks, then held out her arms for a hug.

She was in her late forties, with a motherly streak as big as her waist. She was Oscar Fedder's right hand, but she also considered herself the den mother of the Hampton-Smith gallery girls. Shelby was probably the only serious chaperone left in New York City. The girls didn't know how lucky they were to have her.

'Shelby, one of these days I'm going to get past you. Then you'll find out I'm not the evil predator you think. I'm just misunderstood.' I embraced her ample girth and kissed her on the cheek.

'Misunderstood?' She laughed again. 'Right. Like a fox in the henhouse you're misunderstood. Come on, Oscar is expecting you.' As we walked to the elevator, she glanced at her watch. 'You're late.'

'How's His Lordship's mood today?' I asked. Then I looked at my watch. I was all of three minutes late. Fedder ran a tight ship.

She shrugged, then reached up and smoothed down the collar of my coat. 'Pay the man, Adrian. He thinks you're a comer, some kind of new talent. He can be a good friend, but take my word for it, he's a lousy enemy.'

So, Fedder wanted his money. I thought that might have been why he had summoned me. I tried to decide on the right stalling tactic. What the hell had I told Fedder last time we talked?

I nodded at Shelby and tried to keep the conversation going while I came up with a plan. 'What's new in your life, Shelby? You breaking any hearts?'

'Forget it, Adrian. I'm too old, too fat, and way too smart to fall for your flattery. Save it for the Sandras of the world.' She turned and pretended to glare at me. 'Someone else's Sandras, not mine.'

We rode the next two floors in silence.

When we got to the fourth floor she led me into the library and asked me to take a seat at the large, round mahogany table that filled the center of the book-lined room. I did. She winked at me, smile back in place, and shut the door behind her as she left. Then I twiddled my thumbs for twenty minutes, nervously waiting for Oscar Fedder to make an appearance, still not sure what I was going to tell him.

He blew into the room – there's no other way to describe it. The door suddenly swung open, and Oscar Fedder appeared in the center of the room. He didn't walk in, or make an entrance. One minute he wasn't there, then before I could blink, he was standing in front of me, hand extended, smiling behind his thick glasses. I stood.

'Adrian, so good of you to come. How are things, my boy?'

There is nothing I find more repugnant about the art world than the 'art voice.' Leroy Neiman's paintings don't bother me nearly as much as that slightly bitchy, Northeastern, upper-class drawl that too many art professionals affect, even if they were born and raised in Madison, Wisconsin. Oscar Fedder wasn't from Wisconsin, but he had, over the years, perfected a pared-down art voice. A drawn-out, nasal whining of the simplest words. A William Buckleyish profaning, weighting even an informal greeting with enough pretentiousness to make a normal person cringe.

But I've never thought of myself as a normal person. If I were, I wouldn't be in this business. When I answered him, enough smarm had crept into my own voice to make me wince.

'I'm fine, sir. How about you?' A trickle of sweat ran down my back.

'Sit down,' he said, taking a seat next to me at the table. 'Adrian, we have to talk about your account with Hampton-Smith. You owe us over a hundred and thirty thousand dollars. I understand that you also owe Christie's and Sotheby's substantial amounts of money. We need to do something about it.'

'There have been many times that I've owed you more than that, Oscar. I've always paid my debts.' I wondered where he got his information. McHenry had better fucking well finish soon, otherwise there were going to be more meetings like this with my other creditors. I could almost hear the grapevine humming. Did you hear? Oscar Fedder has cut off Sellars and Ballard.

I kept my voice flat and added, 'Oscar, there's no need to worry, we're just running a little late. We have plenty of inventory and receivables to cover our obligations –

all of them.' I looked him straight in the eye as I spoke, but the back of my shirt suddenly felt plastered to my skin.

He smiled and nodded, but his eyes, magnified by his thick lenses, never blinked. 'That's well and good, Adrian. I'm happy things are going well for you. You have a great eye. I understand you've been buying heavily. I hope you've used your credit wisely and not over-extended yourself.'

I thought about the Matisse.

Fedder continued. 'Once you catch up on your debts, you can begin to take things on the arm again. Until then, I'm afraid you won't be able to borrow from us on consignment anymore.'

'You're cutting me off?'

'I'm sorry, Adrian. In time, I'm sure you'll prove to be one of the great dealers. When that time comes, I hope you will consider me to have been one of your early believers. Someone who helped pave the way. However, bookkeeping tells me that you haven't made a payment to us in almost two months.'

I pursed my lips and pretended to consider the accuracy of his accounting. Then I nodded. The room seemed hot. Fedder sat coiled like an adder.

'Your accountant is right, Oscar. We are almost sixty days late. But I'm expecting payment any day now for a very significant sale. If you would please bear with me a little longer, I'll get caught up.'

He stood and walked to the bookshelves, then turned and faced me. 'Adrian, the art world is a small place. The air gets very thin at the top. Your reputation may be the most valuable asset you have. Hampton-Smith has provided you access to our inventory for several years now. We've proudly watched you grow. I personally couldn't be happier. But I want you to make a good-faith payment to me. Today. Nothing too strenuous. Say ten thousand dollars. Just to show me that I can count on you.'

He smiled, but there was nothing resembling warmth in the upturned corners of his thin lips. All of his talk about reputation would have been fine coming from almost anyone else. True, Oscar Fedder was one of the most successful art dealers in the world, but if I had a hundred dollars for every story I had heard about his underhanded business tactics, and another hundred dollars for every lawsuit from a disgruntled consignor that he had somehow settled, I wouldn't have to peddle art. I could afford to collect it.

The stack of hundreds in my pocket grew heavier as he continued.

'It's a small town, Adrian. I happen to be lucky enough to have a big voice in it. Treat me as you would family, and you'll do quite well.'

His cold smile and the condescension in his voice triggered the streak of defiance in me that had too often led to trouble with authority figures. I knew I should hand Fedder the ten thousand, the same way I knew that I shouldn't have told Judge Luther Alverson, who presided over my last divorce, exactly what I thought of him and his kangaroo court. But knowing and doing are two different things. I tried to push Marta out of my mind and started to reach for the money. Then I looked up at Oscar Fedder standing in front of his books, hands thrust into the pockets of his perfectly creased gray flannels, that superior grin dancing on his face, and I just couldn't do it.

I stood up, the money in my pocket blinking on and off like a beacon. To hell with Fedder. As soon as

McHenry finished, I'd have more than enough money to pay him in full. Until then I had other plans.

'Oscar, I appreciate everything you've done for me. Please bear with me – I'll get a payment to you by the end of the week.' I held out my hand to shake on it.

A look of surprise flashed across his face. I'm not sure anyone had recently said no to him. He frowned, hands still in his pockets.

'You do that, Adrian. You get me a payment by the end of the week.' He shook his head, and walked out of the library almost as quickly as he had come in. I stared after him, then I looked down and realized that I was still holding out my hand.

CHAPTER TWO

My visit to Oscar Fedder had taken longer than planned. By the time I made it back to my place it was five o'clock, and I was running late. I tossed my briefcase onto the bed. No time to change. I checked the clip of the nine-millimeter I kept in the night table, slipped it into the pocket of my overcoat, and walked out of my apartment. I was going to have to hustle to find a cab that would take me up to Spanish Harlem during rush hour.

While I waited for the elevator, I played around with the gun, practicing a couple of 'quick draws' in the mirror. The door to my neighbor's apartment suddenly opened, and Mrs Keene stepped out, a small sack of garbage in her hand. I was crouched in a shooter's position, teeth bared, sighting down the barrel of the automatic at my reflection.

'Good afternoon, Adrian,' she said, then her eyes grew wide. 'What in the world are you doing with that gun?'

'I . . . I'm . . . I'm just making sure that it's safe,' I stammered, standing up and lowering the gun to my side. 'I was checking the safety. You have to be careful with these things.'

'I should hope so.'

'Yes ma'am, you have to be careful,' I repeated as I slipped the gun back into my pocket, willing the elevator to hurry up.

'It's always better to be safe than sorry,' she said as she walked toward the utility room. Then she turned and added, 'Come by for a cup of tea when you have a few moments – I'll show you the forty-four magnum my husband gave me last Christmas.'

On the elevator I decided that it wasn't just me, the whole damned world was mad.

By the time I got to the corner of Second Avenue and 114th Street it was six o'clock. Last month, less than a block from here a fourteen-year-old was shot in the head, left barefoot and dying over a pair of Air Jordans. I tried not to think about the stack of bills pressing against my chest, wishing I had taken time to change out of my suit and tie. Oscar Fedder seemed like someone from another life.

It was thirty-four degrees under a November sky quickly turning from dark gray to charcoal black. The wind was blowing cold off the East River, chasing most of the foot traffic inside. It swirled through the concrete canyons of upper Manhattan, carrying with it the smell of garbage and burned tacos from the vendor carts staked out along Second Avenue. The lights in the barred store windows were coming on, illuminating cheap furniture, glitzy stereos and boom boxes, racks of candy bars, cigarettes, and malt liquor.

I couldn't stop sweating, even with my coat unbuttoned. I was lit up with a heady mixture of fear and anticipation. If I had to pull the gun I carried on these runs, I wasn't sure I could hold on to it, much less hit anything.

I was halfway between the corner and Marta's building when I felt someone behind me. I turned and saw the old man. He was toothless and wore a watch cap pulled down low over his forehead. His mahogany skin looked polished, and his eyes shone as he sized me up.

'Mighty fine coat you're sportin', boss,' he said, taking hold of my sleeve and fingering the material.

I pulled back, then turned away.

'Ain't you got the courtesy to say hello to a man? Young fella like you got the world by the balls. Cain't spare a man a little somethin' to get warm next to?'

He spoke loudly, as if hard of hearing, and kept on coming. Reaching into my pocket, I gave him the first bill I came up with, a twenty, and left him staring after me.

Marta lived in a high-rise brick building that looked more like a prison than the low-income housing project it was. Maybe that was the point. Scarred and covered in graffiti, it was not a welcoming place. I never fully understood why she chose to live there. I assumed it was because of her business.

Whoever her connections were, they had enough juice to help her take over two apartments in a city-owned project and keep them. I wondered if they also controlled the streets. More than once when I approached her building, I had the feeling I was being watched. The kids loitering around the project, wearing colors and flashing signs, scared the hell out of me. But none of them had ever approached or hassled me.

Just the same, I was glad to be armed. I entered the building and crossed the grim lobby, sticking out like a sore thumb in my suit and camel hair coat. While I waited for the elevator, my left hand resting on the money, my right on a gun I hoped I would never pull, two teenage Hispanic girls came out of the stairwell and walked toward me. Neither spoke till after they'd passed me.

'What the fuck's that yuppie dickhead doin' here?'

23

'Be cool, bitch, he's here to see her highness.' Laughter echoed behind them as they hit the street.

The twelfth floor looked like the lobby but smelled worse – of unwashed bodies, cheap perfume, and fried food. I could hear a baby crying and two women arguing in Spanish. Halfway down the narrow hallway, I stopped in front of apartment 12G. I stared for a moment at the door.

I'd stood outside this door more often than I cared to admit. Against my better judgment, my instinct for self-preservation, disregarding the promises I've made myself to stay away, I found myself standing, out of breath and sweating, in front of Marta's door again. Telling myself to turn around and leave, even as I lifted my hand to knock.

It took several hard raps on the door to get a reaction from Marta. I'm not sure whether it was a reflection of her attitude or a result of her reinforced steel door.

'Come in, Adrian – I'm sorry I didn't hear you knocking.'

Marta's voice slays me. Deep and throaty, it hints at her Caribbean origins and her Castilian ancestors. She locked the door behind me, stood on her toes, and without a word kissed me hard on the mouth, both arms encircling my waist, a move I used to think was pure desire. I now understood that her smooth once-over would tell her what I was carrying and where it was on my body. Her hand brushed past the pocket that held my gun, hesitated, then continued on. Marta was not a woman to be taken lightly.

'You brought your end?' she asked, with mock severity.

'Marta, would it do any good to come here broke?'

'For you, sweetie, anything. You know I love you.'

24

Knowing I knew better than to come to her without cash, Marta Batista flipped her shoulder-length dark hair over one eye, blinked, and walked to the back bedroom.

Apartment 12G always dazzled me. It wasn't typical for this part of New York City, certainly not what you would expect in this building. Once you made it through the heavily reinforced door, the smell of the hallway, the decay of the building, and the other tenants all seemed very remote. With flair and a significant commitment of dollars, Marta had taken two low-rent units in a down-and-out building and turned them into a lavish playground, complete with mirrored walls, period antiques, Aubusson rugs, nineteenth-century French paintings. Marta's connections had to be heavy for her to remain untouched, even behind her locked door, in this garbage heap.

'You'll stay all night, Adrian.'

I was never sure with Marta of the difference between a request and an order.

Without waiting for an answer, she opened the tortoiseshell box she had retrieved from the bedroom. Handing it to me, she said, 'A friend brought me this back from Bangkok; it's special, I saved it for you.'

'The weight?' I asked.

'The same as always, but it's the quality that makes it sooo wonderful. Taste it.'

Marta is one of the sexiest and most mysterious women I have ever seen. Forget Hollywood. The sense of danger and forbidden pleasure she radiates is for real. But once she opened that tortoiseshell box, I had eyes only for the bag of China White heroin that filled it. I had never been able to separate the dark compulsion that drew me to Marta's playground from the hunger of my habit. But after two bumps of the dope I didn't care. I removed the heroin from the tortoiseshell box and re-placed it with the ten thousand dollars I had brought. I laid out enough dope to take Marta and me where we wanted to go and carefully put the rest in a special leather case I carried just for this purpose.

I could taste the bitterness of the smack in the back of my throat and feel the heated chill of its embrace. I drew Marta down next to me on the sofa, stroked the hair out of her eyes, and kissed her long and slow, savoring the thrill of her and the release of the smack into my system.

'Stand up,' I commanded.

'Now?' she asked, pulling out the band that held my ponytail.

'Yeah. Stand in front of me and undress. Do it slowly and don't say a word until I tell you.' I read once that eroticism lies in the erection, not in the orgasm. I picked up the silk ropes that were draped across the arm of the sofa and ran my hands along their length.

Marta did as I instructed, silently. She brought to mind a large jungle cat. She slowly, languorously un-dressed, exaggerating every stretch and move till she stood naked in front of me. A light sheen of perspiration covered her skin. She looked at me expectantly as I knot-ted the ropes, waiting for my next order, knowing she would get her turn.

CHAPTER THREE

I came to, late the following morning, in my own apartment, feeling sick. Nights with Marta had a bad habit of bleeding into the next day. At thirty-eight, I was getting old for this shit.

The bag of smack trembled in my hands as I spooned out enough to kill the shakes. I swore to myself for the thousandth time that I would cut back, even as the dope found its way into my bloodstream. I had tried before; I just didn't know how to let go of it.

Hot water sprayed out of the shower head with enough force to sting. While it beat down on my neck and shoulders, I thought about calling my daughter, Caitlin. Thanksgiving was next week; maybe we could spend part of the holiday weekend together this year. I considered the best way to approach her mother for extra visitation, then decided I wasn't really in the mood for another long-distance argument with my ex-wife. I could picture Marilyn holding the phone to her ear with one shoulder, both arms crossed protectively over her comfortless breasts, her hard and brittle voice cocked and ready to fire.

'Adrian, get a life. You'll see her at Christmas, like the agreement says.'

When the hot water started to turn cool, I got out and toweled off. It was time to get my laundry taken care of. Steven would know someone I could hire to do it. The last girl had quit unexpectedly, and I had let things go. My sock drawer was almost empty, down to two pairs. I picked the dark blue ones with the little red seahorses that Caitlin had sent me on my last birthday.

As I lifted the socks from the back of the drawer, I noticed a glossy brochure that had been hidden under them: 'Recovery from alcohol and drug dependence begins at the Stratford Clinic.' Alcohol and drug dependence? Yeah, that about summed it up. I remembered sending away for it shortly after Marilyn and I had separated. Help was just a phone call away, they said. Right. More like twenty thousand dollars away. Twenty grand for a thirty-day trip to a country club loony bin. The brochure shook in my hand. A month in Vermont. There were worse things. Hell, it couldn't be worse than waking up every day feeling like shit. Then I remembered the way Marta had looked as she undressed, the sheen on her dusky skin. The way she had groaned.

Crumpling the brochure, I tossed it into the trash. There were still a few good times to be had.

It took me three tries to knot my tie properly. When I finally got it right, half-moons of sweat darkened the underarms of my shirt. My face was flushed and damp, my stomach on fire. Suddenly, I wasn't so sure how many more good times I could take. The brochure pulled at me. I fished it out of the basket, brushed a couple of damp Q-tips off of it, flattened it out, and tossed it back into the drawer with my last pair of socks. What the hell. I wasn't getting any younger.

It was after noon by the time I left my apartment. On my way out I noticed my gun on the kitchen counter next to a half-empty bottle of Laphroaig. I grabbed the scotch and as an afterthought dropped the nine-millimeter into my briefcase. I felt a little silly bringing the gun, but I was hung over enough to believe I would need the whiskey.

Balancing the bottle and my briefcase, I struggled out of

the cab and into the rain. Gil, the doorman at the Delmonico, took a few steps toward me with an umbrella, but I waved him off. I didn't feel much like talking to anyone.

The Delmonico Hotel was once a posh home to the likes of Diamond Jim Brady. Standing on Park Avenue, just north of Fifty-seventh Street's shopping mecca, it was now a twenty-story mall for the rich and aimless. The old building had been totally gutted and renovated and was now filled with art galleries and antique dealers who benefited from close proximity to one another and the building's anchor tenant, Christie's, the international auction house. The auction giant occupied the first three floors of the old hotel and maintained a separate entrance on Park Avenue, just south of the building's main doors. Whenever Christie's held a major sale, the other dealers in the building threw open their doors, dispensing vast quantities of expensive booze and hors d'oeuvres to the auction crowd, trying to entice additional acts of conspicuous consumption. It was an effort that paid off more handsomely than you might imagine. Art sales in New York City alone are estimated to exceed two and a half billion dollars a year. That's billion with a *b*. A nice chunk of which flowed through the doors of the Delmonico in a seemingly endless stream.

I rode the elevator to the eighth floor, where Steven Ballard, my partner, and I had taken over space once occupied by a rare book dealer. We had used the proceeds of our forgery scam to turn it into a first-class gallery, hoping to divert a small portion of that river of cash into our own pockets. We ran a legitimate art business. None of the forgeries had ever crossed the threshold of our gallery. As good as they were, we saw McHenry's creations as a means to an end, not a career path. I usually got a kick out of seeing our names painted in gold leaf across the double glass doors. Today I forgot to notice.

Steven was leaning over Devon Berenson's desk, a stark glass monstrosity that he had ordered from Milan, which sat just inside the doors at the front of the gallery. She was our only employee. Her official title was receptionist, but she did a little of everything, from handling the day-to-day banking to researching paintings. In the two years she'd worked for us, we'd both come to depend on her. When I walked in, Steven and Devon looked up from the auction catalog they were studying, but neither said anything.

'Good morning,' I offered, trying to make the bottle of scotch look less obtrusive.

'Good morning? Adrian, it's afternoon. I've been looking everywhere for you,' Steven said, his expression serious as he stood up.

'Any calls?' I asked Dev.

She had that vexed look in her eye that drove me crazy. 'Just Marta, but she said not to bother calling back.' Dev picked at some nonexistent lint on her sweater. 'She'll be at the spa. With all the miles on that body, she'll need more than a mud bath.'

'Thank you for sharing your thoughts, Dev.'

'You sure do pick them.' She shook her head, still pulling at her sweater.

'I had no idea you were so interested in helping me pick the right woman.'

'The right woman? Hah! I've seen what you go out with. You wouldn't know a woman if you fell over her.' She turned back to her catalog.

Dev was in her late twenties. She was dressed today in black leggings, cowboy boots, and a long black cashmere V-neck that probably cost more than we paid her in a month. She had long auburn hair, and even sitting you could see that she was at least a head taller than Steven. She wasn't beautiful in a Hollywood sense. Hadn't the features to grace the cover of fashion magazines. Her mouth was a little too full, the line of her jaw a bit sharp. But her eyes were clear and as unlikely a shade of green as I had ever observed.

She studied the catalog with exaggerated concentration, pretending to ignore me. I think she underestimated the effect she had on others. Myself included. She never overdressed or tried to draw attention to herself in any flashy way. But there was something about her, a classic style, a way of angling her head and walking across a room that tended to make you look up from what you were doing and take notice. As far as I knew she wasn't intimately involved with anyone. Which, as attractive as she was, seemed curious. Not that it was any of my business. I'd been smart enough to keep my distance. Devon and I were friends, but what she did with her Saturday nights was something of a mystery.

I watched her turn the pages of the catalog for another minute or two, wondering why she was so down on Marta, then turned my attention to Steven.

'What's got you so nervous this morning?' I asked him.

'I can't find Paul McHenry. I've been calling him since last night. He hasn't shown up here, and there's no answer at his place. Have you spoken to him?'

'No, not since I saw him yesterday.'

'It's not like him to simply not show up, or call,' he said, fidgeting with the collar of his shirt.

'I wouldn't worry, you know how artists are. He's probably got his nose out of joint. I was a little rough on him. Come on in the office, I've got to sit down.'

31

Dev had been sitting quietly behind her desk while Steven and I talked, looking back and forth between us. As far as she was concerned, Paul McHenry was our restorer; she knew nothing about the forgeries. We had been careful to hide that side of our business from her.

I was halfway to the office Steven and I shared when she called after me, 'Adrian, you have Lamar Peterson coming in any minute to look at American paintings. Do you feel up to it?' She dropped the catalog she and Steven had been studying onto a pile by the desk and picked up a different one.

Shit, I'd forgotten all about him.

I turned and took a step back toward her. 'Yes, Dev, I think I can handle it. Pull some things together in the viewing room – don't forget the Severin Roesen still life, and the paintings from California. I need to talk with Steven for a few minutes. If Lamar comes in, tell him I'll be right out. Think you can manage it?''

She sat straight up, tilted her head to the side, and raised one eye brow. The look on her face seemed to say, 'Don't even think about taking me on, unless you're man enough to follow through.' My stomach tightened. I was caught somewhere between wanting to spank her and wanting to kiss her. She unfolded herself from her chair and went to do as I asked.

I caught Steven giving me a funny look as we walked into our office.

'Sometimes I wonder why I put up with her,' I said, shaking my head.

'Bullshit, Adrian, I'm not blind.'

'What you are is full of crap.' A dull throbbing started behind my eyes. I tried a couple of deep breaths, but it didn't help. 'My head is killing me, pal. Do me a favor and grab an Alka-Seltzer.'

Steven moistened his lips with his tongue, 'Adrian, you need to slow it down. You're gonna burn up if you keep on this way.' Looking peevish, he went off to find the Alka-Seltzer.

I set my briefcase and the scotch on top of the desk, then flopped into my chair. My insides felt hollow, empty but nauseated. If you knocked on me, I would echo. The tank was empty except for toxic fumes rising up and floating around my head. I tried several more deep breaths, but it didn't dissipate the fumes.

Steven came back and handed me a cup, then shut the door behind him. He leaned against it, facing me as I forced down the Alka-Seltzer. He was short but well put together, a year or two older than me.

'I'm serious, Adrian. What are we going to do about Paul?'

'First of all, we're going to stop talking about him in front of Devon. Have you already set up the meeting with Tanaka?'

'That's the problem. He's expecting us at six o'clock with the "Monet", and I don't even know if it's finished.'

'We're going to have to stall him.'

'No way, man, you know how Tanaka is, all that samurai honor bullshit.'

'I know what people say about him, but he's always been polite to us.'

'Damn it, Adrian, you heard what Narumi said about him.'

Eiji Narumi had been our other big Japanese client. He happened to walk into our gallery one day just as Ryuichi Tanaka was leaving.

For almost three years, ever since Marta had introduced me to Tanaka at one of her parties, Steven and I had been supplying him with McHenry's French

Impressionist paintings. I was careful to make sure that he knew exactly what he was getting. He bought everything McHenry painted. Tanaka paid us a fraction of what the real thing would be worth, but it still amounted to hundreds of thousands of dollars. We assumed he resold them in Japan as originals.

Tanaka and Narumi gave no sign of recognizing each other. But later, after a long dinner with too much to drink, Narumi told us that Tanaka was well known in his country.

'The man is a beast,' Narumi had said. 'There was a story in the Tokyo newspapers about a cashier who worked for one of Tanaka's hostess bars in the Shin Juku district. Apparently he got caught with his hand in the till. He was found several days later in a Tokyo park with his throat cut. He wasn't alone – his wife and two small children were also found in the same condition.'

'Jesus, you're saying Tanaka did this?' Steven had asked.

'I don't know, there was much noise about indicting Tanaka on murder charges. It was a very big investigation, all of the news media covered it. But it never went any further. Eventually the press stopped writing about it.'

'That doesn't explain why they would try to pin it on Tanaka,' Steven said, not yet convinced that our client could be that dirty.

'He is *yakuza*, like your mafia. He's part of the Hiyashi Gumi, the largest syndicate in Japan. Everyone knows who they are, the newspapers write about them, even publish photographs, but the authorities never do anything.' He leaned forward, elbows on the table, his tongue lubricated by three bottles of Haut-Brion. 'These gangsters are too powerful – let me give you an example. They say in the papers that Ryuichi Tanaka is one of the most ruthless gangsters in the *yakuza*. That he had seven men murdered because he suspected them of cheating him in a card game. One of those killed was a distant relative of the emperor, the royal cousin, Ayanomiya. The whole syndicate took heat for that killing. They say Tanaka was sent to America as punishment – but many think the entire Hiyashi Gumi should be punished. There are still royalists in Japan who think Ayanomiya's death should be avenged.' Narumi paused and took a long drink of his wine. Then he fixed Steven and me with his bloodshot eyes. 'Do you understand me? A member of the emperor's family murdered and nothing has ever been done about it. That's power.'

Narumi had called us the next day to apologize for talking too much, and to ask us to forget the terrible things he had said. A result of too much French wine and an overabundant imagination, he claimed. Whatever it was, we ran into him from time to time at the auctions, but he never came to the gallery or bought anything from us again.

'Steven, I wouldn't take what Narumi said as gospel.'

'If only part of what he said is true, we better hope McHenry shows up with his painting soon. Besides, we need the money. Have you looked at the list of payables lately?'

Devon knocked on the door and opened it a crack. 'The doorman just called. Lamar Peterson is on his way up.' She looked at me and shook her head. 'Damn, Adrian, you can't greet him looking like that.' She crossed the office to where I was sitting and said, 'Stand up.'

I did. She brushed off the shoulders of my coat, then

rearranged my tie so that it looked straight. 'There,' she said, a slight smile, the first of the day, gracing her lips. 'Tuck in your shirt, then at least you'll look like a professional art dealer.'

'Gee, thanks, Devon. Are you sure there's no dirt on my face? I was kind of hoping you'd spit on your finger and rub it off.' I offered my cheek.

She laughed, 'You are not a well man.' She licked her finger and scrubbed my cheek.

'Yecchhh,' I pretended to gag.

'Now, don't let Peterson cry poor,' she said. 'I read last week in *The Wall Street Journal* that a British conglomerate made an offer for Southern Ozark Chemicals.'

'What's that got to do with Peterson?' I looked at Steven.

He shrugged.

'Advanced Coal Technologies is one of his companies, isn't it?' she asked

'Yeah,' I answered.

'Well, Southern Ozark is a subsidiary of Advanced Coal. When the deal closes, Peterson will probably clear thirty or forty million.'

'Very impressive. I didn't know you followed the financial markets so closely.'

She frowned. 'Is it written somewhere that because you have tits and a trust fund, you can't have a brain? I may have inherited money, that doesn't mean I depend upon someone else to watch over it.' She walked out, closing the door behind her.

Steven turned to me. 'Tits and a trust fund?'

I laughed. 'Sounds good to me. Do you think her parents would adopt me?'

'Nah, they must have better taste than that. How

much do you think she's worth?' We had discussed this a hundred times, but it was a source of never-ending speculation between us.

'I'm not sure, but her father's worth bongo-bucks. Hell, he owns half of the gas stations and convenience stores in Massachusetts.' I rubbed my temples, wondering if scotch and Alka-Seltzer was anything like scotch and soda.

'What's she doing working for us?' Steven asked.

We had pondered this question often, too.

'Are you kidding?' I launched into my stock explanation; it usually cheered him up. 'She's a lucky girl. Not only is she in on the ground floor of what's going to be one of the greatest galleries in the world, she gets to hang out all day with a couple of guys like us.'

I got up and walked over to where Steven was standing and chucked him on the arm. 'Come on, pal, stop worrying so much. I saw the "Monet" yesterday at the loft – McHenry's almost finished with it. It's incredible. Tanaka's going to be thrilled. You keep trying to reach McHenry, I'll handle Peterson.'

'All right, but I have a bad feeling about this.' He shook his head and looked thoroughly depressed. Then he changed the subject. 'Adrian, we have to plan the opening for auction night.'

'We have plenty of time. It's not until after Thanksgiving.'

'Are you kidding? Thanksgiving is next week. Auction night is the following Thursday – that's two weeks away!'

'Devon's already booked the caterers, hasn't she?'

'Yeah, but we have to get the invitations out or they'll arrive too late.'

'All right! Stop being such a nag. Tomorrow – without

fail we'll do it tomorrow. That'll leave just enough time for them to be delivered.'

He nodded but didn't look happy. 'I'll stop nagging you – but if something has gone wrong with McHenry, I'm going to need you to be in some kind of shape to deal with it. Go easy on the partying for a while, okay?'

I glared at him, then forced a smile. 'Lighten up, Steven. What could possibly go wrong? You worry about the details, I'll handle the rest.'

By the time I got to the front desk, Lamar Peterson was walking in. He was wearing one of his trademark bow ties, a bright yellow number. I could have sworn he was trying to look down the front of Devon's sweater. She pretended not to notice and smiled up at him as he stood in front of her desk.

'Hello, Mr Peterson. How are you?'

'Well, I'm just fine, you sweet girl. How are y'all doin'?' he asked. He looked around at what he could see of the gallery from the front desk, then focused back on her. 'Devon, you sure are a pretty thing. If you ever get tired of big city life, you let me know. Down in Louisville, we know how to treat a girl like you.'

If anyone else had come in and spoken to Devon that way, she would have cut him off at the knees, but she took Lamar Peterson in stride. 'Mr Peterson, I'll keep that in mind,' she said, looking from him to me.

'You do that, honey,' he said, rubbing his hands together. 'Are you taking care of my boy?' he asked, gesturing toward me. 'You know I depend on old Adrian to be my eyes up here. Don't know anyone else who can look at an auction and pick the winners from the duds the way he does.'

I could feel Devon's eyes on me as Lamar went on, but whatever she was thinking remained unspoken.

'We try, Mr Peterson, but Adrian can be a handful.'

'I can see that,' he said, turning to me, shaking his head. 'Look at all that hair. I'd invite you down to Louisville, but I wouldn't know how to introduce you to my friends. It's not just your ponytail. It's these Italian suits,' he waved his arm up and down at me. 'You look too damned European – more like an artist than a businessman – Adrian, you get yourself a good haircut, a visit to my man at Brooks Brothers, and I bet you double your business. Don't you agree, honey?' he finished, looking back at Dev, trying hard to keep his eyes on her *pretty* face. Which wasn't an easy thing to do even when she wore a more conservative top, as she had great legs and her glass desk did nothing to hide them.

The old boy was more of a goat than I remembered. I made a mental note to get him a date next time he came up. In the meantime, I thought about sending Devon out on some kind of errand before Peterson started drooling on himself.

'Where'd you grow up, Devon?' he asked her.

'Boston, actually just outside of the city. Why?'

'This guy going to give you enough time to go home for Thanksgiving?' Peterson gestured toward me with his thumb.

'Not this year, Mr Peterson. My parents are in France for the winter. I've decided to stay in New York and fend for myself. I think it's time I learned how to cook a turkey.' She looked at me and laughed. 'But after all the important stock market advice I've given Adrian, I suppose I could talk him into some time off.'

He looked at me, eyebrows raised, then back at her. 'I don't doubt that, honey. Not at all.'

The fumes in my stomach had overpowered the Alka-Seltzer, and Lamar's good-ole-boy routine was wearing thin. What I really wanted to do was sit quietly in my office until my head stopped throbbing and my stomach settled down, but I knew he'd buy if I worked on him.

It had cost us a million dollars to renovate the 4,500-square-foot gallery space. We've got the notes to prove it. Oiled teak floors, cream, silk-covered walls, a high-tech, low-voltage lighting system, hand-carved moldings, fireproof storage area. It cost another fortune to operate it – twenty thousand dollars a month just to insure the inventory. A few more 'Monets,' and we'd be out of debt. Until then, every sale counted. I eyeballed Peterson and thought about Oscar Fedder.

'I don't mean to break up old home week, but I want to show this man some art. It's good to see you, Lamar,' I said stepping to his side.

We shook hands and I ushered him around Devon's desk into the gallery. I mouthed at her behind Peterson's back, 'Pull up your sweater,' but she ignored me.

Lamar stopped in front of a small oil painting by Agnes Richmond, a little-known American painter. It depicted a mother walking through a park with a perambulator. It was a spring scene, and the grounds of the park were ablaze with flowers. He pulled a cigar out of his coat pocket and chewed on it, closely inspecting the painting.

'How much?' he asked, pointing at the Richmond with his cigar.

'Forty-five.'

'I hope you mean forty-five hundred, because if you mean forty-five thousand, that dog just won't hunt.'

'Lamar, it's a little jewel. I'll work on the price, but it won't be less than forty thousand.'

'My first house cost less than that,' he grumbled. He walked on.

I showed him everything hanging on the walls, but nothing suited him. Then we went into the viewing room, where most of my significant sales took place. It's a small room designed to allow a client to sit comfortably and view inventory that isn't offered to the general public.

'I had Devon pull a few things out for you to see,' I told him.

One by one I placed paintings on an easel for him to inspect. He was noncommittal until I got to the last painting. I'd saved it for last on purpose; it was an incredible little still life depicting fruits and flowers on a gray marble table. Painted by Severin Roesen, an important nineteenth-century American painter, it was unusual both in its small size and wonderful clarity. The flowers looked as though they had just been picked, the fruits glistened and appeared succulent and sweet; they represented America, in all her newfound wealth and abundance, arranged on the cool, solid marble of the table.

Lamar got up and circled the small panel, chewing hungrily on his unlit cigar. I excused myself, shutting him in the viewing room alone to be seduced by whatever it is great art offers those who can afford it.

I poked my head into our office, where Steven was going over accounts with Devon, and gave them a thumbs-up sign.

'You seem to have made a remarkable recovery since you came dragging in here,' Devon said.

'It's amazing what the smell of money can do, isn't it? If he buys anything, I'm going to get you a turtleneck. Has McHenry called yet?'

'No, and he's still not answering the phone,' Steven replied.

'We'll find him. Listen, if Lamar comes out of the viewing room, don't quote him on the Roesen, I want to handle him myself. I'm going to the bathroom – be back in a minute.'

In the bathroom, I locked the door behind me and pulled the leather case from my pocket. I put a generous line of dope out on the edge of the sink and rolled up a bill to snort it with. The smack ran down the back of my throat, bitter and strong. I did just enough to keep from feeling needy, enough to feel that warm glow, but I was sure no one would notice a change in my behavior. I splashed water on my face and rinsed my nostrils. I wondered if Lamar Peterson would trust his art expert's eyes to pick out his winners if he knew why his pupils were so pinned.

When I walked back into the viewing room, Lamar was still standing over the Severin Roesen.

'This is some painting you've got here,' he said, turning to look at me. 'What's the tariff? And don't quote me any of those damned New York prices that are longer than telephone numbers.'

By the time we arrived at a deal it was almost two o'clock, and we had been going at it for over an hour. Eventually Lamar walked out with the Severin Roesen under his arm, leaving behind a check for $107,000. I walked him to the elevator, trying not to look too happy.

Devon was still at lunch with friends. Steven was sitting at her desk frowning when I walked back in waving the Peterson check.

'What's with the sad face?'

'Adrian, I think something is wrong. I just don't believe Paul would get hinky on us. Not about something this important.'

'You're starting to sound like an old lady. I'm telling

you I saw the painting yesterday, it's a masterpiece. Stop worrying. McHenry's just pissed at the way I spoke to him.'

'Well, what the hell did you say to him?'

'I told him if he wanted to be the next Picasso, to do it on his own time, not ours. Then I told him to finish the damn thing. If he didn't like the tone of my voice, too fucking bad. This is business, not pleasure.'

The lines in Steven's forehead grew deeper. 'What are we going to tell Tanaka?'

'I'll handle it. We'll go over to his place at six, that's when he's expecting us, right?'

'Yeah, but he's expecting us with his painting.'

'I'll explain the situation, I'm sure he'll understand. Then we'll find McHenry.'

I was talking a good game, but the more I thought about it, the more justified Steven's worries seemed. He was right, Paul had never acted like a prima donna before, and now seemed an unlikely time to start.

'Come on, Steven, everything is going to work out. McHenry's probably finished by now. We'll get the painting, and once we deliver it, we'll take a break for a while. Put a hold on the forgery business and play it straight, okay?' I wasn't sure which of us I was trying to reassure.

Steven nodded, still frowning, and said, 'Sometimes I wish we'd never started.'

CHAPTER FOUR

New York is full of wannabe art dealers. Most just like the idea of being in on the game, but a few are serious. They struggle to keep alive, praying for that one coup. The one that will fill their bank accounts and establish them as players in a deadly serious game involving bloated sums of money and egos to match. For most it never happens. I know, I was one of them until about three years ago when Steven Ballard caught up to me one night, and we figured out how to stack the deck in our favor.

I was drinking at Au Bar on Fifty-eighth Street. It was early, and the place was just starting to fill up with its usual crowd of Eurotrash and young professionals who liked to party but didn't want to get too far from their own kind. I was trying to forget a crappy day that began with a call from my banker, informing me that my account was overdrawn, wanting to know when he could expect a deposit. Then my landlord called to remind me, in no uncertain terms, that the rent was late. That was as good as the day got. Until I hooked up with Ballard.

I had spent the afternoon at an auction of paintings held at Sotheby's. Not one of the elegant black tie evening affairs that always get written up. It was just a nuts-and-bolts auction that attracted mostly dealers, and a few truly devoted collectors.

I owned three of the works that were being offered, and to cover my overdraft I desperately needed for at least one of them to sell. If two sold, I could pay my rent.

I watched, trying not to look hungry, as the auctioneer announced and briefly described each of my paintings. He gave them a fair shake, touting them in his refined British accent, but none of them reached the reserve I had set. Two didn't even attract an opening bid.

As if my day wasn't already a walk on slippery rocks, a gynecologist from Atlanta, who had committed to purchase three Victorian drawings I recently bought with money I didn't have, approached me as I was leaving Sotheby's and begged off. He had allowed himself to get emotional during the auction and bid more than he intended, unfortunately not on my paintings. He apologized and promised to give me a call next time he was in the city. I wanted to rip off his bad toupee and make him eat it. But instead I grinned and told him not to worry, an important British museum was interested in the drawings. Keep smiling, no matter how bad it hurts. Never let the bastards know you're down, or they'll eat you alive.

I was bitterly counting my losses over a double Stoli on the rocks when I saw Steven Ballard come in and scope out the room. He worked as an accountant by day and was a small-time coke dealer on the side. At night he always wore a black leather jacket and hung on the periphery of the downtown art scene. He wasn't my favorite person in the world, but he always had good product, was reliable, and didn't seem too crazy. When he sat down next to me at the bar I was mildly pleased to see him.

'Hey, man. What's cookin'?' he asked.

'You are, Steven. When are you gonna get a decent coat?'

'Don't you recognize style when you see it?' he asked, checking out the room for attractive women and potential clients. 'Are you still dealing in art?'

'Yeah, but a few more days like today and I'll probably end up selling time shares in Arizona. Why?'

'Those dead artists in gold frames?'

'I don't generally describe it that way. What's on your mind?'

'Would you look at something for me? I'm going to show it to some of my accounting clients, but I don't know what kind of price to ask for it.'

'Now?'

'Yeah. I'll make it worth your while, but keep it quiet, okay?'

The conspiratorial tone he had taken didn't surprise me. Most drug dealers think of themselves as a cross between Robin Hood and Jesse James. Even though he was in it more for the partying than for the money, Steven Ballard was no exception. But it was still relatively early on a Tuesday night, and for some of Steven's coke I was willing to give him a quick appraisal.

We snorted a few lines in the men's room, and then I walked with him to his apartment in a nondescript building on West Sixty-fourth Street. There is no place in the world like New York City for walking. Steven's coke was humming in my veins, and I felt the spring night around me as though I were wearing it. A thousand eloquent thoughts flashed through my brain only to dissolve before I could give voice to them. Steven, however, was all business. Chugging along in his black leather jacket and cowboy boots, he was a man on a mission.

As we were crossing Fifth Avenue he turned to hurry me along. With his chiseled features and muscular physique, he could have been a model if he hadn't been so short. Even so, he always seemed to have a blonde nearby, and I had enjoyed the few times we partied together. When we got to his place the first thing he did was call someone named Leslie to tell her that he would be late but to wait for him. I hoped she had a friend.

His place was a typical, modern high-rise box. The living room was decorated with black leather sofas, perhaps to match his jacket, and a lot of flashy Italian furniture. Expensive stereo equipment was housed in a tall etagere that also contained a well-stocked bar. The walls were hung with arid contemporary art. If this was what he wanted me to see, it would be a short visit.

After his conversation with Leslie, Steven laid out a few generous lines on his marble-topped coffee table and got us a couple of cold Heinekens. After we did the coke, he led me back into his bedroom. I was surprised to find that it was decorated with cartoon art. Cels of everything from Pinocchio to Cinderella. Who knows about people? Here was a bean counter by day, who turned into a would-be outlaw coke dealer after dark. His living room was straight out of *Penthouse* magazine, but he chose to go to sleep at night looking at Donald Duck. I wondered if he wore pajamas.

'Look at this and tell me what you think,' he said, pulling a small framed painting out from under his bed.

It took my breath away. Art speaks to me. I don't know how or why. I quit trying to figure it out many years ago. The first time I realized the effect art had on me, I couldn't have been more than twelve or thirteen years old. I was spending spring break with my prep-school roommate, whose parents lived in one of those enormous mansions in Newport. It was a rainy afternoon, and we were holed up in his father's library, looking through books for anatomically correct illustrations, when I happened to look up and notice the portrait over the mantel. It was incalculably old, surrounded by a rich gold frame that reflected the watery afternoon light. A portrait of a peasant with a dark and brooding face glaring out from under a floppy brown hat. Shadows covered most of his features, but his eyes gleamed malevolently under the brim of that hat. When I asked about it, my friend informed me casually that it was a Rembrandt. The name didn't mean much to me, but the coarse leer and knowing eyes of that peasant haunted me for the rest of my visit. I snuck into the library every chance I got to steal another glance at him. What did he know so surely? I still remember the fear and delight the portrait awakened in me. I'm no scholar; my stock in trade is my eye. Whenever a painting thrills me the way that Rembrandt had, I stop what I'm doing and pay attention. That's exactly what I did when Ballard pulled his little treasure out from under the bed.

'Where did you get this?' I asked, wanting to take it home and keep it forever.

'First tell me what you think,' Steven said. 'If you like it, maybe we can make a few bucks with it.'

It had to be stolen, I thought to myself. It looked to be a Degas, probably painted in the late 1870s. It was a jewel, and there was no legitimate way someone like Steven Ballard could happen to have it under his bed.

I walked toward the living room holding the painting in front of me to see it in a better light. It was painted on canvas, about twelve by sixteen inches, and depicted a young ballerina bent at the waist, adjusting her slippers. But that doesn't begin to describe it. Degas had somehow imbued his ballerina with life. She looked so anchored in her own flesh that you half expected to hear her breathe. And the light . . . she was backlit by a large window, and the atmospheric quality of the painting evoked dust motes dancing in the columns of sunlight.

It was unsigned, and there were no identifying gallery or exhibition labels on the back.

'You have to tell me where you got this!' I asked again. Steven reached out and shook my shoulder.

'Calm down, Adrian. It's not what you think.'

'Steven!' I exclaimed again, growing more excited. 'Do you realize what you have here? Do you have any idea what it's worth?'

Still clutching the painting, I sat down on one of the leather sofas and tried to figure out how to snort another line of Steven's coke without letting go of it. I'm sure I sounded crazed, as I tried to explain to him what I thought, asking at least ten times, 'Do you know how incredible this is?'

'Adrian,' Steven interrupted. 'I get it. I've got the idea. Have another beer and let me explain.'

He told me about a struggling painter turned art restorer named Paul McHenry, whose taxes Steven had prepared. McHenry was sick and tired of being broke and thought there might be a market for paintings that resembled the work of the masters. He had painted the 'Degas' to test the waters, then showed it to Steven, hoping that he would offer it to some of his better-heeled clients. It was the best damned forgery I had ever seen. Surprised at how completely the work had fooled me, I wondered if it would deceive others as easily. As we worked on the coke, drank beer, and talked, the skeleton of a plan took shape. Steven was right, we could make a few bucks with the fake Degas. But we could make a whole lot of bucks if we teamed up with McHenry and went into business together.

'Adrian, it sounds interesting, but I don't know a damn thing about art,' Steven explained as I put forth my idea.

'You don't need to know anything. You're not a chemist, are you? That hasn't kept you from selling coke.'

'I sell grams, and eight balls. Once in a while an ounce or two. Small potatoes. What you're talking about is big time.'

'You're a CPA, aren't you?'

He nodded, then took a slug of his Heineken.

'That settles it. You'll be in charge of the books.'

'It's not exactly what I had in mind.'

'You have to think big. We can do it. Trust me. I'll handle the art and the clients, McHenry will paint, you'll handle the accounting and bookkeeping. You'll pick it up as we go.'

By early morning the marble-topped coffee table was littered with empty beer bottles and cocaine residue. Steven and I had become partners. Now all we had to do was convince Paul McHenry to come aboard. Judging from the painting I had seen and the money at stake, I wasn't about to take no for an answer.

CHAPTER FIVE

Two men greeted Steven and me at the door of Ryuichi Tanaka's East Seventy-second Street townhouse. Neither of them was exactly welcoming. The senior member of the pair was Yoshio Kotani, Tanaka's right-hand man, who greeted us with a scowl that looked glued in place. Kotani and I had met on at least five different occasions, but he acted as though he had never laid eyes on me. I got the feeling that we had interrupted him, and couldn't help wondering what he had been doing when we rang the doorbell. He was trim and fit-looking. Dressed in a dark blue business suit, white shirt, and tie, he looked more like an accountant with a nasty case of indigestion than a Japanese gangster.

The man who answered the door with him was altogether different. I smiled when he stuck out his hand and introduced himself as Stan. He was Japanese, of medium height, and muscular. But instead of business clothes, he was sporting a powder-blue silk suit over an open-necked shirt, and his long hair was permed and gelled into place. It looked more like a toy poodle perched on top of his head than the funky Elvis look he was trying for. At first glance Stan was kind of goofy-looking, but when we shook hands I noticed that his eyes didn't smile with the rest of his face. They were cold and appraising. As he looked me up and down, I felt like I had been searched for hidden weapons and bad intentions.

The room they ushered us into was decorated from floor to ceiling with exquisite eighteenth-century

French antiques. We were guided across a lavish Persian rug to a pair of Louis XV fauteuils, where we were asked by Kotani to wait. As we sat, Steven pointed toward the large Tahitian Gauguin that hung on the wall behind us. It was the real thing, not one of McHenry's creations.

The room was meant to impress, and it did. Such opulence, so casually displayed, sent a very clear message. He who has the gold makes the rules. A universal truth. Right up there with Murphy's law and alimony.

Once we were seated, Kotani, speaking in Japanese, issued what seemed to be a series of orders to Stan, who listened silently and then left the room. I thought I detected a note of disdain in Kotani's voice.

After Stan had departed, I asked Kotani where I could find the facilities. For the first time he met my eye and looked nonplussed. When I realized that he didn't know what I was talking about, I explained to him that it was the toilet I was looking for. He bowed, then directed me down a long hallway to a bathroom the size of Texas.

The back of my throat was starting to clench, and I could feel the sweat forming under my shirt. I needed some dope. Although I had sworn to cut back, I was afraid I would get sick here and now. Pulling out my case, I laid out enough smack to settle down my system, then added a little extra for good measure. After I snorted it, I was rinsing my face with cold water when I caught my reflection in the mirror over the sink. By what course had I arrived at this place? My face looked pale and burned out, my eyes tired and pinned, more gray than their usual blue. Thinking back, I could trace my path well enough from point A to point B, but there were some pretty large gaps, and too many footprints left behind on people who deserved better. Then the heroin started to kick in, erasing the corners, blunting the sharp edge of my fears and regrets, and I began to feel optimistic. That's why they call it dope.

Walking back down the hallway, I noticed big band music coming from behind a door that was slightly ajar. I peeked in. Tanaka stood in the center of a long narrow room. He was wearing a blue and white warm-up suit, watching with rapt attention as a petite blonde demonstrated a complex series of dance steps. After she repeated the moves a couple of times, he nodded at her and they tried them together. Holding her by the hips as she wrapped her arms around his neck, he lifted her off the ground and in time to the music swung her from side to side, almost violently. His lips were pulled back from his teeth into a wolfish grin, and he let out a high-pitched giggle as they jitterbugged across the floor. As he learned the steps, the blonde laughed and patted him on the cheek as if he were a schoolboy. Unseen, I backed away and continued down the hallway, followed by the sounds of Glenn Miller and Tanaka's squeaky giggle.

I knew his good humor should have encouraged me, but something about the way Tanaka and the woman were dancing unsettled me. I didn't know why. But it was there. Like the name of someone whose face you can picture but whose name you can't recall. I couldn't quite put my finger on it.

Steven was sitting where I had left him.

'You won't believe this,' I told him, trying to ignore the pit in my stomach. 'Tanaka is learning to jitterbug.'

'What?'

'He's dancing. Right down the hall,' I pointed. 'He's taking lessons.'

'Tanaka?'

'Yeah, he's in there dancing up a storm. Smiling like the Cheshire cat. You should see him.'

Steven was bent at the waist, pulling up his socks. 'I'll take your word for it. I still think we shouldn't have come here without the painting.'

'I told you, we'll explain the situation. I'm sure Tanaka will understand. The man's in a great mood.'

'Narumi said –'

'Come on, Steven.' I didn't want to hear any more of Narumi's horror stories. 'I'm sure Tanaka is a reasonable man. As soon as we've finished here, I'll go downtown to Paul's loft. You head back to the office and work the phones. One way or another, we'll track McHenry down.'

Tanaka kept us waiting for another forty-five minutes. Steven fidgeted in his chair the entire time, crossing and uncrossing his legs, tapping his feet. His hands were in constant motion, tugging on the cuffs of his shirt, fooling with his socks and shoes. I closed my eyes, tired just from watching.

'You all right, Adrian? You look . . . I don't know, kind of pale.'

His voice was starting to grate on me. I looked at my watch. 'Jesus, how much longer is Tanaka going to keep us waiting while he does the Fred Astaire thing?'

Steven shrugged. 'You look a little shaky,' he kept on.

'Nah, I'm just a little tired. Don't worry about me.'

'You sure?'

'Let it go, partner. I'm fine . . . I told you I would handle Tanaka, and I will.'

'Chill out, man. You don't have to bite my head off,' he complained.

I tried to apologize, but something in his cocker spaniel eyes tweaked whatever had shifted in me while I watched Tanaka dance. I looked away.

When Kotani returned, he ushered us to a room at the

back of the house where we were asked to remove our street shoes and given soft slippers. He then preceded us past shoji screens and, bowing deeply, led us into the room where Tanaka awaited us.

Tanaka sat cross-legged on a silk cushion in the center of a large traditional tatami room. The space was devoid of any furniture or decoration save the cushion upon which he sat and a spare but elegant flower arrangement on a low lacquered table beside him. Steven and I remained standing, unsure what was expected.

This little ritual was not the way we had conducted business with Tanaka in the past. Usually, McHenry would finish the commission, and I would deliver it by hand to Tanaka's house. Tanaka would inspect the painting, more often than not right in the front hall, then nod his approval. That was it. Simple and elegant. Two days later we would receive, via fax, confirmation of a wire transfer of funds into our bank account. Steven had set up an elaborate bookkeeping system, which allowed us to declare the sale and keep kosher with the IRS without ever actually describing the true nature of the forgeries. Up until now it had been a very nice bit of business for all concerned. This was the first glitch, but it certainly didn't seem insurmountable.

After we stood there for a few uncomfortable moments, Tanaka looked up from the slender book he was reading and studied us. It was hard to believe this was the same man I had just seen laughing and dancing. He was in his mid-sixties, compact, with close-cropped silver hair. Even seated, he radiated a sense of power. His striped warm-up suit was gone. He looked almost imperial, dressed in a kimono of dark green silk, into which was woven his crest of three intertwined cranes. I felt clumsy, out of place, a giant in my stocking feet and loose slippers.

Tanaka gestured toward the floor with an open hand. As we lowered ourselves to a cross-legged position facing him, the shoji screens opened and a young woman, also dressed in a kimono, bowed and entered carrying a steaming pot of tea and three pottery tea bowls on a lacquered tray. Kotani took up a position standing behind Tanaka, close enough to keep an eye on things but just out of earshot.

'Please join me,' Tanaka said as the maid knelt beside him and set the tray on the floor. She picked up the pot in her left hand and hadn't quite filled the first bowl when Tanaka erupted.

'*Damē*,' he barked, 'that is wrong.'

In one fluid motion he was on his feet and reaching for the neck of the girl's kimono. He slapped her across the face. Somehow she managed not to spill the tea as she set the pot down. Then, trembling, she buried her face in the tatami mat as Tanaka drew back his arm to hit her again.

'Don't,' I said, surprising myself. Rising to my feet, I reached out and put my hand on Tanaka's elbow before he could hit her a second time. Out of the corner of my eye I saw Kotani moving toward us with surprising speed.

Steven jumped up, his eyes wide. 'Adrian,' he hissed.

Tanaka loosened his grip on the maid's kimono and turned toward me, his face the color of a plum. I dropped my arm.

'Excuse our ignorance, sir,' Steven blurted. 'We were afraid you might stumble on the tray.' He pointed to where the maid had set it.

Steven bowed low. I followed his lead, the blood sing-

56

ing in my ears. We sat back down and waited to see if Steven's quick thinking would be enough to save face.

Tanaka, with Kotani now at his side, turned back to the maid, his eyes narrowed, his nostrils flared.

'*Densai*,' he ordered her. 'Go.'

Kotani took the ashen girl by the arm and roughly escorted her from the room.

'I am sorry for her lack of manners,' Tanaka bowed to us. 'She is new, a Filipino. *Yabanjin*, a barbarian.' He looked me in the eye, his expression unreadable. 'Thank you for helping me keep my balance. Please allow me.'

He knelt and carefully lifted the teapot the proper way, using his right hand, holding the top in place with his left, then finished pouring the tea. It was an ancient custom, allowing the guest to see that both hands were occupied and therefore could not be holding a weapon. It didn't reassure me, and judging from Steven's pallor, it didn't do much for him either. I wondered where Kotani had taken the maid.

When he finished pouring, Tanaka took up his seat on the cushion facing us. Then he picked up his bowl and slurped his tea.

The shoji screens opened and Kotani bowed as he walked back in. When he saw that the tea had already been poured, he picked up the tray and carried it out of the room. As he reached for it, I noticed that he was missing the little finger of his left hand.

When Kotani had left the room, Tanaka spoke without preamble. 'I understand that you have come without my painting.'

Steven and I exchanged glances. 'Well, sir,' I replied. 'We would like to discuss –'

'I have paid you a deposit of three hundred twenty-five thousand dollars for a painting of water lilies by Monet. Have I not? Since I don't see the painting, I assume that you have some kind of problem which is causing a delay?' He allowed himself a small smile. 'Perhaps the paint is not yet dry.'

'You're closer to the truth than you know,' I started to explain. 'The painting is almost –'

'I'm not interested in excuses or explanations.' He shook his head, emphasizing the point. 'You were aware of my timetable when you accepted this commission. Are you not satisfied with the way our business is being conducted?'

'Of course we are,' I nodded at him. 'We value you as one of our most honored clients.' I felt like I should bow, but I couldn't figure out how to do it sitting.

He picked up his tea and sipped. 'Then I will expect you to keep me happy. I must honor my commitments to the letter. I'm afraid that a delay right now is completely unacceptable.' He stopped. Steven and I waited for the other shoe to drop.

'Ordinarily, when someone doesn't deliver what he has promised me, I would recover my money, perhaps with something added as a penalty. But a refund doesn't interest me. I've already made arrangements for the placement of the 'Monet,' and I am unwilling to change those arrangements. To do so would cause me great embarrassment. I'll give you forty-eight hours to deliver the painting.' He then picked up a thin volume of poetry by Yeats and opened it. As if on cue, the shoji screen opened and Kotani appeared to escort us from the room.

As we walked out, we ran into Stan, who was balancing several shopping bags from expensive women's boutiques as he climbed the front steps. He was whistling an aria from Verdi's *La Traviata*, and nodded to us as we passed.

Outside Steven turned to me and said, 'Some great mood. You really handled him. I feel a lot better now.'

'Come on, Steven, he just wants his painting. I'll go find Paul.'

'Adrian, he's a fucking maniac. You saw what he did to that maid. What the hell did you think you were going to do, act like some kind of hero and save her ass?'

I shook my head. 'He's a sweetheart, all right. Pull it together, pal. I need you to get on the phone and help me track our boy down.'

'You're acting mighty cool now, Adrian. You weren't quite so together back in there.'

'We can discuss it later. Let's just find McHenry and get Tanaka's painting.'

We walked west on Seventy-second Street to Fifth Avenue and caught separate cabs. Steven headed back to the office, and I headed downtown to Triheca. Tanaka hadn't exactly threatened us, but I couldn't shake the ferocity and rapidity with which he'd hit the young maid. Thank God Steven hadn't let me do anything stupid. I looked at my watch. It was seven o'clock on a cold November Thursday. The rain had stopped, but the sky was lowering, and the thickening mist cast an eerie pall over the streets of Manhattan. I was sweating.

CHAPTER SIX

There was a light rain falling by the time the cab left me in front of the narrow building on Lispenard Street. Except for a beat-up Chevy van parked across from Paul's building, the street was empty. Two men dressed in white coveralls stood in the cold drizzle beside the open rear doors of the van, smoking and talking loudly in Chinese. The way they gestured at several large wooden boxes inside the van, waving their cigarettes at each other as they argued, alarmed me. I felt uneasy, exposed. I kept one eye on them in case their disagreement spilled over in my direction.

After ringing McHenry's buzzer repeatedly to no effect, I got lucky. One of the other residents walked up, granny glasses misted, her arms full of groceries. We had been introduced once at a gathering of artists hosted by Paul. I wasn't positive, but I thought her name was Trish Van de Water. Short and well-padded, she had a slight moustache under a nose that reminded me of a potato. She smiled up at me with a mouthful of small, perfectly shaped teeth.

Trish made a living selling the plaster casts she made of erect penises. Her best sellers were the engorged organs of various rock stars.

After exchanging greetings, I asked her if she had seen Paul. Trish shifted her groceries and fumbled with her keys. I couldn't help imagining her pudgy hands at work. Teasing stoned rockers to life, in the name of art. A cold bucket of wet plaster waiting. I wondered if her display case was divided into sections; circumcised and uncircumcised, small, medium, large.

'You know this city gets scarier and scarier each day. Look at them. It's like that all the time down here.' She angled her head at the two Chinese guys, still going at it. I half expected them to pull cleavers and be done with it.

'Yeah, I know. About Paul –'

She interrupted me, pointing out the shiny brass lock on the door as she inserted her key. 'This is new. Some-one tried to break in here last night. I guess something must have scared them away. At least no one has re-ported anything missing.' She pushed open the door. 'If I could afford it, I'd get the hell out of here.' Then she smiled with those pearly teeth. 'Who am I kidding? I love it here. Besides, business is booming.'

'Trish, have you seen Paul since yesterday?' I asked again, wanting to end our conversation and get upstairs.

'No, I haven't. Why?' she asked.

'I've been trying to find him. He hasn't been answer-ing the phone. I'm starting to worry about him.'

'Achh, don't worry.' She waved her keys at me. 'You know how independent we artists can be. Adrian, have you ever posed?' Her eyes traveled up and down my body, coming to rest on my feet. 'You really might make a good model. You should think about it.'

I kept my mouth shut and followed her into the build-ing. In spite of myself, I wondered what section of her case I would fit in.

As a security measure, the elevator required an indi-vidual key to access each floor. Trish didn't have the one for Paul's floor. Neither did I, so I said good night and took the stairs.

The leather soles of my shoes slapped on the metal steps as I climbed, echoing through the concrete stair-well. Out of breath, I cursed McHenry and decided to wring his neck when I caught up to him. He should have been the one standing in front of Tanaka. I'd like to have seen how cool he would have been with the slant-eyed Jitterbug Demon breathing fire at him.

When I got to the second floor I was reassured by the distinctive odor of linseed oil and turpentine. It smelled better than money. I wrinkled my nose and sniffed again. Someone had forgotten to take out their garbage. I rounded the last flight of stairs expecting to knock and find McHenry, paintbrush in hand, having just signed the 'Monet.'

Instead I turned onto his landing and discovered his shattered door. The air was dense with a rank, meaty odor. Inside, Paul lay on his back in a crusted lake of blood. A heavy hand squeezed my heart. I wanted to turn away, but I couldn't. My stomach puckered, but still I stood there, staring until I gagged. Paul's face had been carved into a macabre mask. There was a toothy grimace cut into his cheek where no mouth was meant to be. One milky eye stared blankly up at the ceiling; the other had been slashed. In places the bones of his face were exposed, surprisingly white in the glare of the overhead lights. There was a gaping wound on the side of his neck. I shuddered, my breath caught in my throat, fear rippling up inside me.

Some perverse part of me wanted to reach out and poke at the smooth white bones of his face, to see if they were real, if they were cold, if it was all as final as it looked. The bitter taste of bile filled my mouth and burned my throat. I backed out onto the landing and threw up, vomit splattering all over my shoes. I stood there for a long time, paralyzed, trying to rein in my panic. His body looked so cold, so exposed. I didn't want anyone to gawk at him in that obscene condition, but I was too scared to go back inside the loft. Something had to be done – I couldn't leave my friend laid out like he was.

When I gathered enough courage to go back in, I was overwhelmed by another odor lurking under the pungent smell of turpentine, paint, and blood. It was cloying and metallic. It smelled of terror and rage and hate and other nameless things that come in the dark as we sweat out our nightmares, tangled in damp sheets. I closed my eyes, but the fear I had tried so hard to contain broke free, skittering up and down my spine like a roach trying to find shelter from the light.

Holding my breath, I picked my way carefully around the blood that had dried around Paul's mutilated body. I knelt over him, swallowing quick shallow breaths. My hands shook and my heart was pounding so hard I thought it might jump out of my chest. A streak of green paint was smeared across his forehead, dark, almost black against the bloodless skin of his brow. The hair on my arms stood up. I had never been this close to a dead body. I covered him with a drop cloth that lay nearby, then tried to catch my breath. Somewhere in the loft Paul's phone began to ring.

I jumped up with a start. The 'Monet'! Jesus Christ, I'd nearly forgotten the painting. I turned toward the studio, still shaking, and prayed that the smeared and tattered canvas standing where I had last seen the painting wasn't it. I lunged closer to get a better look, slipping on the paint and turpentine that coated the floor. It was hard to associate what was left on the easel with the canvas Paul had been agonizing over. Then I saw the signature, Claude Monet, in dark blue paint along the bottom of the painting.

I reached out and touched it. Some of the still wet paint came away on my fingers. He'd finished. My eyes filled, blurring my vision. Turning, I wiped away my tears and looked at Paul's shrouded corpse. Tanaka. Mother of God, what the fuck was I going to tell Tanaka? My head filled with static. I turned back to the painting. I couldn't breathe. My gorge was rising again. The phone was still ringing.

With my brain on fire, I stumbled out of the loft, down the stairs, and onto the street. Outside, I leaned against the building and gulped down huge lungfuls of the wet air, but the charnel-house stench of the loft filled my nose and mouth and coated my throat. For some reason I thought about Caitlin. I wanted to hug my little girl. To feel her small arms around my neck, the warmth of her head on my shoulder. I wanted to feel her heart beating steadily, right up against my own.

CHAPTER SEVEN

I pushed away from Paul's building and stumbled along Lispenard Street with no destination in mind. A voice deep inside my head kept shrieking, 'You're fucked,' over and over again, 'You're fucked.' I knew I had to do something, but what? The green neon sign for the Lucky Shamrock Bar caught my eye, and I went in.

A few of the regulars, clustered at one end of the oak bar, looked up as I entered, then went back to their conversation. Otherwise the Shamrock was empty. Dark and smoky, the place catered to career drinkers. No one noticed or cared when I tossed back three shots of the cheap house whiskey within minutes of pressing up to the bar.

It took the whiskey and a couple of good bumps of dope in the men's room to fortify me enough to call Steven. I used the pay phone on the wall outside of the rest rooms. I dropped the quarter on the floor twice before I finally got it into the slot and dialed. When he answered, I told him to drop what he was doing and get downtown right away. Without explaining, I managed to convey the urgency of the situation, and gave him the address of the Shamrock Bar. Then I lurched back into the men's room and barely made it to the stall, where I puked up the warm whiskey I had just guzzled. I ran cold water in the sink and dipped my face into it. I felt dizzy, feverish. I sat on the john. When I looked down and saw my fouled shoes, I panicked. I jumped up and soaked some paper towels, then tried with shaky hands to scrub them off.

When Steven walked in I was back at the bar knocking down shots of whiskey, chasing them with draft. My hands had stopped trembling when the dope kicked in. But I didn't trust my knees enough to let go of the bar.

I was shocked to see that Steven had brought Devon. Both of them looked at me as though I were some kind of an apparition.

'My God, Adrian, what's happened?' Steven asked, breathless, his face drawn and anxious.

I shook my head at him, still not believing that he had brought Devon.

She echoed his question. 'What's happened? Are you okay?'

Both of them were staring at me as though I might burst into flames.

'Shit . . . I guess I'm just surprised to see you, Devon. Steven didn't think to tell me that he was bringing you.' I spoke harshly. She looked back and forth between us. He shrugged and wouldn't meet my eye.

'Don't be mad at Steven,' Devon appealed. 'I made him bring me. He didn't have a choice. The way he was carrying on I was worried about you.'

I nodded at her. There wasn't anything I could do about it now. 'Let's move to a booth.'

Once seated, I couldn't find any words. I looked at Devon and Steven, saw the concern in their eyes, and sat speechless. I could think of a thousand things I should be feeling – anger, guilt, grief, remorse, but that's all I could do. Think about the feelings. I was numb. The only thing I felt was the icy hand that had reached into my bowel and twisted my guts into a frozen knot.

'It's okay,' Devon said, reaching across the table to touch my hand. 'What's happened?'

Her hand was covering mine. Her fingers were long,

delicate. I looked up into her green eyes and found my voice.

'He's dead,' I mumbled.

'What?' they said in unison.

'He's dead,' I blurted out. 'Paul's dead.'

'What do you mean he's dead?' Steven asked.

I looked across the table at him. The drugs and alcohol had chilled my system, and I felt far away, as though I were watching us from across the room.

'He's been murdered. Butchered. His loft looks like a war zone.' Then I looked at Steven. 'The painting is in tatters.'

His eyes widened. He started to say something and stopped, the words stuck somewhere south of his tongue. Devon put both hands flat on the table and looked at me. Her lips were sealed in a thin red line, too much like a gash against her pale face. I doubted that my reference to the painting meant anything to her, but Steven had understood.

I drew in a deep, ragged breath. 'It was a nightmare, a fucking scene from hell . . . you just – I never saw anything like it.' I stopped and ran the back of my hand across my lips, then I held it out in front of me; it was shaking. 'Whoever killed him, they . . . they slashed him to ribbons. Like an animal, they slaughtered him like an animal. Blood everywhere, the smell . . . his throat cut, I . . . I don't, Christ, they mutilated him, they cut his ears off.'

Devon gasped. Steven made a funny choking noise, somewhere between a cough and a squeak. I looked at my hands on the table, two pale islands against the dark wood, waiting for one of them to say something.

'What're we going to do?' his voice cracked. 'Adrian, tell me. What are we supposed to do?'

'Did you call the police?' Devon asked, before I had a chance to answer Steven.

'No,' I replied. The thought had never crossed my mind.

'Well, we need to.' She reached in her purse and fumbled for change.

Steven and I looked at each other. The few times I'd seen him scared he hadn't acted well.

'Shit, this can't be happening. What about Tanaka?' A vein in his forehead began to throb. 'We need to think this through before we call anyone.' He grew pale; a film of perspiration on his face reflected the blinking, red neon BUD sign over the bar.

'What are you talking about, Steven? What could there possibly be to think about? We have to call the police,' Dev explained, as though we were daft children.

She looked beautiful to me at that moment. Her back was straight, her eyes clear, she seemed strong and resolute. Ready and willing to do the right thing. I dreaded telling her what we had been doing.

As she started to rise from the booth, Steven, who was sitting next to her, overreacted, grabbing her arm and pulling her back down, hard.

'Devon, wait a goddamned minute. We need to think this through.' He chewed on his lower lip, the muscles of his jaw flexing. He looked around the bar as though expecting someone to pop up and offer a solution.

Dev, rubbing her arm, glared at Steven and spoke loudly, 'You ever touch me like that again and it'll be a long time before you grab anyone else, you asshole.'

'Jesus Christ, cut this shit out!' I put my hands on the table, as though to separate them. The room was spinning. I started to feel sick again. 'This is bad enough without you two going off on each other.'

Devon was still rubbing her arm, breathing hard. She turned toward me and asked, 'Exactly what's going on here?' Her face had clouded up, her angry gaze flicked back and forth between Steven and me, waiting for a straight answer.

Steven held on to the table with both hands. His lips were quivering, and a thin line of spittle ran down his chin. I wanted to be drunk. Medicated to the gills. But even after all the whiskey I had consumed, I felt wide awake. Locked in, unable to escape.

'Steven,' I said, 'explain to Dev what's going on. I'll get us all a drink.' I was up and moving on rubbery legs toward the bar before he could argue.

'Adrian, wait . . .' Devon called after me. But I pretended not to hear and kept going.

By the time I returned with three bottles of beer, Steven had explained to Dev about the true nature of our business with Tanaka. Her jaw was clenched shut, her mouth pinched into a hard line. Her fingers plucked nervously at her earrings.

'You two have been lying to me all this time?' She faced Steven and then me, as if waiting for one of us to tell her it was all just a bad joke. 'You told me Paul was a restorer. I believed you.' She shook her head. 'What an idiot I am. How could you? How could you just let me be part of this . . . this garbage without even letting me know what I was getting into?'

Her face collapsed into a scared frown. 'First I find out that Paul has been murdered, and now you're telling me that I've been working for a ring of forgers? I don't believe any of this.' She shook her head again. 'Is there anything else I need to know? Any other little tidbits you two forgot to tell me?'

'Devon,' I said gently. 'We never meant to hurt

anyone, least of all you. We thought it better not to involve you.'

'Involve me! Goddamn you, Adrian, just fuck you and
your explanations for everything. How are you going to
explain your way out of this one?'

Steven and I sat silently in the face of her explosion.
His eyes filled with tears. I felt my face tighten. I wanted
her to understand. But I had underestimated her sense
of betrayal.

She thought for a moment. Then she pulled her coat
tightly around herself as she stood. 'Whatever you
decide to do, leave me out of it. Dammit, I wanted to be
an art dealer. I trusted you to teach me. But not this . . . I
don't ever want anything to do with either of you again.
I'll send for the things in my desk. God, I don't even
want my things, you keep them.'

She turned and walked toward the door, stopped and
hesitated a moment, then returned to the booth and
looked down at both of us.

'Paul McHenry didn't deserve you two.'

Her words cracked like a whip. My cheeks burned.
Steven leaned down and put his face in his hands.

The door slammed behind her.

After a while I asked Steven, 'Do you think she'll call
the police?'

'I don't know. I just don't know. Maybe it would be
better if she did. It might be easier to face them than
Tanaka. This shit is way over my head.' He wiped his eyes
and gulped down his beer, then he picked up Devon's
and drank it. 'I keep thinking about what Narumi told us.
Do you think Tanaka's as dangerous as he said?'

'Don't worry about what Narumi said. We aren't
yakuza. We didn't try and screw Tanaka. This isn't our
fault.'

'You're sure?' he asked.

'Yeah, I'm sure. We're going to have to find a way to come up with some big money fast – but I can't believe Tanaka would do anything crazy.' I hoped to God I was right. Stan popped into my mind, then Tanaka's feral grin while he twirled his blond dance partner. I looked at Steven and tried to control the shudder that began in my knees and shook my shoulders.

We talked about it until we ran out of ideas. By then the booze had hit Steven hard. I was still numb.

'What the hell are we going to do if he won't take his money back?' Steven looked at me with bloodshot eyes, pushing with his index finger at the wet rings our glasses had left on the table.

'We'll cross that bridge if we come to it,' I answered.

''S good idea.'

'Let's go home. We'll sleep on it. We'll meet at the gallery in the morning, at eight-thirty, okay? We'll decide what to do then.' I wasn't drunk, but as I stood up my feet felt farther away than usual.

He nodded. 'If you say so.' Then, 'Adrian?'

'Yeah, partner.' I hauled him up out of the booth.

'What're we gonna do about Paul?'

I put my arm around him and half walked, half carried him out of the bar. 'I don't know, Steven. I don't know.' But he didn't answer me. He was too drunk.

We piled into a cab and I took him home. After I got him laid out on his living room sofa, I left.

I walked half a block to a pay phone, then made two calls: one an anonymous tip about Paul McHenry to 911, the other to Marta. I needed a friend. All I got was her machine.

CHAPTER EIGHT

The phone startled me out of a nod in front of the television. After arriving home from the Shamrock, I had left another message for Marta, then snorted enough smack to finally knock me into the dream state I craved. The real world forgotten, I floated, not awake but not really asleep either. Drifting through some in-between place while I vividly dreamt about sailing in water so blue and clear I could see the bottom. Gliding over a crystal sea, I felt the sun hot on my skin, a salt breeze in my face luffing the sails. Heaven. The dope dream faded as I answered the phone. I tried to shake off the blur, but it had been a long time since anything seemed clear.

'I just checked my messages. Are you okay?' It was Marta returning my call.

'Yeah – I guess. What time is it?' I was groggy.

'Just after midnight.' Judging from the background noise, Marta was entertaining. I heard snatches of conversation and the clinking of dishes and glasses. The cheerful noise of her party offended me, and even though I knew better, I felt a mean stab of jealousy.

'Listen, Marta, something terrible has happened and I need to see you.'

'I've got a house full of people, honey. Can it wait till morning? You couldn't have picked a worse night.'

'Marta,' I interrupted, 'a friend of mine has been murdered.'

'Oh, my God. I'm so sorry, Adrian.'

'Yeah, so am I. Marta, I'm not fucking around. I need someone to talk to.'

'Adrian, I can't just leave a house full of people sitting here. Talk to me till you feel better; I'll get there as soon as I can. Tell me what happened.'

'Do you remember introducing me to Ryuichi Tanaka?'

'Of course I do.' Her tone grew serious.

'This thing involves Tanaka. I don't want to get into it over the phone.'

'Jesus, Adrian. How's Tanaka involved?'

'It's a complicated story. I need you to stop what you're doing and come over here.'

'Hold on for a minute, maybe I can.' She put me on hold, then a few moments later came back on the line. 'If it's that important to you, I will. Give me about an hour.'

Something about her reaction struck me as odd, but the whole damned night had been so ugly and bizarre, I couldn't put my finger on it. When I hung up the phone I looked down and noticed my filthy shoes. I kicked them off and threw them into the garbage, but not before that icy hand pinched my insides.

Marta arrived within the hour dressed in her idea of play clothes. She wore white, a sheer silk outfit that set off her dusky skin and left little to the imagination. Around her neck was a multistrand pearl choker that must have set somebody back the equivalent of a new Mercedes.

'You poor thing, I'm so sorry, honey.'

She paused and examined me for a moment. I stood in front of her, wondering if I looked as ragged as I felt. She kissed me quickly, then dropped her evening bag onto the desk in my living room and helped herself to a glass of wine from the kitchen.

'Do you remember me telling you about Paul McHenry?' I asked when she came out of the kitchen.

'Sure I do. The painter.' She walked into the living room and sat on the sofa.

'He was a genius.' I sat down next to her. 'He had more talent than anyone I've ever known. You know he was forging Impressionist paintings for Steven and me.'

She nodded, sipping.

'We've been selling them to Tanaka. He's been buying everything that Paul can produce.' I paused and looked at her, but she sat quietly, curled up in the corner of the sofa, waiting for me to continue.

'Somebody killed him. They fucking slaughtered McHenry like some kind of an animal.' I began shaking. She reached over and touched my arm. 'Marta, it was a nightmare. I got there . . . the door was shattered . . . he was lying there. At first I wasn't even sure it was him. Blood everywhere. They didn't just kill him, they mutilated him.'

'Oh, shit. It must have been horrible.' She took my hand and stroked it. 'Tell me how Tanaka's involved.'

'He was trying to finish a piece for Tanaka when it happened. Paul was trying to make it perfect. Whoever murdered him trashed his place, they cut up the painting. It's a total loss.' The room suddenly felt cold. I wrapped my arms around my middle and squeezed. 'I don't know what to think. Tanaka's already paid us half the money. He's gonna shit.'

'Adrian, you need to call him, let him decide what to do.'

'Tanaka? I'm not ready to talk to him yet. Paul's been butchered, and I have to do something about it.'

'Just how much do you owe Tanaka?' she asked, sitting up.

'Paul is dead! For God's sake, Marta, they cut his

fucking ears off! I never saw so much blood. Tanaka will have to wait.'

'I'm sorry about Paul, but I don't think there's anything you can do about it. I think you better worry about Tanaka. How much do you owe him?'

'We wouldn't owe him anything if we had the painting. He advanced us three hundred twenty-five thousand. God only knows what he'll want on top of that.'

She got up and started pacing around my apartment. Her breasts swayed as she walked, her nipples dark through the silk of her blouse.

'That's very serious money. Have you got it?' She continued pacing, then turned. 'Whether you do or not, you need to call him,' she said emphatically.

'Why are you so worried about Tanaka?' I asked.

She stopped pacing and looked at me hard.

I returned her look and added, 'I know he's your friend, but so am I, and I need to have a plan before I talk to him. I don't know who killed Paul, or why, but I need a little time to work things out before I call Tanaka, or anyone else.'

'Adrian . . .'

'Come on, Marta.' I held out my arms.

She stepped to the sofa, touched my cheek, and agreed to spend the night. Then she walked to the desk and got a bindle of heroin from her evening bag. She laid out a good-sized mound and held out the small silver tube she kept in her bag.

'Come, it'll make you feel better.'

I took the silver straw and did some, but instead of relaxing me, it had the opposite effect. I felt edgy and irritable.

'I just don't understand who would do something like this.' I leaned back against the desk, hugging myself.

'There are a lot of crazies in the world. Who knows.' Marta cut out another line and handed me the straw. I snorted half and offered her the rest. She declined.

'Why? Why kill someone like McHenry? He never hurt anyone.'

Marta didn't answer. She was usually a good listener, but she seemed far away. Distracted.

'Marta, you know what they say about Tanaka. Do you think he had anything to do with this?'

She looked up at me. 'Don't be silly.' She patted the couch beside her. 'Sit, Adrian. Try and relax. It'll all work out.'

When we finally undressed and went to bed, she massaged my neck and shoulders, and eventually I dozed off into a fitful sleep. I had a dream about Paul. He came to me at the gallery, bleeding, unable to speak. Air whistled in and out of the slash in his neck. He silently beckoned me to follow him, but I was scared, unwilling to come out from behind my desk. He beseeched me with frantic gestures, but I was too terrified to budge. Finally he grew angry and started to tear at his ruined face. It came off in ragged strips of bloody flesh, which he threw at me. I screamed and sat up in bed.

I opened my eyes. Marta was gone, the bedroom dark and silent. My heart was pounding from the nightmare. According to the clock by the bed it was a little after 2:00 A.M. I got up and padded into the living room to find her. All the lamps were out – the only illumination came from a crack of light visible under the guest-room door. I walked over and was about to open the door when I heard her voice. She was on the phone, talking so softly that I couldn't quite make out her words. It sounded as if she was about to end the conversation. Just before she did, she spoke loudly enough for me to hear her clearly. It jolted me. She was speaking Japanese, and her final words hung in the air, a reproach to my stupidity.

'*Hai, Tanaka-san, sayonara.*'

Stunned, I stood there as she opened the door and we found ourselves face-to-face. She startled when she saw me, then quickly regained her composure.

'How much did you hear?'

'Enough. Why did you call him?'

'I told you to call him yourself. If you had, I wouldn't have needed to. Now he's on the way. I'm sure you two can work it out,' she said. Naked, her breasts brushed against me as she squeezed through the door and walked to the desk, where she lit a cigarette from her purse.

'Why did you call him?' This time there was an edge to my voice, and I turned and followed her into the living room. I wanted an answer.

'Adrian, my poor Adrian,' she murmured, inhaling on her cigarette. 'You know what I do. Who do you think makes it possible? I've worked for Tanaka for a long time. First in Tokyo, now here. You didn't think I introduced you to him by accident, did you?' She smiled coldly as she spoke, and for the first time I realized who and what she really was.

'What did you do, procure me for Tanaka like some kind of pimp?'

'It's not like that, Adrian. I give my little parties, and whenever I meet someone who might interest him, I introduce them. Anything you and Tanaka cooked up was strictly between the two of you.'

There was an element of truth in her words. But I felt handled, used.

'Come on, Adrian. Stop pouting. You and Tanaka had a good run. Now be a good boy. Sit down and we'll wait for him.' She sat on the corner of the desk and pulled her evening bag closer.

'What about us, Marta?'

'We were business. It was fun, but it was business.'

If I hadn't had my head so far up my ass, I might have seen it. As it was, the news came as a shock. I had thought of myself as a player; it was tough facing the fact that I was a fish. A goddamned bottom feeder. I had swallowed Marta hook, line, and sinker, only to find out it was Tanaka who held the rod and reel. It didn't take long for my surprise to turn to anger.

'Fuck you!' I said, heading for the bedroom. 'I'm out of here. I'll call Tanaka as soon as I decide what to do. You're welcome to wait here for him.' I was almost to the bedroom door when I heard the unmistakable sound of a round being jacked into the chamber of an automatic. When I turned she was standing in front of the desk, holding a small Beretta aimed at my midsection. I almost laughed, but the hole in the end of the barrel looked about the size of a silver dollar. And there wasn't a trace of humor in Marta's eyes. I put up my hands.

'Let's do this the easy way, okay, Adrian?' She gestured with the gun toward the bedroom. 'We'll put some clothes on, then we'll wait here for Tanaka.'

I did as she said, backing into the bedroom with her following me. My heart was bouncing around inside my chest, but for the first time that night I wasn't afraid. I was too busy feeling stupid. As she watched, I threw on some jeans and a sweater and managed to pocket my wallet and keys before she said, 'Enough.' She gestured toward the bathroom and told me to wait inside while she dressed.

In the bathroom I looked frantically for some type of a weapon, but I came up blank. I was jacked on adrenaline. My nerves were drawn tight, the blood was singing in my ears. The tile floor was cold on my feet as I tried to think of a plan. Part of me was outside of myself. I felt no fear, just anger. Anger bordering on rage at all that had happened and at how big a fool I had proven to be.

Soon she ordered me to come out holding my hands in front of me. I had been her puppy for so long, following her lead, never questioning anything, that I don't think it ever crossed her mind to be afraid of me. She was dressed and held the gun steadily. It was pointed at my chest.

She was guiding me into the living room toward the couch when the phone rang. Our eyes met, and for the first time I saw a flicker of indecision flash across her face. I took a step toward the phone on my desk.

'Stop,' she demanded.

'It could be Tanaka,' I said quietly.

The phone continued to ring, and I could see that she wasn't sure what to do about it. I took another step toward the desk. Now she was just out of arm's reach, but she still held all the cards.

'It could be Tanaka,' I repeated. 'One of us should answer it.'

She glanced at the phone as she tried to decide, and I lunged at her. The gun went off, but I had caught her by surprise and her shot went wide. As I crashed into her, the gun flew from her grip and landed under my desk. I scrambled for it and came up with it ready to shoot. Marta got up at the same time and started to say something, but I hit her with a straight left that caught her on the point of her chin. She crumpled to the floor, quiet for the moment.

My only thought was to get out of there. I grabbed tennis shoes and a coat and was out the door before the echo of the shot had completely faded. It wasn't until I was on the street that I realized my dope and my cash were still upstairs. No way was I going back. I tossed Marta's gun into a storm drain, then began walking toward the gallery, where I kept a small emergency stash of heroin and a few hundred dollars' mad money.

CHAPTER NINE

The bottle of Laphroaig sat where I had left it, beside my briefcase on the mahogany partner's desk Steven and I shared. Uncapping it, I took a long pull. The adrenaline rush from my confrontation with Marta had worn off, and in its place a jittery exhaustion settled over me.

The gallery was quiet, the hush broken only by the sound of the all-night traffic on Park Avenue eight floors below. I retrieved my mad money, thirteen one-hundred-dollar bills, and the bundle of heroin I kept stashed in my half of the desk. I thought about calling Steven to tell him what had happened with Marta, but I was still smarting over how naive I had been. We were due to meet in a few hours. I decided to wait and tell him in person.

Walking through the exhibition space and into the storage room, I took a quick inventory of anything I thought might help me with Tanaka. Nothing presented a clear solution. All of the inventory put together added up to more than enough to pay him back, assuming I could sell it quickly. But I wasn't sure how much he would demand.

I walked back into my office, wishing we hadn't put so much money into the renovations. We had nothing put aside for a rainy day, and suddenly it was hurricane season. The teakwood floors, the custom lighting, and all the built-in features we had paid through the nose for now seemed ridiculous. The money from the forgeries had been so good, so easy, I had never even considered the possibility that it could stop. Now I was looking at it from the wrong end of a big stick.

I was scared and angry, and I didn't know which way to turn. One thing was clear: I needed to find someplace to lie low while I tried to work things out. I grabbed my briefcase, threw in my dope and my mad money. The small photograph of Caitlin sitting on my desk caught my eye, and I tucked it into my breast pocket. Then I walked out.

The Hotel Rimbaud was a tattered old European-style hotel on East Fifty-fourth Street. Frank Testa, the night manager, and I had become friends when I lived there after my last divorce. He was on duty when I walked in and seemed more than happy to accommodate me with a guest room for a few hours. Although he was my age, he was bald and at least a hundred pounds over-weight. He came out from behind the counter and stood with his hands on his hips, rocking on his heels. His stomach protruded over the waist of his pants, and every time he shifted his weight from heel to toe his belly rolled like a soft sea. His moon face was pockmarked, his eyes shiny little black glass buttons all but hidden in folds of flesh, but his generous mouth held a welcoming smile.

'Adrian, how long you and I known each other?' he asked, waving away the money I was trying to hand him.

'Too long, Frankie. Way too long.'

'Nah, that's not what I meant. It's good to see ya, man. You still rockin' and rollin' with the babes? Man, you were somethin' else. Remember the time that blond chick called the police?' I looked at him blankly. 'Come on, Adrian. You and she was staying in the penthouse. You tossed her clothes off the balcony and she tried to get you locked up.' He chuckled, a deep rolling sound. 'I never will forget her storming out of here naked as the day she was born. Nothin' but that little blanket 'round her shoulders. How did you get outta that one?'

I had no idea what he was talking about.

'Man, you used to have some wild times.' He tucked his hands in his back pockets and smiled, apparently vicariously enjoying my past exploits. The way he looked made me wish I could remember them as clearly. I was beginning to think that too many of my 'wild times' were stored in someone else's memory bank.

'It's late, amigo,' he said handing me a key. 'I don't expect any other check-ins. The room's on me.' He winked. 'For old times' sake.'

Once in the room I dropped onto the bed and lay there, staring at the cracked and stained ceiling, reliving the last twenty-four hours, wishing it were all a dream. I tried to remember throwing some blonde's clothes off the penthouse balcony, but I couldn't.

My wild times. The stuff of Frank Testa's dreams. Shit, all of my wild times should have come packaged with a physician's warning. I could barely remember a time when getting high wasn't part of my life. I got started in boarding school. By the time I was fourteen, I knew that I wasn't going to win any popularity contests unless I figured an angle. Mary Beth Tollerude's 'Are you serious?' followed by a laughing announcement to all of the other sixteen-year-old girls about my presumptive if misguided advance convinced me of this unfortunate fact of life. Tall and skinny for my age, I was a year and a half younger than my classmates, and decidedly average in most categories. As an athlete I made the soccer team but rarely got in the game. My parents drove a new Mercedes every few years and never complained about the tuition, but by the standards of the Gulfstream Academy in Palm Beach, I was definitely from the wrong side of the tracks. But . . . but . . . but, my life seemed full of buts. Except for Mary Beth Tollerude's.

Then I discovered that I had one talent that set me apart. I knew more about getting high than anyone in the school. By tenth grade I owned a well-thumbed copy of the *PDR*. I may have carried a C average, but I was a kickass partyer. I had the equivalent of a Ph.D. in getting fucked up. Sharing this wealth of knowledge was my claim to fame. Students came to me for advice with the smuggled contents of their parents' medicine cabinets, or their most recent street purchase. Dosages, combinations and effects, the addition of alcohol, I never lost a patient, and I never missed a party. Eventually I even got my yearning fingers on the Tollerude treasure, and what a tightly wound rear end it turned out to be, although I'm a little fuzzy on the exact circumstances of my triumph. Let the good times roll, Frankie.

By 4:00 A.M. the videotapes were playing loops in my head. Close-ups of Paul McHenry wiped to a shot of Marta, her nipples hard, her eyes harder, holding a gun pointed at my chest. Over and over again the images flashed before my eyes, projected straight from my fevered brain onto the stained ceiling. Marta holding the gun. Paul holding his brushes and palette. Then lying in a lake of his own blood, his face cut away, over and over again, until my head throbbed and my eyes burned.

Sleep had denied me solace by the time 7:30 A.M. rolled around on the digital clock perched on the battered night table. I imagined Tanaka and his associates circling the streets of Manhattan like hungry sharks. It suddenly struck me as incredibly stupid to have Steven meet me at the gallery. It was the first place Tanaka's people would look for us. Picking up the phone, I dialed him with one hand and fished in my briefcase for the heroin with the other. His machine picked up on the fourth ring. Assuming he was in the shower, I left word for him to meet me in the lobby of his building at 8:30 instead of at the gallery.

The white paper bindle contained enough dope to last two days – if I was really careful. I snorted just enough to keep the monkey quiet and carefully returned the rest to my pocket. In the elevator it came back to me. Her name was Sherri. I had met her at Nell's. I couldn't remember exactly what she had done, but it had pissed me off big-time. I remembered gathering her clothes and hurling them off the balcony into the night. Her lacy red panties had risen on an updraft and made me think of Mars as they drifted away. That was all I could remember – her name and her red underwear.

It was quarter past eight when I walked into Steven's building. The lobby was empty, with the exception of the doorman sitting behind a desk in front of the elevators.

'I'm sorry, but he's not in,' he responded when I asked him to ring Steven's apartment. 'He left about an hour ago with two gentlemen. Are you Mr Sellars?' he asked, removing an envelope with my name on it from his desk drawer.

My stomach twisted when I tore it open and recognized the three cranes embossed at the top of the short note. Tanaka's personal crest.

Mr Ballard is with us. Contact Marta Batista immediately. We intend to resolve this situation. Please do not doubt our seriousness.

Kotani

I read it twice and then stuffed the note into my back pocket.

'Are you all right, sir?' the doorman asked. 'You look as though you've seen a ghost.'

'I hope not,' I answered, heading toward the street.

On the sidewalk I stopped and looked around, but nothing looked sinister or out of place, just the usual rush hour crowd hustling to get to work. Standing under the awning of Steven's building, I watched the faces pass by, telling myself to be cool, think it through. But my mind felt sticky.

I walked toward Times Square, kicking myself for not warning him. A simple phone call, just a few seconds on the line and maybe we could have avoided this. Think, damnit, think. I walked smack into a man carrying a briefcase and a cake box. 'Watch where you're going, jerk!' he called after me before being swept away by the flow of the crowd. I mumbled an apology and plunged back into the stream.

After about ten blocks I ducked into a coffee shop. Someone had left today's issue of the *New York Post* in the booth I chose. On the front page was a picture of Paul McHenry, under the headline ARTIST'S MUTILATED BODY FOUND IN TRIBECA LOFT. I scanned the article and nearly choked when I read that homicide detectives were looking for me. One of Paul's neighbors had placed me at the scene early last evening. Trish. How could I have forgotten about Trish?

I didn't know whether to laugh or cry. I felt as though I was caught in the flow of a great and powerful river. If I didn't keep swimming, and swimming hard, I knew I'd be pulled under by the suck of the current. I did the only thing I could – kept my head above water and kicked for my life.

I bolted out of the coffee shop, the *Post* under my arm, and spent hours bouncing around Manhattan from bar to bar, worrying about Steven and feeling sorry for myself. I ended up in a clone of the Lucky Shamrock, a serious drinkers' spot named O'Hara's. Over my second Irish whiskey, it dawned on me to call Duncan Marshall.

Duncan Marshall practiced law the way he did everything else – with the ease and confidence peculiar to those born knowing they belong. Tall and slim, in his midforties, he still had the WASPy athletic good looks that must have served him well growing up. He was from an old Georgia family that owned land originally granted them in the eighteenth century by King George himself. The first time I met him, I wrote him off as a dilettante asshole. But our circle of friends overlapped, and after running into him here and there, I got to know him and changed my mind.

Two years ago I was at the opening party for the Winter Antiques show held every January at the National Guard Armory on Park Avenue. It's a major affair. Some of the greatest art and antique dealers in the world exhibit their best inventory to collectors from around the globe. Tickets are hard to come by and expensive as hell.

The show lasts only two weeks, but the exhibiting dealers spend a fortune decorating small booths with everything from wallpaper and moldings to antique carpets and custom lighting. Some bring in painters to add faux finishes, others hire carpenters to install hardwood floors. The cavernous armory, which usually looks like an enormous high school gymnasium, is turned into a series of lavish vignettes worthy of royalty.

The preview party was a mad crush. Designer-dressed, bone-thin women, who spent their days planning the next charity benefit for the 'less fortunate' over lunch, arrived early with their decorators in tow. Their husbands came later, the ruling class out to be seen and envied. I imagined they were fortified by drinks at their clubs, and the benefits of whatever dividends they had wrung from a hard day of trading. Almost to a man they wore smug, self-satisfied expressions on their clean-shaven pink cheeks. They seemed to say: 'We know something the rest of you don't.' But judging from the mannequins they had married, I figured it had to do with interest rates.

Formally dressed collectors vied with one another for the right to have first call on some of the most exquisite objects available anywhere in the world. Rare Fabergé jewelry. Rembrandt drawings. A Chippendale desk once owned by the Prince of Wales. A pair of lingerie cabinets once owned by Marie Antoinette. Price was no object, especially to the newly wealthy collectors, who seemed amazed to find that these things could be had for mere money.

An English marquis bought the Chippendale desk, nodding happily as his wife and their decorator, a swishy-looking Frenchman in a lavender silk suit, congratulated him on his astute eye. I watched as a real estate developer from Milwaukee bought a pair of rare eighteenth-century astrolabes for a cool six hundred thousand, then walked to the bar and ordered a beer. Millions of dollars changed hands in the space of an hour. Trading was based on a nod and a handshake. The funds would come later via international wire transfer. These people didn't carry money.

Neither bone thin nor wealthy enough to compete, I was there as a spectator, trying to learn all I could about the players in a game I very much wanted to be a part of.

No matter how much I despised the artless social climbing that seemed endemic to these affected patrons of the arts, I wanted in. I wanted to smile and shake hands, then call the bank and tell them to expect a wire transfer. I knew I was cut out for this world. I could smell it.

I was standing in the Hyde Park Antiques booth, admiring an incredible Queen Anne lacquered secretary bookcase, when I heard a commotion behind me. It was Duncan Marshall and his wife, Dana. Dana had collapsed in the middle of an antique-porcelain dealer's booth. A crowd gathered around them, but nobody seemed to be doing anything constructive. Duncan was on the floor, cradling his wife's head in his lap. The proprietor of the booth, a small fey man from London, stood looking horrified beside a collector who held an eighteenth-century Meissen squirrel. The dealer mopped his brow with a yellow silk handkerchief, undecided as to where his duty lay. He looked at the unfortunate woman who had picked his booth to faint in. Then he looked longingly at his client. The straining tendons of his thin neck stood out like the cords holding his bifocals, as he swiveled his head back and forth resembling a sideline spectator at Wimbledon. After a few agonizing moments the dealer made his decision. Pocketing the square of lemon silk, he turned his back on the Marshalls and smiled at the collector.

I hustled to the bar and grabbed a bottle of Perrier and several linen napkins. Squeezing through the crowd huddled around the Marshalls, I soaked one of the napkins with the cold mineral water and handed it to Duncan. He bathed his wife's face with it. Her eyes fluttered and she came around. When it became clear that she was all right, he looked up and thanked me. There was such a wealth of concern for her in his eyes that I instantly changed my mind about Duncan Marshall. It turned out that Dana was pregnant. Duncan got her home, and eight months later their fourth child, a girl named Cathryn, was born.

Duncan and I forged a connection that night, which grew into a friendship. We made it a point to grab a beer and a burger together every month or so at P.J. Clarke's and talk over the world's problems. Over the years I discovered that underneath the mild disposition, the blond good looks and soft Southern accent lurked a street fighter with the instincts of a mongoose and a Harvard law degree. He was a good man to have on your side. It was a little past 2:00 P.M. when I fumbled a quarter into the pay phone. I hoped he would be in.

He answered on the second ring.

'Duncan, it's Adrian.'

Silence for a moment, then, 'Adrian, where are you? Can you talk?'

'Yeah, I can talk. I'm in a bar on the West Side. I'm in trouble.'

'I know, I've read about it. Are you all right?'

'Well.' I paused to consider. 'I'm in one piece, if that's what you mean.'

'That's a start,' Duncan answered. 'Why don't you come over, maybe I can help.'

On my way across town to the Chrysler building, where he kept an elegant suite of offices, I made up my mind to tell him everything. I had been drinking for the better part of the day, but I felt strangely sober.

He met me in the reception area as soon as his secretary announced my arrival. Then he ushered me into his paneled office.

'You look like hell, Adrian.'

'Yeah – well, I think I've been there.'

'If I'm going to help you, you need to tell me everything, from the beginning, and don't leave out anything,' he said, lowering himself into a leather barrister's chair behind a desk larger than the one Steven and I shared. He leaned back and picked up a little bronze dog that he used as a paperweight. He sat still, turning it in his hands as I spoke. He carried a quiet air of confidence and strength. Just the sight of him reassured me.

Across the wide expanse of his desk, I watched his face as my story unfolded. For the first time since that night at the antique show, he looked upset when I described the bloody scene at McHenry's loft. His usual good color faded, and his mouth turned down at the corners. I told him that Tanaka had Steven, and handed him Kotani's note. He put the bronze dog down, read the note, then blew his nose. When I finished he sat there, resting his chin on his steepled fingers, the note in front of him on the desk, a strange faraway look in his eyes.

'I knew you had a problem when I read about Paul McHenry this morning. I didn't think you were a murderer, so I was confident we could straighten that mess out.' He paused and tapped his lips with his fingers. 'This business with Tanaka is another kettle of fish. Now he has Steven? To be honest with you, Adrian, this entire mess stinks all to hell.'

I started to interrupt him, but he held up both hands as though surrendering, then continued.

'I'm not going to judge you, but you've really stepped in it this time.'

'Duncan, you're preaching to the choir here. I'm real clear on the problem, it's the solution I can't figure out. What the hell should I do?'

'Adrian, I don't know. I just don't know. As an officer

of the court, I can't advise you to do anything illegal, but I'm not sure I like your other options. I'm going to have to chew on it for a while.'

'Chew on it as long as you want.' I got up and walked over to the bookcase behind his desk. He had several books about art standing next to the heavy case-law volumes that lined the shelves. I took down one on the abstract expressionists.

'You know, sometimes I look at these things and it all seems a little bit like the emperor's new clothes. Imagine, millions and millions of dollars for these canvases.' I shook my head. 'Other days I look and it seems to me that no amount of money is as important as these paintings.' I held the book out for him to see.

'You're getting philosophical on me, Adrian. I think we better concentrate on reality. Have you got a place to stay?'

'Yeah,' I answered, shelving the book.

'Why don't you go get some rest. I'll think this through, try and come up with some ideas for you.' Duncan stood and walked me to the elevator.

Before I left and headed back to the Hotel Rimbaud to chill out, I promised to call him later that evening.

Back at the hotel, Frank wasn't on duty. So I checked in under the name O'Hara and paid cash in advance for two nights.

At eight o'clock I called Duncan at home. Dana answered, and when she put the phone down to go get him, the sounds of family life came flooding over the line. A child scolded someone or something named Max, the noise of a television show blared in the background.

It reminded me of my failures on the domestic front. Knowing Duncan, but never having been in his home, I pictured a tastefully done interior, with a sprinkling of low-country antiques, on top of which sat framed photographs of his blond children with pert noses, who attended the right schools. The perfect American family at home.

In each of my three marriages, I had tried to create the type of life I now pictured myself connected to by miles of telephone wire. I hadn't come close. My first marriage had been the defiant act of a child attempting to prove he was a man. It lasted six months. I came home from a fishing trip one day and found our apartment stripped bare. All she had left were my clothes, and a note that said: 'Enough is enough. Go to hell, Adrian.' My second hadn't been much better. A drug-soaked exploration of how to destroy a friendship. And the last was a continuation of the first two, broken by infrequent periods of lucid sobriety, into one of which was born my daughter, Caitlin, six years ago. That marriage ended in a bitter divorce soon after Caitlin turned two.

But it had been worth it. Becoming a father was one of the greatest moments of my life. The day she was born, the first moment I laid eyes on her, Caitlin Sellars lifted my heart with winged fingers and has been in possession of it ever since.

Within a year of our divorce Marilyn had picked up stakes and moved with Caitlin to Arlington, Virginia. Since then, I hadn't seen Caitlin nearly as much as I wanted to. The enmity between Marilyn and me came to the surface whenever we dealt with issues of custody or visitation. Exercising my rights as Caitlin's father had proved to be a constant and exhausting legal battle. A battle that, without meaning to, I had ceded to Caitlin's mother. For a while the drugs had done their job and kept me from thinking too much about it. But listening to the Marshall family, I suddenly wanted to think about it. I wondered what Caitlin was doing – was she already in bed? Did she still sleep with the stuffed hippopotamus that she named Señor Popomo? I wanted to kiss her forehead and know that she was all right.

Duncan finally picked up, and his businesslike tone brought me back to the problems at hand.

'Adrian, you okay?'

'The same. You?'

'Fine. Listen, one of my partners does quite a bit of tax work for a couple of Japanese companies. At my request he made a few discreet inquiries. You're right, Adrian, this Tanaka is a heavy hitter.'

'You should hear some of the stories I've heard about this guy.'

'Yeah, from what I've been told, they're probably true. Your friend Tanaka has been implicated but not charged in at least seven different homicide cases, in Tokyo alone, over the past five years. In one of the cases an entire family, the parents and two small children, were killed. This guy is very bad news.'

'Jesus, how the hell am I supposed deal with someone like that?'

'I wish I had a brilliant idea. Where Tanaka is concerned, there's not much I can do for you. The police are another story. I've called in a few chips downtown. The homicide detective handling McHenry's murder is a guy named John Carstairs. He's a friend of a friend, and I have it through pretty good sources that he doesn't believe you were the perpetrator. Apparently their witness placed you at the scene well after forensics estimates the time of death. This Carstairs wants to talk with you, but I think I can keep him off your back for a while.'

'What if I just went and told him everything? The for-geries, Tanaka, everything.'

'That's an option, but it's probable that you would end up charged with a felony. At a minimum, you'd be looking at criminal fraud charges, theft by deception – Christ, Adrian, I'm not even sure what other laws you may have violated. The feds would probably get in-volved, and they might throw a RICO charge at you. But that's not what worries me most. Once you were in custody, I seriously doubt the authorities could protect you. Someone like Tanaka could reach out and touch you anytime he wanted. Your life would be a nightmare. You would always be looking over your shoulder, and under your car, waiting for the day he decides to re-member you. Believe me, Adrian, guys like that never forget.'

'I believe, Duncan, I believe. I don't have very many options, do I?'

'My advice is to try and work it out with him. Do any-thing it takes to make him go away. I don't think the world is a big enough place to run and hide from his kind.'

I felt light-headed. The room seemed airless. 'You're saying I should just sit down with this bastard and try and work it out? How the hell am I supposed to do that?'

'I'm not sure. I've never negotiated anything quite like this. My instincts tell me to try and follow their lead, do as they say up to a point. If you set up a meeting, you should do it in a public place. Ask them to show some good faith.'

'Shit, Duncan, they have all the leverage. How can I make them show good faith? Tanaka writes his own rules.'

'Then play by his rules, but remember, you have

something they want. Tell them you'll only meet if they agree to bring Steven. Don't push too hard, but don't act terrified either.'

Easy for you to say, I thought. 'Any other suggestions?'

'No. Just be careful and call me, let me know what happens. And Adrian . . .'

'Yeah?'

'Good luck, man.'

Alone. He hadn't said it, but that was the simple truth of the matter. I was on my own. I got out the smack and spooned out a fat line. Then I took several deep breaths and dialed Marta's number.

'Adrian, you're a fool,' she spat when she realized it was me.

The tone of her voice set my teeth on edge.

'Shut the fuck up and listen,' I hissed into the phone. 'If Tanaka wants to meet, set it up, but I don't want any more of your crap.'

The deadly edge in my voice seemed to subdue her a bit.

'Tanaka wants to see you right away,' she informed me.

'All right, tell him I'll meet him at nine-thirty tonight, at the China Grill on Fifty-third Street.'

'I'll have to verify that. Give me a number and I'll call you back in five minutes,'

'Right, Marta, you want an address, too? I'll call you in exactly five minutes.'

I waited an extra few minutes before I called back, trying as Duncan had suggested not to appear terrified.

'Well?' I asked.

'He'll meet you at nine-thirty, but he says either his place or mine.'

'No way, Marta. It'll be in public or not at all, and tell Tanaka to bring Steven. I want proof that he's all right.'

She put me on hold for a moment, then came back on the line. 'Where exactly is the China Grill?'

'It's across from MoMA on Fifty-third, in the CBS building. Tell him to bring Steven, and not to try anything crazy. I'll have friends in the restaurant,' I lied.

'I'm sure that will make him very nervous,' she answered sarcastically, then added in a more serious tone, 'Don't do anything stupid, Adrian. If you do what he says, everything will work out. He'll be there at nine-thirty with Steven.'

CHAPTER TEN

The China Grill occupies the street level of the CBS building. It had been a trendy spot for a few years now, and Steven and I had celebrated more than one big sale over a long, wet lunch there. I arrived at eight forty-five, and as I had expected, the place was crowded. A quiet talk with the hostess and a fifty-dollar tip secured me the table I wanted, in the center of the raised dining platform looking toward the Fifty-third Street entrance. I was surrounded by other patrons and hoped that was enough.

I ordered a double Stoli on the rocks and settled in to wait. The restaurant was filled with a typical Friday-night group of attractive couples, businessmen on the make at the bar, and suburbanites in from New Jersey and Long Island for an evening on the town. I didn't notice any Japanese faces, but that wasn't proof that Tanaka didn't have the place covered.

I had snorted some smack before leaving the Rimbaud, and although I had been careful, I would soon run out. The second Stoli was going down smoothly as I pondered where to safely score some clean dope. Then I saw Kotani walk in and look around. As usual, he was dressed like an accountant, in a blue suit and trench coat. When he spotted me he nodded, then continued his survey of the room. Then he walked back out. He returned a few minutes later with Steven, who looked worn and frightened but otherwise okay, and Stan, with his poodle do and hard eyes, which automatically swept the restaurant. Steven looked at me and mouthed something, but I couldn't make out what he was trying to tell me. They were followed in by Tanaka and Marta, who was unable to disguise the smirk on her face.

Tanaka whispered something to Kotani, who then led Steven, Marta, and Stan into the bar area. Then he approached my table and sat down without any greeting. Before words were exchanged the waiter appeared and offered drinks; Tanaka asked for a Perrier, I ordered another Stoli.

'Adrian, you know who I am and what I do, so why have you acted so foolishly and caused us all so much trouble?' he asked after the waiter left us.

'Mr Tanaka, I didn't plan any of this. I assume Marta's told you by now what happened to McHenry and to your painting. If she hadn't acted so heavy-handed, pulling a gun and threatening me, I'm sure you and I would have already resolved this situation.' I lifted the empty drink I held and sipped at the ice cubes, which tumbled out of the glass onto my face and down the front of my shirt.

He watched as I wiped my face on the cocktail napkin and brushed the ice cubes out of my lap, tapping out a cadence on the tabletop with his fingers. Tanaka was the picture of a twentieth-century mogul, dressed in a Savile Row suit and tie. But he still looked like an ancient Japanese warlord to me. His lined face and hooded eyes were unfathomable. If he was angry, you couldn't tell it by looking at him. Only the persistent tapping of his fingers revealed any feeling at all.

Finally I broke the silence. 'Mr Tanaka, I don't intend to run and hide from you. I'll pay you every cent I owe you.'

At this, his lips twisted into a nasty smile.

'Plus whatever interest you want,' I added hastily. 'I just need a little time.'

He continued to grin at me, still tapping his fingers. His eyes reminded me of the cat's-eye marbles I had owned as a kid. They glinted in the light, expressionless and disconcerting as hell. He sat there silently smiling at me. What he was waiting for, I couldn't guess. His speechless tapping was starting to unnerve me, and I was beginning to get angry when the waiter suddenly appeared with our drinks, babbling about the evening's special, sake-cured salmon rolls. I asked him to come back later, and he departed. Still not a word from Tanaka.

Finally I couldn't stand it anymore. 'Goddamnit, my friend's been butchered, I don't know which way to turn, and you and Marta play games with me.'

His smile faded. He slapped the palm of his hand down on the table hard enough to make our glasses jump and startle our neighbors. People turned and then quickly looked away. We were in New York.

'I do not play games. Now stop your whining. I told you before that I had already made plans for the "Monet." Nothing has changed. I'm not interested in a refund of my money.' His tapping had stopped, but his face had hardened into an implacable mask lit from within by a burning intensity that surprised me. I preferred the tapping.

'What do you want?' I asked. 'The painting is gone. Without Paul McHenry I have no way to produce another one.'

'I think you do, Adrian.'

'There are other forgers around, but none of them are as good as Paul was.'

'You misunderstand me. I don't want another forgery.

I doubt there is anyone in the world who could produce as good a fake as your McHenry,' he said. 'Certainly not within my time frame.'

He continued to study my face, as it slowly dawned on me what he meant.

'No way, Mr Tanaka.' I shook my head emphatically. 'An original "Monet" *Water Lilies* would cost over six million dollars. I can't come up with anything near that. You might as well ask for sixty million.'

'Adrian, I only expect what you have already agreed to deliver. I'm going to hold you to that agreement.'

'It's impossible,' I stated. 'Impossible. I can't come up with that kind of money.'

'No one has asked you to come up with any money. You're a professional, Adrian. Go use your talents and find me a "Monet". Certainly you know other dealers who possess such works. Get one on consignment, then deliver it to me. Believe me, Adrian, you would rather owe one of them than me.' The threat implied by his words hung in the air and reverberated. He looked at his watch, then took a sip of his Perrier. 'I'll be traveling next week; you have until the end of the following week to deliver a "Monet". No games, Adrian. Don't disappoint me twice.'

He stood up and gestured to Kotani at the bar. Then he looked down at me.

'My people tell me you have a beautiful little daughter. She lives with her mother in Arlington, doesn't she? Don't even consider approaching the authorities. They can't help you.'

My heart froze. I sat there gaping up at him, speechless.

Dropping a hundred-dollar bill on the table, he turned and without another word walked out of the

China Grill, followed by Stan. By the time I stood up, Kotani, Marta, and Steven were waiting for me outside the door. Steven and I hurried down the street headed east, Marta and Kotani on our heels.

'You all right, Steven?' I asked as we walked away from the immediate vicinity of the restaurant.

'Yeah, they took my watch and my wallet, but they didn't knock me around or anything.'

He was mumbling something else when Kotani, without warning, pulled from his trench coat a small-caliber automatic fitted with a silencer, grabbed Steven and forced him into the shadow of a doorway. Steven struggled, but Kotani subdued him easily with a vicious blow to the throat. Kotani held him upright by the collar of his jacket, the gun pointed at his head, and looked up at me. Steven's eyes bulged in terror as he fought for air. The night clicked into slow motion. I heard him gasping for breath, otherwise the world had grown deathly quiet. Even Marta looked surprised, eyes wide, the smirk gone. Staring straight into my eyes, Kotani pulled the trigger; he shot Steven once in the side of the head without so much as blinking. Steven's face contorted, then his body collapsed in a heap; a small fountain of blood jetted from his wound, puddling on the sidewalk around his head. His left foot shook spasmodically and his body shuddered, then lay still.

Kotani leveled the gun at me without saying a word. He stepped from the doorway, grabbed Marta by the elbow, and together they walked off into the night.

The marrow of my soul froze. I screamed for help, as I knelt over Steven to see if there was anything I could do. I couldn't tell whether or not he was breathing. I put my ear to his chest, listening for a heartbeat, but all I heard was the sound of his leather jacket scraping on the pavement as I shook him, trying to get him to respond. When I realized that he was really dead, I let go of him and stood up.

A small crowd quickly gathered around us. Voices asked, 'What happened?' Someone shouted, 'Call an ambulance.'

But my friend was beyond help. I slowly walked away and left Steven with the crowd of onlookers. Nobody stopped me or even seemed to notice me.

I walked all the way to the Village and back on Broadway. The hookers and pimps plying their trade up and down the Great White Way approached me as I crossed from one's turf to another's, but one look at my face seemed to convince them that I wasn't a likely john. The porn shops and triple-X-rated theaters were doing a lively business. Hollow-eyed kids roamed in groups of two and three. Teenage street dealers hawked their wares with calls of 'Rock. Got rock. Nickels and dimes. Right here, man, got what you need.' The neon cast a surreal light on everything. I fit right in.

I wanted to just keep walking until I couldn't walk any farther, to be a part of the night, a shadow that would disappear with the light of day.

CHAPTER ELEVEN

The shabby hotel room grew smaller each time I paced its length. My thoughts flared, then flickered out as I took four steps, then turned, four more steps, then turned again. Steven was dead, and it was my fault. No way around it. My heart felt like it was tightly wrapped in rubber bands, my mouth dry. If I'd moved quicker, seen it coming, I might have been able to stop Kotani. I would have tried. 'I swear to God, Steven, I would have tried. But I didn't see it coming.'

Just when I thought I could swallow the fear and grief, stuff them down so deep that I could breathe again, the guilt would stir like a worm, and I felt like I would explode. As dawn lightened the sky, I looked out of the window and tried to pull myself together. If I didn't do something to keep Tanaka off my back, I would be next.

'Put him out of your mind for now, and concentrate,' I told myself. But it wasn't that easy. The look of terror on Steven's face just before Kotani fired was going to haunt me for the rest of my life. Maybe longer.

I called Marilyn to warn her about Tanaka's threat.

'I'm telling you, Marilyn, the man is dangerous. Until I get him what he wants, Caitlin could be in danger. *Please* take her to your mother's house – just until I get things resolved.'

'If you think I'm going to live my life around your problems, you're crazy. Don't call here and try and scare me again. It won't work. I don't believe anything you tell me.'

'Marilyn, wait –'

But she had already hung up on me. I drank some water.

A Monet.

I had to find a painting for Tanaka. But where? There were a handful of galleries in Manhattan that might have one in inventory. Hefflenberg was the first that came to mind.

I called Dominick Pastore the minute Hefflenberg Galleries opened for business at 9:00 A.M. Without asking why, he agreed to see me, providing I could be there at 10:30 sharp.

Dominick managed the New York branch of the Hefflenberg empire – the world's richest and most powerful family-owned art dynasty. He had no real authority. Old man Hefflenberg, actually the grandson of the original founder, ran the place with a tight-fisted authority that Mussolini would have admired. Whether he was on his ranch in Kenya, sailing off the island he owned in the Grenadines, or merely in Paris or London visiting one of his branch galleries, no business was ever transacted in any of the far-flung Hefflenberg locations without the express consent of Nathan Hefflenberg. He had a son, Nathan junior, now in his forties, who was nominally the director of the company. Little Nate, as he was known behind his back, and I got along. But old Nathan had pretty well castrated him by the time he was twenty. Without the blessings of Nathan himself, you simply didn't exist as far as Hefflenberg Galleries were concerned. I didn't relish the idea of tangling with the nasty old bastard, but it had to be safer than owing Tanaka.

What would Steven have thought about trying to hustle Nathan Hefflenberg? I wanted to have the chance to discuss it with him. To argue about it. His death was still too raw, too fresh. I couldn't quite get my hands around it. I still expected to hear his voice the next time I called our gallery.

'What're we going to do now?' he'd ask in that worried tone, expecting me to know.

Well, he'd found out exactly how little I really did know. How do you tell a dead friend that you're sorry?

Dominick greeted me at the front door of the mansion that old man Hefflenberg's father had built in the late teens, to accommodate the American arm of the family business. The neoclassical building was six stories of pale limestone, fronting on East Sixty-second Street. It was almost as opulent as Malmaison. When you walked in off the street, you stepped into a rarified atmosphere of privilege and substance. The objects on display in the front hall practically whispered their history. Many of them had passed from the hands of royalty into the hands of the world's most influential families before coming briefly to rest at Hefflenberg when the money ran out. The enormous, walnut-paneled hall was dominated by a sweeping staircase of pure white marble. On either side of the stairs hung a pair of rare antique Flemish tapestries, depicting lions and unicorns. Under the tapestries stood a pair of Louis XV lacquered cabinets, made by the *maître ébéniste,* Martin Carlin, which had once been owned by the Churchill family. Hanging above the stairs were paintings by Vigée-Lebrun and Ingres. Opposite the tapestries and cabinets, facing the sweep of the staircase, hung a life-sized portrait of Napoleon Bonaparte, by David, which had decorated Napoleon III's study in the Tuileries in 1871, when he made the decision to abdicate his throne. This one hall, just a small part of the six-story mansion, held a handful of objects worth more than most museums could afford to spend in a decade. God only knew what the Hefflenbergs had buried in their vaults.

All of this treasure was watched over by the most discreet security personnel I had ever seen. They were dressed in morning coats and wore little earphones, like the secret service. But even the well-cut civilian dress they affected failed to hide the telltale bulges under the arms of these late-twentieth-century palace guards. Whenever I walked into Hefflenberg Galleries I automatically started whispering.

This morning I didn't even lower my voice. 'Thanks for seeing me,' I called to Dominick as I walked in.

He was wearing a black suit and as usual projected the demeanor of a funeral director. When he saw me, he clasped his hands together and looked me up and down.

'*You* look a bit rough this morning, Adrian. Burning the candle at both ends, I *suppose*. Have you even been home yet?'

The art voice. I wanted to grab Dominick by the shoulders and shake the shit out of him. But I kept the thought to myself and tried to smile.

'Just out a little late, Dominick.'

'Hmmm. From what I hear, later than you ought to be out. You might consider hiring a new public relations person. Everyone knows it's not easy getting good press, but don't you think the *Post* is a bit – well, it's not exactly the *best* paper.'

Shit! I'd forgotten all about it. Everyone in the trade had probably read the article by now. It was hopeless. No one was going to give me the time of day. I wanted to run – to find a deep hole somewhere in South America and lie down in it until this nightmare passed. Then I thought about Caitlin. I held out my arms, palms up. But my hands were trembling. *Calm down. It's just a painting – all you need is a goddamned painting. You can do this.*

'A mix-up, Dominick. Somebody got it wrong. It's been straightened out.' I forced a chuckle.

He studied me for a moment, then must have decided I wasn't as dangerous as I looked.

'Well, come in. *Come* in. What can I do for you today? You sounded positively possessed, or something, on the phone. What's so *bloody* urgent?'

'I have a new Japanese client. He wants a Monet. A *Water Lilies*. If I can get one in front of him quickly, he'll buy.'

Dominick pursed his lips, then nodded. 'Let's see what we have *floating* about.'

We took the oak-paneled elevator to the fourth floor. Dominick ushered me into a viewing room, then asked me to wait. The room was long and narrow, furnished with four large, wingback chairs, lined up facing three empty easels. Everything was covered in a dusty maroon velvet – the walls, the drapes, the chairs, the easels. Even the carpet was a burgundy color. It was like being inside an enormous wine bottle.

Dominick returned after a few minutes, followed by a porter who wore white cotton gloves and a butler's uniform. The porter carefully placed a large Monet *Water Lilies* on the center easel, then made four more trips in and out of the viewing room until a total of five Monets were lined up in front of me. I was impressed, in spite of the circumstances that had brought me here.

'Jesus,' I blurted. 'I didn't think anyone in the world had five of these for sale.'

Dominick grinned. Just a little curl at the corners of his mouth. Almost, but not quite, lending a pleased look to his serious face.

'Most people would be absolutely *shocked*, if they knew what we have sitting in the cellar vaults. This is just a *small* group of our Monets. You *know*, the old man's father dealt directly with the artist. Used to drive to Giverny for lunch, then buy these things over coffee and cognac. Must have been something – dining with Claude Monet. What do you think?' He gestured at the easels.

'I think it must have been a hell of a lunch.'

'I *meant* about these. Have you *ever* seen such light?' Dominick asked, pointing again at the Monets.

'He was the master – no doubt about it,' I answered, stepping closer to the paintings.

'Nathan's father wrote *the* book on Monet. He once said, "Monet practically stole the light from the heavens." *Rather* poetic, isn't it?'

I looked up to see if he was being serious.

Dominick was staring at the paintings, a far-off look in his eye. I cleared my throat, then couldn't help commenting. 'He was a regular thief, all right. A thief of light.'

My apparent blasphemy broke the sanctity of the moment. Dominick turned to stare at me, then sounding a little petulant, asked which of the five paintings my client might go for.

After looking them over, I pointed at the first one the porter had brought in. 'How much?'

'Eighteen-five.'

'Eighteen and a half million dollars?' I choked.

'It *is* the best of the lot,' he answered, looking surprised, almost hurt that I would question such a fair price.

I lowered my sights. 'How about that one?' I asked, pointing to the smallest and least finished of the five.

'Let me check,' Dominick answered. 'Nathan just sent it over from Paris. I'm not sure of the price.'

He opened the door and stepped from the room, leaving me alone with the paintings. Ordinarily, I would have welcomed the opportunity to examine each as closely as possible. Today I just wanted to grab one and leave. If it hadn't been for the guys with the earphones and bulging underarms, I might have tried. I looked at my watch. Almost noon. God, I needed something. The dope wasn't helping at all. Marta had probably stepped on it too many times.

Dominick came back in. 'Seven-five, Adrian. And don't even *think* about making an offer. That is as low as Nathan will go. I'm sure of it.'

I glanced once more at the painting. 'Okay. Wrap it up. I'll give it a try.'

He didn't move, just stood there and studied me like I was some kind of an alien.

'Well?' I asked, growing impatient.

'I can't let you take it on the arm. You'll have to bring your client here to see it. We'll protect your commission.'

'Bring my client here?' I exploded. 'Since when have I ever brought a client here? You always let me take paintings on consignment.'

'Calm down,' he said, not seeming in the least flustered by my outburst. 'You don't *usually* ask for seven-million-dollar paintings. The rules change at that level.'

'Calm down!? Bullshit! I come in here trying to sell a painting for you, and you tell me to calm down. I've done too much business with Hefflenberg to be treated that way. You call Nathan, wherever the hell he is, tell him I have a live one, but I need to take the painting on the arm.'

'Adrian, he's not going to let you.'

A voice in the back of my head told me to chill out, but I couldn't. 'Call him, Dominick.'

He frowned, then walked out, closing the door behind him, I supposed to do as I had asked. My palms were sweating. This was not going the way I had hoped it would. I jerked open the door and motioned to the surprised porter, who stood in the hall like some kind of medieval footman.

'The bathroom – where's the bathroom?'

He directed me to it. Once inside, I locked the door and snorted a third of the dope that was left. I felt like I was going to burst apart at the seams. My fingers were numb, my chest constricted. I soaked a towel and held it to my face until my breathing slowed. Then I went back into the viewing room and waited for Dominick, hoping he knew CPR.

As soon as he walked back in, I could see by his face that I wasn't going to get the painting.

'Nathan says you're *welcome* to take the painting, *providing* you escrow the funds first,' he said, confirming what I already knew.

'Fuck Nathan,' I said, barging past Dominick, then the shocked porter.

I took the stairs two at a time, then hurried out onto the street. I walked half a block, then stopped and just stood there. For a moment, nothing looked familiar. I turned and looked back in the direction from which I had come, but nothing came into focus. I turned a circle, then closed my eyes and held my breath.

'What're we going to do now?' I whispered. Steven didn't answer.

During the course of the day I called on Acquavella,

Billy Beadleston, Hammer, and Stephen Hahn. All of them were dealers with whom I had an existing relationship. If you wanted to find a Monet for sale in New York, these were the people to see. They all asked about the damned *Post* article. My throat was sore from all the hearty chuckling. Beadleston and Acquavella actually had a Monet in stock but weren't willing to let me take it on consignment. Stephen Hahn had access to a *Water Lilies* but the bottom line was always the same. 'Bring your client here – we'll make sure your end is covered,' or 'Escrow the money – then you can take anything you want.' I didn't get my hands on a painting, but I did succeed in pissing off practically everyone I saw, much as I had Dominick Pastore.

I was exhausted and depressed by five-thirty, when I walked into Mary Lumpkin's gallery in the Fuller building on Fifty-seventh Street. In her late forties, Mary had started out twenty years ago as a salesperson for a small gallery in Palm Beach, then worked her way up the ladder. During the late eighties she had set up shop in Manhattan, and within five years had built an international clientele of her own as a dealer in French Impressionist and modern paintings. She was well respected, as smart and as tough as any dealer I had ever met. What really set her apart, though, was her reputation for honesty. When you dealt with Mary, you always knew where you stood. Unfortunately, she didn't have what I was looking for.

'I just can't fucking believe it's this hard to get my hands on a goddamned Monet.'

'Adrian, if you're going to act like a boor, do it somewhere else.'

'Ahh, shit.' I rubbed my eyes, then looked down at her. 'I'm sorry, Mary. It's not been a good day. I don't think Billy Beadleston or Stephen Hahn will ever speak to me again.'

'Go see Connatser,' she said, hands on her hips. 'Why not be rude to everyone, Adrian? Make a clean sweep of it.' She frowned, then shook her silvery head. 'I've heard on the street that Anthony's mortgaged his soul to Rosenswieg, the art factor, to buy a Monet. Supposedly he found it in an attic. Belonged to some little old lady in Newport, who only drove it on Sundays.' Her way of saying the painting was fresh – that it hadn't been offered around. 'I don't know how good it is, but it's worth a visit.'

'Thanks for the tip. I'll go see him.'

'Do that.' Her frown grew deeper. 'I don't know what's bothering you, but lighten up – it can't be that bad.'

'Can't it, Mary?' I wanted to say. But I bit my tongue and thanked her again. Then I headed uptown to call on Connatser Fine Art.

Anthony Connatser was about my age. He had built his business on elbow grease and commitment, after discovering that he hated practicing law. The gallery he ran with his wife, Julie, was everything Hefflenberg wasn't. It was small and somewhat dingy, poorly lit, and not at all chic. Not the sort of place you would think of if you were trying to locate a Monet. The thing that made the place viable was Anthony himself. He stood at least six foot seven, with an unruly mop of curly brown hair and a quick smile. He looked like a handsome Ichabod Crane but was nobody's fool.

Julie was at the front desk doing some paperwork when I walked in.

'Hello, Adrian.' She smiled warmly. 'I'll let Anthony know you're here.'

She didn't mention my name in the paper. I leaned against her desk as she went to get him. The place looked smaller than I remembered, but it seemed cozy. A nice place to spend an afternoon looking at art. The type of gallery where you expected to be offered sherry.

'Adrian, come in. You look beat, man. Can I get you anything?' Anthony asked, walking with Julie to where I waited by the front desk. He seemed genuinely pleased to see me.

'No thanks, Anthony. It's just been a long day.' I explained why I had come.

'Well, you may have saved the best for last. I have something to show you.' He put his arm around my shoulders, then led me into his small office. 'What do you think?' He gestured proudly to a small gem of an oil study of water lilies hanging behind his desk. 'Had to deal with Arthur Rosenswieg to come up with the money to buy it – practically had to sign my children over to him. But it's a beauty. Don't you think?'

'How much are you asking?'

'I'll split anything over four million dollars with you. I think it's worth closer to five and a half – maybe six.'

He was right. It was much nicer than the unfinished study that Hefflenberg was offering for three and a half million dollars more.

'It's lovely,' I said, backing into a chair and dropping into it.

'Sit there for a minute,' he said, looking concerned. 'I'll get you some water.'

He came back a moment later and thrust a glass into my hands. I drank it down and felt a little better.

'Is your client willing to act quickly?' he asked.

'Yes. I think he's a very decisive man.'

114

Anthony nodded. 'Why don't you take it with you? Show it as soon as you can.'

I looked up into his long, sincere face, and my stomach turned. If it had been Oscar Fedder or Nathan Hefflenberg, I'd have danced out of there, the Monet tucked safely under my arm, willing to worry about paying for it later. But Anthony Connatser wasn't like Fedder or Hefflenberg. He had meant it when he said he'd practically signed his children away to buy the damned painting. Arthur Rosenswieg was just this side of a loan shark. If I took the painting, then couldn't pay Anthony, Rosenswieg would destroy him. Then he'd come after me, too.

Julie Connatser poked her head into the office. 'Adrian, can I get you some more water?'

I shook my head, afraid to speak. Afraid that if I opened my mouth, I would ask Anthony to wrap up the painting. Somehow, I knew if I did take it, I'd regret it forever. It wasn't a matter of principle, or some deeply felt moral dilemma. It wasn't at all rational. It was crazy. I'd seen what Tanaka was capable of. I didn't know why, but I knew in my gut, as sure as I knew my name, that if I took that painting everything would turn to dust.

'Something stronger?' she asked again. 'You really do look pale.'

'No thanks, Julie. Really, I'm okay.'

She nodded. 'Shout, if you change your mind. I'll be up front,' she said, turning to leave.

Anthony smiled after her with obvious pride. Something clicked in my head. Sitting in his office, cold-bloodedly contemplating his ruination, something turned over inside of me. I couldn't do it. It was as simple as that – I couldn't smile and then knife him in the back.

I stood up. 'I'll give it some thought, Anthony. But I think this painting is a little too small.'

He looked momentarily disappointed, then nodded. 'You look sick as a dog, Adrian. Can I do anything for you?'

I walked toward the door. 'You have, Anthony. You have.'

Outside, I looked up at the sky. 'What now? What're we gonna do now?'

A man in a turban, walking past me on the sidewalk, paused and stared at me. I hurried down the block. If only I could clear my head. There had to be a way out of this. I just needed time to catch my breath and think.

By ten o'clock I was jonesing. It started with a tightening of the throat, a cold soaking sweat, and a hunger that had nothing to do with food.

Standing barefoot on the faded carpet of the thread-bare hotel room, holding the dope, unable to part with it, I came face-to-face with a man I no longer knew. I couldn't decide which I hated more, the white powder in my hand or the fool that had fallen in love with it. I could taste it – the bitter drip that would untie the knot in my throat. My hand shook, the bindle fluttered like it was alive, alternately light and heavy in my sweaty palm. There was no place to hide. No pretty blonde's eyes to seek shelter in. Just me and my old friend the dope. With trembling fingers I started to unfold the package of smack. Then I remembered the humiliation of facing Marta as she held the gun, and the scorn, the utter contempt for me on Kotani's face as he shot down my friend. A storm tide of shame and self-loathing swept over me. I sat back down on the bed. Rivulets of cold sweat ran down my face; the dope whispered to me.

I tried not to listen, but the damage was done. I had already lost, and in the losing I had misplaced something precious, something I had willingly set aside long ago. I had lost myself. In the clarity of that moment I understood the gravity of that loss. Adrian Sellars, gone and almost forgotten. Buried somewhere in Manhattan, under a mountain of China White heroin. I tried to summon tears for his passing, but I had none to give him. And that terrified me. Soaked in my own sweat, and stinking of fear, I crawled into the bathroom. I flushed what remained of my stash down the toilet.

Kicking cold. I didn't think I could do it alone. Too bad I hadn't called the Stratford clinic when I'd had the chance – it was a little late in the game to think about it now. There was only one person in New York I could imagine going to. I didn't know how she would react when she learned what had happened to Steven. I wasn't even sure she would listen long enough for me to explain and ask for help. But there was one way to find out. I picked up my briefcase, took a last look around the room, and left the Rimbaud. I headed uptown to Devon Berenson's.

It was almost midnight when I rang her apartment from the street entrance.

'Hello?' Her voice was small, tinny over the intercom.

'Devon, it's Adrian, I need to see you.'

'Now?'

'Please, it's important.'

She hesitated, then without answering she buzzed me in.

She opened her door as I came up the steps. She was wearing a pink, terrycloth robe; her long auburn hair was pulled back, her face clouded with sleep.

'You look like shit. Marta throw you out?' She

yawned. 'Whatever you have to say, make it quick. I told you I don't want anything to do with you – Steven.'

It was worse than being struck with a fist. I looked at her, and even though I tried to hold back, I started to cry. Blubbering like a goddamned child. My face was hot, my nose running. I tried to stifle my tears, but I couldn't turn off the faucets now that they had opened. 'Devon, I need your help.'

Her mouth opened slightly. She took me by the elbow and pulled me into her apartment. 'My God, Adrian, what now?' she asked. 'Sit here.' She patted a spot on the middle of the large couch that dominated her living room.

'I can't do this alone,' I mumbled as I sat. I took a deep breath and tried to pull myself together.

She sat in a large, overstuffed chair facing me and asked, 'What? What can't you do alone?' She leaned forward, elbows on her knees.

I looked down at the floor, the words caught in my throat. 'Devon, I'm a junkie . . . a fucking dope addict . . . I've got to stop.' I couldn't meet her eye.

She sat straight up in her chair, a look of surprise washing across her face. 'A heroin addict?'

I nodded, hating the sound of fear and loathing those words assumed in her voice. I put my hands between my knees and squeezed, trying to hold on to the little control I still had over myself.

'Do you want me to call a doctor? The hospital?' she asked.

'No, no doctors. I just need some help.'

'Adrian,' she said leaning toward me again, 'I have no idea how to help you.'

She studied me, looking for a clue. Then she stood up and walked into her bathroom. I was beginning to regret coming. She came back into the living room holding a box of tissues. She sat back in her chair and pushed them across the coffee table to me.

'What do you want me to do?' Her hands plucked at the sleeves of her robe.

'I don't blame you for being pissed off at me. I'm going to be sick – but it'll pass. I need a place to wait it out.'

'What kind of sick? Are you sure you don't need to call a doctor?'

'No. It won't be pretty, but there's nothing a doctor can do.' I was starting to feel light-headed, dizzy and edgy at the same time. I blew my nose, then wiped my face with a handful of tissues. 'Two – three days. It's like having a bad flu,' I told her. My mouth was dry, my skin damp and cold. I wanted to lie down.

'Two or three days,' she repeated. 'Then what? You just walk out, and I send you a bill?' She sat back in the chair rubbing her face.

'There's more.'

She lowered her hands and looked at me.

'I've fucked up, Devon. Big. Not just me, everything. Tanaka's man shot Steven. He's dead.'

'What?' She erupted out of the chair, paced around behind it, then stopped and faced me, keeping the chair between us. She raised her arm and pointed her finger at me. 'If you hadn't been so damned greedy . . .' she bit off the rest. 'When? When did this happen?'

'Last night,' I answered.

The room was too bright. I was shivering, but the apartment felt hot, airless. I crossed my arms in front of me and tried to breathe deeply. I couldn't get enough oxygen. Devon sounded as though she were talking through a drainpipe.

'Adrian, we're calling the police right now. We have to . . .' her words were starting to break up into bits and pieces of cartoon voices that didn't make sense. The room, which had seemed too bright a second ago, suddenly seemed shadowed. Her face was dark, I could see her lips moving, but all I heard was a rushing noise, like the wind.

'No . . . Tanaka . . . I'm sorry I came,' I mumbled, my voice echoing in my ears. I stood to leave, then the floor tilted and rose up to meet me.

I came to in Devon's spare bedroom, undressed and in bed. I had no idea how I had gotten there. My head was throbbing. I reached up and felt an egg on my forehead.

'Devon?' I called.

She came to the door, dressed in jeans and an old Boston University sweatshirt. 'You gave me a scare, Adrian. If you hadn't gotten up and managed to get into bed, I'd have called an ambulance. You'd be in a hospital now. Maybe that's where you belong.'

'Thanks.' I didn't know what to say.

'You're here now.' She stood framed in the doorway, her arms crossed, one hip cocked. 'I'll get you back on your feet. Rest for a while, then we have to talk. You need something to drink.' She turned and walked away.

She returned a few moments later with a tall glass of water and slapped it down on the nightstand. The water sloshed over the rim of the glass and puddled by the lamp. 'Damn it!' She grabbed a hand towel from the bathroom and mopped up the spilled water. 'If you need anything else, call. I'll check on you in a little while.'

Within a few hours I knew my skin would never fit again. Every nerve in my body was vibrating, carrying too much current. Bugs were on the march under my skin, biting and stinging as they pushed their way up my arms and down my legs.

Dev appeared in the doorway, holding a tray. 'I've made you some soup.'

'Please, Dev,' I waved her away. 'I can't eat anything. I'm so fucking cold. Have you got another blanket?' I was shivering, feeling miserable and ashamed. She put down the tray, got a blanket from the closet and threw it over me, then left the room.

There was an old-fashioned alarm clock on the night-stand whose hands refused to move properly. Flushed and hot one moment, shivering and cold the next, I watched, a captive audience, as that clock moved in slow motion, seeming to register only five minutes of every hour.

Against the wall facing the foot of the bed stood a pine chest, over which Dev had hung a print of Edward Hopper's 'Cat Boat.' I grew to hate that print as much as I hated the clock. Hopper's boat rode a smooth swell, neither gaining nor losing headway, over the marching blue waves rolling toward it from the distant horizon. I looked at it a hundred times, a thousand, as I tossed from my right side to my left, then back again. But it never moved. The cat boat was as stuck in that blue sea as I was in this withdrawal, and I despised it for mocking me. Then the itching started.

By the end of the next day I was ready to die. I had thrown up so much I thought I might have torn something in my stomach. The sheets were wet and stank of sour sweat and puke.

Dev came in with fresh linens and asked me to get up so she could change the bed. I crawled out from under the blankets and stood wrapped in a towel, shaking, bent at the waist from stomach cramps, as she tore the soiled sheets from the bed. I mumbled, 'I'm sorry.' She tossed them into the hallway, holding the damp sheets away from her with two fingers, the way you would grab a dead rodent by the tail. She wrinkled her nose and worked silently but efficiently. As soon as she finished I flopped back into the bed and drew the blankets around me again.

'Thank you,' I said from my cocoon.

'Are you ready to try some soup?' Her voice was cold, her face flat, expressionless.

Another day, I told myself. One more day and I'd feel well enough to leave.

'No,' I grunted at her. 'I'll be okay. I'll go tomorrow. Please just let me rest awhile.'

She looked down at me and bit her lower lip. 'Okay, but call if you need anything.' She walked out. Then a minute later she returned. 'Listen, I may not be the best at this Florence Nightingale stuff, but I'm trying. I want to help you. I really do.'

I nodded at her, but I couldn't quite manage a smile.

She walked to the bed and put her hand on my shoulder. 'Friends?'

'Yeah,' I answered, 'friends.'

She withdrew her hand, and I closed my eyes. The phone rang, and I heard her walk off to answer it.

The muscles in my arms and legs, my back, were still cramping and wrapping around each other like a nest of lovesick pythons. I had every blanket in the apartment on the bed and was sweating like a pig, but I couldn't get warm. I lay in a fetal position, grunting whenever she offered anything, unwilling and unable to be polite.

The physical symptoms of kicking cold are bad enough to push most junkies right back into the arms of the white lady. The psychological impact is a fucking nightmare. While my body waged war on itself, my mind fought a more subtle and terrible battle on ground that was both familiar and alien. Devon was in and out, helplessly watching, as I gritted my teeth and waited out the storm. The hardest fought engagement was with the fear, the soul-wrenching anxiety that gnawed at me like a hungry rat. I felt an overwhelming sense of desperation, a panic attack as deep as the Pacific. I couldn't separate the withdrawal from reality. I relived the last four days of my life over and over again. Steven, Paul, Marta, Kotani, Tanaka. I wanted to wail and gnash my teeth, scream like an Arab woman at a funeral. But I huddled deeper under the blankets, knees drawn to my chest, the stubble of my unshaven face scratchy, praying for the panic to subside so that I could breathe again.

When the stomach cramps got bad, I must have started thrashing. Devon came in and wiped my sweaty face with cool washcloths. She was hovering near the bed when, without warning, my stomach spasmed. I jumped up but didn't make it to the bathroom in time. I stood mortified, a few feet from the door, hot, watery shit running down my leg, puddling on the floor.

'It's okay,' Dev said, hurrying into the bathroom. She ran hot water into the tub for me. 'Don't worry, it's not a big deal,' she insisted, but her voice was tight.

I soaked in the tub, unable to look at her. When I got out and toweled off, I looked in the mirror and caught her reflection just outside the open bathroom door. She was on her knees with a bucket, scrubbing at the carpet with a soapy sponge. Her expression was grim, determined, as she assaulted the shit-stained rug. But her face was damp with tears running down her cheeks and dropping onto the soapy mess. I wanted to crawl into a hole. She didn't know I could see her. I cleared my

123

throat before coming out, and she quickly rubbed her sleeve across her face.

'Let me help.' I tried to kneel beside her, but another spasm sent me scuttling like a crab for the toilet.

When I came out she was still working on the rug. I started to try and kneel down again.

'No, please. Get back in bed. Get well.' She tried to smile but wasn't able to erase the stricken look in her eyes.

Shivering and unsure what to make of her, I crawled back under the blankets. I turned my face to the wall, unable to watch her scrub.

If Devon hadn't been there, I would have fought the withdrawal until I exhausted myself. Then I would have stumbled into the streets and scored some dope. It wouldn't have been the first time. Something about her presence, her grim acceptance of me, changed everything. I stopped trying to beat this thing and tried to rest. Once I quit fighting it, the fear diminished.

By Sunday night I had cleared a big hurdle. It had only been two days, I was still feverish, sick to my stomach and suffering diarrhea, but I no longer felt so afraid. I got up and showered. When I got out, I couldn't find my jeans, so I wrapped a towel around myself and went to look for Devon. I found her in the kitchen.

'You need some clothes,' she said, smiling for the first time in days.

I agreed. We walked back into the guest room. She opened the pine chest and handed me my jeans and one of her sweatshirts, then turned away as I dropped the towel and slipped into them. Her sudden modesty made me smile, too.

'There's not much left to be modest about,' I teased.

'Come into the living room. I'll fix you something to

eat.' She took my arm and led me back to the couch. Her hand felt warm on my skin. 'I do believe the patient might live after all,' she said.

She brought me a bowl of chicken soup. As I stirred it around and tried to swallow some of it, she took a seat in the chair.

'How did you get so far into it?' she asked.

I looked up from the soup. 'The drugs?'

She nodded. 'Yeah, the drugs.'

I swirled the broth with my spoon, watching the little globs of chicken fat spin around the bowl. 'They opened doors for me, Devon. Got me into places that I didn't think I could go on my own. Even when I was a kid, they made everything easier.'

'What I'm seeing doesn't look so easy.' She sat back in her chair and thought for a minute.

'There's not a better way of explaining it. The drugs worked for me. I could be anybody I wanted. Talk to anyone – measure up. I don't know . . . it sounds so trite to say it, but I never felt like I was whole. The dope helped for a while.'

She nodded, but I don't think she really understood. We sat quietly while I played with my soup.

'Do you really think you can stop?' she asked.

'I don't have a choice. If I keep on, it'll end up killing me.'

She looked around the room, as if wrestling with something she wanted to say, then seemed to think better of it. The silence dragged on.

'Adrian, we need to call the police,' she said, changing the subject.

'We can't!'

'I don't see that we have a choice.'

'Dev, I know it's the right thing to do, but Tanaka's

threatened Caitlin. He knows where she lives. Even if the authorities take me into protective custody, how could they keep her safe? We'd be sitting ducks.' I told her about my talk with Duncan Marshall and described in detail all that had happened since the night she walked out of the Lucky Shamrock. By the time I finished, I was feeling sick again. The muscles in my shoulders were pulling tight. I felt jittery, depleted.

'Marilyn wouldn't even listen to your warning?'

I shook my head.

She sat very still in her chair, hugging her knees to her chest. I wanted to crawl back under the blankets and stay there for a very long time.

'Devon, I need to lie down.'

I got up, and she followed me back into the guest room, then helped me into bed.

'Don't Steven's parents live near Utica? One of us should call them,' she said, adjusting the covers, trying to tuck me in.

I sat back up. 'We can't! God knows what they would do – at the very least, they would call the police.'

'Well, I can't stand the thought of him lying in some freezer. No one knowing.' She shuddered.

'I agree. But I don't want to join him.'

Her face pulled into a scared frown. 'Duncan really believes that the authorities can't protect you and Caitlin?'

'That's what he said. I'm going to have to find some way of dealing with Tanaka. He's not going away.'

'What are you going to do?'

'I'm not sure yet.'

She stood by the bed for a while, her face pale, her eyes puffy and tired. Then she said good night.

As she turned to leave, I stopped her. 'Tanaka's not

going to get away with this. I don't know how, but they're going to pay for what they've done.' My threat sounded hollow in my own ears. A would-be Clint Eastwood, ready to rain fire and death down upon the bad guys. But I was starting to shake again. My body was craving the dope.

She came back into the room and stood at the foot of the bed.

'What are you going to do about the gallery? Do you want me to go in and open up tomorrow?' she asked.

'No. It'll just have to be closed. Tanaka probably has somebody watching the place. For now, nobody knows where I am. I want to keep it that way.' I pulled the blankets tighter around myself.

She thought for a moment, then came around and sat on the edge of the bed. 'Steven was my friend. I want to help you get this thing resolved. You're right, one way or another those bastards can't get away with what they've done.'

'Devon, this isn't your battle.' I reached out and put my hand on her knee. 'I don't want you to be a part of this insanity.'

She pulled away. 'You said that before. In the bar the night Paul McHenry was killed. You said you didn't want to involve me. Well, you have involved me. I'm in it now, and I'm not walking away.'

'These people are murderers. It's too dangerous.'

'Oh, so you're telling me it's okay for me to clean up your shit, but not okay for me to do anything else.' She stood up and walked to the door. 'Well, you're mistaken. I didn't ask you to come here, but I took care of you anyway. Now I'm in this with you, and I'm going to see it through.'

'Devon –'

'Don't even think about arguing with me. You can't win.' She crossed her arms and stood rigidly staring at me.

'I don't even have a plan.'

'All I'm saying is that when you figure out what to do, I'm going to help.'

I looked at her, standing framed in the doorway. Not a bit of bluster or bullshit about her. 'All right, Devon. Fine. You want in, you're in. Whatever happens, you're part of it.' I put my head down on the pillows and prayed I wouldn't live to regret those words.

Later, after she had gone into her room, I picked up the little picture of Caitlin I had propped on the nightstand. I held it on my chest and stared at it for a long time, feeling lost as I waited out the sickness in my body and soul.

CHAPTER TWELVE

By Tuesday I had been in bed for three days and Dev's apartment was beginning to close in around me. I felt old, sapped of energy. Chilled to the bone no matter how high Devon turned the thermostat. But Steven haunted my thoughts. A compulsion to do something, anything, drove me to get moving. Information. I needed to know what I was up against. All the rumors about Tanaka were true as far as I was concerned, but I wanted to know as much about him and his syndicate as I could possibly learn.

For lack of a better place to start, I headed to the New York Public Library. If there was anything in print about the Hiyashi Gumi, it was likely that I could find it there. I bundled up as best I could, adding a few over-sized T-shirts of Dev's to the limited wardrobe of jeans, sweater, and tweed sport coat I had with me. I moved slowly.

Dev walked me to the street. 'You take it easy,' she said. 'Are you sure you don't want me to come with you?'

'You've already done too much,' I answered.

'Well, there are a few things I need to get done today. I'll go by the gallery to pick up messages, the mail. While I'm there, I'll redo the answering machine, say that we're closed for the holiday. What time will you be back?'

'I don't think it's a good idea, Devon. I'd rather just leave it closed.'

'Dammit, you've worked too hard to let your real

clients believe you pulled some kind of disappearing act. Nobody's going to bother me.' She stood beside me, hands on her hips, looking as glad as I was to be out of the apartment.

It was a sunny day, the first I had seen in a week. Standing on the curb waiting for a cab, New York bustling around us, it was hard not to feel like the whole thing was a bad dream.

'Why don't you call the front desk, let the doorman know that we're closed. He'll tell anyone who comes by,' I said.

Her smile faded. 'You're really convinced he's watching the gallery?'

'Yes,' I answered. 'I am.'

'You know, auction night is next week – what are we going to do?'

'Nothing. We'll have to miss the fun this year.' I shook my head. 'Steven and I never got around to sending out the invitations. I doubt we'll be missed.'

She nodded, then handed me a key to her apartment. 'Use this if you get back before I do.' She studied me for a moment. 'Be careful, okay?'

Without thinking I pulled her to me and kissed her on the cheek. 'I'll see you later,' I said, surprised by a little surge I hadn't felt for a long time – that quickening of the pulse, a loosening somewhere deep inside that's scary and thrilling at the same time. Powerful enough to make itself felt in spite of the withdrawal.

My time at the library was well spent. I found a periodical in English, *The Pacific Rim Economic Report*, which had written extensively about the *yakuza* over the last decade. Among articles detailing the *yakuza*'s expansion into international money laundering, their ties to the Colombian cocaine cartels and American banking and real estate conglomerates, I found an in-depth profile of the Hiyashi Gumi and its leadership. It included organizational charts, which actually named Tanaka as one of three men who answered directly to the leader of the organization. Narumi had been right – they even published photographs.

Tanaka's boss was named Noburo Nakamura. From what I read, Nakamura was even more ruthless than Tanaka. He carried himself and lived like a feudal lord. A far cry from the streets of Osaka, where he began his career as a common thief. Nakamura's rise within the Hiyashi Gumi had been meteoric. By the time he was forty, he had wrested control from his predecessor in a violent coup. Since then he had maintained absolute control of the syndicate for almost three decades. Little was known about his personal life, aside from the fact that he bred and raised exotic birds. There was much speculation about Nakamura's political connections, both in Japan and abroad, but according to the article he lived a simple life, receiving visitors but rarely leaving the grounds of his estate outside Tokyo.

Nakamura had quietly and effectively expanded the Hiyashi Gumi's operations into Europe and both of the Americas. Without ever having been implicated in a serious crime, he ran a syndicate that by official estimates had yearly revenues greater than McDonald's and Reebok combined.

I needed to know if Nakamura had sanctioned Tanaka's art dealing or if it was a side venture. Compared to Nakamura's money laundering for the cocaine cartels, the art scam seemed like small potatoes. Why would he even bother? Maybe he didn't. Maybe it was Tanaka's franchise. How the hell was I going to find out? What *did*

Tanaka do with the forgeries? Questions, questions, and more questions. I was getting a headache.

By the time I left the library with copies of my research, I felt weak and shaky. I stopped at a coffee shop and forced down a bowl of chicken noodle soup. Its warmth eased my stomach and put a little strength back in my legs. Using the pay phone, I checked in with Duncan Marshall.

'Jesus, Adrian, I've been worried sick about you. What happened?'

'I'm okay, but Steven's dead. They killed him.'

'Oh no,' he groaned. He drew in a deep breath, then said, 'I think it's time to see Detective Carstairs.'

'Not yet, Duncan. I've seen what these people are capable of. They've threatened Caitlin. I don't want to make her a target. I won't directly involve you in this anymore. But I would like to ask for a favor.'

'I'll help you as best I can. But you're not going to be able to avoid Carstairs for long, he still wants to talk to you about McHenry. I don't know what he'll do when he connects you to Steven Ballard.'

'I doubt they've made a connection between Steven and me. Tanaka's people took his wallet. I don't think he was carrying any identification when they shot him.'

'That may keep him off your back for a while, but eventually someone's going to add it all up. When they do, you'll be at the center of the whole thing.' He sounded worried.

'Yeah, I know. If it's possible, buy me some more time with Carstairs. One way or another this thing with Tanaka is going to be settled by the end of next week. I've been at the library reading up on him and his people. Shit, I have more questions now than I did before I started. Do you think your partner with the Japanese contacts could put me in touch with someone knowledgeable about the *yakuza*?'

He asked me to hold, then came back on the line a few minutes later.

'Adrian, Hiro Okuba is the head of security for Mishima International's North American operations. My partner plays racquetball with him. Wait about ten minutes, then call him. He'll be expecting to hear from you.' He then gave me Okuba's private phone number.

'I'm staying at Devon's, if you need to reach me.' I gave Duncan the phone number, then added, 'You've been a good friend to me. Thank you.'

'I wish there were more I could do. Listen, I know you don't want to tell me what you're up to, Adrian, but if you need me, call. I mean it.'

I killed a few minutes reading the graffiti in the phone booth, then unable to wait any longer, I fed more coins into the slot and dialed Okuba's number. It was answered on the first ring by a man with a British accent, which surprised me.

'Hiro Okuba.'

'Mr Okuba, my name is Adrian Sellars. I was given your number by Duncan Marshall.'

'Right, you're the man who wants to know about the *yakuza*. I'm up to my ass in alligators right now. How about meeting me tonight for a drink?'

'Sure, where and when?'

'Seven o'clock, the Kansai Sushi Bar on East Forty-eighth Street, okay?'

'I'll be there,' I replied. 'And Mr Okuba . . .'

'Yes?'

'Thank you for seeing me on such short notice.'

'I'm going to let you buy me a beer, Mr Sellars, and if

you still feel like thanking me after the first beer, then you can buy me another.' With that he cut the connection.

By the time I returned to Dev's it was almost 4:00 P.M. When I walked in, I heard her clattering around in the kitchen and smelled something sweet, a cake or pie baking, and the greasy odor of sausage frying. Just the smell of it sent me reeling into the bathroom. When I came out, she was stepping out of her tiny galley, talking on her cordless telephone to someone named Marion.

'Hey, I didn't hear you come in,' she said, disconnecting. She was smiling, but fatigue showed in the lines at the corners of her eyes. Strands of her hair had come loose from her ponytail and hung on either side of her face.

'Dev, what's going on? What are you cooking?'

'Thanksgiving is in two days. I was just asking a friend how to make cranberry relish,' she said. 'Since my parents are in Europe, you're stuck with me. We're going to celebrate it, regardless of what's happened.' She placed the phone back on its cradle.

'Thanksgiving? Hhmmph.' I shrugged. 'Fuck it. I'd just as soon forget Thanksgiving this year. There's nothing to be thankful about.'

Devon looked at me. She frowned and shook her head. I didn't like what I saw reflected in her eyes.

'Adrian, you're alive. I know you're scared to death. I'm scared too. But a million things can happen between now and next week. Let's not give up yet.'

'Give up? Do you have any idea what I'm up against?'

'Of course I do.'

I pulled the copies I had made of the article at the

library out of my pocket and waved them under her nose. 'Look at this.' My voice sounded shrill. 'Read this and tell me not to give up.'

She snatched the article out of my hand and waved it right back at me. 'I don't give a damn what it says here, or anywhere else.' Her voice was low, determined, her jaw thrust forward. 'You have a fighting chance. That's more than Steven or Paul had.'

'A fighting chance – huh. You can take my fighting chance and shove it. I wouldn't give a rat's ass for my odds.' I walked over to the chair sitting next to her sofa and fell into it. 'Fuck my fighting chance.'

Devon followed me into the living room and tossed the article down on the coffee table. 'You're alive, Adrian. You have a daughter to think about. You can get through this.' She pulled at her hair, capturing the loose strands, gathering them into a new ponytail.

I looked at the article sitting on the coffee table and nudged it with my foot. Then I looked up at her. 'Life's a beach, ain't it, Dev?'

'That's right, Adrian. Life's a beach.'

'And then you die,' I added, turning away, hoping my soul wasn't as shriveled and ugly as it sounded.

She shook her head at me, then went back into the kitchen. I got up and walked into the guest room. I picked up the phone and dialed Caitlin's number in Arlington. At least for now my daughter was safe and far away from this nightmare. Maybe if I asked calmly, her mother would listen to reason and take her to Grandma's for a while.

Even on her answering machine Marilyn's voice somehow managed to sound cold, unyielding. 'I'm sorry but I'm unable to take your call right now, if . . .' I left word that I would call again tomorrow, then hung up. Devon was banging around in the kitchen. I wanted to go to her, apologize and hold her. Instead I let myself out of the apartment and went outside for some air. There was always Anthony Connatser. I pushed the thought out of my head.

CHAPTER THIRTEEN

The Kansai Sushi Bar was almost empty when I arrived, about ten after seven. There were two American couples at one end of the bar and a young Japanese man reading *The Wall Street Journal* at the other end. I took a seat in the middle and sipped green tea while I waited for Hiro Okuba.

The raw slabs of tuna, barbecued eel, and octopus tentacles displayed at the bar didn't help my treasonous stomach. They looked too much like bait. After about ten minutes I was starting to get antsy when I noticed the young man with the newspaper looking at me through round, tortoiseshell glasses.

'Mr Sellars?' he asked.

'Are you Mr Okuba?'

'Call me Hiro,' he answered, picking up his paper and moving to the chair next to mine. He was of medium height, and slender. He looked like a junior stock analyst, not at all what I had pictured.

'On the phone you sounded – well, I was expecting someone older, more official-looking. More like a policeman.'

'Yeah? Didn't mean to be short with you. I had people in my office.'

I nodded. 'You're really in charge of security for a company as large as Mishima?' I asked.

'I'm only the head of Mishima's American operations,' he laughed. 'My looks have proven to be a great advantage to me. I suppose you could call it a disguise.'

'Well, you fooled me,' I admitted.

'It's preferable to be young and single in my department.' He grinned, and toyed with the chopsticks resting on the tray in front of him. 'No sane wife would put up with the hours or the moves. I've been posted in four different countries over the last five years.'

'How old are you?' I asked.

'Thirty-four. And yes, that's young to be head of an important territory. How about you?'

'Thirty-eight. An old thirty-eight.'

He nodded. 'Are you married?'

'The scars show, huh?' I smiled and shook my head. 'No, I'm single these days. But I've been married a few times.'

He looked around, trying to attract the attention of a waitress. 'I've only been in New York for a few months. Some city. But the women' – he shook his head – 'great to look at, but they're all starstruck.'

'Don't get me started on New York women, we'll be here all night.'

We both laughed.

'You mind if I ask you some questions about the *yakuza*?'

'Of course not, after you buy me that beer.' He flagged down the waitress and ordered an Asahi draft, then waited for me to order.

I picked up my tea. 'This is fine, I'm just getting over the flu.'

He nodded. 'I picked this sushi bar to make a point. It's owned by a family from Kyoto who work very hard to be successful. But too much of their profits go to the *yakuza* for them to ever really enjoy the fruits of their labor. The *yakuza* take a monthly percentage of the gross as an "insurance" premium. In Japan we refer to this as *tera sen*. It means "bodyguard fee."' He sipped his beer.

'I thought the *yakuza* was into big-league stuff, money laundering, things like that. How much money could they take from a place like this?'

'Enough. It adds up. There are a lot of places like this in New York.' He eyed the display of seafood.

'Do you know of Ryuichi Tanaka?' I asked.

'Of course I do.'

He interrupted our conversation long enough to discuss in Japanese the day's offerings with the sushi chef. He ordered for himself, then offered to order for me. I declined. Although I was up and around, it was all I could do to watch him eat. Just the thought of putting raw seafood in my stomach had me squirming in my seat, looking around for the bathroom.

Okuba picked up a shiny red slice of tuna with his chopsticks and held it up. 'Tanaka is a big fish.' The tuna waved at the end of the chopsticks as he spoke. 'Why do you ask about him?'

'I've had dealings with him that have gone bad. I want to know if those dealings were a sideline for him, or if Nakamura was involved.'

His eyebrows rose. 'You've done your homework. How much do you know about the Hiyashi Gumi?' He dunked the tuna into a dish of soy sauce mixed with green horseradish and popped it into his mouth. Appreciation lit his face as he chewed and swallowed.

While he ate, I laid out for him what I had learned.

'What did your deals with Tanaka involve?'

'Very expensive works of art,' I replied.

He sat back, took off his glasses, polished them and held them up to inspect his work. The sushi chef handed him a second wooden tray of sashimi, and he sampled two pieces before he spoke again.

''S good,' he said, still working on a piece of yellowtail snapper. 'You sure you won't eat?'

'No, thank you,' I replied, sipping my tea, trying to remain patient.

'Are you trying to get the works of art back?' he asked.

'Possibly,' I hedged. 'What I really want is to find out what Tanaka has done with them.'

'You don't think he bought them to look at?'

'He doesn't strike me as much of a collector. At least not an art collector.'

Okuba picked up another slice of fish. 'No, I suppose not. Do you suspect he's resold the paintings?'

'Maybe. I don't know what else to think. Are there any other options?'

Okuba thought for a moment before answering. 'Have you ever heard the term *za e teku*?'

'No.'

'Mr Nakamura is not known as a patron of the arts, but he is known to have several important business leaders and politicians in his pocket.'

'What do you mean?' I asked, confused.

'In Japan, the giving of bribes and kickbacks has been honed to a science. One of the most innovative ways to buy influence involves gifts of expensive items, like diamonds or works of art. They're portable, they can be expected to grow in value if kept, or they can easily be turned into cash. These gifts are very difficult to trace. This form of bribery is known as *za e teku*. I'm not saying this is the case with your paintings, but Nakamura is an expert at *za e teku*.'

Now it was my turn to pause and think. Maybe I had misread Tanaka's art scam. Instead of reselling

McHenry's paintings as originals for huge profits, maybe he had discovered a new angle on this *za e teku*. The possibilities were interesting.

'Would there be any way to find out if Nakamura has been giving away any art recently?'

'It wouldn't be published anywhere. But these days a Picasso, or a Renoir, for that matter, almost any important work of art, conveys such status upon the owners that sometimes the recipients of these illegal gifts actually display them in public.' He shook his head, then sipped at his beer. Wiping the foam from his lips with a napkin, he continued, 'I could ask a few of my contacts in Tokyo if they know of any art-related deals involving Nakamura. Why don't you call me on Friday afternoon?' He put down his napkin and handed me his card.

'I appreciate your help, Hiro. Are you ready for another beer?'

'Adrian, I hate everything about men like Nakamura and Tanaka. They represent the worst of Japan. If helping you ends up hurting them, I'm more than happy to be of assistance. I'll take a raincheck on that beer. Next time let's talk about something more pleasant.'

'Like women?'

'You got it. New York women, the more the better.' He lifted his beer to toast the thought. 'It's been a long couple of months. Haven't even had a date yet.'

I smiled at him. 'Give it a few months, Hiro, by then you may change your tune.'

We shook hands, and I left him with his newspaper and sashimi. On the way back to Devon's I wondered what Duncan Marshall's partner had told Okuba about me. I knew he would never divulge the details of my situation, but I could picture some buttoned-down lawyer commenting on my social life. 'Adrian's a little on the wild side. You'll enjoy him. Get him to introduce you to some of the women he knows.' I smiled to myself. New York women, vastly overcriticized creatures.

Za e teku – I rolled the syllables around in my mouth. Okuba had been helpful. Maybe, just maybe, there was a chink in Tanaka's armor.

Dev was lying on the sofa watching 'N.Y.P.D. Blue' in the living room. She was wearing men's flannel pajamas with little green whales on them. When I walked in she wiggled her toes.

'There's soup on the stove, if you're hungry,' she said. 'Want me to get you some?'

'No thanks. I don't think I can get any down right now.' I flopped into the chair next to where she lay. Her head was propped on a pillow at my end of the sofa. I reached over and touched her hair, then said, 'Dev, I'm sorry about the way I acted this afternoon. I used to think I had a grip on things, now . . . I just don't know. I feel like I'm in the fucking twilight zone.'

She sat up and faced me. 'It's okay, Adrian. It'll get better. What happened with Mr Okuba?'

'He was pretty damned knowledgeable about the *yakuza*. I think he'll help us to some degree.'

'How?'

'Bribes. It might be about bribes. He thinks Tanaka's boss may have used McHenry's paintings to buy influential people. He's going to ask some of his friends in Japan to look into it. They even have a fancy expression for bribing people with art – *za e teku*.'

'Do you think that's what's going on?' she asked, drumming her fingers on her knees.

'I don't know. But it could get interesting if the people who have the paintings don't know they're fakes.'

142

'What's the next step?'

'We wait. Okuba told me to call him on Friday. By then maybe he'll know something.'

'Well, at least it's a possibility. You seem a little better than you did this afternoon.'

I could feel the blood rush to my face. 'Listen, I'm sorry about the way I acted. I didn't mean to sound like such a pitiful jerk.'

Her lips turned up in a slight smile. I could smell her, all sweet spice and summer, sitting on the couch in front of me. My heart started beating a little faster.

Our eyes met and we sat quietly looking at each other. Minutes went by without a word. The moment stretched on.

Finally, Devon broke the silence. 'I'm glad you're here.'

'Thanks for taking care of me, Miss Nightingale.'

Her smile grew. I felt weightless. Something was vibrating inside my chest.

'Devon, I'm tired of being scared. Let's just pretend everything is going to be all right.' I couldn't stop looking at her.

'Adrian, even if it's not all right – it's going to be all right.' She reached across the coffee table and traced my lower lip with her finger. The vibration in my chest spread to my arms, my legs. My ears felt hot.

I moved onto the sofa next to her and put my arms around her. She reached up and stroked the back of my neck. I nuzzled my face in her hair and breathed her scent in. Her hand was cool and soft, first on my neck, then on my cheek. Then she disengaged, got up, leaned over and kissed me good night and went into her bedroom, shutting the door behind her.

I stayed on the sofa, trying to make sense of the

million feelings suddenly awake in me. I was shaken to the bone. I felt as though Devon had reached inside me and touched some silent, hidden place that I had forgotten. I got up and stood outside her door for a few minutes before going into the guest room. I lay there trying to remember the last time I had felt this way. Of all things, my grandfather came to mind.

'Grab it, boy. Go ahead.' He had laughed, silhouetted by the morning sun. Little pinpoints of light poured through his straw hat, coming to rest like tiny yellow diamonds on his face. He stood, head tilted back, hands on his hips. A rag gathered in one fist was flapping in the light breeze.

'Like this,' he said, the laughter still in his voice. He leaned over and pinned the still flip-flopping fish to the rough boards of the pier with his foot. Then reaching down with the rag, he picked it up and held it for me to examine.

One huge glassy eye stared at me. The fish opened and closed its mouth, silently gasping. I looked up at my grandfather. The fish struggled in his grip, but its movements were slower now.

With my grandfather's help, I pulled the hook from the lip of the fish and then carefully wrapped my hand around the rag, taking the fish from him. It looked at me and flopped weakly. It seemed much larger in my hand. There was a story I remembered about a boy who caught a great big, magical fish and was granted three wishes for turning it loose. I carried my fish to the railing of the pier and looked out at the dazzling blue Atlantic. Then I looked up again at my grandfather, who stood watching, his face shadowed, only the yellow diamonds visible under his hat. Holding my fish out over the rail, I let it go. Rag and all. He tumbled down and down, reaching for the sea. Finally he splashed in and disappeared in a quicksilver flash. I watched the spot where he had hit. Within seconds the rag floating on the current was the only sign that anything had ever happened.

My grandfather's huge hand felt warm on my shoulder. Turning, I saw that he had taken off his hat. He wore an enormous smile, all white teeth against his tanned face.

'That was some fish, boy. I'm proud of you.'

I beamed at him, delighted myself.

'Now that fish will live to fight another day. You and he are joined forever.'

I squared my shoulders and stood a little straighter.

'You hungry after all that work?' he asked.

'Yeah,' I answered.

'Come on.' He held my hand and together we walked to the snack bar at the base of the pier, my grandfather greeting several of the other fishermen by name as we passed by them.

'Mornin', Ray, doin' any good?' he said to one of them.

Then to another, 'Jake, long time, how's the back?'

In reply to their questions he would hold up our hands and answer, 'Yup, this is my boy, Adrian. My partner.'

Over cheeseburgers I asked him what he had meant by me being joined together with a fish.

'Adrian,' he said, 'there are some people and some events that become part of us. Part of the fabric of our being.' I had no idea what he was talking about. 'Take you and me, we're joined together by blood. Nothing can ever change that. We are part of each other's fabric. A few minutes ago you held the life of that fish in your hands. You chose to let him live. Now that might not seem very important to you. But I'll wager it's damned important to the fish. The two of you connected. That can't be changed.'

I took a bite of my cheeseburger. I didn't understand him at all, but it sounded very deep, very, very wise. I hadn't been thinking about connections or anything like that. I had been thinking about how I would spend my three wishes. First, I wanted to live with my grandfather. Second, I wanted a million dollars. Third, I wanted more wishes, but since I knew that was against the rules, I wished never to have to go back to boarding school again.

'Grandpa, why can't I just come and live with you? I hate that crappy school. Mom and Dad are never around, they won't even know.'

He put down his cheeseburger and swiveled around on his stool, so that he could face me.

'You're nine years old now, aren't you, Adrian?'

'Yes.'

'Well, sometimes when we're young we have to do what our parents tell us. They want what's best for us,' he said. But I could tell by his eyes that he didn't really believe it.

'I only see them at holidays. They don't care. I want to live with you. We should always be together. I'm your partner, aren't I?'

He put his hand on top of my head and tousled my hair. 'In here' – he tapped his chest – 'we are together, always. Right in here.' He smiled and tapped on my chest. 'Right, partner?'

'Seems to me we'd be more connected if we lived together.'

He smiled at me. 'Eat your cheeseburger, Adrian.

You're going to need your strength. There are still plenty of fish out there waiting for us.'

I looked up at him, wishing I were older, and swore to myself that I would be just like him when I grew up.

According to the clock by the bed it was after 3:00 A.M. Somehow I could still smell Devon's scent. I longed to go and wake her. Sleep was out of the question.

I looked at the photograph of Caitlin propped by the clock and wished she had been lucky enough to know Grandpa Charley. He died of a heart attack when I was still nine, not long after our fishing adventure. I hadn't thought about him in so long that I was shocked at how vivid the memories were. He had been right, though. He was a part of me and always would be. I could see his face smiling down on me like it was yesterday. 'We're partners, Adrian. Right in here.' I put my hand on my chest where he had tapped me all those years ago and said a silent prayer. I asked him to please help me now. I didn't get an answer. But I thought of Devon and the place inside me that she had touched, and wondered about the warp and weft of my fabric.

CHAPTER FOURTEEN

It was becoming obvious that sooner or later I needed to go back to my apartment and retrieve some clothes and other essentials. The prospect of being seen on the streets was not appealing. I was more worried about Tanaka's people than I was about the police. But how the hell was I supposed to deal with Tanaka, if Carstairs pulled me in? I rationalized to myself that I was still well within Tanaka's deadline. If he wanted a Monet, he was going to have to give me room to operate. It was Wednesday; that left me about ten days to come up with a plan, or a painting. In the meantime I was just going to have to avoid Carstairs. Dev and I bundled up and walked the eight blocks to my place. She looked like a teenager in her baggy jeans, parka, and baseball cap.

On the way my stomach started to cramp. I had spent most of the day lying down in Dev's guest room, using the phone, trying to track down articles and additional information on Japanese art collectors between trips to the bathroom. Columbia University listed two articles in its library that I had missed at the public library, but neither seemed promising. By evening I felt better, having forced down some rice and dry toast, but not well enough for this hike.

'This walking is killing me,' I complained. 'Let's get a cab.'

'Oh, come on. The exercise will do you good. Get your blood moving. You'll feel better soon.' Dev, the drill sergeant.

She adjusted her pace to match my septuagenarian stride. We walked arm in arm, pretending we were normal people with normal problems, out for a stroll. Our breath formed clouds in the frosty air as we talked. The streets were crowded with couples walking off their dinners, laughing, enjoying. I felt like a fraud, a specter moving among them. I kept a lookout for Kotani. Tanaka was never far from my thoughts. Neither was Steven, or Paul.

'I've been thinking about something, Adrian. When you explained the drugs to me, you told me they opened doors, gave you access to places you didn't think you could go on your own.'

'Yeah, that's true.'

'Is that what the forgeries were about? Helping you get somewhere you were afraid you couldn't go on your own?'

I stopped in my tracks. 'Yeah . . . I hadn't thought about it that way. I guess that was part of it.'

'Why did you think you needed a shortcut? I've seen you in action. You're good, Adrian. Trust me, you're very, very good.'

I wanted to believe her. I touched her cheek. 'If only it were that easy, Devon.'

We started walking toward my apartment again.

'I still don't understand why you don't just give Tanaka his money back,' she asked.

'If he would accept his money back, we wouldn't have a problem. But he doesn't even want to talk about the money. He wants a Monet. Since I can't deliver Paul's, he's demanding a real one.'

'What made Paul so good?'

I thought for a minute – no one had ever asked me that before. 'Paul was special. Most forgers make the mistake of either copying an existing painting or taking elements from several existing works and trying to put them together into a new composition. They end up with a flat, lifeless imitation. Paul understood that. When he decided to paint a "Monet," he studied the master's work for weeks, sometimes months. He spent a lot of time looking at the artist's sketches and pastels. He used to brag, "Show me a drawing, and I'll read it like a diary, tell you exactly what the artist was thinking. Show me three drawings made in the same afternoon, and I'll tell you what he had for lunch." When Paul painted a "Monet," he became Monet. He did it so well, both technically and aesthetically, that the experts couldn't tell the difference.'

'So why was he always buying those awful paintings?'

I laughed. 'You knew about that? Sometimes I thought he was crazy. Once he bought a huge old painting of a flock of sheep. It was the ugliest damned thing I ever saw. When he got it back to his loft, he cut the blue areas of the sky into strips and started boiling them in some kind of chemical. Stunk like hell. Later, he explained that he was capturing old pigments, dissolving them in a solvent, then reconstituting them. I've seen him buy old paintings just to scrape the paint off and have period surfaces to work on. The man was incredible.'

'Too bad he couldn't have used those talents honestly.'

I looked over, but Devon was being matter-of-fact, not taking a cheap shot.

'I'm not saying what we did was right, but Paul was a genius. That's why Tanaka won't accept anything short of an original.'

'Then why don't you just get him a real Monet?' She stopped and waited for an answer.

'Shit, Dev, you make it sound simple.' I pictured Anthony Connatser, then tried to dismiss the thought. There had to be another option. Still, to tell the truth, it was comforting to know that Anthony was just a few blocks away.

'What about another fake?' she asked.

'If there was anyone who could paint one that would convince the experts, I'd do it.' I slipped my arm through hers and got us going again.

'Have you thought about old Dr Fulton? He's the one who taught Paul in the first place.'

'Dev, he taught Paul how to be a restorer, not a forger. He's not going to fake a painting for me. My God, the man's an institution. If it hadn't been for him, the Metropolitan Museum would still be sending its paintings to Europe to be restored. I can't even imagine anyone having the balls to ask him.'

'Yeah . . . but he loved Paul. You ought to at least talk to him.'

I thought about what she said as we walked along Madison Avenue, window shopping like the other couples. We were standing outside of a gallery, looking at a painting by Maurice de Vlaminck, when Dev jumped back in fright.

A stack of cardboard against the building had suddenly come to life. 'Goddamned city's got so you can't find no peace.' The cardboard parted, revealing a filthy old man, his grizzled face and hands caked with grime. He had built his cardboard home on the grate outside of the gallery. Pissed that he had scared her, Dev clutched my arm as we made our way quickly up Madison. His soggy voice followed us, 'This is my corner, goddamned bastards.'

'It really is Bombay on the Hudson,' Devon said, holding on tightly to my arm.

'Maybe, but you have to admit there's something obscene about that man sleeping on a grate beneath a painting worth hundreds of thousands of dollars. I wonder if he knows what's behind that half inch of glass?'

'Do you think he cares?' Dev asked.

'Nah, but when you see all that wealth just out of his reach, it makes you wonder.' I looked over my shoulder, but the old man had disappeared back under his cardboard.

As we approached my building, I scanned the street, looking for anyone who might be looking for me. Nothing seemed out of place or unusual – no suspicious characters loitering about, nothing resembling a cop or a Japanese gangster.

Aside from a stack of mail, mostly bills and Christmas catalogs addressed to Occupant, Omar, the doorman, had no messages for me. If Detective Carstairs had been here, he hadn't introduced himself.

Inside the apartment there was nothing to indicate the scene with Marta had ever taken place. Someone had cleaned up, a little too well. I didn't know who, or how they had gotten in, but someone had come calling while I was at Devon's. My place had never been as neat as it looked now. It appeared to have been thoroughly searched, then put back together. It gave me the creeps.

I packed some clothing and toiletries, and as an afterthought threw a couple of suits and ties into a hanging bag. The cash and dope I had left on my dresser were gone. While Dev used the bathroom, I went through my desk, taking my Rolodex. I was closing the top drawer when I noticed an envelope under the phone. Opening it, I discovered a good-sized bindle of heroin and a note.

Adrian,

I'm sorry. I never knew Tanaka would hurt Steven. Please believe me. Call me, maybe I can help.

Marta

P.S. The enclosed should hold you until we get together.

I refolded the note and replaced it in the envelope. The heroin sat on top of the desk, staring at me. The sight of it made my stomach cramp again.

'You ready?' Dev called from the bathroom.

The door opened. Before she stepped out I snatched up the drugs and the note and stuffed them into my pocket.

'Are you okay? You look funny,' she asked.

'No. I'm all right,' I lied.

'Have you got everything you need?'

'Yeah, let me check the answering machine.' There were no messages.

After a brief discussion about whether or not we were pushing our luck, we decided to detour and stop at the gallery.

If anyone followed us, we didn't see them. I took all of the records that pertained to the paintings I had sold Tanaka. The files included full descriptions and photographs of each. I didn't think Paul McHenry kept records, but in case the police had found any in his loft, I wanted the files of Sellars and Ballard to be clean.

While I pulled it all together, Dev cleared the gallery's answering machine and recorded a new message, saying that we would be closed through the holidays.

'Anything important on the machine?' I asked.

'Nothing that won't hold. Oscar Fedder called. He sounded snippy.'

Damn, I'd forgotten all about him. Fuck it. He didn't seem quite as dangerous as he used to.

'He'll wait. Anybody else?'

'Anthony Connatser. He wanted to let you know that the painting he showed you is no longer available, he sold it. He sounded pretty happy.'

'He ought to. Let's get out of here.'

As we locked up, I told myself that I wouldn't have called Anthony, regardless. But now that it wasn't even a possibility, I realized how much better I had felt knowing his Monet was there, if I needed it.

The note from Marta, and the package of smack, burned in my pocket.

CHAPTER FIFTEEN

When we got back to her apartment, Dev kissed me and said good night, then retreated to her bedroom, leaving me sitting in her living room, brooding. I prowled her apartment, restless and irritated. Connatser's Monet had been a fail-safe option that I had tried not to think about. Now that it was gone, it was hard to think about anything else.

It was a bad habit of mine to examine other people's possessions. Up until now I had felt too sick or too pre-occupied to explore. Maybe it had to do with being an art dealer. I had always loved going into collectors' homes and viewing the possessions by which they defined themselves. It was surprising how many otherwise mild-mannered businessmen went for paintings that depicted bold acts – Indians and cowboys going at each other, or Napoleonic soldiers preparing to charge. On the other side of the coin, some of the really macho types expressed themselves by collecting sweet French paintings. I once sold a Miami speedboat designer a very expensive sugary painting depicting a naked cherub, by Adolphe William Bouguereau. He was a big muscular man, with a hairy chest, gold chains, and a beautiful blond wife. Almost a year to the day after I sold him the Bouguereau he was mowed down. Ambushed in a parking lot by drug dealers angry at him for selling the DEA boats that were as fast as the ones he had designed for their drug runs. I would have expected him to collect Remingtons and Russells, gunfighters and broncobusters. Instead he loved cherubim and pink flesh, the silken romance of an earlier society. There's no predicting taste.

Maybe I was just a voyeur. Either way, it wasn't meant as a violation. Given the choice of an apartment with a view of the park or one with a view of interesting neighbors who didn't close their curtains, I'd choose the neighbors.

Two walls of Dev's living room were lined with built-in bookshelves crammed with all manner of books. Well-thumbed novels and classics were stacked with art books, cookbooks, volumes about photography and music. Robertson Davies novels stood next to the works of Anaïs Nin and James Joyce. I was surprised to find Jonathan Carroll's *Sleeping in Flame* on top of a pile of auction catalogs. She even had Jim Harrison's *Dalva* set aside with an Alice Waters cookbook.

The furniture could only be described as eclectic. An overstuffed chair sat next to a couch, obviously chosen for comfort, flanked by a fussy pair of painted Venetian end tables, carved to look like dolphins. The hardwood floors were scattered with good antique Persian prayer rugs. Against one wall stood a satinwood Biedermeier curio cabinet, displaying a pair of old eyeglasses on a stand, two small African fertility carvings, antique tarot cards, the porcelain head of an old doll staring out at the world with vivid blue glass eyes, an ivory elephant, and several fossils. Somehow the objects looked as though they belonged together. There were fresh cut tulips and freesia placed around the room in vases.

Framed photographs of family and friends were everywhere. Devon was an only child but came from a large extended clan. If the pictures weren't lying, her parents and grandparents, uncles and aunts and more cousins than I could count had all doted on her. There were photographs of happy-looking family get-togethers. Devon smiling at birthday parties, weddings, anniversaries, holidays. I studied each, imagining the conversations her family must have had about everything from grades to politics. 'Did you see what our Devon made in math last semester?' her father would ask her grandfather. 'Of course, son, we couldn't be prouder,' grandfather would answer, a twinkle in his eye. 'Anyone for more dessert?' her mother would interrupt, holding a small bell with which she could summon the cook.

I thought I was feeling a certain sarcastic superiority at how normal, how like white bread the Berensons looked in the photos. The longer I looked I realized that what I felt was jealousy. The few memories I had of my family gatherings were dominated by bitter arguments about who did what first to whom and why. By the time I was a teenager, our meals were usually judged either a success or a failure by whether or not the number of empty wine bottles outnumbered the guests, and by what margin. Three to one usually meant a smashing success. Devon's pictures were of a world I wasn't sure I believed in.

I looked for photographic evidence of a boyfriend, expecting to find glossy prints of shots taken in Aspen or Rio or any of a dozen other romantic places I could imagine taking Devon. Shots of some blond jock with his arms draped all over her. Photographs that would explain how she had actually spent those Saturday nights I had wondered about. There were several pictures that included men; however, none seemed terribly intimate. But there was a shot of Caitlin and me, taken on her fourth birthday. I winced at how stoned I looked. The Sellars family tradition, alive and well in another generation. I thought about Marta's note and the heroin, still glowing in my pocket. But the slack look on my face as Caitlin blew out the candles on her cake sickened me. Why would Devon keep a photograph of my daughter and me? Especially such a bad one? I'd have to ask her in the morning.

One item nailed my attention and held it. A small black and white photograph in a dusty silver frame, sitting on one of the Venetian end tables.

It was of a little girl, six or seven years old, dressed in a cowgirl outfit complete with hat and six-shooters. Dev, sitting on her grandfather's lap, pointing both six-shooters at the photographer, and laughing with childish glee. Her grandfather held her with obvious pride. Both their eyes shone, and there wasn't a hint that anything bad could ever happen in the world captured forever by that snapshot. I was mesmerized. Much of that little girl still lived in the woman. Dev's smile, and that light in her eyes, hadn't changed a bit. Looking at that picture, I thought of my grandfather and wished that Dev could have met him.

Carrying it over to the chair by the couch, I sat and gazed at it, trying to remember if I had ever been that innocent, that convinced anything was possible. I wasn't sure what it was like to live in a world like the Berensons'. Maybe I had been born cynical.

Staring at Dev's photograph, I didn't see her grandfather, I saw mine. Holding my fish in his huge hand, smiling bigger than big. And I found myself at the age of thirty-eight wanting more than anything to tell him that I was lost again. Scared, and lonely, and lost. I wanted to bury my face in his shoulder, smell his aftershave, and know that everything would be all right.

I hadn't realized that I was sobbing until I looked up

and saw that Dev had come out of her room and was watching me. She wore a strange expression. A mixture of concern and affection and something else I couldn't name flickered and sparkled behind her pale green eyes.

'I saw this picture and it made me think of my grandfather,' I explained. I put the photograph down on the coffee table and picked up a tissue and wiped my face.

Dev knelt beside the chair, took my face in her hands, and kissed me with enough tenderness and passion to melt the ice that had clogged my heart for longer than I could remember. The tip of her tongue slipped into my mouth, then traced my lips. I reached up and touched her hair. Whatever barrier I had imagined kept us apart dissolved. Wordlessly she pulled me up by the hand and led me to her room. While she was undoing her robe, I unbuttoned my jeans and stepped out of them.

Her bed was rumpled and warm. I drew her to me, kissed her again and got lost in her lips. She tasted like she smelled, of spice and sunlight, and the sea. We were gentle, tentative. We explored, and stroked, finding each other's rhythms and sensitive places. Aroused, we grew more sure of each other. When I entered her she murmured something, and without hearing her words, I understood. We moved together. I felt her rising to me as if to draw me deeper inside her. As her nipples hardened against my chest she twisted her fingers in my hair and urged me on. Her legs spread wide and she pushed herself up at me, all slippery heat. She called my name, then opened her eyes and looked into mine. She was ready. My world filled with incandescence and white noise, and I exploded inside her.

We held on to each other, neither wanting to be the first to let go. Then we kissed, and I knew that I had discovered something. I couldn't explain it or put it into words. But some part of me that had been murky and confused became clear. Then I drifted off to sleep, all tangled up with Dev.

CHAPTER SIXTEEN

I started awake an hour or so later, surprised to hear Dev crying.

'What is it?' I asked, reaching over and placing the palm of my hand flat on her warm stomach.

'What are we doing? We . . . no, I must be crazy. Adrian, I don't know if I can do this.'

'Dev, what do you want me to say?'

'I don't want you to say anything. I've wanted this. Us. But not like this. My God, Adrian, the whole world is upside down, and we're in bed like it doesn't matter.'

I moved my hand up and rested it between her breasts, over her racing heart. 'It matters, all of it matters.'

She stiffened, then asked, 'What if it doesn't work out? What if Tanaka does something awful to you? To us?'

'Shhhh. Don't talk like that. Everything is going to work out. It's going to be okay.' I tried to sound brave, but the words came out of my mouth sounding foolish.

'Stop it,' she snapped. 'Don't act like it's all under control. Nothing's under control and you know it.'

She pushed my hand away and lay there, stiff as a board, staring up at the ceiling.

'You're right,' I admitted. 'It's a fucked-up situation – we'll do the best we can.'

'And if that's not good enough?'

'Do you want me to leave?'

'Is that what you want to do?' She raised up on one elbow and searched my face.

'No. I want to stay as much as I've ever wanted anything in the world.'

'Then hold me,' she said, sliding up against me. Then she added, 'Don't fuck with me, Adrian. Whatever happens, don't fuck with me.'

I held her tight, until her breathing quieted and she fell asleep in my arms. *Life* magazine once published an article about heroes, stating that during moments of great fear and danger the best of the human spirit often surfaces, allowing us to act in ways that are better than we might normally behave. They included stories of great and enduring love affairs begun under the worst possible conditions – war, natural disasters. I slid my arm out from under Devon's head, kissed her parted lips, and wondered if I could be that lucky.

When I opened my eyes again, it was morning. It had been days since I had slept for more than a few hours at a time. I almost felt human again. Dev was in the kitchen. Lying still a while longer, I listened to her clatter around, savoring the softness of her bed and the lingering scent she had left on the pillows. I wondered what her mood would be. After what she had said before we fell asleep, I didn't know what to expect.

Reluctantly I left the warmth of Dev's bed for the chill of her bathroom.

It was obviously a woman's bathroom. Not that it was frilly or overdone. To the contrary, it was spare and functional. But unlike in the guest bathroom, Dev's presence was everywhere. Jars of cosmetics were lined up on the marble counter. Perfumes stood beside them on a small mirrored tray. There were sponges and scented bath soaps. I felt like an intruder, and was careful to lift the seat, then put it down again.

When I picked up my jeans from the floor by the bed, the forgotten note and the smack tumbled from the pocket and landed at my feet. I stared at them for a moment, jolted by the ugliness of their reality lying next to my pale toes. Bending, I scooped them up and stuffed them back into the pocket they had fallen from.

I wondered how much heroin the bindle held. At least five, maybe six or seven grams. Pretty generous of old Marta. I needed to get rid of it. Fingering the pocket, I thought about flushing it, even though it was a terrible waste. Later, I told myself. I'd do it, but later. I considered the note. Devon would have a good feel for it. What would be the best way to broach the subject? The phone rang, interrupting my thoughts. Pulling on my jeans, I headed for the kitchen, the envelope light in my pocket.

Devon was holding the phone to her ear with her shoulder while she wrestled the turkey into the oven.

'All right, Mom. I've got it . . . mm-hmm, three-fifty, fifteen minutes a pound. Yes, I'll cover it toward the end. I promise. I love you . . . yeah, me too. Tell Daddy. Bye-bye.'

I watched as she hung up the phone and turned back to the oven.

'Good morning,' I said cautiously.

'You're up.' Her smile was tentative.

'Happy Thanksgiving,' I said.

'You too. Are you in the mood to watch the parade?'

'I don't know, what's it like out?' I asked, crossing to the window.

'Cold, but we could watch it on TV.' She adjusted the temperature of the oven, then busied herself picking over a bowl of cranberries.

'Devon . . .'

She looked up from the cranberries.

We stared at each other. I searched her face, hoping to find an invitation, afraid she might have decided that it was all too much for her. Instead, her look was as penetrating as my own. Searching, but for what I didn't know. I opened my mouth to ask, but she shook her head and put her fingers against my lips.

We stood like that for a long moment, each of us trying to see inside the other. Then we kissed, pressing hard against each other. She bit at my lower lip and fumbled with the buttons of my shirt. Dropping my jeans to the floor, I backed her up and lifted her skirt. I went after her like she was a drug.

Her response was equally intense, as if she had overcome some sense of caution and decided to dive in hoping the water was deep enough. She groaned as I pulled off her panties and buried my face between her legs. She rubbed and bucked against me, urgently digging one heel into my back. More, I thought. I wanted to breathe her in, to inhale until I had absorbed her. Then I wanted still more. My cock stiffened and rubbed against my belly. I wanted to push it into her. Had to push it into her. To push and thrust until I lost myself inside her. I lifted her onto the counter, and she spread her legs. Her hands were in my hair, her teeth biting at my nipples as I pounded into her. We knocked over a bag of flour, and then the cranberries, shifting and straining to get deeper, to get more.

By the time we'd had enough, it was hard to tell who looked worse. We were both caked in flour. Devon giggled like a schoolgirl while we cleaned up the mess. When she bent to gather up the cranberries, I laughed until my sides hurt at the sight of her perfect ass imprinted with the pattern of the spatula she had come to rest on. We didn't talk about what was going on between us. For once I wanted to let it happen, without the burden of words or explanations. There would be plenty of time for both. We wound up naked on the couch, Devon still laughing as she tried to get the flour out of her hair.

'I need a shower. Want to join me?' I asked.

'Go ahead. I'll be there in a minute.' She sat back on the couch, a distant look settling on her face.

'Are you okay?'

'I'll be fine,' she said, but a weight seemed to have suddenly descended on her. 'Go ahead, you're getting flour everywhere.'

'You sure?' I turned to her.

'I'm fine,' she insisted, getting up and walking toward the kitchen. 'Now go and start the shower. I'll be there in a minute.'

Most of her soaps were perfumed, but I found a square block of white stuff that looked like it had oatmeal suspended in it. It was the only one that wasn't scented, but I wasn't sure whether you were supposed to eat it or wash with it. I shampooed twice to get the flour out, then began to wonder what had happened to Devon.

Stepping out of her shower, I toweled off. 'Devon?'

No answer.

'Hey – I thought you were coming in,' I called.

I walked out of the bathroom and found her sitting on the end of the bed. My jeans lay across her lap, the note from Marta and the dope were in her hand. Her face was gray, her eyes molten.

'In the kitchen . . . I picked up your jeans, these fell out of the pocket.' She waved the note. 'Get dressed and get the fuck out.'

I stood there for a moment, stunned by the heat of her anger. Then I started to talk, and talk fast.

'Devon, I found them on my desk last night,' I explained. 'I was planning to flush the dope – show you the note – we got sidetracked.'

She threw the jeans at me, sending them flying over my head. 'I don't want to hear it. You should have said anything you had to say last night. I want you out.'

'Please. You have to believe me.'

She snorted derisively. 'Believe you? I couldn't trust you to tell me what day it is.'

'Devon, listen to me for a second. You've seen with your own eyes what I've been through. Do I look high?'

She studied me, a flicker of indecision in her eyes.

'I was going to get rid of the dope. I'm through with it.'

'You need help.'

'Then help me.'

'I can't give you the kind of help you need.'

'Just get through this with me, Devon. Give me a chance. Then I'll get whatever type of help you think I need.'

She got up and walked to the window, then peered out through the drapes. The note and the bindle were clutched in her right fist.

'Why? Why should I put myself through this?'

'I need you.'

Silence.

'Don't make me beg.'

Her back stiffened. Her fist tightened around the note.

My heart dropped. Standing there dripping with a towel wrapped around my waist, I desperately tried to think of something more to say. Some way to convince her. But my brain was filled with wool. The best thing I'd been near for longer than I could remember was slipping away.

She turned and glared at me.

'No. I can't live with this,' she said shaking her head. 'Everything you do, everything you say . . . I'd have to wonder. Is he lying to me? Is he using? It's too much to ask. I don't know how to put you back together. Even if I wanted to.'

'Devon, on all that matters to me, on Caitlin's life, I swear that I'm not lying to you. Don't cut this off just when it's starting to mean something.'

She looked at me, her mouth working. 'This? *This?*'

'Give it a chance . . .'

She turned away. 'I can't. I just can't.'

I picked up my jeans from where she had thrown them and carried them into the guest room to dress.

It was cold, and everything seemed too hard-edged and bright, too real. My legs felt heavy as I gathered my clothes. I was pulling on my shirt, dreading the walk back to the Rimbaud, when she appeared in the doorway. Her eyes were red; the note and the dope were still in her hand.

'You swear to me you didn't do any of this?'

I nodded, hope rising. 'On everything I care about.'

'Flush it.' She threw the bindle at my feet.

I walked into the bathroom, tore it open, and dumped the white powder into the toilet, then crumpled the paper bindle and tossed it in too. The powder formed a slick on the surface of the water, then started to filter down. The paper was still floating as I pushed the handle. I watched it swirl and disappear. A little smudge of the dope was smeared on my thumb. Out of habit, I started to lick it off, then realized what I was doing and rinsed my hands in the sink. I could feel Devon watching the whole thing. She was silent, intent upon my actions, observing it all as though I were performing a pagan ritual.

Turning, I waited for her to speak.

She regarded me steadily, then nodded. 'If I ever even get a hint that you've lied to me, or that you're using drugs or drinking, you're on your own.' She looked at her feet. Then she tossed Marta's note onto the bed. 'I'm going to shower.'

After she left, I picked up the note and tore it in half. I made coffee. There wasn't much on TV, but I sat in front of it anyway, until Devon finally came out of her room.

She walked straight into the kitchen without saying a word and started banging around. I let her be.

'You aren't foolish enough to believe Marta, are you?' Devon asked, coming out of the kitchen.

'No. She's a snake,' I answered. 'You read the note. What do you think?'

She sat down on the couch. 'I think you're right. She's a snake.'

'The question is, can we use her in some way? Is there any advantage to meeting with her? We don't have a hell of a lot of other options.'

She twisted a strand of her hair as she thought. 'I hate this. The thought of you two together makes me sick. But maybe she knows something. You should see her, Adrian, but . . .' An unspoken warning was in her eyes.

'Why don't we see her together?' I offered.

Dev flashed me a scornful look. 'Because if I sat in the same room as that . . . that sleaze, I'd probably have to tear her tits off.'

We sat on opposite ends of the couch, lost in our own thoughts. The distance between us was only a couple of feet, but it felt like the Grand Canyon.

'I still think you should call Dr Fulton,' Dev said, out of the blue.

'I appreciate your advice, but he's not going to forge a painting for us. No matter how close he and Paul were.'

'I'm not saying he would. How long did he run the restoration department at the Met? Twenty years, thirty? He knows everyone in the art world. If he wanted to, he could help us in some other way.'

'He could probably help me right into a jail cell.' I shuddered thinking about it.

'Come on, he's going to he angry when he finds out what you and Paul were doing, but don't underestimate how close the two of them were.' She paused. 'He and Paul were lovers, you know.'

'Lovers?' I sputtered. 'Dr Fulton? Paul? I never gave it any thought. You think Paul was gay?'

'Of course he was. You never noticed?'

'I guess not.' I sat back on the couch to consider this new slant on Paul McHenry's life. 'I always thought it was a mentor relationship. Kind of an apprentice thing. My God, Dr Fulton's an old man. You really think they were lovers?'

'Mm-hmm.'

I shook my head. 'I just don't see it. Have you ever met him?'

'No. I only know what Paul told me about him.'

'When? I didn't know you knew Paul McHenry that well.'

'We talked. He used to come by the gallery. I think he was lonely.'

'He never said anything when I was around.'

'You get pretty intense, Adrian. There are a lot of things people don't tell you. He was probably worried about what you would think if you knew.'

'I just can't believe I never picked up on it.' I shook my head again. My world was getting stranger by the day. It was as though I had stepped into the mirror and come out in never-never land. The landscape looked the same, but all the rules had changed.

'Let's go see him tomorrow,' Devon said again.

Reluctantly, I agreed to call and ask if Dr Fulton would see us, but I didn't think it would do much good. Moving to her end of the couch, I put my arm around her and attempted to give her a hug. She pushed me away.

'I'm trying, Adrian. But it's not that easy.' She got up and retreated back to her bedroom.

Later, as we settled into an uneasy silence in front of the TV, watching the Macy's Thanksgiving Day parade, the phone rang. Dev answered, looked at me with a shrug, and handed me the receiver.

'Adrian? Hiro Okuba here.'

'Hiro,' I stammered. 'How did you find me here?'

'It wasn't terribly hard. It was quite simply a matter of looking at the options. Anyone could do it.'

I listened dumbfounded, not sure what he was telling me. Up until that moment I had believed Dev's apartment was safe. Hiro shattered my illusion. It couldn't have been *that* damned easy to track me. I didn't know how he did it, but if Okuba could reach out and touch me, I had to believe Tanaka's sharks were circling Devon's building as we spoke. I picked up the phone and walked with it to the window. I looked down at the sidewalk, but nothing seemed out of place. Shit, for all I knew, Carstairs was out there too.

Hiro sounded pleased with himself. 'I've received a short list of art collectors in Japan who could be in Nakamura's pocket.'

'How many are there?'

'Four in all. Two politicians, and two bankers who might interest you. All of them very influential and powerful men.'

Asking him to hold, I gestured to Dev for a paper and pen. As an afterthought I covered the mouthpiece and asked her what she thought about inviting Okuba to our Thanksgiving dinner. She picked up a pen from the night table and shrugged.

'Hiro, rather than doing this over the phone, why don't you join my friend and me for Thanksgiving dinner?'

'Thanksgiving? Damn, I'm sorry. I don't know what I was thinking. Mishima does business seven days a week, including holidays. When I got this fax from Japan, I couldn't resist calling you right away. I won't put you to any more trouble.'

'It's no trouble at all. We would really love for you to come.'

'Thank you, but I couldn't possibly impose upon your hospitality.'

'Listen, Hiro, it's no imposition. It's just going to be the two of us, and we'd welcome your company.' With Devon acting so chilly, I'd have welcomed Charles Manson.

'Well . . . to be honest with you, I've never had a real Thanksgiving dinner.'

'Then let's plan on it. Come at seven o'clock. The address is –'

He cut me off. 'I already have it. Can I bring anything?'

'Just an appetite,' I said, wondering if it had really been that easy to track us down. 'And that list.'

Devon frowned as I hung up. 'How did he find you here? Are you sure about this?'

'What do you mean?'

'You hardly know this Okuba. Do you think it's smart to invite him here?'

'Duncan Marshall gave me his name. I trust Duncan.'

She tapped her front teeth with the pen. 'I thought one of Duncan's partners gave him the name. Does Duncan really know this Okuba very well? You think he gave him my phone number?'

'Come on, Dev. Okuba's all we've got. You want me to call Duncan and double-check?'

She thought for a moment. 'Nah – I'm just getting paranoid. It's Thanksgiving. Let's not bother the Marshalls.'

Just after noon I got Marilyn on the phone.

'Stop it, Adrian. Stop trying to run our lives,' she said when I asked her to take Caitlin to her mother's.

I tried again, this time calmly, to explain the situation.

'Get a life,' she responded, her usual brilliant come-back to anything she didn't want to discuss. 'Now, talk to your daughter. I've got things to do.'

Caitlin sounded relieved to hear my voice.

'Daddy, where have you been?'

'I've been staying with a friend, honey. How are you doing?'

'I'm fine. But I miss you. We're having a big turkey and I made the stuffing. You know what, Dad?'

'No, tell me what.'

'Mom says I'm spending Christmas with you this year. I left a message on your machine. I want to go to the beach, like we did last spring.'

I couldn't think that far ahead. Tanaka's deadline was a wall I hadn't tried to look beyond.

'Caitlin, I would rather go to the beach with you for Christmas than anything in the world.' My chest was tight.

'Okay. I'm gonna get a new bathing suit. Mom said I could pick it out myself. I think it'll be a bikini. A pink and green bikini . . . Is it okay with you if I hang up now? I need to help stuff the turkey before Mom does it without me.'

'Sure it is. I love you, Caitlin.' I had tears in my eyes.

'I love you too, Daddy. I'll call soon and leave another message. Bye-bye. Oh, Dad?'

'Yeah, honey.'

'Akka Bakka Beecha.'

'Akka Bakka Beecha to you too.' I held the phone to my ear and listened to the silence when she hung up.

Then I put the receiver down and started toward the kitchen to see if Devon needed any help. Christmas at the beach. A pink and green bikini.

CHAPTER SEVENTEEN

The doorbell rang promptly at seven. Before Devon buzzed Hiro Okuba in, she turned to me. 'We need his help. Let's give him some time to get to know us. Promise me you won't jump him with a million questions the minute he walks in.'

'He's coming to show us the list,' I grumbled.

Dev ignored my comment and made a last-minute inspection of the dining table she had spent an hour setting. She had been tense and distant all afternoon. I hoped Okuba's presence would lighten things up a little.

As she bent to move a glass until it was just so, her short denim skirt rode up and revealed the back of her thighs. She was wearing a white T-shirt. Her nipples formed little peaks where they pressed against the thick cotton. Even pissed off, she looked like ripe strawberries taste.

When I opened the door to greet Hiro, I could barely see him behind an enormous bouquet of Parrot tulips.

'Happy Thanksgiving,' he said, holding the flowers out to Devon as he walked into the apartment.

'Where did you find anything so beautiful on Thanksgiving day?' she asked.

He smiled at her. He wore a blue blazer and a striped tie. With his tortoiseshell glasses he looked like an Ivy League grad student. I felt old, tattered around the edges.

'Hiro, this is Devon Berenson.'

She offered him her hand. 'We're pleased you could come.'

'You and Adrian were kind to include me.' He bowed slightly as they shook hands. 'I'm very happy to meet you.'

'Adrian, show Hiro around. I'll put these in some water.'

We walked through the apartment, for the most part silently. I felt awkward showing someone I didn't know around an apartment that wasn't mine. He stopped in front of the curio cabinet and seemed fascinated, then moved on to the photos on the bookshelves. I glanced at my watch and wondered how long I should wait to ask him about the list. It read five after seven. I tapped the dial to make sure it was working.

'A glass of wine, Hiro?' Dev offered from the kitchen.

'White, please.'

'Anything for you, Adrian?' The shadow of a chill lingered in her voice.

A cold glass of white wine sounded good. It might take the edge off the evening and settle my stomach. But the tone of Devon's voice helped push the thought from my mind. 'Ginger ale, Dev. You need any help?'

'No. I'll be out in a minute.'

'Adrian, tell me about the art market. What should a guy like me' – Hiro tapped himself on the chest – 'a beginning collector of limited means, be looking at?'

Devon brought him a glass of wine and me a ginger ale, then disappeared back into the kitchen. We sat down on the couch, and twenty minutes later I was just warming to the topic when she called us to the table.

We continued the conversation over a salad of wild mushrooms, sauteed and served over lightly dressed field greens. While Devon picked at her food, I told Hiro about the last, no-holds-barred arena of free enterprise.

'Now, you have to always be alert at the auctions.' I

gestured with my fork as I spoke. 'I've seen people get stuck for tens of thousands of dollars, simply because they didn't double-check the accuracy of the catalog. Once –'

Devon put down her glass and interrupted. 'Hiro, where are you from?'

I looked up, surprised.

'Kyoto,' he answered, sounding glad to be asked. 'My family has lived there for over four hundred years.'

I tried to work out how many generations of Okubas that represented.

'Do you have a large family?' she asked.

'My parents, two brothers,' he hesitated. 'Actually one brother, my oldest brother is no longer alive.' His mouth hardened for a fleeting second, then relaxed. 'Too many cousins to count.'

'Your accent sounds English.'

He swallowed, wiping his lips before answering her. 'That's where I learned your language. Oxford, part of an exchange program.' He looked down at his plate and smiled. 'Devon, this salad is incredible. You're a wonderful cook.'

She smiled, her first genuine smile of the evening. 'Save room. Adrian tells me you've never had a traditional Thanksgiving dinner. I don't know how traditional this will be, but there'll be plenty of it.'

As she cleared the salad plates and walked into the kitchen, I turned to Hiro. 'How are you settling in? Is New York all you thought it would be?'

He picked up his wine and nodded, a funny smile passing over his lips. 'It's taken a while. Hell, it was a year before I really knew my way around. Sometimes it gets a little lonely. I miss Japan.'

Something he said struck me as wrong, but I couldn't think what.

'Well, it's a great City. I wish you much success here.'

We clinked glasses.

'A little success with women, that's what I need.' He tilted his head back and laughed.

'You really haven't met any women?' I asked.

'Shit, Adrian, it seems like all of the great-looking New York girls are either taken or they're waiting for Tom Cruise. You can count the dates I've had in the last two years on your fingers.'

I looked at him, confused, but he seemed not to notice. I could have sworn he'd told me he hadn't had a date since moving here. Devon interrupted before I could pursue the thought.

'Well, don't ask Adrian about dating.' Devon's voice, loud and clear, came from the kitchen. 'You'd probably do better without his help. At least you'd be safer.'

Hiro looked at me.

I shrugged. 'Women,' I whispered.

He smiled.

'Do you need any help in there?' I offered Devon. 'Or are you happy listening and providing commentary?'

'No, thanks,' she answered. 'But try not to lead Hiro too far astray.'

I got the distinct impression that he would like nothing better. Somehow I managed to refrain from asking him about the list. Instead we talked about New York, until a loud crash followed by a yelp from Devon brought us both to our feet.

'Are you okay?' I asked, hurrying into the kitchen, Hiro fast on my heels.

Devon was leaning against the counter, holding a wet dish towel against her left forearm, biting her lip. The turkey lay in a puddle of its own juices in the middle of the floor. The pan in which it had been roasting lay upside down beside it.

'I burned myself,' she said, holding out her arm for me to see.

'Let's put some ice on it.'

She looked up at Hiro, tears streaming. 'I'm sorry. Some Thanksgiving dinner this is turning out to be.'

'Don't worry about it,' he said. 'I know you guys have a lot on your minds.'

I bent and lifted the turkey with a pair of kitchen tongs. 'I think we can still get a meal out of this.'

Devon slammed out of the kitchen toward her bedroom. I poured Hiro another glass of wine and set about salvaging the turkey. By the time Dev returned, I had rinsed it off and carved it.

'I'm okay now.' She had fixed her makeup, and her lips were pressed into a determined smile. 'Hiro, please forgive me. We've not had a good week.' She looked at him; her face was composed but she looked drained.

He nodded.

We returned to the dining room with the salvaged turkey and the somewhat congealed bowls of sausage-and-sage dressing and gravy. Devon had also made candied yams, and haricots verts. After we'd loaded our plates, I looked at Hiro.

'So, tell me what you found out about Nakamura's art dealings.'

He cracked a smile. 'I'm impressed. You waited over an hour to ask. Very Oriental of you.'

I glanced at Devon. 'We aren't all barbarians, *yabanjin*.'

He laughed so hard that the turkey fell off his fork. 'Where did you learn that expression?'

'Our friend Tanaka.' My smile faded. 'Did you find out anything that might help us with him?'

I pushed the food around on my plate, waiting for him to answer.

'I'm afraid I can't confirm anything. But I have the names of a few collectors who are thought to be in Nakamura's pocket.' He put down his fork and pulled a typewritten list out of his blazer. There were four names on it.

'The first two are bankers,' he said, pointing with his finger. 'The other two are politicians. They're all in Tokyo. Unfortunately, I can't get you a list of their collections. They may have nothing at all to do with your situation.'

He handed me the sheet of paper. The names meant nothing to me. I thought about who might know these collections, hoping it wasn't a dead end.

'This stuff is amazing,' Hiro said, helping himself to his third serving of the cranberry-and-orange relish. 'Where can I buy some?'

A faint smile lit Devon's face, the first since the turkey crash-landed. 'You can get the berries in any grocery store. They come in bags. I'll give you the recipe.'

'Good,' he said, wiping his plate clean with the last of the rolls.

He'd kept his word, bringing not only the list but as healthy an appetite as I'd ever seen on someone his size.

Devon got up to clear the table. 'Let's have coffee in the living room. I'll try not to drop it,' she said, rolling her eyes.

We all laughed.

By the time we pushed back from the table, I knew I wanted more from Okuba, but I didn't know how to get it. I thought about telling him the whole story – the murders, the forgeries, everything. Dev was right, he could be an important ally. I helped her clear the table, and when we were alone in the kitchen, I asked her opinion.

'Do you think we can afford to trust him?'

'I don't think we have much choice.' She put down the dishes she held and placed her hand on my chest. 'Adrian, we need help. Who else can we trust?'

No one came to mind. I nodded.

Sighing, she stood on her toes and kissed me lightly on the lips.

We moved into the living room. I took a seat on the couch next to Hiro, and Devon sat in the chair facing us. I stirred my coffee.

'Hiro, I'm not sure what you're going to think of this, but I need help. There are some things I didn't tell you in the sushi bar.'

He leaned forward. 'Go on.'

'A friend of mine . . . my partner, has been murdered over this. The paintings we sold Tanaka were forgeries.'

Hiro's face hardened, his eyes narrowed. Suddenly he looked wary.

'For some reason I was thinking of you as an innocent victim, Adrian. Apparently I was wrong.'

'Don't misunderstand me, Hiro. Tanaka knew what he was buying.'

He sat back, alert but willing to listen quietly as I told him the rest of my story.

'Let me be sure I understand this,' he interrupted. 'Tanaka knew that the paintings were forgeries, and he bought them anyway?'

I nodded. 'That's why he bought them. I'm not sure what he's done with them, but he never bought anything from me except the forgeries. Like I told you at the sushi bar – Tanaka's not a collector, he's a hustler.'

'How many paintings in all has he purchased from you?'

'Nine. The "Monet" would have been the tenth.'

'Has anyone else ever been present when you and he negotiated these purchases?'

'Steven Ballard, and Tanaka's man Kotani.' My stomach twisted at the thought of him. 'Someday that bastard is going to be sorry. All of them are.'

Hiro ignored my threat. 'Never Nakamura, or anyone else in Tanaka's organization? Never Stan?'

'No. Why?' I asked, wondering why he'd ask about Stan.

'I just want to get a clear picture of your dealings.' He sipped his coffee and settled deeper into the couch. Then he removed his glasses and rubbed his eyes.

'Adrian, you did the right thing by not going to the police. You'd be a dead man by now if you had. No one has ever survived to testify against these people. I'm sorry about what happened to your partner, but I suggest we concentrate on resolving your situation. Not on getting even.'

Devon and I exchanged worried looks.

'What do you think we should do?' she asked him.

'It seems that Tanaka has done one of two things. Either he's resold the forgeries as originals, or he's passed them on to Nakamura to use in some *za e teku* scam. If he's simply resold the forgeries and taken his profit, they could be anywhere in Japan. I don't see how that scenario can offer you a way out.' He sipped his coffee again. 'If, however, the paintings you supplied Tanaka ended up as bribes, and the recipients of those bribes believe they have been given valuable originals – '

Dev broke in. 'I understand the meaning of "face" in Japan. If we could prove to the people on your list that Nakamura had used forgeries as gifts to bribe them, what would happen?'

Hiro thought it out. 'It's a two-edged sword, Devon. It would cause great loss of face to Nakamura. But if he ever found out who brought his scam to light . . . well, I wouldn't want to be that person. But you're getting ahead of things. We don't know that he's used the paintings as bribes. We don't even know where the paintings are.'

Dev freshened his coffee, then he continued. 'It doesn't make sense. Substituting forgeries for originals would be too risky for Nakamura. Eventually the fakes would be discovered. The loss of face would be incalculable. It would cripple him next time he needed to buy influence.'

'What if he thought they were originals?' Dev jumped in again.

'Yeah,' I echoed, 'what if Tanaka hustled Nakamura into believing our paintings were the real thing? What if Tanaka paid us for forgeries, then passed them along to Nakamura for the price of originals? He could have pocketed millions by now.'

Hiro sat forward. 'If Tanaka was greedy enough to pull a stunt like that, and you could prove it . . . you would own him. But until you find the paintings, there's nothing to go on. This is all speculation.'

The three of us sat in Dev's living room thinking about the possibilities. Any way you cut it, we needed someone in our corner. I hated to beg, but so far Hiro Okuba was the only horse in a one-horse race. I got up from the couch where I had been sitting next to him and walked over to the bookcase. I leaned back against the shelves and cleared my throat.

'Hiro, we're in over our heads. We never intended for this to go so far. Do you think you can help us?'

Devon also got up and came to stand beside me.

Hiro thought for a few moments before answering. 'I don't know what I can do for you. Maybe you should have thought about this before you got involved with such heavy players. I'm not sure of the legalities, or of my moral obligation to the new owners of the forged art.' He paused, his mouth softening. 'I'd like to help the two of you. My older brother would be alive today if he hadn't joined the Hiyashi Gumi. He died trying to get out. I'd like nothing more than throwing a wrench into Nakamura's machine. But this is a very serious matter.'

'We know. We need a friend.' Devon spoke softly.

'Yes, I believe you do.' He pressed his hands together as though he were about to pray, and seemed to wrestle for a moment with some internal decision. 'In Japan we have something like your FBI, it's called the National Police Agency. The NPA handles any investigation concerning the *yakuza*. From time to time information that may be of use to them crosses my desk. As long as there's no conflict for my company, I pass along what I hear. As a result, I've developed a few good contacts. That's how I acquired the list of collectors I gave you. I don't completely trust them, but if you don't object, I'd be willing to use my sources at the NPA to find out more about Nakamura.'

'Can you do that and leave us out of the picture?' I asked.

He hesitated. 'This is a nasty mess you're in. I'm not sure how far I can go for you.'

Devon and I stood and waited.

He shook his head. 'I don't know how much I can get out of them without telling your side of the story. But if I ask the right questions, who knows what we might find out.' He looked up and smiled, then held up his cup of coffee as though toasting us. 'But I want that cranberry recipe.'

Devon looked at me. Then we all started speaking at once.

We talked long into the night. By the time Hiro left we had distilled the information we needed down to four important questions.

We needed to find the paintings in Japan. The list of art collectors Hiro had provided was as good a starting point as any. The four individuals he had chosen were not only powerful and influential men but also very public collectors. The type who loan their collections to museums and exhibitions, or even allow a catalog of their holdings to be published. I needed to find someone who knew the contents of their collections.

If we discovered the locations of McHenry's forgeries, we would probably answer the second question. Whether or not Nakamura had used them in a *za e teku* scam.

The third question, perhaps the most important one, seemed impossible to answer. Did Nakamura pay Tanaka for originals, or did he know the works were forgeries?

The fourth question was how to prove the paintings were fakes, if we did find them.

Paul McHenry's work was good. So good, that to my knowledge no one had ever questioned one of his forgeries. They were painstakingly executed, using materials consistent with the period each given work was meant to represent. And all of them possessed carefully created provenances, which would be very difficult to disprove. They also had certificates of authenticity purchased at considerable expense from the appropriate 'art experts.' Steven and I had spared no effort in creating plausible circumstances for the 'rediscovery' of these 'lost' masterpieces.

But Paul McHenry had always been vain about his work. Perhaps all artists maintain an interest in their creations, even long after they're sold. Paul always marked his paintings with a hidden cipher. A secret mark that would enable him to prove his authorship if he ever needed or wanted to.

We argued often about it. I considered it to be an unnecessary risk. An egotistical pirouette that had no place in our business. But Paul was adamant. Whenever I thought I had him backed into a corner, he would smile and tell me about the case of Hans van Meegeren, the great Dutch forger.

During World War II, van Meegeren, an art dealer, managed against the odds to keep his business open and thriving in spite of the Nazi occupation.

When the war ended, he was charged by the Allies and jailed as a German collaborator. His accusers maintained that he had helped the Nazis plunder Dutch art treasures, particularly the rare works of Jan Vermeer, several of which van Meegeren was known to have supplied to Goering himself.

At his trial van Meegeren loudly proclaimed his innocence. He swore that all of the paintings he had supplied to the Nazis were forgeries. Creations of his own hand. Furthermore, he asserted that the bulk of the profits from his dealings with the Germans had been funneled back to the Dutch Resistance movement.

Unfortunately several art experts testified that the paintings in question were indeed originals. And the leader of the resistance, to whom van Meegeren claimed he had given his profits, had been killed in the closing days of the war. With no evidence to support his story, Hans van Meegeren was found guilty and sentenced to a twenty-year prison term.

In jail, he hatched a final desperate scheme to prove his innocence. Using the last of his resources, he managed to bribe guards into bringing him art supplies. Then, in his cell he completed a painting by 'Vermeer' that so impressed his jailers, they helped him convince the court to submit it to the same panel of 'experts' that had condemned him.

After carefully examining the painting without knowing the circumstances of its 'discovery,' the art experts declared it to be an original. Amid much publicity, the delighted van Meegeren was given a new trial. Several members of the Dutch Resistance, who did not testify at his first trial, came forward now, confirming that although they couldn't swear to the details, van Meegeren had indeed met on a regular basis with the leader of their underground group.

On the basis of his skill as a forger and the new testimony, Hans van Meegeren won his case and was immediately released. A minor hero, his reputation restored, he lived out the rest of his life as a successful art dealer, although he never sold another Vermeer.

Paul loved that story. We even talked about trying to write a screenplay based on van Meegeren's exploits. Like so much whiskey talk, it never happened. Paul McHenry considered himself to be a lot like Hans van Meegeren, although I wasn't sure how he related the *yakuza* to the Nazis.

In any case he had been convinced that it was necessary to be able to prove beyond a doubt which paintings were his. Now it looked as though he had been right all along. Unfortunately, he refused to tell Steven or me where he hid his cipher, and how. Given time to look for it, I was confident I could locate it. But first I had to find the damned paintings. Back to square one.

I lay sleepless next to Devon, circling the questions, unable to get my hands around them. For some reason I couldn't get Stan's face out of my mind. Something about his icy stare under that curly Elvis hairdo, and the way he had whistled Verdi, lodged in my memory. Eventually I gave up on sleep, quietly got out of bed, and went into the living room. I turned on the television and listened to late-night talk shows until I finally dozed off.

CHAPTER EIGHTEEN

By ten o'clock the next morning we stood outside Dr Anthony Fulton's apartment in an old-moneyed Fifth Avenue building overlooking Central Park. At Devon's urging, I had called him and introduced myself as a friend of Paul McHenry's. Although he had agreed to see us, I didn't expect him to be very sympathetic.

An elderly maid, complete with uniform and apron, answered the door and showed us into his study. He sat in an old wingback chair placed in front of a crackling fire in a room that looked like something out of an Edith Wharton novel. It was a wood-paneled library, lined with leatherbound volumes and carpeted with an old wine-red Sarouk. A fine antique Chinese lacquered screen stood in one corner, and a worn leather sofa, draped with a plaid cashmere throw, faced the fireplace and Dr Fulton's chair. The study had that frayed elegance new money couldn't buy. You had to inherit a room like Dr Fulton's study.

'So, you're Adrian Sellars,' he greeted me as we walked in. He took me in at a glance, then turned and studied Dev. 'You must be Devon Berenson.' His voice rumbled up from deep within his chest, sounding as though he began each day by gargling kerosene.

Dr Fulton had been a bear of a man. Now, pushing eighty, he still looked more like a retired bricklayer than one of the world's foremost authorities on art restoration. Vestiges of his strength were still evident in his broad shoulders, only slightly bowed by time, and his thick chest. He possessed a full head of silvery white hair, which he wore long, pushed back over a blunt-featured, florid face that looked like it had gone a few rounds in the boxing ring.

He picked up a copy of the *Post*, the one with Paul's picture, that had been sitting in his lap. He waved it at me. 'You mind explaining to me exactly what the hell you had to do with Paul McHenry's murder? Why are you mentioned in this article?'

I glanced at Dev.

Dr Fulton gestured impatiently at the sofa that faced him. 'Sit. Sit down, I haven't got all day.' He looked at the photo of Paul, then dropped the paper onto the floor by his feet. He picked up a cane that had been propped against his chair and laid it across his knees. He was glaring at me.

I took a deep breath and began. 'Dr Fulton, it's a long, ugly story. I know you and Paul McHenry were friends. Please believe me, I had nothing to do with his murder. But I'm afraid that's not all of it.'

'You just start at the beginning, Mr Sellars. I'll decide what I believe and what I don't.'

'A mutual friend, Steven Ballard, introduced Paul and me about three years ago.'

I told him everything, from the first forgery, the 'Degas' ballerina, right up to my meeting with Hiro Okuba. We were interrupted once, when the ancient maid brought in coffee. The heavy tray she carried wobbled in her hands. Dev jumped up to help her. I noticed Dr Fulton smile.

Then he sat holding an elegant Spode cup in his large hands, listening intently as I finished. He sipped occasionally but otherwise was as still as a statue. I could feel his disapproval, his contemptuous disregard for me. But I told him the truth as plainly as I could. There was nothing he could say that was going to make me feel worse than I already felt. And there was nothing I could do to bring Paul back.

He shook his head when I stopped talking. 'I'm truly sorry to hear that Paul got himself involved in any of this. He should have stayed at the museum. 'He carefully set down his cup, then he looked at me. 'What makes you think I should want to get involved?'

'We need help,' I answered, looking at Devon.

'I talked Adrian into calling you,' she added. 'We came because of Paul. He was our friend, too.'

He peered out at us from under his bushy white eyebrows. First he looked at Dev, then he turned to me.

'Mr Sellars,' he said, frowning, 'I've been in the art game for longer than you've been alive. I've dealt with the likes of Duveen and that crook Valentiner. Negotiated with old man Wildenstein in the days when a dollar meant something. Even drank with Picasso, in Paris, back before the war, when Paris was still worth a damn. Thought I'd seen about all there was to see. But Japanese gangsters, near-perfect forgeries, murder. You're talking about a world that's left me behind, and I'm glad of it.'

'Dr Fulton, it's true, all of it.'

'Oh, I don't doubt it. Not a word of it . . . I wish I did,' he said shaking his head. 'How much did you say you were paid for Paul's work?'

'About ten percent of the value of an original. We would have gotten six hundred fifty thousand for the "Monet" he was working on.'

Dr Fulton whistled, settling deeper into his chair, fiddling with the cane that lay across his knees. It was made of ebony with a chased silver head shaped like a griffin.

'The whole world's gone crazy,' he mused. 'Hell, I

guess that amount of money would tempt about anyone. But if it was money he needed, why didn't he come to me?' He grasped the cane in his right hand and hauled himself up out of his chair, then crossed the room to a window that looked out across Fifth Avenue toward the Metropolitan Museum of Art and Central Park. He stood quietly gazing out the window for a moment, then turned and stared hard at me.

'Do you think Paul McHenry had the heart of a thief?'

'No sir,' I answered quickly. 'I don't think it was just about the money. I think he was a frustrated artist who finally found a way to have his work appreciated.'

'Hmmph,' was all he said. He turned back to the window before continuing. 'I believe you have the heart of a thief, Mr Adrian Sellars. Never met an art dealer who didn't . . . must be in the blood.'

He was right, but still his words stung. I kept my mouth shut.

'No excuses, eh? Well at least you're an honest thief.' He turned and chuckled as he walked back across the room.

'I'm still not sure why you don't just go to the authorities,' he said, settling back into his chair.

'I've been advised that if I were to do so I wouldn't live to testify.'

He looked at Devon and his face softened. 'Please tell me how a young lady like you got mixed up in something like this.' The cliché actually sounded original coming from him.

She frowned and crossed her arms. 'I didn't know what they were doing, Dr Fulton. If I had, I would have walked away a long time ago.' She shook her head. 'What Adrian and Paul did was wrong. It was stupid.'

She glanced from Dr Fulton to me. 'Adrian made a mistake. I don't think he'd do it again. I want to help him.'

'You sure he deserves your help?' Dr Fulton grumbled.

'Yes, I'm sure. If you give him a chance, you'll see why.'

Sitting next to Dev on the sofa, listening to the two of them discuss me as though I weren't in the room, I felt more and more uncomfortable. I was beginning to doubt that Dr Fulton's help, which was by no means guaranteed, would be worth the abuse he was heaping on. But Devon had insisted on coming, and I didn't have any other brilliant ideas.

He turned his attention back to me. 'Surely you aren't going to ask me to forge a Monet for you?'

'Of course not. But we hoped you might be able to point us in a direction. We need to find the forgeries. I need to buy some time to search for them. Hell, I don't know what we thought you would do . . . it was a mistake to come.' I started to get up. 'Come on, Dev, we're wasting Dr Fulton's time.'

'Wait a minute, sit back down. No need to be in such a hurry,' he said, toying with his cane, turning it over in his blunt, age-spotted hands. 'I don't like the idea of those fakes floating around out there. You say they're all in Japan?'

'We think so,' I answered him.

I wondered why he was prolonging our visit. Regardless, Dev clearly wasn't budging until either she had gotten what she had come for or she was completely sure he wasn't going to help us. Still standing, I gave her a frustrated look, anxious to be out of there.

Dr Fulton sat stiffly in his chair, still twirling the cane.

Dev looked him straight in the eye and asked, 'Will you help us? Please.'

He returned her gaze and held it. I felt like a fifth wheel.

'If I decide to help you, it will be to root out those damned forgeries and expose them.' He looked from Dev to me. 'Not because I feel any compulsion to save you. The world would get by just fine with one less art dealer.' He waved at me with his cane. 'Sit back down, dammit. Go ahead, sit.'

I lowered myself onto the couch, my face burning.

'Let me see those files you brought,' he said, putting aside his cane.

I handed him the files. He scratched his ear as he examined the eight-by-ten transparencies.

'You're right, they are good. Damned good.'

Dev and I kept quiet as he looked through the files.

'You should have seen the paintings, Dr Fulton. Paul put his heart and soul into them,' I said.

He looked up, a queer expression on his face. 'I wish I had. Maybe I could understand this whole thing a little better.'

I nodded.

He handed back the files. 'I taught him well, didn't I? Maybe a little too well.' He sank further into his chair and for the first time looked his age.

'We were close once, you know. It seems like a long time ago, but it couldn't have been much before you got to know him.'

We leaned forward to hear him better.

'God knows he was a talented young man, lovely to watch.'

I looked at Devon, but she refused to meet my eye.

'I'm going to miss him. I truly will ... what a

goddamned tragic waste.' His face, which had looked hewn of red granite, grew slack; the folds and wrinkles of his ruddy skin seemed deeper, his eyes unfocused. He sat like that for what seemed a long time, then he shook his head and picked up his cane.

'This Japanese gangster, what's his name?' he asked.

'Tanaka, Ryuichi Tanaka.'

'He's demanded that you deliver a Monet *Water Lilies*?'

'Yes, sir. By next week.'

'Has he specified size, or the date?'

'I don't think it matters now.'

'And if you don't make the delivery?'

I shrugged.

He held up the cane. 'I'm not promising you anything, but I may be able to help you. I want to think it through, then I have a few calls to make.' He looked at his watch. 'It's eleven-thirty now. Call me after lunch, say two-thirty; we'll talk then.'

I said thank you, but he ignored me.

He rang a small bell summoning the maid. As she was preparing to show us out, Dev walked over to where Dr Fulton was sitting and took both of his hands in hers. They looked at each other for a moment, then he smiled. She leaned over and kissed him on the cheek.

'Thank you, Dr Fulton,' she said.

He squeezed her hands, then frowned and admonished me from his chair. 'Remember, Mr Sellars, I'm not doing this for you. Damned art dealers.' He scowled at me, then waved us out of the room. 'Two-thirty, I'll speak to you then.'

As we walked out of the building onto Fifth Avenue, I turned to Devon and said, 'Jesus, he really can't stand me.'

She laughed. 'He just doesn't know you yet, Mr Sellars.'

We had time to kill, so I dragged Dev across the street to the Met. For the day after Thanksgiving, the place looked crowded. It was sunny, a little warmer than it had been, and from the number of people wandering around the outside of the museum you had to believe that a little culture went down well with leftover turkey.

'He really did love Paul, didn't he?' I asked.

'Yeah, I think he's trying to get why Paul made the forgeries. If he helps us, that will be why.'

'That, and because of you. I thought he was going to try and adopt you. Let's hope he doesn't change his mind.'

'He's a sweet old man. He seems lonely.'

'Yeah, a real charmer,' I muttered.

'What?'

'I said, I hadn't realized he was so wealthy.'

'He was the only child of Ashby and Clarissa Fulton. You've heard of them, haven't you?'

'No.' I shook my head.

'The mining and timber baron? You never heard of Ashby Fulton?' She looked at me as though I had been deprived of something important.

'No.' I shook my head again. 'I'm sorry, but I doubt they've ever heard of me either. I'll just be your ignorant friend, you can be the one who knows all about the Ashbys and Clarissas of the world. I'll settle for an occasional poke and the right to see you naked.'

She laughed so loud that heads turned as we walked into the museum. 'I must sound a little bit like a snob,' she said, squeezing my arm.

'A *little* bit? Are you hungry?'

'As a matter of fact I am.'

I stopped short, pulling her to a halt beside me.

'What's the matter, Adrian?'

Barely, just barely, in the echo of the crowded marble-clad entrance hall, I heard somebody whistling the finale of *La Traviata*. I turned and stood on my toes, scanning the crowd.

'What is it?' Devon tugged on my arm.

'Shhhh. I thought I heard something.'

Again, I caught the strains of Verdi's opera. Now it was coming from my right. I grabbed Devon's hand and pulled her toward the entrance. There, standing not fifty feet away, separated from us by a group of German tourists, was Tanaka's thug Stan. He caught my eye and winked, then turned his back, pretending to study the museum directory.

My blood ran cold. I grabbed Dev's arm and rushed her out of the museum and into a cab. Breathless, I explained to her who I had just seen. The cabby waited for our destination.

We decided not to return to Dev's, in case he was following us. Instead, I ordered the cab to take us through the park to the West Side, and then back around to the East Side via Fifty-ninth Street. I didn't think we would lose him that easily, if he was tailing us, but I hoped to at least pick him up and find out for sure if we were being followed. Neither of us saw any sign of him, or anyone else following us. They were either very good, or we were clean.

We were still not comfortable going back to Dev's, so I had the cab drop us at La Goulue, a little bistro on East Seventieth.

Getting out of the cab, I turned to Dev and said, 'Jesus, he scared the hell out of me.'

She nodded. 'Are you positive it was Stan?'

'Yeah, I'm sure. Maybe it was just a friendly reminder from Tanaka. Sort of like that postcard the dentist sends to remind you of your appointment.'

'Very funny. How did he know we would be in the museum?' She stood on the curb, looking pale and worried.

I shook my head. 'Maybe they've been watching us all along. Hiro found us easily enough.'

She shivered. 'God, what should we do?'

'There's not much we can do right now. Come on, let's go inside.' I took her hand and walked into the restaurant. 'What time is it anyway?'

'It's only twelve-thirty. Are you going to eat?'

'I guess,' I answered, eyeing the bottles that lined the bar. My confidence had been shaken. A shot of Stoli would take the edge off nicely. I thought of all the reasons I could give Dev for ordering just one drink. But they all sounded hollow.

When the waiter came, Dev ordered a cheese soufflé and a Perrier. I asked for the onion soup and, gritting my teeth, a Coke. It took forever for two-thirty to arrive. But by the time it did, I no longer craved a drink. Both of us had pushed our food around and tried to keep up a brave front. Neither of us had fooled the other, but somehow the vodka stopped calling my name. While we pretended to eat, I decided to set up a meeting with Marta. Stan's little surprise convinced me that we needed some idea of what Tanaka was thinking. She was our only contact. I planned to call her when we got back to Dev's.

At exactly 2:30 I used the pay phone to call Dr Fulton. He answered on the first ring.

'Adrian, set up a meeting on Monday or Tuesday with

Tanaka. Make it sometime around noon, at the Day &
Meyer warehouse on Second Avenue, okay?'

'What's the plan, Dr Fulton? Should I tell him you'll
be joining us?'

'Yes. Tell him you have something to show him.
Something I'm working on, that can be delivered to him
as soon as I've finished with it.'

'You're not painting a "Monet," are you, Dr Fulton?'

'Don't be stupid, boy,' he snapped. 'I'm going to have
the real thing to dangle in front of him. He'll never actually get his hands on it, but he won't know that. I'd be
willing to bet my last dollar that once he sees it he'll be
willing to wait for it. If he knows anything at all, his
tongue will be hanging out. Come around to my apartment on Sunday morning at eleven, we'll discuss the details then. Bring the files on Paul's paintings. Oh, bring
that lovely young woman with you.'

'Thank you, Dr Fulton. We'll be there.'

'Don't forget, Monday or Tuesday midday, no earlier.
And be vague, don't tell him too much.'

Back at the table I told Dev what he had said. Smiling,
she took my hands and squeezed them. 'This is going to
work out, I know it is.'

CHAPTER NINETEEN

Saturday passed in a blur. The day had dawned brighter and warmer than usual for this time of year. If anyone was watching Dev's building, or following us, we didn't see them as we walked to the Frick Art Reference Library, where we spent the afternoon searching for anything that listed or illustrated French paintings in private Japanese collections. Nothing we found related to the forgeries. When we left the library I asked Devon if she wouldn't change her mind and come with me to meet Marta.

'Are you kidding? I don't even want you to go. Don't let her get near you. Okay?'

I held my index fingers out in front of me crossed like a crucifix. 'I'll keep the evil bitch away.' I laughed.

Dev knocked my hands away. 'I'm not kidding. You watch yourself.'

'Come here.' I pulled her to me. 'I haven't forgotten my promise to you. I'll be back as soon as I've finished. Don't worry.'

She bit her lower lip. 'I don't like this. Not at all. You be careful.'

I nodded. After putting Dev in a cab, I walked over to the Plaza Athenee Hotel.

Marta had agreed to meet me at four-thirty. But by five o'clock, I was the only patron in the hotel bar, and I was thinking seriously of blowing the whole thing off.

I was sipping mineral water but tasting vodka. I'd been clean for a week. The withdrawal had left me feeling hollow and exhausted; otherwise it was mostly just a bad memory. But in spite of how miserable it had been, and how fresh the memories of the whole ordeal were, I'd developed a wicked thirst. It first hit me yesterday, after running into Stan at the museum. Now it was back, with reinforcements. The thought of vodka, icy cold, burning its way into my gut was almost more than I could bear.

It hadn't been a good idea to meet in a bar. I carried enough baggage where Marta was concerned, without the familiar, dark ambience of a fancy watering hole smacking me in the face.

She finally breezed in at half past five, wearing all black.

'Hello, Adrian.' She stood, one hand on her hip, looking down at me. 'Order me a Stoli Gibson, up, with extra onions, honey.'

Then she went straight on to the ladies' room. When she got back, her drink was waiting for her. Standing in a sweating martini glass a few errant ice chips floated in a slick on the surface of the clear liquid.

'So. How are you doing?' She raised the glass to her mouth and sipped.

I watched silently. What a stupid goddamned place to meet. I could taste the vodka on her red lips.

'Did my package hold you? Do you need anything?'

'Cut the crap, Marta,' I said, finding my voice. 'Why did you want to see me?'

'You read my note. I never knew that Kotani was going to . . . to . . . Well, I never knew anything like that would happen. I want you to know that I'm sorry.'

'It's a little late for apologies now.'

'Adrian, I want to help you.'

'That's rich.'

'I mean it. I've done a lot of things that I'm not particularly proud of, but I've never ever been involved in anything like this. I'm scared.'

We sat quietly eyeing each other. Then she noticed that I was drinking Perrier.

'Adrian, don't you want a drink?'

'I'm fine with what I have.'

'Oh, come on, I know things are bad, but a drink isn't going to hurt anything. Let me get us something good to drown our sorrows in.' She pushed the point, looking for a waiter.

'I said I'm fine. You want to help me, what have you got in mind?'

'Have you come up with a painting for Tanaka yet?'

'Come on, Marta,' I said, shaking my head. 'If you're here to help, then offer me something. I'm not going to play twenty questions with you.'

'I know Tanaka will be back in New York soon. He'll be expecting to hear from you.'

'Where is he now?'

'Tokyo.'

'What's he doing there?'

'Jesus, Adrian! You think he tells me his business? The only reason I'm involved in this at all is because I introduced you to him. He thinks I can help control you.' She smiled at me over her drink. 'But we both know that's not true. Don't we.'

I didn't bite.

'You know he's had Stan keeping an eye on you, from time to time, while he's been away.' She tilted her head and ran her finger along the rim of her glass as she spoke.

'Yeah, I know. We bumped into each other yesterday.'

'If you saw him, it was because he wanted you to see

him. He's scary. Even Tanaka's a little wary of old Stanley.'

'Why does he keep him around?'

'Who knows. He came over from Tokyo about a year ago. I get the feeling Tanaka is stuck with him.'

'What does that mean?'

'It means, I don't know!'

The conversation wasn't leading anywhere, although Marta had seemed forthcoming. I decided to push it a little.

'Do you know Tanaka's boss, Nakamura?'

Her eyes narrowed as she swallowed the rest of her drink. I had hit a nerve, and it didn't look like I was going to get an answer. Instead she sat forward in her chair, flagged down the waiter, and ordered another Gibson. As she settled back in her seat, her skirt, short to begin with, rode higher. I found myself staring at the inner curve of her thigh. She caught me, and slowly, tantalizingly, tugged the hem higher until I could see the top of her stocking, and the garter that held it in place.

We had been together for less than thirty minutes, and already she was playing the old games. Even so I felt a stirring, a tightening between my legs, at the sight of her smooth flesh. It was offered up on a platter. All she needed was a rose in her teeth.

With some effort I tore my eyes away and laughed out loud. 'Jesus, you're slick, Marta.' I shook my head. 'But it won't work this time. Why don't we play straight with each other for once? No more games, okay? I have something to show Tanaka. Can you set up a meeting on Monday or Tuesday?'

As I spoke her mask dropped; the practiced smile disappeared, no longer hiding the coldness that I had first seen in her the night I found Paul McHenry's body. She was angry that I had refused the bait. Maybe she had forgotten that I already knew the sting of the hook embedded in her flesh.

'Well, you want to set up the meeting, or not?' I asked again.

She glared at me for a moment, then looked at her watch. 'He'll be leaving Tokyo in a few hours, I'll ask him when I see him. Call me tomorrow, I'll know then.'

She frowned at the waiter as he delivered her second drink. This time I didn't ache, watching her drink it.

'What's going on between you and lover girl?' she asked, after knocking the drink back in two swallows.

'Lover girl?'

'Come on, Adrian, is it love?'

At first I was surprised by the nature of her taunts. Then I realized that it had nothing to do with jealousy. It wasn't that she wanted me – she wanted me to want her. She craved the control she could exert by simply flashing her legs. I smiled to myself as I realized that I had hit her hard, where it really hurt.

'Lighten up, Marta, I thought you were here to help me.'

She continued to glare for a moment longer, then straightened in her chair, adjusting her sneer into a smile.

'I *am* here to help. I was just curious,' she said, effortlessly slipping back into character. It was scary to see her good girl bad girl act come and go so fluidly. Still, as she played with the bowl of nuts sitting in the middle of the table, her elbow slipped, and she knocked her empty glass to the floor.

The second drink seemed to have hit her hard, and Marta was no lightweight. Knowing her habits, I assumed she was high on a mix of drugs. A pharmaceutical cocktail, blended to take her to a certain place and keep her there. The alcohol must have upset the balance of chemicals. She got up, swaying slightly, felt for something in her pocket, and excusing herself, headed back to the ladies' room again. She left her purse hanging on the back of her chair.

As soon as she was out of sight, I picked up her bag, opened it, and quickly rifled through the contents. Lipstick, keys, a wallet, a compact, some tissues, a brush, a small, red leather address book, and an ugly little .22-caliber automatic. I took the clip and made sure that the chamber was empty, then I replaced the gun and looked through her wallet.

It was filled with cash, almost three thousand dollars, mostly in hundreds. There were also several credit cards, all in Marta's name. Tucked away behind her driver's license, I found a small slip of paper. Written in her hand were the words 'N and T, 10:15 A.M. Sunday, JFK/JAL, Stan to drive.'

By the time she returned from the bathroom, I had replaced the contents of her bag as I had found them, with the exception of her address book, which I pocketed, along with the clip from her gun.

Her eyes were glassy and pinned, her lipstick askew.

'Adrian, why don't you come back to my place, we'll pick up some moo-shu shrimp and have a picnic in bed.' She didn't give up easily. She was playing with her skirt again as she spoke.

'I thought I was strictly business.'

She attempted a seductive smile, but it came off looking like a crude leer on her messy lips. 'You know I like to mix business with pleasure.'

She must have been off in her dosage; she was beginning to slur. I wanted to laugh, but the whole thing was so sad. So absurd.

I'd had enough. I dropped a twenty on the table as I stood up. 'Marta, you're all fucked up. Go home and sleep it off.' I walked out, wondering how she had sucked me in so completely.

From the Plaza Athenee back uptown to Dev's wasn't far, so I decided to walk. The sun had set, and the city seemed poised between two moods, suspended between night and day, the shifts about to change. The air was crisp, hinting at winter just over the northern horizon, somewhere in Canada. Wood smoke came from someone's chimney. Traffic was less aggressive than usual; Thanksgiving weekend was winding down. The clip from Marta's gun went into the first trash can I passed.

I had this weird feeling that time was flashing past me at the speed of light and standing still at the same time. I was in limbo, no longer even nominally calling the shots. A sitting target, waiting for something to happen. My life, as I had known it, had ceased to exist.

Dev was sitting on the couch reading the new issue of *Vanity Fair* when I walked in. She was wearing her B.U. sweatshirt. Her hair was pulled back into a thick ponytail. Her long legs were bare, propped up on a pillow.

'How'd it go?' she asked, putting down her magazine.

'Fine. Marta was her usual charming self. I had to listen to a lot of crap, but I learned a few things,' I said, lifting her legs and slipping under them on the couch next to her.

'What was she like?'

'Like?'

Glaring at me, she pulled her knees up to her chest

and wrapped her arms around them. 'You know what I mean.'

'She was fucked up. It wasn't a pretty sight.'

'I know. I've seen what it looks like.'

I winced and looked to see if she was trying to pick a fight. But there was no malice in her eyes; she had been merely pointing out a fact.

'I found a note in her wallet. I think Tanaka is flying in tomorrow from Tokyo. Nakamura may be with him.'

'How did you manage that?'

'She was in and out of the bathroom. The second or third time, I can't remember which, she left her purse at the table. I couldn't resist. I found this too,' I said, tossing Marta's address book onto the coffee table.

'Did she have anything else to say?' Dev asked, picking up the little red book and starting to thumb through the pages.

'Nothing worth listening to,' I answered, getting lost in her legs.

Devon looked up from the book. Under the sweatshirt, which had gathered around her waist, she wore nothing but a lacy pair of black panties that were almost transparent. It seemed natural to see her half dressed. Her body was firm and athletic, but it was the body of a woman, full-grown and ripe, not the body of a girl. She was proud of her looks.

'Damn, you look good enough to eat.'

She put down the address book and reached for me. Our lovemaking was fast and hard, almost violent. Full of need. Then totally spent, we lay at opposite ends of the couch, facing each other, our legs intertwined.

'Jesus Dev, I think you've killed me.' I was panting, trying to catch my breath. 'Where'd you learn to fuck like that?'

'Me? You did all the work.'

'Admit it, you're some kind of sex ninja, aren't you?'

She laughed and wiggled her toes, seeing if she could prod me back to life.

'No,' I groaned. 'No more, you've conquered me. I surrender. I'll do as you say, just let me rest, please.'

She laughed again, and it was good to hear. We showered, then ordered in a pizza.

CHAPTER TWENTY

Either Dr Fulton was a slave driver, or Sophie, his maid, had no other place to be on Sunday mornings. She greeted us in full livery, looking exactly as she had the last time we were there. I thought it entirely possible that she never left the apartment, that Dr Fulton kept her hanging in a closet, like an old but cherished coat, and when he needed her, he took her down, dusted her off, and put her to work.

We had brought with us a box of pastries from Zabar's. After Dev greeted Dr Fulton, she followed Sophie into the kitchen, leaving the two of us alone in his study. He was sitting on the sofa; I stood by the mantel and waited for him to say something.

He held an unlit pipe by the stem in his right hand and rhythmically slapped the bowl into his left palm. He avoided my eyes.

Finally he cleared his throat. 'Well, well. The con-artist art dealer. Discover any new talent since we last spoke?'

'Dr Fulton, you've made it clear that you don't think much of me. Fine, I've got a few problems with the way I've been acting myself. But let's not play games with each other.'

He smiled in a cockeyed way at my little speech.

'What makes you think I'm playing games?'

'Whatever you want to call it. I'd like you to stop sniping at me. I'm glad you're helping us. I'm grateful. But let's clear the air between us. If you've got something to say to me, say it.'

He looked up at me from his chair, his eyes clouded with anger. He just stared at me for a while, then finally broke the silence that had settled over the room like a dark cloud.

'I want to know if this is your fault. Did you persuade Paul to create these fakes?'

'I encouraged him. But he was already creating paintings that were intended to deceive. I told you about the "Degas" I was shown. It was better than most of what Degas actually painted.'

Dr Fulton leaned forward.

'It was the first time I heard the name Paul McHenry. When I met him, I told him what I thought of his work.'

'And what was that? What did you tell him?'

'I told him there was a market for it. I explained the kind of money we could make.'

'What share did he get?'

'There were three of us – we split the money equally.'

'Ah, your partner Steven Ballard. I'd almost forgotten.' He sat back and thought about what I had just told him.

'You say that Paul had already been experimenting with these forgeries, and that once he got involved with you he was an equal partner?'

'Yes, sir. He was a partner. What we did, we did together.'

'And none of these so-called experts ever called into question one of his paintings?'

'Not to my knowledge. He was *that* good.'

He relaxed a little, and took his time filling his pipe.

'I want to blame you, Adrian. It's easier for me to accept Paul's actions if I blame them on you. If he had been unwilling, somehow coerced, or persuaded by you to become a forger . . . well, it would have been easier for me to understand. I guess you're the only one around that I can vent my anger at.' He lit the pipe, then sighed as he exhaled a cloud of gray smoke. 'I'll try and lighten up.'

'Dr Fulton, if I could go back and undo what I've done, I would. I know apologizing doesn't get it. But I'm sorry, truly, deeply sorry, and I'll do what I can to make it right.'

'I'll have to believe you,' he said, his voice softening as he tried to let it go. 'Let's get a look at those files you brought. Someone in Japan must know where these paintings are. It's one thing to fool these modern *experts*. Hell, computers and lab tests – that's what they rely on now. Those damned ivory tower dunces wouldn't know how to look into the soul of a painting if their lives depended upon it. Anyone with half an eye could fool them. I want to see for myself how good Paul was. I want to get my hands on those paintings.'

I handed him the files, just as Dev and Sophie brought in the coffee and pastries.

Sophie poured us each a cup, then left. Dev and I sat on either side of Dr Fulton on the sofa.

'Hmmm.' He looked from Dev to the stack of transparencies in his lap. 'I'd like to fax these to a Dr Otani, at the Tokyo National Museum. I've known him for years. He's head of their European paintings department. I doubt if anyone in Japan knows the private collections better.'

I started to object, but Dr Fulton continued.

'I understand we don't want to tip our hand yet, so I won't let him know why we want to find the paintings.'

'Won't he want to know?' I asked.

'If he asks, I'll just have to finesse him a little.'

'These four collectors are of particular interest to us,'

I said, handing him a copy of the list Hiro Okuba had given us.

'Where do we stand with your friend Tanaka?' he asked, taking the list.

'I'll know this afternoon. What have you got up your sleeve?'

He chuckled, a disturbing rasping sound, then picked up a cheese danish, took one enormous bite and set the rest down.

'You've heard of Aynsley Bishop?'

'Of course, I saw her collection when it was on loan to the Met.'

'Remember the Monet on the cover of the catalog?'

'The *Water Lilies*?'

'That's the one. She's been after me for years to clean it. It'll be delivered to the security vault at Day & Meyer in my name, tomorrow morning.' His eyes lit up as he told us this news.

'You can tell your Japanese friend that you can acquire it for him. If he likes it, you'll promise to have it delivered to him on approval, just as soon as I've finished cleaning it. I'll confirm all of this, as agent for the owner. I doubt he'll question me.' He half snorted, half laughed, then went on, sporting a big smile. 'Of course there's no way of knowing how long it'll take me to finish. Who knows what kind of technical problems I might run into once I get started? That ought to buy us some time to find those forgeries.' He was looking very pleased with himself.

'Do you think Tanaka will go for it?' Dev asked, looking at me. 'It sounds plausible, especially with Dr Fulton there to back you up.'

'I think it'll work. I don't believe Tanaka would try to take the painting by force. Certainly not with Dr Fulton standing there. I think he'll jump at the bait. But Dr Fulton, don't underestimate these people. By becoming part of this, you'll be at considerable personal risk.'

'Nonsense, boy. I'm too old and too well known to be of any interest to them. Besides, this is the most exciting thing I've done in years. I feel a little bit like Sherlock Holmes. Maybe I'll get some cards printed up: *Anthony Fulton, crime fighter/problem solver*. What do you think, Dev?'

The two of them laughed, but I wasn't quite ready to share in their levity. If I closed my eyes, I could still see the look on Steven's face when Kotani shot him.

We left the photographs for Dr Fulton to fax to his friend in Tokyo. As we said good-bye, I promised to call the moment I confirmed our meeting with Tanaka.

Out on the street, Dev seemed pensive. 'He's really focused on getting Paul's paintings back. What do you think he'll do with them?'

'You mean, if we get them back.' I shrugged. 'Who knows?'

That night I called Marta. 'Have you arranged the meeting?'

'You took my book.'

'What are you talking about?'

'You know goddamned well what I'm talking about, Adrian. You stole my book. Yesterday at the bar. I want it back.' She wasn't only angry, she sounded scared. I had actually forgotten all about her address book.

'Marta, you've got it wrong. I don't have anything of yours. I called to find out about Tanaka. Did you set up a meeting?'

I could hear her breathing, but she didn't say anything. She must have been trying to retrace her movements, wondering where else she could have lost her book. She had been too high when we met. She might have been 99 percent convinced I had taken her book, but I knew she couldn't be sure.

'Marta, you still there?'

'I'm here, and I know you took my book. If you return it, I'll make it seriously worth your while.'

Whatever was in that address book was sounding more and more interesting by the minute.

'You're not listening, Marta. I don't have whatever it is you're looking for. I just want to confirm a meeting with Tanaka.'

'Adrian, I'm going to get it back one way or another. Why don't you just make it easy on yourself and hand it over?'

'Tanaka, Marta. I called about Tanaka.'

'Okay, I heard you the first time. Tanaka will meet with you tomorrow,' she said. 'Where and when do you want to set it up?'

'I've found a Monet. It's perfect. But I want him to see it and approve it before I go any further. Tell Tanaka that Dr Anthony Fulton from the Met is cleaning it; he's the best in the business. As soon as Fulton's finished I can have the painting delivered. It's at the Day & Meyer warehouse on Second Avenue, at Sixty-first Street. Ask Tanaka to meet me there at one o'clock.'

'Good boy. I'm glad to see you're wising up. But Adrian, I'm going to get that book back.'

'Yeah, Marta, I'm sure you will. But you'll have to find it somewhere else, I don't have it. Tell your boss I think he's going to be very pleased.'

'I'll tell him. One o'clock tomorrow. Adrian –'

I hung up on her before she could start in again. Then I called Dr Fulton to confirm the meeting. He asked me

213

to meet him half an hour early, then told me to get a good night's rest.

When I finally got off the phone, I explained to Dev how agitated Marta had sounded about the loss of her book. I went into the living room to retrieve it.

We went through it page by page, not once but several times. Aside from some telephone numbers that meant nothing to either of us, we couldn't make anything out of it. What wasn't written in Japanese characters seemed to be in some kind of code. After about an hour we gave up trying to decipher it and decided to call Hiro Okuba in the morning. Maybe he could make some sense of it.

I tossed the book onto the night table and joined Devon under the covers.

CHAPTER TWENTY-ONE

The Day & Meyer warehouse squats on the east side of Second Avenue between Sixty-first and Sixty-second streets. In spite of its height, twelve stories of colorless concrete, the building seems a low and heavy thing plopped down as an afterthought among the fancy shops and modern high-rise apartment buildings that make up this neighborhood. The entrance, a heavily reinforced steel door, stands behind a barred gate mounted with electronic and video surveillance equipment. At one time there had been windows on the first three floors; now they were brick-filled anomalies in the smooth surface of the otherwise featureless facade. It seemed much later than twelve-thirty by the time Devon and I arrived at the warehouse to meet Dr Fulton.

Neither of us had slept well. We were up before dawn, sitting in the living room drinking coffee while we watched the early news. I had tossed and turned, trying to imagine being face-to-face with Tanaka again. What if he showed up with Kotani? I hadn't laid eyes on either of them since the night Kotani shot Steven.

As I poured my second cup, I wondered how the local media would cover the story if things turned out badly. Some smiling, lacquer-haired morning anchor with a name like Flip or Johnnie would tease the audience with raised eyebrows before a commercial, '. . . and when we return, a terrifying story about greed and forged art, a story that crossed international borders from the United States to Japan, eventually ending in a brutal series of killings here in Manhattan. Then, our own Storm

Jackson will check in and tell us what we can expect from today's weather.' That ought to slow down the old bran muffin's trip from plate to mouth, at least for a second or two.

Dev and I started to argue when she made clear her intention to accompany me to the warehouse.

'No way,' I said shaking my head. 'It's out of the question. What possible reason is there for you to come?'

Devon scowled and set down her cup. 'If you think I was asking your permission, you're sadly mistaken. I thought we were clear on the fact that I'm part of this.'

'Dev –'

'Don't Dev me. And you can lose that worried look. I hate when you wrinkle up your brow like that.'

'It doesn't make sense for you to come,' I complained, even though it was already clear that I was on the losing side of this discussion. I might end up as a footnote on the early news, a juicy tidbit tucked in just before the morning weather report, but that didn't mean I had to go down without a fight. 'There's no upside to your being there,' I added defiantly.

'Bullshit,' she retorted, her face coloring. 'You know goddamned well, calling Dr Fulton was my idea in the first place. I'm coming whether you like it or not.'

With that she stomped out of the living room and slammed the bedroom door behind her. Goddamn, she was stubborn. The sound of running water penetrated the walls. Cursing under my breath, I stubbed my toe walking into the guest bathroom, where I showered alone.

By nine-thirty we were ready to leave the apartment, but we had nowhere to go. Devon had put on a dark blue dress and heels; I wore a suit and tie. At least we'd show up on time, dressed to play. Woody Allen would have approved, but I doubted it would make any difference to Tanaka if we showed up in bathing suits. Briefly, I considered carrying my gun, but if I pulled it and used it or worse, pulled it and didn't use it, it would cause more problems than it would solve. I left it where it was, in the guest room, under the bed in my briefcase.

We sat on opposite ends of the couch watching television, attempting to ignore each other. The morning dragged on. Flip or Johnnie was interviewing some basketball player recently out of rehab. I knew how he felt.

'Okay,' I finally broke the silence between us. 'Obviously you're going to do whatever you want anyway. Let's stop arguing.'

'Arguing?' She looked up from the television. 'Who's arguing?'

'You know what I mean.'

'Apologize.'

'What?' I spluttered.

'You heard what I said.' She examined her fingernails.

'Why the hell should I apologize?'

'Didn't you say you wanted to stop arguing?'

'Yeah.'

'Then apologize.'

'Jesus Christ! Are all women nuts?'

I got up and walked into the bedroom. Marta's address book lay on the night table where I had left it. I grabbed it and walked back into the living room.

'I'm calling Okuba,' I announced.

His voice mail picked up, and a recording informed me that he would be out of his office for the day but would return on Tuesday. At the beep, I left a message asking him to return my call, then hung up.

Devon studiously ignored me while she made invisible repairs to her fingernails. The lacquer-haired broadcaster droned on. I made a show of ignoring her back while I studied the address book, acting as though I had miraculously learned to read Japanese. After about twenty minutes my eyes started to cross. I slipped the book into my coat pocket and stood up.

'Okay,' I said. 'Enough. Are you hungry?'

'Okay what?' She looked up at me with just the slightest look of triumph beginning to light her face.

'Okay . . . I'm sorry. I'll stop trying to tell you what to do.'

She nodded her acceptance, unable to keep a straight face as she tried not to gloat. 'I am hungry. Let's go someplace for a bagel. You buy.'

Dr Fulton arrived in front of the warehouse right on schedule, in a black Lincoln town car. He dismissed the driver with a wave and stepped onto the sidewalk.

'Good, good – you're here on time,' he rasped, smiling at us.

His long silver hair was carefully parted and slicked back. He wore a well-tailored, if old-fashioned, charcoal-gray suit with a white carnation in the lapel. A black wool overcoat with a fur collar was thrown over his shoulders, and he carried his cane.

'Let's go in. No time to waste.' He led the way.

Once through the security doors we found ourselves in a small reception area, carpeted and spotless but devoid of furniture or decoration. A female receptionist sat behind a thick pane of bulletproof glass, to the left of which was the only door in or out of the area, save the one by which we had entered. She greeted Dr Fulton by name through an intercom, then slid a sign-in sheet attached to a clipboard through a drawer like the ones used by drive-in bank tellers. Dr Fulton logged us in.

'Now don't forget,' he addressed the receptionist. 'When our guests arrive, I want you to notify us and then keep them waiting for twelve minutes.'

The receptionist nodded at him. 'Okay, Dr Fulton.'

'Twelve minutes exactly,' he repeated. 'Not ten, not fifteen.'

'Yes, sir, I understand.' She looked at her watch and noted the time, then hit a button that opened an electronic lock, allowing us to enter the inner door where we were met by a uniformed guard.

The guard walked us to the elevator and rode down two floors with us to the high security vault.

On the elevator Dr Fulton explained his twelve-minute theory: 'Ten minutes isn't quite long enough, and fifteen minutes tends to get them a little too antsy,' he said, punctuating with taps of his cane. 'But twelve minutes usually does the trick. Keep a client waiting twelve minutes and he has time to remember why he's come to see you. Lets him know he's not the only thing on your mind.'.

Twelve minutes. I shook my head in admiration. Listening to Dr Fulton explain his philosophy, I tried to imagine him as a young man, drinking in prewar Paris at the Deux Magots with Pablo and Dora Maar. It might have been around the time Guernica was bombed. I made a mental note to ask him if he had been invited to Picasso's studio to see the painting. 'Paris when it was still worth a damn,' he had said. The man was something else.

Two floors below street level, the guard ushered us into a brightly lit conference room adjacent to the actual vault. We waited while the guard, now joined by two white-uniformed vault attendants, went to retrieve the painting. The room was furnished with a long walnut table, surrounded by a dozen reproduction Chippendale armchairs and a matching sideboard, on top of which sat a telephone. The three of us stood quietly, wrapped up in our own thoughts. Devon looked pensive.

The two attendants entered the room carrying a large painting wrapped in plain brown paper. They were followed by the guard, who carried a heavy folding easel, which he set up at the far end of the table, facing the door.

'Go ahead and unwrap it,' Dr Fulton instructed.

They removed the wrapping paper without tearing it, then placed the canvas on the easel. A low whistle escaped my lips. My fingers started to itch. I thought about Paul McHenry. He would have fallen head over heels in love with the Monet now shimmering in front of me. Hell, McHenry had understood the master's intentions completely.

The canvas was almost four feet square, originally painted as part of the *Water Lilies* series Monet completed in 1908. Known in the art world as the 'Bishop' Monet, it was regarded by many to be one of the artist's best. In it Monet had captured the effects of the late-afternoon light as it played across the surface of his pond at Giverny. He had harnessed the water and the air to serve as conduits for the sun's luminescence. Under his hands the paint had come alive. The slanting light was reflected on the undulating surface of the water in all of the colors of the sky and clouds and surrounding trees. This depiction of light as color was almost abstract, held in place only by the static weight of the lily pads. Monet's powerful brushwork made me think of the way Miles Davis played the trumpet.

The Monet reminded me of the reasons I had become an art dealer. Not to be rich and famous; those affectations came later. I really had loved the art. For as long as I could remember, it spoke directly to me. I wanted to be able to touch it and handle it, to live with it, not visit it in museums or other people's houses. I thought art was the highest calling. Man's closest imitation of God. So, what the hell had happened? I stood in front of Aynsley Bishop's Monet asking myself why. Why had I let it all go so wrong?

Turning, I realized that both Dr Fulton and Devon stood watching me react to the painting. I shook my head.

'It's incredible,' I whispered. Approaching the canvas, I lightly brushed my fingers across the impasto of the paint. With the exception of varnish, which had yellowed and darkened with age, it looked exactly as it had when it left Monet's studio. I had seen it once before when Aynsley Bishop had lent her collection to the Met. But it hadn't looked the same in the crowded, sterile atmosphere of the museum. Even with the old coat of varnish that Dr Fulton had been hired to remove, it was magnificent.

Dr Fulton nodded in agreement. 'I think it should catch our gangster's attention.'

The three of us put our heads together and decided that when Tanaka arrived it would arouse the least suspicion if I did the talking. Both Devon and Dr Fulton would act as though Tanaka were an important client of mine. Devon would remain quiet. Dr Fulton also agreed to stay in the background. If asked, he would confirm my offer to deliver the Monet on approval, but otherwise he would simply nod and look official.

At one-fifteen the receptionist phoned to notify us of Tanaka's arrival. My stomach puckered. Exactly twelve minutes later the guard escorted him, accompanied by

Stan, into the conference room. Tanaka was dressed impeccably. As usual he looked like the chairman of Nissan. Stan looked ridiculous in a pale green leisure suit, open at the neck, revealing a tangle of gold chains draped over the hairless muscles of his chest. Wraparound sunglasses finished his ensemble. It was as though he were trying to call attention to himself.

The two of them stood just inside the door while they took in the layout of the room. Seemingly satisfied, they conferred briefly in Japanese, then Stan stepped out of the conference room, accompanied by the guard, who closed the door behind them.

The room shrunk. I had tried to prepare myself for what it would feel like to meet with the man responsible for my partner's murder, the man who was casually destroying my life. But the reality of breathing the same air in that small room was worse than I had imagined. It felt like the bagel I had eaten for breakfast had come halfway up and lodged in my throat. My fingers itched in a different way than they had when I first saw the Monet. I wanted to wrap them around Tanaka's throat and choke the fucking life out of the bastard. I wanted to see his eyes bulge and his tongue swell, then turn black. I regretted not bringing my gun.

'Adrian,' Tanaka nodded at me. He stood there, relaxed, as though nothing untoward had happened.

Cold sweat ran down the back of my neck and soaked my armpits.

He looked at Dr Fulton. 'You must be Dr Anthony Fulton. I've heard many great things about you.' He bowed and took a step toward Dr Fulton, extending his arm.

'That I am, at your service, sir,' Dr Fulton replied,

taking Tanaka's hand and shaking it. 'You must be Adrian's client, Mr Tanaka.'

The two of them nodded at each other, two gentlemen ready to do business. Dr Fulton was hamming it up a bit but was playing his part to perfection. Devon stood across the table observing. Neither Dr Fulton nor Tanaka paid her any attention.

'This is what I wanted you to see.' Pointing at the Monet, I addressed Tanaka, struggling to keep my voice flat. Someone had turned off the air conditioner.

Dr Fulton stepped back so that Tanaka had an unobstructed view of the painting.

Tanaka moved closer to the easel and studied the Monet intently. His expression was unreadable, his face impassive. Save for the movement of his eyes as they swept the canvas, and a slight tightening at the corners of his mouth, he could have been a statue. After a few minutes he nodded.

'It's very interesting. However, I'd like to live with it before I decide whether or not to purchase it.'

I glanced at Dr Fulton before responding. 'As you can see, the painting needs to be cleaned. You can have it on approval as soon as it's been restored.' I turned from Tanaka to face Dr Fulton. 'When do you think you'll be finished?' I asked him.

He smiled, clearly enjoying his role in our little charade. 'It's a hell of a painting, isn't it?' He stepped to Tanaka's side, shifted his cane to his left hand, and clapped Tanaka a little too hard on the shoulder. 'Not many Monets of this quality on the market. Make quite an addition to any collection, eh, Tanaka?'

Tanaka recoiled from Dr Fulton's jocular slap and attempted a smile that looked more like a grimace.

'Yes . . . it's very impressive,' Tanaka said, confused,

glaring in my direction. 'When do you think it will be ready?'

'Not so fast, sir. Are you sure it's the right size, the right date?' Dr Fulton asked him.

Dev and I exchanged looks, wondering what the hell Dr Fulton was up to. Tanaka stared at him, perplexed. Then he turned to me.

'Is the painting for sale or not?' he demanded.

'Of course it is,' I answered. 'Dr Fulton, will you please tell us when the cleaning will be finished?'

He laughed, that disturbing rumble of his magnified by the hard walls of the underground room. Suddenly I wasn't sure who I wanted to throttle first.

Devon brought him back to earth. 'Dr Fulton, didn't you tell me that it would take at least two or three weeks to properly clean a painting of this stature?'

We all turned and looked at her. She smiled innocently at Dr Fulton.

Looking sheepish at having gone too far, his smile dimmed and he cleared his throat before answering. 'Well, yes, that's about right. No less than that certainly. I'll work quickly, but with paintings of this importance, you have to be painstaking about each detail.'

Tanaka's eyes narrowed. He thought for a few seconds, then addressed Dr Fulton. 'Would you and the young lady excuse us for a moment? I would like to speak privately with Adrian.'

Dev's head snapped around to me. Dr Fulton's mouth opened slightly, but he said nothing. We hadn't anticipated this request.

'That would be fine,' I broke the silence. 'Would the two of you wait right outside the door?'

Dev started to object, but Dr Fulton shook his head, and the two of them filed out.

Tanaka and I were alone, the distance between us a matter of feet. I wondered if he was armed. His pulse throbbed with every beat of his heart, visible just above his collar. My thumbs would press there until the throbbing stopped. Then it would be over.

'You've done well, Adrian.' His cold voice shook me out of my fantasy. 'This painting will do nicely.' He gestured toward the Monet. 'However, two or three weeks won't be possible. I can't wait nearly that long.'

I couldn't speak. I opened my mouth, but nothing came out. Tanaka seemed not to notice. His eyes were glued on the painting.

'No games, Adrian. I'll extend your deadline, but make no mistake, there will be no further delays. You will convince Dr Fulton to finish quickly. I want this Monet delivered to my home by this weekend. Do we understand each other?'

He turned from the painting and faced me, waiting for my answer. He stood still, his chest rising and falling slightly with the rhythm of his breath. He smelled of garlic and wine. Steven wouldn't be lunching on Italian anytime soon. Violence whispered darkly through my veins; something ancient stirred below my navel. My own pulse pounded in my ears, nearly deafening me. I stood at least a foot and a half taller and outweighed him by sixty or seventy pounds. I stretched my fingers, gauging the distance between us, and took a half step toward him. Should I? My vision narrowed to that area above the collar of his shirt where his pulse was still visible. Would it solve anything? Yessss. Do it! Do it now, the blood whispered. Now!

I ordered my body to pounce. To leap at him. I could feel his soft throat in my hands. But I hesitated. I stood frozen, unable to move. As I raised my eyes from his throat and looked into his eyes, cold and glittering, observing me with the faintest expression of distaste, I could see that he had known that about me all along. The gulf between us was even wider than I had thought. All of my dark fantasies of violent revenge were going to remain fantasies. Exhaling, I nodded and felt the tension in my hands flow back up my arms, knotting the muscles of my neck and shoulders, unable to find an outlet.

'Yes,' I croaked. 'We understand each other.'

He looked into my eyes for a moment longer. 'Good. I want you to keep me informed as to Dr Fulton's progress through Marta,' he said, striding to the door. 'Call her every few days.' He grasped the knob and turned it, but stopped before he pulled the door open. Turning, he spoke softly, his eyes boring into mine. 'Adrian, don't ever look at me that way again.' He smiled dryly. 'It would be a mistake to think you can become something you're not. Someone who didn't know you for the junkie you are might take offense.'

He opened the door and stepped out of the conference room. In the hall he was joined by Stan and the guard. I heard him bid a pleasant good-bye to Dr Fulton as the elevator doors slid shut.

Devon and Dr Fulton came into the room.

'Well?' Dr Fulton asked.

Rubber-kneed, I pulled out one of the chairs and collapsed into it. 'That bastard. That fucking, low-life bastard,' I whispered in a trembling voice that sounded hollow in my own ears.

My hands were shaking. I clenched them on my lap under the edge of the table and waited until my heart slowed before continuing. 'I almost attacked him. I swear, I could feel my hands around his throat. I wanted to kill him. I came this close.' I held my fingers a fraction apart. 'But when it came right down to it, I couldn't. I just couldn't do it.' I pounded my fist on the table, my vision blurred by tears. 'Fuck!' I shouted. 'I just couldn't do it.'

Devon stepped over to me and put a hand on my shoulder. 'I'm glad you couldn't,' she said softly. 'You're not like him, Adrian. I wouldn't love you if you were.'

It took a second to register. Then I looked up at her. 'I'm afraid you may have picked a bad bet, Devon.'

'I'll judge that.' She leaned over and kissed me.

'Ahhh-hmmm,' Dr Fulton cleared his throat. 'She's right, Adrian. Don't put yourself on Tanaka's level. You did well today.'

He looked down at me, smiling. Then he circled the table and stood in front of the Monet.

'It's hard to believe that a simple idea, even when it's executed by a genius like Monet, can result in something as enduring as this.' Dr Fulton touched the painting. 'Even Tanaka felt it.'

'He went for it all right. He's given me till the weekend to deliver it. Wants me to push you to finish, and call Marta to report on your progress.'

'Very well,' Dr Fulton said, walking over and pulling out the chair next to mine. 'We've accomplished our first goal. We've bought some time.' He laid his cane on top of the table and lowered himself into the chair. 'I've faxed the photographs and descriptions of Paul's forgeries to Mr Otani in Tokyo. He should have them by now.'

'What do we do next?' Devon asked him.

'We wait, Devon. We hold our breath and we wait.'

CHAPTER TWENTY-TWO

'Who?' I felt like a stranger in my own office.

'Oscar Fedder. He's left five messages. He wants you to call him immediately,' Devon shouted from the storage room where we kept the answering machine.

'Anyone else?' I yelled back to her from where I sat on Steven's side of the desk.

After leaving Dr Fulton at the warehouse, we had come to the gallery to check the messages and mail. For the first time I took no pleasure in the gallery. It didn't seem like mine anymore. The place felt like a dusty memory of someone else's wish that never came true.

I sat in Steven's chair and remembered how he had looked in his black leather jacket the night we came up with the forgery scam. It seemed a lifetime ago. No, two lifetimes. God, it was hard to believe it was only three years ago.

His chair was comfortable but too high. The tops of my knees bumped against the desk. I'd never sat in it before. Never wanted to. I opened his top drawer. It was as neat and orderly as mine wasn't. A dozen pencils, freshly sharpened, were lined up in neat rows on one side; pens and paper clips had their own space on the other. His address book was placed just so, beside an even stack of business cards. 'Sellars and Ballard – Fine Art.' Not anymore. A small pad of paper, with his neat accountant's script on it, sat toward the back of the drawer. Curious, I reached in and pulled it out.

At the top he had written, 'Things to do.' What followed was a list that anyone might have compiled: 'dry cleaners, haircut, check Xmas flights, kitty litter . . .' I didn't even know he had a cat. The list went on, reminding him to do this or that, mostly chores related to the upcoming holidays. The second item from the bottom caught my eye; 'FAO, something special for Caitlin.' I bit my lip.

My friend and partner was, for all I knew, lying in the morgue with a tag wired to his toe. How long did they hold on to unidentified corpses before they were buried in a pauper's grave? Maybe Duncan would know. My stomach felt queasy. I dropped the pad back into the drawer and shut it.

'Devon, you about ready?' I asked, walking into the storage room where she was sorting through the mail.

'Yeah, just a minute. Are you going to call Fedder back?'

'No. Not today. Let's go back to your place. I don't want to be here.'

She looked up from the stack of bills she was organizing. 'You're white as a sheet, what happened?'

'Nothing. But if that can wait, I'd like to get out of here.'

It was a frigid, sunny day. The unusually cold autumn air should have had a cleansing effect, but as we walked back to Devon's I felt more and more depressed. I couldn't stop thinking about Steven, and the piss-poor way I had dealt with Tanaka.

'What the hell was Dr Fulton thinking? He sure laid it on thick. I couldn't believe it when he slapped Tanaka on the shoulder. Does he think this is some kind of a game?'

'I don't know.' Devon looked concerned. 'It scared me, too. He probably hasn't had much going on since he retired. Maybe he just got excited.'

'I guess we'll have to watch him.'

She nodded. 'We don't have much choice now.'

The streets were crowded with shoppers for a Monday afternoon, holiday bargain hunters in from the suburbs to take advantage of the after-Thanksgiving sales. The bright and overly cheerful Christmas displays in the windows of the shops we passed depressed me more.

'Shit,' Dev growled when we got to her apartment building. The front door was standing wide open. 'I'm going to have it out with that little s.o.b. This time I'm telling his mother.'

'Who?'

'That kid on the fourth floor. He never shuts the damned door. You know. The one with the skateboard and the pierced eyebrows.'

I looked at her blankly.

'Little Eddie Carlisle. Come on, you've seen him, the stupid-looking kid.'

I knew a stupid guy named Ed Carlisle, but he wasn't a kid, and I didn't think he lived in her building, so I just nodded, not really paying attention.

As we climbed the last of the stairs to her apartment I asked her about the kitty litter. 'Steven didn't have a cat, did he?'

'Of course he did, why?'

'It's not important.'

It was her turn to give me a strange look.

'I didn't know. That's all.' I wondered what else I didn't know about him. The thought made me sadder than I already was. Some friend I must have been. 'Maybe we should call Steven's doorman. Tell him Steven is traveling – ask him to feed the cat.'

She smiled. 'Good idea. I'll take care of it.'

I wondered if that meant we had inherited the creature.

As I fumbled with the keys to Devon's apartment, I found that the door was closed, but not locked. I flashed on Paul's studio.

'We locked it this morning, didn't we?'

'You had the keys,' she whispered. 'Shhhh, I think I heard something.'

We listened for a moment, but nothing stirred. Quietly, I pushed the door open.

The living room had been turned upside down. Books scattered, the sofa overturned, drawers pulled out and emptied onto the floor. Devon stiffened, a low groan escaping her lips as we stood just inside the door, surveying the mess.

A thump from her bedroom startled us. We froze. I started to move to push Dev back out the door, but I was too late. A kid stepped out of the bedroom and into the living room holding a large semiautomatic pistol leveled at us.

'Shit!' his voice was muffled by a blue bandanna wrapped around his face. He wore another bandanna on his head, pirate-fashion. Just over five feet tall and skinny as a whip, he looked young. I couldn't tell how young, but he held the gun in a steady enough grip.

'What?' A second burglar followed the first into the living room. He also wore blue bandannas. 'What the fuck, Peewee? Nobody's supposed to be here.'

'These two – they just walked in,' the boy with the gun explained.

The second burglar, much larger than the gunman, motioned us in. Dev and I exchanged glances.

'Now!' he ordered.

Pivoting, I shoved Dev out into the hall. 'Run,' I

shouted. It caught the gunman by surprise. He hesitated but quickly recovered and brought the gun up aiming at my face before I could follow Devon.

'No!' shouted the larger of the two. 'No shooting. She said no shooting.'

He lunged at me as I tried to back through the door, grunting as we collided. We both went down, rolling around in the wreckage of Dev's living room. He was strong as a bear. The muscles of his shoulders bunched and knotted as we grappled, each straining to overpower the other. Over and over we rolled, neither one of us able to gain the upper hand. We ended up side by side, my back against the kitchen door. I got a firm grip on his denim shirt, the fabric thick and stiff in my hands, then using my hips to gain enough leverage, I rolled on top of him, pinning his ass to the floor. All of the fear and frustration I had felt with Tanaka erupted in a spasm of pure burning rage. I straddled his chest and started to pound at him with my fists. He twisted and turned, struggling to avoid the blows, but I had no mercy in me. He'd made a bad choice coming here today.

The bandanna covering his head slipped off. He was bald, his angry brown eyes defiant. It seemed like we had been locked together like this for hours, but only minutes had passed since I had pushed Dev out into the hall. As I pummeled him the bandanna covering his face fell down around his neck. He couldn't have been over nineteen or twenty. A thin moustache grew over his lip, and he snarled up at me, revealing a gold incisor set with a small diamond. I hesitated, then lashed out even harder, connecting solidly with his chin, sending a painful jolt up my arm, quenching the fire in his mongrel eyes.

Dev screamed behind me. I looked up just in time to

see the gunman raise his pistol and swing it like a hammer at my head. I tucked my chin into my chest and jerked to my left, too slowly. He caught me with a glancing crack above my right ear, and I tumbled off his friend, stunned.

'The book, man. Give it to us, now.' He waved his gun around, the whites of his eyes large in the gap between his bandannas.

Dev stood in the doorway shrieking at the top of her lungs. I tried to get up and managed to gain my knees. Everything was moving. I couldn't get my balance.

'Let's go! Let's get the fuck outta here, R.J.,' the gunman yelled, clearly unnerved now by the screaming. He pulled his dazed friend up from the floor with one hand, trying to cover both Devon and me at the same time, swinging his pistol back and forth between us.

The apartment was rocking like a boat in a storm. I swayed on my knees. The two burglars stood together by the upside-down sofa.

'Go! Get out!' I called to Devon. She ignored me and kept up her deafening cries.

The floor shifted and flowed under me. Something wet and warm dripped into my ear. I reached up and touched my head, my hand came away bloody. I hadn't had time to be scared; now I wanted out, but the floor was quicksand.

'Come on, man. We got to go,' the gunman urged his partner.

Ignoring him, the one I had tangled with turned back to me, his bleeding mouth twisted into an ugly smirk, a flash of gold catching the light. The bastard pulled an ugly collapsible police baton from his pocket and snapped it open. Dev screamed louder. I raised my hands and tried to duck the blow, but he was faster. I heard the swoosh of the baton as it cut the air. Then everything exploded. The world smelled like the old varnish on Devon's floor, and tasted like dust.

Ammonia. I was suffocating. Coughing, I tried to wave the fumes away and draw a clean breath. Then I blinked and saw Devon swimming above me, behind a man with a thick red beard, who waved a bottle under my nose.

'No more,' I managed, weakly. 'I can't breathe.' I tried to push him away and sit up. 'Stop.'

'Easy, man.' Redbeard's voice was calm and soothing. 'Stay down.'

Devon's voice repeated his words. 'Please, Adrian, stay still.'

They weren't making sense.

'You've got a nasty little cut on your head. Maybe a concussion. You're going to be fine.' Redbeard again; this time I heard a little Brooklyn in his voice. 'Don't fight us, we're going to strap you onto this stretcher so we don't drop you. Just relax. Okay?'

'Whaa . . .?' I tried to sit up again and see what he was talking about, but firm hands pressed me down.

'Adrian, please stay still,' Devon said over his shoulder. Her face was pale, her eyes swollen. She looked scared. 'Everything is going to be fine. Just do as Sean says. Please?'

Sean? Redbeard? What the hell was happening? He wore a green and tan uniform. I couldn't quite focus on the tag embroidered over his breast pocket. I squeezed my eyes shut hoping to stop the spinning. He and his partner, a heavyset black woman he called Rita, lifted me easily and strapped me onto a narrow gurney.

'Easy,' I complained. My head felt the size of a weather balloon.

'We got you,' Rita said. 'Just be a good boy and lie still.'

As they wheeled me out of Dev's apartment, I noticed the mess. The burglars! 'Jesus Christ!' I tried to sit up again, fighting my restraints. 'Dev, the burglars. Where are they?'

'It's okay. It's okay, they're gone.' She walked beside the stretcher.

'Are you all right?' I asked her. 'Did they hurt you?'

'No. Don't worry about me.' She patted my arm. 'They ran out after they hit you. I'm fine, you just stay quiet. We're going to the hospital.'

The lights in the stairwell were brighter than usual. The stretcher bobbed with each step. I wanted Redbeard and Rita to stop and let me rest for a few minutes, but down we went bumping our way to the ground floor. I felt seasick. As the gurney hit the last step with a jarring thump, I remembered what the gunman had said.

'The book,' I clutched at Devon's arm. 'They were after the book.' It seemed like I was looking at her through the wrong end of a telescope. 'Dev, you look so far away . . .' The lights stopped bothering me, and I was falling. Light as air, I slipped down.

When I came to I was looking up the nostrils of an immense black man. Bald, with a walrus moustache and even white teeth, he clucked to himself as he shined a penlight into first my left, then my right eye. My brain quivered. My head was full of tomato aspic. The light didn't help.

'How are you feeling? Can you remember anything?' His deep, melodious voice owned a shadow of the South, hidden under the baritone.

'Are you kidding?' I started to sit up, but he pressed one hand against my chest and pushed me back down on the examining table as easily as he would have handled an infant.

'What do you remember?' he asked, slipping the penlight into the breast pocket of his white lab coat. 'Henry Givens, M.D.,' was etched on a black plastic name tag pinned over the pocket. He dwarfed a stethoscope draped like a scarf around his thick neck.

'Not much . . . I got hit. Is Devon here?' I asked, suddenly worried about her. I tried again to sit up.

'Yes,' he answered, pushing me back down. 'She's right outside. You've given her quite a scare, passing out like that. You're going to be all right. Now please lie still. I need to bandage those stitches.'

He did so, then turned and looked closely at an X ray tucked into the brackets of a light box mounted on the wall. The gray skull he was so carefully studying looked thin, the neck bones supporting it too flimsy and frail to be mine. He turned and gently probed the right side of my head, then referred back to the X ray.

'Nothing broken,' he muttered to himself. 'Are you nauseated? Dizzy?'

I nodded. 'A little of both.'

'You have a concussion. I'm going to admit you for observation. I want you off your feet for a day or so.'

'Is that necessary? I'm not . . . How bad is it?'

He looked down at me, a slightly bemused expression animating his grand face. 'I think you'll be fine, I just want to be on the safe side. We'll monitor you, give you something for the nausea, the pain, if you need it. Tell me something, Mr Sellars, what does the other guy look like? Your hands are bruised and swollen – I assume you got in at least one or two shots of your own.' He chuckled, a soft round sound that filled the corners of the examining room.

'Last I saw of him, he looked a helluva lot better than I feel,' I answered. 'Where am I? Can I see Devon now?' The throbbing in my head was a living thing, growing and shrinking with a rhythm all its own.

He picked up what I supposed was my chart and smiled benignly, king of his domain. 'You're in my emergency room.'

'I guessed that. Which hospital?'

'New York Hospital. I don't believe there are any finer.' He clucked a few more times as he completed his notes, then set the clipboard down by my feet. 'Lie still, Mr Sellars. I'll go get your friend.'

He shut the door of the examining room as he left. It was cold. I was lying on the table shirtless, my pants were loosened, and although I wore socks, no shoes, shirt, or suit coat was anywhere to be seen. The book had been in my coat pocket. I didn't know whether they had gotten it or not.

The door opened with a squeak, and I looked up expecting to see Devon. Instead a pleasant-looking man about my age, with curly brown hair and long drooping features, stuck his head in. 'Mr Sellars, I'd like to talk with you for a few minutes. Feel up to it?'

Before I could answer he stepped into the room and shut the door behind him. He flashed a gold shield at me, then introduced himself. 'I'm Detective John Carstairs, Mr Sellars.'

My heart missed a beat. He was the last person I wanted to see. Where was Devon? Damn, I tried to think of a reason not to talk with him, but nothing came to mind. For lack of a better plan, I rolled my eyes back into my head, pretending to pass out. A little drool slid from the corner of my mouth, tickling my chin. I don't think Carstairs bought it, but he had no choice other than to go and get help. I felt like an idiot, lying there freezing, with my eyes closed, spit dribbling down my face.

He returned quickly with a woman, judging from her voice, who hovered over me for a moment, then instructed Detective Carstairs that he would have to go back to the waiting room. He snorted. I imagined a disgusted look settling over his hound-dog features. His footsteps receded.

Then the nurse paged Dr Givens, using the phone on the wall by the door. After I heard her replace the handset, I held my breath, trying to listen to her movements. An eternity passed. I had no idea where in the room she was. Miming some childhood idea of delirium, I rolled my head from side to side and moaned, trying to get a fix on her, but it didn't work. My act, something any self-respecting sixth-grader would scoff at, was wearing thin. My brain was sloshing around inside my skull; I couldn't keep it up much longer. Still I couldn't hear the nurse. What the hell was she doing?

Finally I had to take a look. Slowly I opened one eye to see what she was up to, and found myself staring right into her face, not three feet from my own.

'Yoww.' I let out a yelp.

'Hardly an Academy Award performance, Mr Sellars. Along with your other injuries, did you neglect to tell the doctor that you're allergic to the law?' She stood over me, arms crossed, her lips pressed into a sardonic little smile, not the least surprised by my sudden and miraculous recovery.

'Please.' I reached up and grasped her elbow. 'I

haven't done anything wrong. I need to see my friend. She could be in danger, I have to warn her.'

The nurse unfolded her arms and put her hands on her narrow hips. She was tough, in her fifties, and her lined face looked as if there was little that would ever surprise her again. Her frosted hair was short and lay flat on her head. A pair of bifocals dangled on a silver chain around her neck. Dr Givens might claim the place, but I was looking at the real owner.

'Please,' I appealed. 'I need to see my friend before I talk to anyone else.'

'Relax, Mr Sellars. You remind me of Reid, my oldest.' She smiled broadly. 'A real talker, that one. A story for everything. I don't mind making the cops wait their turn. Close your eyes, I'll bring her in.'

'Thanks . . . nurse?'

'Nurse Gaylin, Betty Gaylin.'

'Reid's a lucky guy.'

'Reid's doing twenty-to-life in Attica. Now close your eyes and keep quiet. See that you don't make an idiot out of me. Carstairs is nobody's fool.'

The door squeaked as she closed it.

It squeaked again, but I kept my eyes shut.

'Adrian. It's me.' No voice ever sounded sweeter.

I squinted, barely opening my eyes. Devon and Nurse Gaylin stood just inside the door.

'I'll be in the hall if you need me. But talk quietly. Detective Carstairs is waiting down the corridor.'

Devon practically threw herself on top of me. 'I've been worried sick. Until that nurse came and got me, no one would tell me anything.'

I stroked her hair. 'I've been in here worried about you. Are you all right?'

She held me tighter. 'I'm okay. Those two scared the

239

hell out of me. I thought they were going to kill you.' She started to tremble. 'I wanted to help, but that gun. He kept pointing that gun at me. I was terrified.'

She buried her face in my chest and sobbed. I held her until the trembling eased, then she sat up and I got a good look at her. Her hair was disheveled, and her mascara had run, leaving dark vampire circles around her eyes. She was way too pale.

Slowly, I dropped my legs over the side of the examining table and managed to sit up. The room tilted for a second or two, then righted itself. My head boomed like a bass drum.

'You did fine, Devon. Your screaming is what scared them away. I'm just glad they didn't hurt you.'

She started to cry. 'Damn them.'

'We're okay, Dev.' I took her hand and stroked it. 'They were after Marta's book.'

Her tears stopped. 'I know. If I ever lay eyes on that bitch again, I'll kill her, Adrian. I swear it.'

'The address book was in my suit coat, did they get it?'

She opened her purse and extracted the book. 'It fell out in the ambulance.' She handed it to me, then rummaged further in her bag and pulled out a tissue. After she dabbed at her eyes and blew her nose, I handed the book back to her.

'You keep it in your purse for now. I need you to call Duncan Marshall. Carstairs wants to talk to me about Paul McHenry.'

'I've already called him.' She took a deep breath and looked at her watch. 'He should be here any minute.'

In spite of how obviously upset she was, she had done everything right.

'You're a fucking champ, Devon Berenson.' I smiled at her. 'A thoroughbred. Thank you.'

She smiled back at me, a little color returning to her cheeks. 'Look at us,' she laughed. 'Some team we are.'

'Hey, I think we did pretty well . . .' The image of her standing in the door, screaming at the top of her lungs, was indelibly etched in my memory. Her apartment was no longer even marginally a safe place to be. 'You can't go back there.'

Her smile faded. 'I know.' She nodded, tears welling again.

'You have money – credit cards with you?'

She patted her purse. 'Both, I have my wallet.'

'Good. Go to the Hotel Rimbaud, on Fifty-fourth Street. You'll be safe there. Check in, then wait for me, okay?'

She nodded. 'Are you going to be all right here?' She seemed reluctant to leave.

'I'll be fine. Do you know where they put my clothes?'

She looked around the room. 'In here,' she said, pointing to a plastic garbage bag next to the door.

'Go, now. Just walk out, don't stop to talk with anyone. I'll either call you or come to the hotel.'

She looked as if she might start crying again but visibly stiffened and seemed to pull herself together. Leaning over, she kissed me lightly on the lips, then walked out. I lay back down and closed my eyes.

With Nurse Gaylin's help, I remained unconscious, at least as far as Detective Carstairs was concerned, until Duncan Marshall arrived.

'Devon called me,' he said, as soon as he walked into the room. 'What happened? What's this all about?'

'Thanks for coming, Duncan.' I sat up. A sharp pain,

241

like a jagged blade, ripped through my head. I inhaled sharply.

'Jesus, want me to call the doctor?' Duncan asked.

'No, it's okay.' I took a few breaths, and the pain eased back to its dull throb. 'Carstairs is out there. What should I tell him?'

He put down his briefcase and thought for a minute.

'First things first. What happened to you? Devon said you two surprised some burglars at her place.'

'That's the extent of it,' I told him, not wanting to get into details.

'Did it have anything to do with Tanaka?'

'Not directly. Listen, Duncan, I told you I wouldn't involve you in this thing where I didn't have to. I'm not sure how to handle Carstairs. That's how you can help.'

He shook his head, a little put out. He wanted to know what was going on with Tanaka. It was eating at him, but we both knew he couldn't cross that line without risking his career, and neither of us wanted that.

'I'll help you however I can, you know that. You can refuse to talk with Carstairs. That's within your rights. But he'd know you were hiding something. Right now he may think it, but he doesn't know for sure. I say we talk to him.'

'But I do have something to hide.'

'Adrian, you didn't kill Paul McHenry. That's what Carstairs wants to know. I'll stop him if his questions stray too far from that topic.'

After the introductions had been made, and cards exchanged, Detective Carstairs came right to the point.

'Any idea what the burglars you surprised were after?'

'No. I figured they were crackheads – would've taken anything they could get.'

He nodded. 'Probably. You remember anything distinctive about them?'

'No, it's mostly a blur.'

He nodded again. 'Now that you're feeling better, I have a few questions about Paul McHenry, Mr Sellars.' He looked at me closely. 'You are feeling up to it, aren't you?'

'Yes.'

'Good. I understand you and McHenry knew each other both socially and professionally. What were you doing at his place on the night he was killed?'

Duncan interrupted. 'Certainly you don't think Mr Sellars is a suspect, do you?'

It hadn't taken Carstairs long to stray from whether or not I had killed Paul.

Carstairs shook his head. 'Come on, counselor. You know I'm not going to discuss who is and who isn't a suspect. Assuming your client and McHenry really were friends, he'll want to help me figure out what happened.' He turned to me. 'Right, Mr Sellars? You and Paul McHenry were friends, weren't you?'

'Of course we were,' I answered defensively.

Then I caught myself. Carstairs was smart. It dawned on me that I had no idea how he had found me. Maybe he'd been following me, watching all along. *But if he's been watching me, why hasn't he pulled me in?* He stood, fiddling with something in his pocket, waiting for me to continue. The three of us filled the examining room. The stale smell of tobacco and nicotine clung to Carstairs. When he realized that I wasn't going to say anything more, he asked the question again.

'Then tell me what you were doing at the loft the night he died.'

'He hadn't returned my calls or come to the gallery. I

went down to Lispenard Street to find him. I was worried.'

'Why were you worried? Was he expected at the gallery?'

'Yeah,' I nodded. 'When he didn't show, or answer the phone, I decided to go and find him. When I saw the broken door . . . his body . . . I guess I panicked and ran out. I didn't know what to do. I have no idea who killed him, or why.'

Carstairs had pulled a small notepad from the inside pocket of his coat and was scribbling notes as I spoke. If I had felt better, it would have seemed like bad television; as it was I felt nauseated and claustrophobic.

'I just don't see it,' he said, digging in his ear with the end of his pen. 'If I had discovered the body of one of my friends like that, all that blood, cut up like some kind of sacrifice, I would have called the police.' He examined the pen, then not finding anything of interest he looked down at me. 'Why didn't you?'

'I told you, I panicked.'

'What time did you arrive at the loft?'

'I'm not sure. Sometime after seven.'

'Were you alone?'

'Yes.'

'Did you leave the gallery and go straight to McHenry's loft?'

Now he was too close for comfort. I had left Tanaka's with Steven, then headed downtown to the loft. 'No. I ran a few errands, then went to find Paul.'

'Errands?' He shook his head in wonder. 'I thought you were worried about him. When you got to the loft, did you see anything suspicious?'

'No . . . well, there were a couple of Chinese guys arguing by a van, and Trish, the neighbor who let me in.'

Eyebrows raised, he scribbled something on his pad as he spoke. 'Chinese guys? A van? Come on, Mr Sellars, do I look like Columbo?'

'Seriously, there were two guys, Chinese, they were parked across from the loft. I noticed them because they were arguing over some wooden crates in the back of the van.'

'You notice a license number, anything specific?'

I shook my head no.

'Right. So, aside from a couple of mysterious Oriental guys, you're telling me you haven't got a clue as to who killed McHenry, or why?'

The way he said it, the whole thing sounded absurd. I was beginning to think I sounded guilty to him.

'None.' I held out my hands as if the sight of them empty would convince him that I was telling the truth. 'If I could help you I would. I just don't know anything.'

Carstairs met my gaze. His flat brown eyes were the color of a muddy creek. 'Why was McHenry expected at the gallery? Was he working for you?'

Duncan answered for me. 'Detective Carstairs, Mr McHenry was often employed as an art restorer by my client. You already pointed out that they were also friends. Mr Sellars has been injured. If you wish to ask more questions, we'll be happy to set up an appointment when he's feeling better. He's already told you that he has no knowledge of Paul McHenry's murder. Is there anything else you need to ask that can't wait until he's recovered?'

Carstairs ignored Duncan. 'One more thing, Mr Sellars. Why haven't you been opening the gallery?'

Duncan jumped in again. 'He's taken some time off for the holidays. Is that a problem, Detective?'

'What about your partner? Ballard, right? Is he taking a vacation, too?'

My heart stopped beating. Duncan looked stricken.

'Yeah,' I finally answered. 'He's taking some time off. Traveling.'

Carstairs's eyes never left mine. He slowly closed his pad and returned it to his pocket. 'When he gets back, I'd like to have a word with him. Have him call me. One of the uniformed officers has taken a statement from Miss Berenson about the break-in. I'd like you to tell him what you remember.'

He started toward the door, then turned back to me. 'The lab boys found chemicals and materials in McHenry's studio that seem out of the ordinary for a freelance art restorer. Hell, they found stuff in there the Met doesn't even have.' He shrugged. 'I don't understand people like you, Mr Sellars. A friend gets dusted like McHenry was, and you don't call the police. Somebody did a job on him. Brutal. Too damned brutal. I want the animal that did it off the streets. If I believed you had anything to do with his death, I'd bust your ass here and now.' He looked down at his feet and shook his head. 'But I sure am curious about what McHenry was up to. I'm going to do a little digging, see if anyone else has any ideas. I'll call Mr Marshall if I think of anything else you can help me with.' He laughed. 'Yeah, I'll make an appointment. Maybe next time we'll do lunch.'

After he left, Duncan sighed loudly. Carstairs's speech had left me feeling like a piece of garbage.

'We haven't heard the last of Detective Carstairs.' Duncan's voice interrupted my self-flagellation. 'I wish he hadn't asked about Steven.'

'Do you think they've identified his body?'

Duncan shrugged, then started pacing. He looked

thoroughly unhappy. I was getting dizzy watching him. I pressed both hands to my throbbing temples. A greasy film of sweat covered my face.

'How did he find me here?' I looked up at Duncan, noticing for the first time the dark circles under his eyes.

'Luck. I'd be willing to bet it was blind luck. When Devon called nine-one-one to report the assault on you and asked for an ambulance, the dispatcher notified both the police and the paramedics. Somehow Carstairs was in the right place at the wrong time and heard about it. Just rotten luck.'

'I wish to hell that it hadn't happened now. Do you think he knows about the forgeries? I wonder if that's what he was getting at when he brought up what the lab boys found?'

'What did they find?' Duncan asked, looking even more worried.

'Probably enough to put two and two together.'

He rubbed his face. 'Maybe we should come clean with Carstairs. Talk to him before he puts it all together.'

'I can't do that, Duncan. If Tanaka even suspected that I'd talked with the police, he'd have me killed.'

'You want to tell me exactly what's going on?' Duncan asked.

'No. I can't. Hand me my clothes, they're in the bag by the door. I've got to get out of here.'

'You can't just walk out of a hospital. What did the doctor say?'

My shirt was bloody, my coat worse. I pulled them on anyway. In the mirror over the sink I examined the bandage over my right ear. Not much to look at.

'Adrian?'

'A concussion. He said I may have a concussion. Wants to admit me for observation.'

'Aren't you going to stay?'

'Come on, Duncan. Walk me out of here. I've got too much at stake to lie around here while they poke at me.'

Together we walked out of the emergency room. It was getting busy and no one noticed us. Two uniformed cops stood near the door, deep in conversation with three nurses. They never even looked up as we passed in front of them.

'You going to be all right?' Duncan asked.

'Yeah, pal. Thanks again. You keep showing up when I need you.'

'Damn it, Adrian. I don't think I've helped much at all.'

We clasped hands. 'Is everything all right with you? You look beat, Duncan.'

'Me? Have you looked in the mirror lately?'

'Seriously.'

He exhaled, his breath forming a cloud in the frosty air. 'I'm just a little worn out, Adrian. Dana hasn't been feeling well. We're not sure why yet.'

'Is there anything I can do?'

He looked at me like I was out of my mind. 'Haven't you got a few problems of your own? I appreciate it, but we'll be fine. You worry about yourself.'

'Give her my best. I'll call you.'

He waved as he got into a cab, then I flagged down my own.

'Ay mon, dis cab she is clean,' the driver said, looking at me with obvious distaste. 'You still bleedin'?'

'No.' I waved a twenty under his nose. 'You know the Hotel Rimbaud, on Fifty-fourth Street?'

He nodded, snatched the money, and took off down Second Avenue, adjusting his rearview mirror so that he could keep an eye on me.

CHAPTER TWENTY-THREE

At the Rimbaud the desk clerk hadn't given Devon the same room I had occupied a week and a half ago, but the rooms looked remarkably alike, right down to the threadbare carpet and the stains on the ceiling. Frankie Testa wasn't on duty yet. I wondered what he'd think when he got a look at Devon.

We sat side by side on the edge of the bed, our combined weight creating a deep valley in the cheap mattress. I held the telephone away from my ear so that Devon could listen.

'Marta, what the hell is wrong with you?' Confronting her was the only way we could think of to try and back her off.

'I don't know what you're talking about,' she answered, an exaggerated lilt of innocence coloring her voice.

'Those two assholes you sent almost killed me.'

'You're not making sense, Adrian. Did you fall and hit your head or something?' She laughed, a high-pitched, mirthless giggle.

Devon tensed up and frowned. I held my finger to my mouth.

'They were after your book. They said so. I've already told you that I don't have it. That was a stupid stunt you pulled.'

'Adrian, I told you I'd get it back. I meant it. Are you ready to return it?'

'If I had it, I wouldn't return it now. Does Tanaka know about your precious book?'

Her silence was an eloquent answer. Before she could think of anything to say, I continued.

'Let me tell you what I'm going to do. I'm going to hang up and call him. Let him know exactly what happened, all about your lost address book, and how upset you are. What'll he think about that, Marta?'

Devon smiled. Whatever was in the book had Marta scared enough to take wild chances in order to get it back. I was bluffing, but I had to believe that Tanaka wouldn't like the fact that she had been keeping such a document, and would be even less thrilled to learn it was floating around somewhere.

'You wouldn't call him,' she said, after digesting my threat. 'It's you he'd go after to get it back.'

'Maybe. But do you think he'll give up a six-million-dollar Monet by hurting the one person who can get it for him?'

Marta was silent as she weighed her options. Devon looked as happy as I'd seen her in a long time.

'You stay the hell away from Devon and me, and I'll stay out of your business – agreed?'

'What do you mean?' Marta asked.

'I mean exactly what I said. No more break-ins. No gang-bangers showing an unhealthy interest in us. You back off and I won't tell Tanaka about the book. But if anything happens to either of us, Tanaka's going to hear all about your book. My lawyers will see to that.'

'Will you return the book if I agree?'

'Are you crazy? If I had it, your morons would have found it. They practically destroyed the place looking. Do we have a deal or not?'

'Okay,' she answered, reluctantly. 'But if I find out you have it . . .' Her words trailed off.

'No ifs. We either have a deal, or not.'

'Okay, okay. I already told you we have a deal.'

'Good. You call Tanaka, tell him that Dr Fulton is making good progress. I'll try and keep him moving.'

'I need to see you, Adrian. We need to talk.'

I hung up without giving her a chance to finish. Devon stood and wandered around the room.

'Do you think it's safe to go home now?'

'No. Not until we get the book to Okuba. Come, sit with me.' I patted the spot on the bed she had just vacated. My head hurt, but the pain wasn't unbearable. 'Have I told you how much you mean to me?'

'As a matter of fact, you haven't.' She sat down beside me, draping an arm over my shoulders. 'I'm scared, I don't like this. Not at all, so make it good.'

I looked around the seedy room. 'In spite of all the luxury I've subjected you to.' She followed my eyes to the mottled ceiling. 'And even though I haven't exactly been the best houseguest you've ever had, as awful as everything has been, I'm glad you and I are together. I think you're the most wonderful woman I've ever known.'

She pushed me onto my back and rolled on top of me. 'I love you,' she declared, looking at me with such a depth of feeling that my pulse quickened. 'If it's too much for you, Adrian, you better tell me now.'

'It's not too much. But everything is so fucking strange. You must think I'm completely out of my mind. There's more to me than this, the forgeries, the dope. I did them, no denying it, but there's more. I want you to see me, to see what's inside. I don't know . . . I've always tried to project this image. I don't want to do that with you.'

Devon looked at me strangely. 'You don't know, do you?'

'What? What don't I know?'

'All this time I thought you knew.' She rolled off me and lay back on the bed, smiling. 'Did you think I worked for you just because of the incredible salary and benefits? Shit, you barely paid minimum wage. You never noticed me looking at you? How jealous I got over Marta, and all the other women that called or came by the gallery?'

I looked at her with my mouth open. 'No. I never suspected.'

'Well, now you know. I've wanted you for a long, long time. I saw through the fancy suits, and the attitude, and all of the bullshit. I saw what you were doing to yourself with the drugs. But I also saw a man who had brains and an imagination, and who in spite of himself actually cared about people. Don't get me wrong, I've seen you act like a total asshole, but I've also seen you regret it. I've seen you with Caitlin. Do you understand what I'm saying? I saw you when you didn't know anyone was watching. That's the man I love.' She rolled onto her side and propped her head on her elbow. 'Why did you come to my apartment, if you didn't know?'

I didn't know what to say. Her speech had caught me by surprise. 'I'm not sure. I just wanted to come to you.'

'I wish you'd come sooner.'

'To tell you the truth, if I'd known how good you look naked, I'd have been there a long time ago.'

She picked up a pillow and threw it at me.

'Hey, watch the stitches.' I stood up, laughing. 'I'm an injured man.'

'In that case, come back to bed. I'd better nurse you back to health.'

Sleep came only in fits and starts. Around two in the morning I woke with a blinding headache. Devon went

252

down the hall in search of ice but came up empty-handed. The machine was broken. She laid a cool washcloth over my eyes, and eventually the pounding eased up. By morning it had subsided to a dull roar, and although I still felt nauseated, I hoped the worst was over.

We left the Rimbaud well before 8:00 A.M., dressed in the same clothes we had arrived in. Two businessmen shared the elevator with us, and although neither commented, I was aware of their sidelong glances at the dark brown stains matting my shirt and suit jacket. Neither Devon nor I had thought to grab coats when we left her apartment in the ambulance.

Winter had tightened its grasp on the city overnight; the day was dark and strangely hazy with a wind that held an icy edge and threatened snow. Blowing out of the north, it came snarling down Madison Avenue with bared teeth, tugging aggressively at Devon's dress and my bloodied suit. Both of us shivered as it found its way under and through our clothes. We turned our backs to it and walked south toward Hiro Okuba's office in the Mishima Tower. Most of the other pedestrians had had enough sense to wear heavy winter coats and scarves. I turned up my collar and held my jacket closed at the throat, but it did little to keep me warm. Devon's blue dress offered even less protection.

The only store we found open that offered any type of clothing was a combination newsstand and gift shop on the corner of Madison and Fifty-first. We stopped and I bought a 'Big Apple' sweatshirt, the least offensive of those available. It wasn't much of an improvement, but I took off my ruined jacket and carefully pulled the sweatshirt over my head, hoping it would get me through the lobby of Mishima's midtown skyscraper without too much notice. I draped my jacket over Dev's shoulders as we left the shop and once again turned our backs to the wind.

Eighty-four stories of gleaming red granite, covering a square block of some of the world's most expensive real estate, the Mishima Tower had been designed by Stone Hickman, the I. M. Pei of the nineties, and had set the standard for high-tech luxury. It had received rave reviews in the architectural press, but some of the tabloids continued to run stories about ghosts roaming the halls at night. Six Canadian Indians, who had come from Saskatchewan to hang the high steel, had died during the building's construction. A freak windstorm knocked them from the girders and sent them reeling through space, falling until the sidewalk of East Forty-third Street put a sudden stop to their descent. The ghosts of the Indians were often seen by the building's janitors, who worked late into the night.

The place didn't look haunted to me. Devon shrugged off my jacket and handed it back to me. Turning it inside out and draping it over my arm, we entered the building through the massive Forty-third Street portico with the other early arrivals, who formed a steady stream through the ornately columned postmodern entrance.

We signed in at the reception desk built into the polished granite of the atrium lobby. The uniformed guard made a notation on the console of his computer, glanced quickly at a bank of video monitors, then waited. Within moments a young woman appeared through a doorway that opened behind the reception desk. She was perfectly turned out, not a flaw or distinguishing mark on her. She held name tags for Devon and me.

'Welcome to the Mishima Tower. If you'll follow me, please, I'll take you upstairs.' She smiled stiffly, and if she noticed my strange outfit, she gave no outward sign. She escorted us to an elevator and rode in silence with us to the eightieth floor, where she turned us over to another young woman, seemingly a clone, who was waiting for us as the doors whispered open.

'Good morning,' said our new escort. 'Won't you please follow me? Mr Okuba is expecting you.' Devon and I exchanged glances. Were these girls real or some kind of advanced Japanese robotic inventions? I wondered if they were warm to the touch.

She led the way down a sterile hallway with hard white walls and plush white carpeting. The only sound was the muffled hiss of the air handlers as they switched on and off. There were several closed doors along the way, each unmarked. We turned a corner after about a hundred yards and the hallway dead-ended at an open door.

It revealed a large corner office with floor-to-ceiling windows that afforded a dizzying view of lower Manhattan, the East River, and beyond that Brooklyn. Hiro stood in the center of the office, smiling. Behind him was a large mahogany desk with a contemporary black leather swivel chair. Two richly upholstered sofas sat at right angles in front of him, facing respectively the desk and the windows. There was no art, no awards or certificates, no photographs, no books – nothing personal anywhere to be seen. With the exception of a telephone and a neXt PC that looked like it belonged to Darth Vader, the desk was bare. There was nothing in this office to indicate who occupied it. For that matter there was nothing beyond Hiro's presence to indicate that the office was occupied at all.

I meant to ask about it, but something about the hushed atmosphere and the uninterrupted view suddenly had me teetering on the edge of a dark gulf. The room started to spin under my feet, and Hiro's smiling face swam in and out of focus. I stumbled over to one of the sofas and fell into it.

'Good Lord, Adrian. What's happened to you?' Hiro asked. He turned to Devon when I didn't answer immediately. 'Is he okay?'

'Yes. Yes, I'm all right. Just a little dizzy.' I took several deep breaths. 'Some water. May I have some water?' The spinning slowed, and the crinkles at the edge of my vision unfolded.

The girl who had escorted us from the elevator hurried off to get me something to drink, her starched smile still in place. While she was gone Devon sat next to me.

'Do you want to go back to the hospital?' she asked. She searched my eyes, trying to gauge my condition.

'No. The view.' I gestured at the windows. 'I guess it overwhelmed me. Made me lose my balance. I'll be okay.'

The girl returned with a glass of ice water. As I sipped it, then held the glass to my forehead, Hiro stepped behind the desk and punched a series of commands into his sleek black computer. The windows went from clear to a milky white, and the lights in the office dimmed slightly.

'Is that better?' he asked.

I nodded. 'Thanks. I guess I got hit harder than I thought.'

'Who did this to you? I want to know what happened.'

'That's why we're here. Devon, show him the book.'

She dug the small, red leather address book out of her purse and held it out to him. 'I hope you can make more sense out of it than we could. It appears to be in Japanese, maybe some kind of code as well.'

He reached for the book, looking puzzled as he took it. Then he thumbed through it twice, stopping a few times to reread a page or two. When he got to the last couple of pages, he stiffened and actually did a double take.

'Where did you get this?' he asked. 'Who wrote it? Can it be verified?'

'Whoa, slow down. Is it that important?' I asked him, looking at Devon who seemed as surprised at the intensity of his reaction as I was. 'What does it say?'

Hiro, through some enormous act of will, seemed to calm down. His shoulders fell back from around his ears, and he forced a smile. But his eyes gave him away. I'd had enough experience in the art world to recognize pure unadulterated greed when I saw it. Behind his glasses, Hiro looked like a man who had just won the lottery and couldn't wait to get rid of his guests so that he could go and claim it.

'I . . . well, I can't say for certain until I've had some time to study it, but what I can make out appears to be a record of Tanaka's and Nakamura's dealings in America. Parts of it are in some kind of numerical code. I'll have to get it deciphered.' He waved the book in front of us. 'If it's what I think it is, it could he very helpful. Now, please tell me how you came by it.'

'I borrowed it from Marta Batista's purse.'

'Does she know you have it?' His demeanor turned serious.

'She suspects. She's certainly anxious to have it back.' I sipped some of the cold water. 'A couple of thugs who work for her broke into Devon's place looking for it. Unfortunately, we walked in on them.' I reached up and touched the bandage. 'It could have been worse; they had a gun.'

Hiro grimaced as though it was his head that had been stitched up. He stood and walked over to the window, looked for a moment into its opaque glow, then thumbed through the book a third time.

'Next time you won't be so lucky,' he stated flatly, as he closed the book.

Devon and I looked at each other again.

'What are you saying?' she asked.

'There are names, dates, some very specific and damaging information in this book. Not only to the Hiyashi Gumi. This book lists a number of their American contacts. Most of it's in code, but we're probably talking about some very powerful and scary people here. If Tanaka or Nakamura knew you had this, your troubles over the forgeries would seem like a welcome relief.'

This wasn't what I had expected to hear. I had thought the book might make Tanaka uncomfortable. But I hadn't considered the possibility that Marta could have compiled such damaging information.

'She must have been looking for a way out. Why else would she keep such a dangerous insurance policy?' Devon asked.

Hiro didn't answer. He seemed lost in thought, his brow wrinkled, his lips a tight line.

'Isn't there some way we can use it?' I asked him.

He walked around his desk and sat down in his chair. Something had changed in his demeanor. Nothing too obvious. A hardening around his eyes – a new arrogance in the set of his shoulders that belied his earlier friendliness. Even the tone of his voice seemed colder.

'Oh, there will be a way to use this, no doubt about it.'

He waved the book. 'But we're not talking about getting you out from under at this point. This book changes everything. I'm just trying to decide where to keep you and Devon until I make up my mind how to handle this.'

'Keep us? Hiro, we don't want anything to do with it. All I ever wanted was to get Tanaka off my back.'

He snorted. 'I wish it were that simple. Adrian, whether you like it or not, you and Devon are in this up to your eyeballs. There is no simple way out.'

'We can use the book as leverage – that's our way out,' Devon said.

'Exactly,' I echoed. 'We'll use Marta's book to back Tanaka off. What happens then is between him and Marta. Let me have it, Hiro.'

He placed the book on his desk and covered it with his hand. Fixing me with an icy stare, he leaned back.

'Don't be so goddamned naive, Adrian.' His voice was sharper than I had ever heard it. 'Even if I let you have the book, he'd never believe you hadn't made a copy, or shown it to someone else. Have you forgotten that he's had you followed? I wouldn't be surprised if he knew you were here right this minute.'

I wasn't sure that I had heard him correctly. 'What do you mean, if you let me return it? I don't remember asking your permission.'

'Adrian, let's be smart about this. Let me help you and Devon.'

'You can help us by returning the book.'

'Devon, would you please talk some sense into him? I think that bump on his head might have affected his thinking.' He looked at Devon as he spoke, a 'let's be reasonable' appeal in the half smile he flashed at her.

She shook her head. 'No, Hiro. I think Adrian is right.

259

If Tanaka knows we're here, it's all the more reason we should just return the book.'

Hiro looked from Devon to me and bowed his head. 'You're both talking like fools. This will be much easier on all of us if you'll cooperate.'

'Cooperate with whom?' I asked.

He sat there looking at me. Then he shook his head.

'Adrian, haven't I shown you and Devon that I can be a friend?'

'Maybe. But if you'll hand over the book, we'll keep that friendship intact. Then we'll get out of your office and let you get back to work.' I stood.

'No!' He slapped his hand down hard enough to make the phone jump. 'The book stays with me. I'll decide what to do with it, and when. And you, my friends, will do exactly as I say. Assuming you want my help and protection. I don't see that you have a hell of a lot of choice. You wouldn't last ten minutes out there once Tanaka finds out about this.' He came out from behind his desk, but not before placing the book carefully into one of the drawers.

Devon looked dumbfounded. I stood gaping at his sudden transformation.

'What the hell is this?' I asked.

He shook his head. 'Come on, Adrian. Haven't you figured it out?' Reaching into his pocket, he pulled out an official-looking notebook and flipped it open, revealing an I.D., which included a photograph of an unsmiling Hiro Okuba, what I assumed to be his fingerprints, and a good bit of written information. Unfortunately it was in Japanese.

I looked at him, still confused. 'I don't understand.'

'I'm head of the NPA's organized crime task force in America. We're here in New York by the invitation of your State Department supposedly to help the FBI wage war on our common enemy.' He twisted his lips into a sarcastic smirk. 'For all the good it's done.'

'What about Mishima, this office?'

He ignored my question and continued, his voice full of bitterness and anger.

'Sounds like quite a job, eh? Head of the NPA task force.' He snorted derisively. 'It's not, it's the fucking boondocks is what it is.' He crossed his arms in front of him and bent forward at the waist, as though to whisper a secret to us. 'It's a dead-end assignment. At least it was, until you handed me that book.'

My initial shock at his sudden change in attitude gave way to an uncomfortable realization that to Hiro Okuba, Devon and I were no more than a couple of extra pawns on the game board. I glanced over at her to see if she understood how little we meant to him.

She looked at me out of the corner of her eye, brows raised, her mouth pressed into a hard, tight line. Her hands were knotted into fists.

Hiro ignored her. He went on to confirm our status in no uncertain terms.

'You're nothing but a lucky break.' He shook his head in wonder. 'When you fell into my lap – and that's what you did, Adrian – I lit some incense and thanked my ancestors. I've been chasing after Tanaka and his cronies in New York for almost two years. For nothing. Every time I get close,' he snapped his fingers, 'poof – he squirms out of it. Hell, I've had agents on the inside, but never quite close enough. Your little forgery scam opened up some possibilities. Hell, I was overjoyed to help you, thought it might be a crack in Tanaka's wall. A way to put a wedge between him and Nakamura. But this little book that you've brought me . . . this is a different story.

Careers are made on much less than this. I'm not letting it get away from me, not under any circumstances.'

'Hiro, what about the forgeries?' Devon asked. 'What does this mean?' She stood by the coffee table, her face flushed.

I understood what he was saying, but I wanted her to hear it from him. My blood was racing, the adrenaline surging through my system. I felt my pulse ticking under the stitches in my scalp. Keep him talking, Devon, I thought, moving closer to the desk.

'The forgeries are unimportant. I'm through with this bullshit assignment. It means I'll be going back to Japan.'

'What are you going to do about us?' she demanded.

'First I'm going to clear it with the FBI, then I'm going to take the two of you into protective custody. You're both going to have to testify – about Steven Ballard's murder, about Marta Batista's little red book – it'll all come out, even your precious forgeries. This time I'm going to nail Tanaka and Nakamura to a cross they can't wriggle off.' He grinned, a faraway look in his eyes.

'You said we wouldn't last five minutes in custody,' I spat. 'For over two years you've been trying to bust Tanaka. You haven't even come close. Now you're going to use us to do it? Even if it means we could get killed in the process? No fucking way, Hiro. It's not going to happen.'

I stepped around the coffee table to where Devon stood on the opposite side of it. Hiro faced us, a few feet beyond my reach.

His face hardened. 'Things have changed, Adrian. You don't have a choice. We'll do everything humanly possible to protect you. If you're helpful enough, maybe you won't do any time. You might even be a candidate for the federal witness protection program. Think of it as a fresh start.'

Devon looked horrified. 'We trusted you, Hiro.'

He shrugged, then turned and reached for the phone.

'You can't do this,' I said softly, inching closer to Devon.

Something in my tone made him hesitate and turn back to face me. 'I can and I will. Don't make it worse.' He turned back to the phone.

The blood was pounding in my head. I grabbed for Okuba, but Devon stepped in front of me. She held the brass ashtray from the coffee table cocked in her right hand; her face was crimson. Without a word she swung the ashtray at the back of his head, connecting with a nasty crack. He stood there for a second, his back to us, swaying. Then the phone fell from his hand and he crumpled across his empty desk, knocking his fancy computer to the floor. It hardly made a sound as it hit the carpet.

Devon stood perfectly still, shock draining her face. She dropped the ashtray.

'Is he dead?' she asked, barely whispering. 'Did I kill him?'

Walking around the desk, I returned the receiver to its cradle, then rifled through the drawers until I found the book. Slipping it into my pocket, I reached over and felt for Hiro's pulse. It was strong and even, but it looked like he'd be out for a while. Bastard.

'Come on,' I said, gently taking Devon by the elbow. 'We have to get out of here.'

We closed his office door behind us and walked to the elevators. The security guard at the reception desk thanked us as we handed him our name tags. Then we hurried out of the building.

CHAPTER TWENTY-FOUR

Out on the street, in stark contrast to my own weariness, I felt the energy of the city: the stink of the buses as they blew clouds of black smoke into the already gray morning air, the bellowing of the automobile horns, the roaring murmur of throngs of pedestrians pushing and plowing their way through the packed sidewalks. New York pressed down on me, a jangling current that echoed and reverberated inside my head, ricocheting off the walls of my skull like shards of glass. Devon stood beside me on the curb, caught somewhere between sheer exaltation and fearful shock at her own capacity for violence. There wasn't a cab to be had.

The wind had died down to occasional gusts, but the morning was, if anything, colder. Dark laden clouds were streaming out of the north, visible in the long rectangle of sky above Forty-third Street, low and fat, ready to make good on the threat of snow before lunch. I took Devon's hand and we turned west. Her fingers, curled against mine, vibrated as we forced our way into the flow of foot traffic and walked to Fifth Avenue. We turned north. I didn't have a destination in mind, I just wanted to get us away from the immediate vicinity of Okuba's office.

'Did you see? Did you see what I did to the little liar?' Devon's face was pale, but her eyes were shining. 'At first I was scared that I might have killed him. Now I'm glad I did it.'

'You surprised the shit out of me,' I answered. 'I'll be real careful about turning my back on you the next time we argue.'

'He had it coming. He was going to arrest us, make us testify. Even after we trusted him.' She shook her head at the injustice of it, then flexed her arms, as if to loosen them up after a session of vigorous exercise.

By the time we had walked four or five blocks, the color had returned to her cheeks.

'I think I'm hungry,' she said. 'You?'

I looked at her, surprised. 'Now?'

'Yeah, now.' Her expression still held a childlike look of wonder, as though she had discovered a new and not unlikeable side of herself.

'In here.' I led the way into a coffee shop on the corner of Forty-seventh Street.

We sat quietly in a booth at the back of the crowded restaurant, and when a waitress finally approached I ordered two coffees. Neither of us spoke while we waited for her to bring them.

'We can't do this anymore,' I said after we had been served.

'What?' Devon asked, cupping her coffee in both hands, trying to warm them while studying the menu lying on the table in front of her.

'We can't be stupid. Everything I've done has been laughable. Not anymore.' A hard knot of anger had formed inside of me.

She sipped at her coffee, the liquid sloshing out of the cup as her hands shook. Then, carefully placing the cup on the saucer, she closed the menu.

'What can we do?' she asked, her voice trembling. 'There's no place to turn, nowhere to go. Between Hiro, the FBI, Carstairs, and Tanaka, we're fucked.'

'Maybe not. Hiro's going to play things very close until he gets his hands on this.' I pulled Marta's address book out of my pocket and tossed it onto the table. 'He wants it so badly he can taste it. There's no way he's going to let some American FBI agent get to it first. I doubt he'll let anyone know about the book until it's in his hot little hands.'

Devon stared at the book for a moment, then picked up her coffee and looked over the rim of the cup around the coffee shop. 'Do you think Hiro was right? Do you think we're being followed?'

I turned and looked over the crowd. They all looked like regulars, not a Japanese face in sight. If there was a cop in the place, I couldn't spot him – or her.

'Let's assume we are.'

She stiffened. More of her coffee sloshed into the saucer in front of her. 'Shit! Shit, shit, shit. I can't believe this is happening to us.' The anger that had driven her to brain Okuba was rising again. Her hands tightened around the cup as she drained the rest of her coffee.

'He's a son of a bitch, that little bastard,' she exclaimed, looking around the restaurant again.

'To hell with Okuba. To hell with all of them.' I reached across the table and gripped her hand. 'No more stupid. We have to get out of the city. But first, we need to be sure that nobody's following us.'

'How are we going to do that if we can't even see them?'

I rubbed my eyes. The bandage over my ear was starting to itch. Tenderly, I probed around the edges with my index finger. She was right. How would we know if we lost whoever was following us, when we weren't even sure they were there in the first place? My head started to hurt.

'Let's walk up to Saks. Inside we'll separate. We'll zig-zag through the store, then leave by different exits. Then we'll meet back at the Rimbaud. Later we can decide where to go.'

'We need clothes, do you think we can risk a trip back to the apartment?'

'No. We'll buy some things at Saks. I've got credit cards, but not much cash. How about you?'

'The same. We'll need some if we're leaving town – how much do you think?'

'A few thousand. I don't have a check with me.'

She hesitated for a few seconds. 'I have mine. I'll stop at my bank after I leave Saks.'

I nodded.

She looked at her watch. 'It's almost ten. Let's do what we have to do, then meet back at the hotel at noon.'

The walk up Fifth Avenue to Saks was a long and cold experience in frustration. We stopped often, pretending to look in every other window, entering one or two stores on every block, hoping to flush out anyone who might be following us. Our actions were to no avail. If, as Okuba had said, we were being followed, it was being done well enough to stymie our clumsy efforts at discovering the tail.

Once inside Saks we kissed, then went our separate ways. Waving away the fragrance girls, I walked to the elevators, looking over my shoulder repeatedly at the entrance. No one had followed us into the store.

In the men's department I selected a pair of jeans, a thick wool sweater, a couple of long-sleeve T-shirts, two changes of socks and underwear, and a forest-green three-layered Gore-Tex anorak. It was a little much for the city. Hell, I looked like a goddamned reject from Robin Hood's merry band when I tried it on. But I liked the color and the way it felt, so I kept it. In the shoe department I added a sturdy pair of hiking boots to my new wardrobe. I paid with a credit card and decided to wear my new clothes. I was ready for whatever might lie beyond the Lincoln Tunnel, including Sherwood Forest.

The thought of leaving New York had lifted my spirits. I felt sure that Marta's book would turn everything around. If it contained half the information Okuba seemed to think it did, all we had to do was figure out the best way to use it. I left Saks through the Fiftieth Street exit, carrying my old clothes in a shopping bag, and hurried east. Swollen clumps of snow, the size of fifty-cent pieces, were beginning to drift from the sky, sticking wherever they hit. It was almost eleven, and my stomach was growling. There was a trendy Italian restaurant on the corner of Madison Avenue, called Paper Moon. I ducked in and sat at the bar where I could keep an eye on the street through the window. The bartender approached, and I ordered an espresso and a couple of biscotti.

When he returned with a steaming cup and a small plate of the crisp almond biscotti, he shook his head. 'Cold as hell out there, isn't it?'

'Yeah, it'll be coming down hard before long.' I stirred the strong black coffee and turned my back to him as I sipped it.

The sidewalk was almost empty. Gusts of wind stirred the litter on the street, swirling it against the curb. The restaurant was warm and smelled of roasting lamb, garlic and rosemary, cheeses and baking bread. Turning to pick up one of the almond cookies, I noticed that the bartender had set a neat snifter of clear liquid beside the plate. I looked up at him, surprised.

'Grappa. On the house, it'll warm you up.'

Without a second's thought I emptied the rough

brandy into my coffee and swallowed a slug. It burned clean and bright all the way down. My eyes watered. I brought the cup back up to my lips, the coffee redolent with the fumes of the grappa. Then I hesitated. The warmth rolling in my belly was a welcome friend. Still, I held the cup to my lips but didn't swallow. A voice in my head explained that it was really quite all right to finish it, after all, it was only one, and I hadn't actually ordered it. I opened my mouth and the grappa stung my tongue. Stung it warmly, a sort of nipping kiss from an old and comfortable lover. The voice droned on: You deserve it – the way things are going, if you don't have reason enough to take the edge off, who does? My throat clenched, and suddenly without warning I sneezed violently, slopping most of the coffee onto the bar.

'Shit!' I jumped up, apologizing to the bartender. 'Clumsy,' I muttered as I brushed off the front of my new anorak, and he wiped up the puddle on the bar.

'You want another?' he asked.

Throwing a ten on the bar, I declined. 'Where's the men's room?' I asked. My hands were shaking. I stuffed them in my pockets so he wouldn't notice.

At the back of the restaurant I found the bathroom and locked the door behind me. Then I stood for a few seconds at the sink, waiting for the shaking to subside. I splashed cold water on my face and rinsed my mouth clean. In the mirror my eyes were clear and blue, the pupils normal. I shuddered when I realized how close I had come to blowing it. A damned sneeze had kept me from getting shit-faced. A sneeze. Not much to rely on. But it was that simple. If I hadn't spilled it, I would have drunk it. And I knew in my heart that one wouldn't have been enough. An old drunk once told me that this shit creeps up on you. At the time, I hadn't understood what he was trying to say, but now I saw the truth in his words. Feeling raw, I headed for the street. I was going to have to be a hell of a lot more careful about what I put in my mouth.

As I walked out, I nodded to the bartender. He shook his head as though I had in some way let him down, then gave me a dismissive half-wave. The snow was beginning to fall in earnest now, slanting on the wind, which was blowing harder out of the northeast. It had begun to collect on the street and the sidewalk. A grizzled old woman hurried past, clutching a large red-and-white striped golf umbrella, which threatened to lift off and carry her away.

On the way back to the hotel, I stopped at a drugstore just down from the Paper Moon and bought some breath mints. Standing inside the door, out of the wind and snow, I unwrapped them and popped two into my mouth. Chew or suck? I couldn't decide which would most effectively remove any lingering trace of the grappa from my breath. A mind is a terrible thing to waste, so I chewed one and sucked the other. As I fumbled the remaining mints into my pocket, I glanced up and noticed a flash of movement across the street in front of an empty store.

A face quickly turned away. The man, dressed in a gray coat, stood with his back to me, looking into a soaped window as though mesmerized by the display. My stomach jumped into my chest. Taking a deep breath, I tried to gather my thoughts. The last thing I wanted was to lead him back to Devon. Then I remembered the gallery was just around the corner. Hurrying, I left the warmth of the drugstore and walked quickly in the direction of the Delmonico, feverishly trying to decide what to do when I got there.

As I turned north on Park Avenue, I realized that I didn't know who was having me followed, Tanaka or Okuba. It could be either. I hesitated outside of a luggage store, and my tail did the same several shops down. The knot of anger inside me pulled tight, stirring my blood. I wanted to confront him and find out who he worked for. Continuing up Park Avenue, I crossed Fifty-ninth Street and entered the Delmonico.

With a quick wave at Gil, the doorman, I hurried through the lobby and used the employee exit, which led to the loading dock. The Delmonico was serviced by a private driveway that led from the dock at the back of the building to Fifty-ninth Street. The heavy iron gate that secured the drive at night stood open. Staying close to the building, I circled up to Park Avenue and peeked around the corner. My man had continued on past the door and taken a position outside the bank half a block north of where I stood. He looked as if he might be waiting for someone inside the bank and had a clear view of anyone who came or left the Delmonico.

Ducking back around the building, I saw Bernie Leibovitz, the man who ran the loading dock, walking out of the mouth of the driveway.

'Hey, Bernie. Over here,' I stage-whispered to him.

'Adrian. Where you been, man? I've got two, t'ree deliveries for you.' A broad smile spread across his homely features. He looked around to see who might be within earshot, then added softly, 'The cops have been askin' 'bout you. You'se okay?'

'Yeah, Bernie, I'm hangin' in there. I got a few problems though. You want to make a quick hundred?'

He rubbed his meaty hands together, and if possible, his smile widened. 'Hey, you know it. Chanukah's around the corner.' He dug a small cigar from his pocket and stuffed it in the side of his mouth. Bernie had worked the docks in Jersey, before retiring from the union with his full package of benefits and coming to work at the Delmonico. He stood about five eleven, with a barrel chest and short, powerful arms that were covered in a thick mat of black curly hair. He rarely wore a hat or a jacket, no matter the weather, and as usual was in his shirtsleeves today. He pushed one hand back across his bald pate, brushing off the snow that had settled there, and asked, 'What's the situation?'

'There's a guy been following Devon and me.' His cigar twitched at the mention of her name. 'He's standing in front of the bank. I want a word with him, but not on the street. Do you think you could get him over to the loading dock so I could have a few moments with him privately?'

His eyes glittered as he considered my proposition. The cigar waved up and down. Together we walked to the corner of the building and peered around it; I pointed him out.

'You mean the Oriental guy? This guy's been bothering Devon? What is he, a Jappo?'

'Yeah. Think you can help me?'

'Does the pope shit in the woods?' He held out his hand, palm up.

I withdrew my last hundred-dollar bill and handed it to him.

'Go wait in my office. I'll be there in a couple of minutes,' he said, striding around the corner, cigar bobbing.

Bernie's office was a small cubicle just inside the loading bay. There were two old metal filing cabinets, and a beat-up steel desk, covered with bills of lading for the various crates and boxes the Delmonico's tenants were shipping all over the world. A fluorescent fixture hung from chains. I pulled the door shut, brushed the snow off my clothes, and after clearing a space, sat on the corner of Bernie's desk. I didn't have long to wait. Within minutes a stream of indignant Japanese filled the loading dock, accompanied by Bernie's grunts. 'Yeah, yeah, tell it to your mother, Mac.'

The door swung in, followed by the man who had been following me. A red-faced Bernie Leibovitz held him by the neck of his coat, with one of the man's arms twisted behind his back.

'My friend here tells me you been following him and the girl that works for him,' Bernie said, kicking the door shut behind him.

The man's eyes grew wide when he saw me. He struggled briefly but in vain. Bernie's grip was powerful.

'Be careful, he might be armed,' I warned.

Bernie chuckled, releasing his grip on the man's coat but keeping our reluctant visitor's left wrist in a hammer lock. 'Now you tell me! Check this,' he said, taking a boxy-looking H&K nine-millimeter out of his back pocket and tossing it onto the desk. 'Our boy didn't want to give it to me, so I had to take it.' He tightened his hold on the man's wrist for emphasis, eliciting a wince and gasp of pain.

'Who are you working for? Why are you following me?'

The man grunted something incomprehensible. He was short, about five foot six, and slender. He looked to be in his mid-thirties. A sprinkling of snow was melting in his dark hair. I didn't recognize him.

'Answer the man,' Bernie ordered, squeezing again.

But the man stood there silently, his eyes full of spite.

'Is he carrying any identification?' I asked.

273

Bernie gave a half-shrug and loosened his grip slightly as he checked the man's pockets.

It happened so quickly, I'm not sure exactly how it went down. One moment Bernie was checking the man's pockets, the next moment the man had whirled around and Bernie was on the floor.

Stunned, I looked to see if Bernie was okay, and in that second the man went for his gun. I pounced on it at the same time, and we both ended up with one hand on it. We wrestled for a few seconds on top of Bernie's desk, scattering bills of lading like confetti. Then Bernie was on his feet, dragging the man off me and literally throwing him against the filing cabinets. The man's feet never touched the floor. He bounced off the steel cabinets, and Bernie hit him on the side of the head with a fist the size of a ham hock, as hard as I've ever seen anyone get hit. The man went down in a limp pile.

'Jeez,' Bernie complained, rubbing his hand. 'The guy used some kung fu shit on me. Never saw it coming.'

'You okay?' I asked. I bent over the man, going through his pockets.

'Yeah,' Bernie answered.

When he saw that I came up empty-handed, he asked what I wanted him to do with the guy.

'He doesn't look like he's going anywhere soon, at least not under his own power. What do you think?'

Bernie's face lit up with a wicked inspiration. 'I got a big empty crate back on the dock. I think I'll put him in it and ship the little fucker back to Tokyo.'

'You're not going to kill him?'

'Nah. I'm all for fair is fair. I'll cut some airholes. He'll make it.'

'Fine with me, but who's going to pay the freight?' I asked, stooping to pick up the gun, which had dropped to the floor during the scuffle. I shoved it into the waist of my jeans, under the anorak.

Bernie's face darkened. He scratched his chest, took a deep breath, then brightened again. 'I'll send him collect, that's what I'll do.'

We walked out of his office and shook hands. 'Thanks, Bernie.'

'Hey, you call me whenever you need help.' He smiled and rubbed his thumb and first two fingers together. 'I'm always available. You tell Devon I asked about her, okay?'

'Sure. Whatever you decide to do with him, be careful.'

'Shit, Adrian, that's my middle name. You think he's got any friends out there?' he gestured toward the street with a jerk of his thumb.

'I'll keep my eyes open.'

'You do that. Remember, call me you need any odd jobs done. I still got friends on the docks over in Jersey.'

Nodding, I made my way off the loading dock and headed down the drive toward Fifty-ninth Street. I looked back over my shoulder once and saw Bernie manhandling a large wooden box in the direction of his office. He looked like he was whistling.

'Devon, it's me.'

'Where the hell are you? I've been worried sick.'

I looked at my watch. It was almost one o'clock. 'I'll explain when I see you. We were followed. Now, listen to me carefully. I'm around the corner in a telephone booth on Fifty-fifth and Park. Grab what you need, nothing more, and leave the hotel. We won't be coming back. I'll be watching you. Walk over to Park and go

275

north. I want you to walk all the way around the block, then back to the hotel. Don't look behind you.'

'You're okay?'

'I'm fine. But it's important that we do this right. You understand so far?'

'I've got it.'

'Good. When you get back to the Rimbaud, get a cab and go to the public library. When I'm sure you're not being followed, I'll meet you in the cafeteria. Now, repeat what I said.'

'You want me to walk around the block, not look behind me, then get in a cab and wait for you in the cafeteria of the public library?'

'Exactly.'

'It sounds a little melodramatic.'

'Do it. Exactly as I've asked. Trust me.'

'It sounds crazy, but if that's what you want me to do –'

'Hurry up, Devon. It's cold out here.'

'It'll take me less than five minutes. Be careful, Adrian.'

'That's my middle name,' I told her, hanging up.

The wind was whipping the snow into a white froth. What had started as a mild shower was now beginning to look like a damned blizzard. I pulled up the hood of my anorak and eased back into the shadowed doorway of a closed shop. The gun was a reassuring weight at the small of my back.

CHAPTER TWENTY-FIVE

Fifteen minutes had passed since I had spoken to Devon, and still no sight of her. Visibility was down to about half a block, and the snow was falling harder. I breathed on my hands, regretting not buying gloves, then stuffed them back into my pockets and stomped my feet. The first week in December was early for this kind of a storm.

The traffic was already snarled with surprised commuters trying to get out of Manhattan while they could still navigate the streets. Pedestrians either leaned into the wind, heads down, collars up, or shuffled along with their backs to it, hurrying as fast as they could toward whatever warmth and shelter their destinations offered. An emaciated homeless man wearing layers of old clothes and a bright red knitted scarf stood erect in the middle of the sidewalk, announcing to no one in particular the end of the world. He was flapping his elongated arms, trying either to fly or to conduct a symphony only he could hear.

Devon emerged from the swirling snow and walked toward me. I backed further into the doorway. As she came abreast of me she looked up and recognized me. Startled, she started to say something, but I shook my head and gestured for her to keep walking. With a frown on her lips, she did.

Just before the snow obscured her retreating figure, a man appeared, following her footsteps. Something about the timing was a little too perfect to be accidental. I waited until he passed, then fell in behind him.

I could no longer see Devon, but when the man turned left off Park Avenue onto Fifty-fifth Street, my suspicions seemed confirmed. It wasn't the sort of day one takes a casual stroll around the block just for a little exercise.

I followed him down Fifty-fifth Street, and when he turned left again onto Madison, I knew I had my man. Which presented a whole new problem – I hadn't a clue what to do about it.

I quickened my pace until I was only twenty or thirty feet behind him. He was approaching the corner unaware of my presence. At that point I caught sight of Devon, who was turning onto Fifty-fourth Street. Whatever I was going to do, it was time to act.

I broke into a trot, the snow muffling my approach, and as he turned the corner I pulled the gun, holding it concealed against my right side. With my left hand I reached in front of me and grabbed the man by the shoulder.

'Excuse me,' I said, planning to ask directions, or some other innocuous question, in the unlikely case he turned out to be an innocent passerby.

He jerked to a stop and spun on me quick as a cat. Startled, I jumped back, recognizing the one face I hated and feared above all others. Yoshio Kotani.

'You,' he hissed.

He swung at me but slipped on the snow-covered sidewalk, missing by inches. Bringing up the gun, I aimed it point-blank at his face.

'Don't move an inch. Don't even fucking breathe,' I told him.

No one was close enough to see what we were doing. My breath came in ragged gulps, but I held the gun steadily pointed at Kotani's mouth.

'What now?' he asked. 'Are you going to shoot me?' A faint smile formed on his lips. He wore on his face the same look of cold disdain that had hardened his features the night he shot Steven.

My finger tightened on the trigger. Something pulled inside me. I looked into his flat brown eyes and wondered if I could.

'Get on your knees and face the building,' I ordered.

He stood there looking at me as though he didn't understand. I waited a second or two, then repeated my order. When he refused to comply a second time, whatever had pulled so tight in my belly snapped. I drew the gun back a few inches and brought the butt down hard on the bridge of his nose, too quickly for him to react. There was a satisfying crunch as I made contact, and Kotani staggered under the blow. Blood spurted, and by the time he had raised his hands to his face I had the gun pointed at his left eye.

'Now!' I ordered again.

Holding his flattened nose cupped in both hands, blood streaming past his lips and dripping from his chin, he sank to one knee. I drew the gun back intending to hit him again when I heard Devon scream. 'Adrian, don't!'

I jerked around and saw that she hadn't caught a cab, as I had asked. She was standing not more than ten feet away.

'What . . .' I cried out.

It was all the diversion Kotani needed. He was up and running along Madison Avenue, back in the direction from which we had just come. Splotches of bright red blood were splattered in the fresh white snow where he had knelt.

'Goddamnit!' I roared at Devon. 'Why? Why didn't you do what I asked?'

Her cheeks were red and her nose was running. She looked cold and shaken. But I was too angry to have much sympathy.

Kotani's figure quickly disappeared into the wall of snow that was falling harder and harder.

'I . . . I just –' she began to explain.

'Later,' I cut her off, turning to chase Kotani. 'I'm going after him. Get over to Dr Fulton's. I'll meet you there,' I called over my shoulder.

The wind tore at me. The snow, which had been wet and soft, was mixed with sleet now, and scoured my face as I ran. Visibility was down to about a hundred feet, traffic on Madison Avenue was at a standstill. I dodged the other pedestrians and moved as quickly as I could, slipping and sliding on the icy patches. I went down hard outside an optical boutique but picked myself up and continued after him. Within four blocks I had Kotani in sight. He turned and saw me gaining, then picked up the pace. Every hundred feet or so his spoor was visible, a bright red flower of blood staining the snow on the sidewalk.

At Fifty-ninth Street he cut in front of a huge semi and crossed to the west side of Madison. I followed. Then he angled back into the middle of the street and continued north, running between the cars and buses that were lined up like they were parked. I stayed with him, neither gaining nor losing ground. I realized how out of shape I'd gotten when I found myself gasping for breath after about seven blocks. Kotani kept up the pace.

We passed Sixty-second Street without slowing. I put the last of what I had into my legs and slowly began to gain on Kotani. On and on we went, into the wind and the snow until I thought I couldn't go any farther.

My chest was burning, my legs starting to get rubbery. The stitches in my scalp felt as though they were about to split open. He was less than fifty feet away now. I could hear him breathing. He crossed Sixty-fifth Street and abruptly stopped. He turned, saw how much ground I had gained, then darted between a van and a limousine and dashed headlong into the Grantham Hotel.

The lobby of the hotel was pandemonium, filled with people escaping the storm. I pushed my way through the crowd just in time to see Kotani run up a sweeping flight of stairs that led from the lobby to the second floor. The second floor of the Grantham was designed for meetings and banquets. There was also an art gallery up there, which fronted on the Madison Avenue side of the hotel and was owned by a friend of mine. I'd made and lost more than a few dollars trading paintings on the second floor of the Grantham Hotel. Kotani had picked the wrong place to try and shake me.

As I started to follow him up the stairs, a fur-clad matron pointed at me and screamed. I looked at her, confused, then realized I still had the gun clutched in my right hand. Luckily, no one paid her the slightest attention, they were all too intent on securing a room, or more importantly a space at the bar. Slipping the gun into the waist of my jeans, I took the stairs two at a time, thinking I had Kotani cornered.

When I got to the top, he was nowhere to be seen. The second floor was quiet; the only voices came from the fire exit at the far end of the hall. The door was propped open, and as I approached I could see two workers arguing about whether to finish the painting job they had started or call it a day on account of the blizzard.

'Hey,' I interrupted. 'I'm looking for a guy who just ran up here. Either of you see him?'

The older of the two shrugged and pointed to a portable compressor they had been using. 'No. Ain't seen or heard nobody. Not with the racket that thing makes.'

Kotani hadn't had a chance to catch the elevator. That left the meeting rooms or the gallery. I walked down the hall to check the gallery first, but my friend must have closed early – the door to his space was locked, the interior dark. That didn't leave too many options. Kotani had to be in one of the four banquet rooms that were across the hall. I took a minute to catch my breath, then checked the clip of the gun.

The doors to each of the banquet rooms were open, but the rooms themselves were dark. Starting at the far end of the hall, I held the gun ready and entered the first room much more cautiously than they did on television. No sign of Kotani. I checked the second, the third. The fourth room was also empty. He couldn't have doubled back past me. So I went back through each room again, slowly, turning on all the lights, checking under tables, behind curtains. Where the hell was he?

On my third trip through the rooms I noticed a red smear on one of the windowsills. I grabbed the window's handle and pulled. It swung open easily, revealing an old iron fire escape bolted to the wall, which descended into a dead-end alley that serviced the hotel. Kotani must have known about the fire escape – the rest had been a piece of cake. I slammed the window shut, then stood there breathing hard, trying to figure out my next move.

I was about to hang it up and head for Dr Fulton's, when from my vantage point at the window I noticed that a police car was parked at the mouth of the narrow alley, blocking the only way out. The cop was standing next to a woman in a black-and-white waitress uniform, under the awning of what I assumed to be the employee entrance. It seemed as though he was doing the talking. The woman stood stiffly beside him, arms crossed, looking up at the frozen sky. From the accumulation on the windshield of his cruiser, it looked like he had been there for a while. It seemed possible to me that he might have unintentionally bottled Kotani up somewhere in the alley. But from where I stood, there was no sign of Kotani.

I put the gun under my anorak and hurried back down the stairs through the lobby to the back of the hotel. By the time I found the employee exit, the cop was in his car backing onto Sixty-fifth Street. The waitress stood for a moment looking after him, then brushed past me without so much as a nod as she walked back into the hotel. Her cheeks were red, and mascara tracked from the corners of her eyes to the sharp line of her jaw. She slammed the door shut behind her, leaving me alone in the alley.

The alley was sheltered from the wind, but the snow falling in heavy spirals covered every exposed surface. I looked for Kotani's footprints, some of his blood, anything that might point to where he was hiding. There were plenty of tracks, unfortunately I couldn't tell Kotani's from my own. Cold and tired, angry at Devon for causing this ridiculous chase in the first place, I was about to give up when I heard a muffled squeal from inside one of the large hotel Dumpsters.

'You gets outta here. This my spot. Don't wants to wake up and find the likes a' you sittin' in my spot.'

This was followed by the sounds of a short scuffle, then a grunt and a dull thud. As though something heavy had fallen into a pit. I waited but heard nothing more.

Circling the Dumpster quietly, gun extended, I made sure that the sounds had indeed come from within it, not behind it. Then I approached the Dumpster and threw back the lid.

Kotani was crouched in the back corner holding a bloody switch blade. His face was a mess. Blood and snot bubbled from his ruined nose, he was breathing hard from his mouth. On the floor of the almost empty Dumpster lay the body of an old man. His wrinkled face was tilted at an odd angle toward the sky, the way a child might hold his head if he were trying to catch the falling snow on his tongue. His throat had been slashed. The gaping wound still leaked the last of his blood onto the old newspapers, orange peels, egg cartons, and other refuse that he had died trying to protect.

'You bastard,' I spat.

'Come and get me, you fucking junkie.' Kotani gestured with his knife, straightening his back but remaining in a fighting crouch.

'Get out of the Dumpster, Kotani,' I ordered, holding the gun on him.

He laughed. Not a chuckle or a small laugh, but a full, deep, belly laugh. As though my order was the most ridiculous thing he had ever heard. I stood there in the snow, listening to that laugh echo around inside the Dumpster, trying to understand what he thought was so funny. He shifted the knife to his left hand and started to reach for something in his coat pocket with his right.

I jerked the gun. 'Don't! I'll fucking blow you away where you stand.'

He laughed again, but froze. 'You're going to have to come in and get me.'

'Don't be stupid. One way or another you're coming out of there.'

'In that case you better go and get some help.'

'Now, Kotani!'

He drew back his foot and delivered a vicious kick to the homeless man's head, sending up a spray of blood. 'Looks kind of like your pal, doesn't he?' Kotani taunted.

Sickened, I lowered the gun a fraction. He saw it and shuffled through the garbage a step closer.

'Don't,' I warned.

He grinned, then shifted the knife back into his right hand and made a sudden grab for his coat pocket.

My gun went off with a deafening roar, magnified by the Dumpster. It bucked in my hand a second, then a third time. I don't remember making a decision to shoot, but at that range I didn't miss. The impact straightened Kotani up and hammered him against the far wall of the Dumpster. He leaned there for a moment, his smile wiped away, his legs splayed at an impossible angle, then he slid down and joined the homeless man, blood gouting from his chest.

I looked around the alley. Nothing stirred. The snow fell in sheets, softening the contours of everything. It was beautiful, something out of a picture book. I could almost hear the individual flakes as they fell. My ears were ringing from the shots, but that didn't seem to affect the sound of the snow. I stepped back from the Dumpster, feeling a little dazed. Then it dawned on me that I had just killed a man. I shoved the gun into my jeans.

Turning quickly, I surveyed the alley again, then looked into the Dumpster and was surprised by how peaceful Kotani and the homeless man looked. Almost as if they were embracing. Minutes went by as I stood there and stared. The snow was beginning to collect on their clothes. I had to tear myself away.

There were a couple of flattened cardboard boxes leaning against the Dumpster. I tossed them on top of the bodies, took a last look around, then closed the lid. Making my way to the mouth of the alley, I stood for a moment looking out at Sixty-fifth Street. I felt like I was standing outside of myself. My ears were still ringing, but otherwise I felt numb. Then suddenly I started to shake, violently. I gagged, then vomited. Coughing, I leaned against the wall and puked, again and again, until I had the dry heaves. I sat on the curb for a moment until I could breathe normally. Cupping my hands, I scooped up some snow and wiped my face. Then I pulled myself up and walked away into the storm.

CHAPTER TWENTY-SIX

Dr Fulton bent and put another log on the fire. Then he turned and faced the couch where I was sitting and shook his head.

'I don't know what happened, but talking about it might help,' he offered.

I looked up at him. He stood, arms folded, in front of the fire, wearing an old green cashmere cardigan. His study was almost too warm, but still, I shivered. Somewhere in the direction of the kitchen, a door slammed, then Devon walked in with a steaming mug of hot chocolate that she had insisted on making. I smiled at her, but I wasn't ready to talk about it. It was too fresh, too new.

A wave of shocking clarity had washed over me at the mouth of the alley. But with it came a moment of soul-wrenching, abject terror. Terror not of being caught, or from any misplaced feelings of guilt or remorse for killing Kotani. Deep down, I didn't see myself as a murderer. The world wasn't going to miss the likes of Yoshio Kotani. No, what shook me to the core was how good it had felt. That moment after shooting him was one of the most crystalline moments of my life. I was sure that I had heard the snow as it hit the ground. A faint, ringing song, like silver wind chimes, only more beautiful. More delicate.

I felt the raw power of it. A few pounds of pressure on the cold trigger – and boom. That was it. No more Kotani. Such an elegant solution to such an ugly problem. I sipped at the hot chocolate, its sweet richness scalding my mouth, while Devon and Dr Fulton waited for me to say something. At some level I knew not to try and explain myself. I didn't understand what I was feeling. How could they be expected to comprehend it? And what if it didn't last?

'This is good,' I told Devon, setting down the mug.

'Well?' She studied me as if I knew what she wanted to hear but was holding it back on purpose.

She and Dr Fulton both seemed worried. Did I look as strange as I felt?

I took a deep breath. 'Listen, there's not much to tell. I caught up to Kotani, he was hiding in an alley. He knifed a bum to keep him quiet. When he saw me, he went for his gun and I shot him. I don't really want to say any more about it.'

'Did you kill him?' Dr Fulton asked.

I nodded.

'Were you seen?' he persisted, staring intently at me.

'No. I don't think so.'

'My God, Adrian. You could have been killed.' Devon eased down beside me and put her hand on my knee.

'I'm fine,' I insisted. 'He got what he deserved.'

I drank some more of the chocolate.

They looked at each other, concern creasing Devon's brow.

After walking out of the alley I had wandered in the snow for almost two hours. I walked far up Madison Avenue, past where the fancy shops and boutiques gave way to bodegas and cheap liquor stores, then back beside the park on Fifth Avenue. By the time I arrived at Dr Fulton's apartment, I understood why Eskimos kiss with their noses; they're too fucking cold to even think about opening their mouths. But even the blizzard conditions hadn't blunted the intensity of the way I felt. It was almost a floating sensation.

'Adrian, are you still with us?' Dr Fulton was squinting curiously at me again.

'Yeah, I'm just a little tired. Why?'

'I was just saying that Devon's brought me up to date on all that's happened, including the break-in at her place and this morning's commotion with Okuba. A nasty bit of business, eh?'

I nodded.

'What are you planning to do about it?'

I shook off the lethargy that seemed to be creeping over me and tried to focus on his question. The room seemed to be getting warmer and warmer, but my insides felt icy and numb.

'We still have this . . .' I began. But when I stood to pull Marta's book out of my hip pocket, the gun slipped out of my waist band and clattered to the floor. Devon's eyes widened. 'Shit!' I stuffed the pistol back into my jeans and handed Dr Fulton the book.

He started to say something, but suddenly I didn't feel so good. My hands started to shake, then my arms and my legs. My entire body began to quiver. I couldn't stop. My mind was clear, but the rest of me seemed to belong to someone else.

Devon gripped my hand. Dr Fulton stepped closer, looming over me.

'I shot the bastard!' I exploded, jerking away from Devon and jumping to my feet. 'He deserved it. Goddamnit, I watched him kill Steven. I had to do it.' My fists were clenching and unclenching, seemingly of their own accord.

The two of them exchanged glances. Devon stood up.

'We believe you,' she said, taking my arm and leading me closer to the fire.

The warmth of the flames radiated out toward me. I raised my trembling hands and held them closer to the open grate, but the heat only went skin deep.

'I enjoyed killing him. It felt so right, so clean. It scared me. I didn't think that's what it would be like – killing a man. So – I don't know – just so right.' I turned my back to the fire and faced them. 'It all happened too fast; it was like watching someone else do it.'

Dr Fulton nodded. 'Well, it's done now. And I'm glad it didn't happen differently. It could be you lying out there in some alley – in that.' He pointed to the window, which revealed a whirling curtain of white snow. 'Don't waste time second-guessing yourself, Adrian. You did what you had to do. If doing it felt good' – he shrugged – 'so be it.'

Devon put her arm around me. 'He's right. Thank God it wasn't you.'

Their words comforted me, but the floating feeling, the euphoria that I had felt, was gone, replaced by a leaden heaviness. I felt tired, and not a little frightened at how unpredictable and utterly unchangeable my actions had turned out to be.

'I have news from Tokyo,' Dr Fulton announced, slowly lowering himself into his wingback chair.

Devon and I waited for him to elaborate, but he had opened Marta's book and seemed to be studying it in earnest. I returned to the couch, picked up the mug, and drank deeply. Devon moved closer to the fire, standing with her back to us.

'Well?' I asked, putting down the mug, having drained it.

Dr Fulton lowered Marta's book from in front of his

face, then cleared his throat. 'Kotani, er, no, Otani, these damned Oriental names can be so confounding. Otani, my friend in Tokyo, called this morning. He's located three of Paul's paintings in a private collection in Osaka. They belong to one of the collectors on your list, Adrian.' He paused, seeming pleased with the news. 'The owner is some big-wheel politician named Mori Miyatomo. Otani doesn't know the paintings are forgeries yet. But he's anxious to know why I'm so interested in them. I've put him off for now.'

'That seals it. Nakamura definitely used Paul's paintings as *za e teku*. Damn, I knew it! He's going to shit when he finds out they were fakes.' I couldn't help laughing out loud at the thought.

Devon turned from the fire. 'Will this Otani help us, if we tell him the truth?'

'Who knows?' Dr Fulton answered. 'His first concern will be Miyatomo.'

'Before we tell Otani, I'd like a little time to think it through,' I said.

Devon nodded. 'Let's be sure we know what we're doing before we act.'

We sat there in silence. The only sounds were the crackle of the fire and the low moan of the wind as it blew across Central Park and wrapped around the building.

Eventually, Dr Fulton stood and, grasping his cane, walked to the door of his study. 'You two make yourselves comfortable. It's time for this old relic to take a little rest. Devon knows where the guest room is – with this snow, it looks like you two are going to be here for a while. Make yourselves at home.' He held up the address book. 'I want to look this over. You don't mind if I take it to my room, do you?'

'Of course not,' I answered.

'Have a good nap,' Devon added.

'Hmmph,' he grumbled. 'One of the few pleasures left at my age. I'll see you in a few hours.'

After he left, Devon joined me on the couch. We sat in front of the fire looking into the flames, listening to the wind. I sank deeper into the couch, and she leaned against me. The study smelled of the applewood Dr Fulton had fed the fire, and soon I was drowsing.

The bum sat up in the Dumpster and untangled himself from Kotani's body. He tried to brush the crusted blood from his filthy clothes, but it refused to come off. He looked around, the snow swirling about his nappy head. His features were not much larger than a child's, with the exception of his eyes, which were enormous, and shockingly green against the dark ebony of his skin. When he saw me, he did a double take and opened his mouth to speak. But no words came out. His facial muscles contorted as he tried again, and again, to tell me something that he seemed to think very important. I climbed into the Dumpster to better hear him. Stepping over Kotani's supine form, I put my hand on his shoulder and leaned close. Then his eyes lit with comprehension. Raising his hands, he pinched together the grotesquely flapping wound in his neck, and whispered my name. 'Adrian,' he said. Then repeated it again. 'Adrian – revenge me.' His voice rang, not unlike the chimes of the falling snow I had heard earlier in this alley. Then something cold fastened itself to my ankle, and I leaped back in terror. Kotani had gripped my leg with his right hand.

His lips were drawn into a wide sneer. 'Sounds like your buddy, doesn't he?'

I screamed and jerked away from him, scrambling out of the Dumpster, landing flat on my ass in the snow. Backing away, I saw that the bum was trying again to tell me some-

thing, while Kotani wrestled to pull his hands away from the gash in his throat so that he couldn't speak. The two of them seemed to be performing a macabre dance, swaying and staggering around the inside of the Dumpster as they grappled with each other. Kotani slipped and fell back. The bum faced me, green eyes bulging, mouth working, and managed one word before Kotani pulled him down. 'Nakamura,' he said emphatically, a ghastly smile stretching his mouth after he had formed the word. Then the lid of the Dumpster came crashing down, and all I heard was the echo of the two of them struggling inside.

I awoke with a start. The fire had burned low, and the light, dim to begin with, had all but faded from the room. According to the clock on the mantel it was just after four o'clock. I was alone in Dr Fulton's study.

'Nakamura!' What the hell had he meant? I sat on the couch and stared into the glowing coals of the fire, letting my mind drift. The room was gloomy, full of too many shadows, perhaps too many memories. I wondered how long Dr Fulton had lived there. From the look of the place, it was far longer than I had been alive. Sitting in that murky room, I thought about Paul's work hanging in a bent politician's collection. Did Nakamura know they were fakes or not? According to the note I had found in Marta's wallet, he was in New York. But for how long? The realization dawned on me that if the forgeries were the key, then Nakamura was the lock. Somehow I had to exploit what I knew. If that didn't work, there was always Marta's book. I sat there for a while longer, then went in search of Devon and Dr Fulton.

Sophie had abandoned ship early, not long after the snow had started to fall in earnest. But before she had left, she had prepared a large pot of beef stew that had been simmering slowly all day. Devon spooned the stew, fragrant with bay leaf and thyme, into a porcelain tureen and sliced a baguette for our dinner. Dr Fulton was already at the table, still preoccupied with Marta's book. He had opened a bottle of Chambertin to go with the stew. My mouth watered as I watched him sip from a large crystal goblet while he sat studying the book with an illuminated magnifying glass.

We ate by candlelight; the mood was quiet, almost surreal. While I had been sleeping in the study, Devon must have set the table. Everything glowed by the light of ten or twenty candles, standing singly and in candelabras placed around the small but elegantly furnished dining room. It seemed somehow appropriate, as if the dining room were a shelter from both the weather and the circumstances that had brought us there. We ate off fine Derby plates with heavy Georgian sterling, and drank from Baccarat crystal. Everything reflected the flickering candlelight. The whole effect was of timeless grace. Devon, seated across the linen-covered table from me, looked like a long-necked beauty Modigliani might have painted. It all seemed too fragile. I tried to etch each detail into my memory, as I doubted I would ever experience anything like the feeling of such sheltered beauty again.

After we had each helped ourselves to some of the stew, Devon broke the silence.

'I thought we were getting out of the city. Where are we going?'

'Nowhere in this weather. It's like Antarctica out there,' I answered.

'Adrian's right. Wait until tomorrow – you wouldn't get far tonight,' Dr Fulton added.

Devon sipped her water, then nodded. I poked at the stew. Dr Fulton watched us eat but didn't touch the food on his plate. He drank his wine, looking old in the flickering light.

'I've been thinking about this politician, Miyatomo,' I said, spearing a hunk of beef with my fork. 'I think we should wait to call Otani – put some pressure on Nakamura before we go public with the forgeries.'

'What kind of pressure can we put on him?' Devon asked.

I shook my head. 'I'm not sure. But now that we know for certain about the *za e teku*, we have a few options that we didn't have before. We know something Nakamura doesn't know. Those forgeries are a potential time bomb. Imagine Miyatomo's reaction if he finds out that Nakamura bought him off with a fake. How much would it cost Nakamura to regain face?'

'How do you know Nakamura didn't tell Tanaka to buy forgeries in the first place?' Devon asked.

'I don't *know* for sure. But it doesn't add up. Why would Nakamura risk losing so much face? I think the forgeries were Tanaka's idea – a scam within a scam.'

'Assuming you're right – and that's an enormous assumption – how are you going to pressure Nakamura?'

Devon's questions were beginning to annoy me.

'By illuminating the problem for him, then offering a solution,' I answered sharply.

'You're assuming that Nakamura will believe you,' Dr Fulton said, over the rim of his goblet. 'The Japanese aren't known for trusting outsiders.'

Devon nodded her agreement.

'It would take some selling,' I admitted.

'Let me pose another question.' Dr Fulton put down his wine. 'What kind of solution can you offer him?'

'Time. Time to straighten out the mess before it becomes a public scandal.'

He raised his eyebrows. 'And for this – you think he'll be grateful?'

'I don't want his gratitude. I want him to make Tanaka back off. It's the only card we hold – other than the book. I don't see any other options.'

We lapsed back into silence. I had thought leaving New York would buy us time to decide how best to use Marta's book. With both Okuba and Tanaka breathing down our necks, it had seemed the only smart thing to do. Now I wasn't so sure. Finding even a few of McHenry's paintings had changed things. If Nakamura really didn't know they were forgeries, maybe I could talk us out of this dilemma. I needed to look him in the eye and give it a shot – before he left town. If he didn't believe me, then I could threaten him with Marta's book. But threatening a man like Nakamura wasn't something I looked forward to. No – I'd much rather finesse him.

'What do you think about the book?' I asked Dr Fulton.

'Can't make hide nor hair out of it,' he said. 'But it would be easy enough to copy.'

'Why would we want to do that?' Devon asked.

He shrugged, then held up his wine and looked at it in the candlelight. 'Seems to me that we have two people who want the book. Okuba wants it now – Nakamura will want it when he finds out about it. Can't give one book to both of them. Wouldn't do much good to act like King Solomon and offer to cut it in half. Don't you think we'd be better off with two books? A matching set?' He emptied the goblet and chuckled.

He was enjoying this game a little too much. It reminded me of how he had acted with Tanaka. I looked at Devon to see if she had noticed.

'Dr Fulton, are you being serious?' she asked him.

He looked up, surprised. 'Of course I am.'

After we cleared the table we sat in the study and talked about it.

'The book came from Tiffany's – leather-bound, quality paper, they've been making them for years,' Dr Fulton explained. 'I'm sure they still have them in stock. The writing would be simple enough to copy. The trick would be to get this right.' He held up the book and pointed out various smudges and scrapes on the leather cover, both front and back. Then he opened it up and showed us where something had been spilled, leaving a brownish stain across several pages. 'Nothing too difficult, if you know what you're doing. Assuming of course that Tiffany's does have the book in stock.'

'How long would it take?' I asked.

'A day, two at the most. I think I have everything I need right here in the apartment.' He rubbed his chin. 'Give me two days and even Marta wouldn't be able to tell the books apart.'

'You sound just like Paul McHenry, bragging about his abilities,' I said.

'Bragging!? I'm telling you a simple fact, my boy. When I say no one will be able to tell my work from the original, you can put it in the bank.' He shook his head and frowned. 'Bragging,' he muttered.

I walked to the window, thinking about it. The snow was still falling hard, but the wind had died down considerably. In the reflection of the glass, I watched Devon put another log on the fire. Dr Fulton was sitting in his chair, fumbling with his pipe. Kotani and the bum lay at the bottom of the Dumpster. I wondered where Tanaka and Nakamura were. Revenge? Was there really such a thing? I had wanted to believe so. Especially as I watched my bullets slam Kotani against the steel wall of the Dumpster. But it hadn't brought Steven back. Then I thought about the man Bernie Liebovitz had crated up at the Delmonico. I hoped that he and Kotani were missed by now. It would be nice to think that the other side, or sides if you counted them, were wondering what the hell had happened to the two of them. Time was running out. There was no percentage in waiting for Tanaka to make the next move. I had to get to Nakamura.

Turning back into the room, I nodded to Dr Fulton. 'Let's do it. We'll make a second copy of the book, then see if we can't play both ends against the middle.'

A match flared, illuminating his smile as he lit his pipe. 'Indeed.' He nodded, exhaling a gray cloud. 'Both ends against the middle – sounds rather Sicilian.'

CHAPTER TWENTY-SEVEN

We had gone to bed separately, each of us occupying one of the twin beds in Dr Fulton's guest room, but after about an hour Devon crawled in with me. I was glad for the company, even though she seemed to think the blanket was solely her property. We slept wrapped around each other, with my ass hanging out of the covers freezing for most of the night. I don't think I dreamt at all, except for a brief nightmare about gluteal frostbite. It was almost seven by the time the first gray light of day seeped through the plantation-shuttered windows and woke me. Devon was spooned against my glacial backside, which was just beginning to thaw. She mumbled something as I crawled out of bed, then rolled over and pulled a pillow over her head. I slipped on my clothes and went to make coffee.

I was surprised to find Dr Fulton in the kitchen, dressed and looking as if he had been up for hours. Lined on the counter in front of him were six or seven cups of coffee that varied in color from a reddish brown to a deep black. He had several pieces of paper arranged in front of the cups and was using an eyedropper to stain the paper with various mixtures of the coffee. Marta's book was opened to the pages that had been marked by a spill. Each time he stained a piece of paper he would blow on it, then hold it up to Marta's book to compare results. He made notes on a small pad as he worked. I observed, unnoticed I thought, until he barked at me to get out of his light.

'Make yourself useful and fix us a fresh pot of coffee,' he added.

'Should I make it any special way?' I asked, pointing at the cups lined up on the counter.

'What do you mean?' he replied, not looking up from his notes.

'For the experiment – do you want it dark, or light?'

'Follow the instructions on the can, Adrian. I want to drink it.'

Embarrassed, I did as he asked. When we both had steaming mugs of strong black coffee in front of us, he put down the eyedropper and grinned at me.

'I've got it.' He gestured at the pad. 'Now all we need is the book. Can't do anything about that until the stores open.' He picked up the mug and took a swallow. 'Tell me about this Detective Carstairs. Devon said when he showed up at the hospital, he alluded to the forgeries. How much do you think he knows?'

'He's a homicide detective – works out of the Fifth Precinct. He didn't actually mention the forgeries, but he asked about some of the materials in Paul's studio.'

As we drank our coffee I told him all about my hospital visit with Detective John Carstairs. When I finished, he shook his head and got up to refill his cup.

'Sounds like a smart cop. City could use a few more like him,' he said, picking up Marta's book and disappearing behind it.

I raised my eyebrows and tried to think of a nasty retort, but it was too early. 'How long before we hear back from Otani?'

'A day, two maybe. I lit a pretty good fire under the old boy.'

Devon wandered in, her eyes half open, tucking her hair into a ponytail.

'Morning,' she said, stifling a yawn. 'Still snowing?'

I walked to the window to check. 'Not much.'

It was a gray and windy day, but the snow had diminished to an occasional flurry. The park was glazed in a pristine white mantle.

By nine o'clock Devon and I had showered and dressed. The bandage over my ear had come loose, the split in my scalp was puckered and angry-looking; the thick black stitches that held it together resembled the seam of a baseball. Devon had found some adhesive tape, and while I sat on one of the twin beds, she fashioned a new bandage, which itched so badly that it was about to drive me crazy.

'Keep your hands off it,' she ordered. 'You'll just make it worse.'

'Right, Nurse Ratched. Isn't there someone else on the ward you could torture?'

'Nobody as fun as you,' she said, smiling. She plopped down on the bed opposite the one I sat on, and her smile faded. 'I want to say something. It's important to me, okay?' Her voice grew serious.

'Sure.'

'I'm sorry about yesterday. I should have done as you asked. I put us both in a bad spot. It won't happen again.'

'Forget about it,' I said magnanimously, starting to get up. 'It's done with, don't worry about it.'

'Wait!' she said sharply. 'I'm not finished.'

I sat back down, surprised.

'Kotani was following me, not you. Obviously both Tanaka and Okuba know all about me. I'm in as much danger as you are.'

She paused and waited for me to respond.

301

'I don't doubt it,' I said, scratching at the bandage, which suddenly itched more. 'I'm sorry to have gotten you into this mess.'

'That's not what I mean.' Standing, she paced to the dresser, then continued. 'I'm in this by my own choice. You didn't force me to do anything I didn't want to do. No matter how this turns out, I won't blame you. But I don't want you to think that because of what happened yesterday I'm willing to sit on the sidelines while you go charging around trying to fix everything. I have as much at stake now as you. Wherever you go, I go. We're a team. We do this together. Agreed?'

A team? I pulled at the edge of the bandage.

'Devon, we've been through this before, I don't want to see you get hurt.'

'It's a little late for that sentiment.'

'Yeah, maybe late, but I can't believe we're discussing it again. This topic is getting old, Devon. Would it do any good to argue with you?'

'No.'

'Of course not. Why the hell am I wasting my breath? You're without a doubt the most bullheaded woman I've ever met.' I rubbed my eyes, then looked up. She was standing by the dresser looking down at me, her face expressionless. 'Fine. You've convinced me. We don't need to talk about this again. We're a team.'

Satisfied, she turned away and took a deep breath, then exhaled.

When she turned back I added the only thing I could think of to say, 'I love you, Devon Berenson. You damn well better not get yourself killed.'

She nodded at me. 'I won't, Adrian. You have my word on it.'

★

Later, we sat watching Dr Fulton practice Marta's handwriting. He was seated at his desk in the study with several sheets of foolscap spread in front of him. Next to the desk, he had opened a brass-bound mahogany case the size of a small steamer trunk. He referred to it as his 'toolbox.' I couldn't imagine how he had gotten it into the study – it looked like it weighed more than the three of us combined. Its interior was fitted with drawers and cubbyholes. It looked like the world's largest or at least most expensive fishing-tackle box. It was filled with jars and tubes of paints, brushes, bottles of solvents and lacquers, varnishes and emulsions, as well as scalpels and probes and shiny steel hand tools of varying functions and sizes. It was a traveling version of Paul McHenry's studio, and must have cost Dr Fulton a small fortune.

One drawer had been pulled out of the case and set on top of the desk. It seemed to contain about a thousand pens, twenty or thirty of which were laid out on the desk, while Dr Fulton compared the marks they made to the writing in the address book. His blocky hands moved with the confident grace of a surgeon or a musician, as he sorted and sampled the various pens. He wore a pair of headband-mounted magnifying lenses, the sort that jewelers use, and he kept up a heated conversation while he worked, mostly complaining that Sophie was late and that she damn well knew he expected her at eight-thirty on weekdays, not at lunchtime.

When she came in at nine-fifteen to greet him, he grumbled and complained to her, but he was clearly glad to learn that the weather hadn't caused her any significant trouble.

At nine-thirty Dr Fulton poked his head up from his work and asked who was going to go to Tiffany's to buy a matching address book. I volunteered, but Devon brought us up cold.

'Assuming we've been followed for quite a while now, doesn't it seem to you that if anybody was looking for us they would keep an eye on this place?' she asked.

Dr Fulton took off the magnifying lenses.

'Shit!' I slapped myself on the forehead. 'I wasn't thinking clearly when I sent you here.'

She said nothing.

Dr Fulton stood and stretched beside the desk. 'In that case, I'm afraid you two need to stay out of sight for the time being.' He looked at his watch. 'I'll go buy the book. I'll pick up some other things I need while I'm out.'

He called downstairs to the doorman and asked him to summon a cab. Then Devon helped him on with his overcoat and off he went, clutching his cane.

Stepping to the hearth, I began building a small fire on the grate. By the time the kindling caught and the first flames were licking the split applewood logs I had stacked, Devon was standing at the window seemingly absorbed in her own thoughts. I wandered over to Dr Fulton's desk. His practice sheets were spread over the top, Marta's book propped up beside them. I studied his work with growing admiration.

'He's really going to pull this off. Look at it, you can't tell the writing apart.' I held one of the sheets so that Devon could see it.

She swiveled her head to look. Then she scratched at her nose. 'I'm so damned turned around I don't even know what day it is. It seems like Thanksgiving was a month ago.'

'It's only Wednesday, Devon. Tanaka thinks he's getting Aynsley Bishop's Monet by the end of the week.'

She shook her head as if to clear it, then looked again

at the paper I was holding. 'What are we going to do when he finishes?'

The rough outline of a plan had been forming in my head ever since Dr Fulton suggested copying the book, but it was only the first step, and there were too many variables to really even call it a plan. It was actually a wild gamble. But I outlined it for her anyway.

'Time is running short. Sitting and waiting for Tanaka or Okuba to make the next move won't get us anywhere. I'm going to go ahead and set up a meeting with Nakamura.'

'Are you crazy?'

'Just listen to me for a minute. I'm the only one who can keep the forgeries under wraps long enough for him to do something about them.' I took a deep breath and continued. 'Nakamura is here in New York – just a few blocks away. I don't know how long he'll be here. I need to go and see him. Convince him that he needs us.'

'You're dreaming, Adrian,' she said, her voice loud. 'I thought you said we were through with acting stupid. Shit! Nakamura is never going to side with us over Tanaka. Even if he thought the paintings were originals. For all we know, he told Tanaka to buy fakes.'

'It's not a matter of Nakamura taking our side over Tanaka. It's simply in his own best interests to keep the forgery scam quiet.'

'So, you think you can just threaten him, and he'll make Tanaka back off?' She was practically shouting.

'You have a better idea?' I shot back at her.

'As a matter of fact –'

Sophie poked her head into the study and cleared her throat.

Devon tried to reassure her, lowering her voice. 'Everything is all right, Sophie.'

'Well, if you need anything, call me,' Sophie said, glaring at me as she retreated from the room.

'Let's stop shouting,' Devon suggested.

'Fine! You were about to offer a better idea.'

'What would happen if you just told Tanaka to go to hell? Show him a copy of Marta's book – tell him you'll arrange for the authorities to get it if he lifts a hand against you.'

I shook my head. 'You've been watching too many movies, Devon. Tanaka plays for keeps. He'd bide his time, then take a shot at us when we least expected it. You want to live with that hanging over you?'

'Shit! Shit! Shit!' She stepped closer to the fire. 'This is insane. Why don't we just run away? Go to Tahiti – someplace they can't find us.'

We stood quietly for a few moments.

'I know,' she said, shaking her head. 'They'd find us.'

'We have to try and get to Nakamura while he's still here in New York. We'll never have a better chance.'

'I don't see the difference between threatening Tanaka with the book and threatening Nakamura with the forgeries.'

'I won't threaten Nakamura – I'll try and convince him. We didn't cause his problem, but we can help him solve it.'

She looked up at me, her mouth hard. 'You're sure?'

I nodded.

'How do you plan on getting to him?'

'I'll call Marta, have her set it up. If she balks, I'll threaten to tell Tanaka about the book.'

She thought for a moment. 'What if she goes to Tanaka and tells him the truth anyway?'

'Would you?' I asked.

'No. I don't think so.'

'If push comes to shove and Nakamura doesn't believe me, or doesn't seem to care about the forgeries – we show him the book. I'll make sure he understands that if anything happens to us, a copy of it will be forwarded to the authorities along with information about the fakes. Hopefully he'll think we're less trouble alive and in one piece than dead and the whole story made public. I don't see any other way. Either we come to terms with Nakamura, or we run from these bastards for the rest of our lives.'

Devon looked grim. 'What about Okuba?'

'Fuck him! You heard what he said. He'd sell us out in a second. Force us to testify, regardless of the danger it would put us in. He's not any better than Tanaka. I'd rather take my chances dealing with Nakamura myself than hand our future to Okuba. If we make a deal with Nakamura, we're out of the woods. Okuba can't prove anything, no matter how much he thinks he knows. Plus we'll have Dr Fulton's copy of the book if we ever need it.'

'What about Marta? What do you think they'll do to her if we tell them about the book?'

I looked down at my feet. An uncomfortable moment passed.

'I don't know,' I said, finally. 'We have enough to worry about without adding her to the list. If she's smart, she'll get the hell out of town after she sets up the meeting.'

I shook my head, then added, 'I'm going to have one shot at Nakamura, either I convince him or . . .' The rest of the thought caught in my throat.

Devon started to say something but stopped and simply nodded. The sheet of foolscap shook in her hand.

There were a thousand holes in my plan. Hell, it

sounded pretty far-fetched in my own ears. But the alternatives seemed even worse. I threw another log on the fire and tried to relax. Nakamura was going to do whatever he wanted. All I had to do was sell him on wanting to do the right thing – and selling had always been my strong point. Only this time there wouldn't be any shortcuts.

It was almost midnight by the time Dr Fulton put the finishing touches on the phony address book. I called Marta anyway.

She answered quickly, sounding wide awake.

'I don't know what you've done, but the shit is coming down hot and heavy over here.' Her voice was tight.

'Is Nakamura still in town?' I asked, hoping that she was referring to Kotani's unexplained disappearance.

She hesitated, then answered, 'Why?'

'I want to see him, but I don't want Tanaka to know about it.'

'What!? Are you out of your fucking mind?'

'Set it up for me, Marta. If you don't, I'll go public with what I know about your book.'

'What the hell do you know about my book?'

'I know enough to wager you haven't told Tanaka anything about it.'

Only the sound of her breathing convinced me that she was still on the line. The silence lengthened.

'Marta –'

'Give me a minute, I'm thinking.'

'There's nothing to think about.'

'Easy for you to say. If I help you – what's in it for me?'

'You happy with the way things are?' I asked.

Silence again. The very existence of her book had

convinced me that she wasn't, but I wanted to hear it from her lips.

'Are you?' I repeated.

'What if I'm not? I don't see that you could do anything about it.' Her voice was brittle.

'If you help me, Marta, I'll do what I can to help you.'

'That's a laugh. You can't even help yourself.'

'Gotten any better offers lately?'

She laughed, a bitter cackle that sent shivers down my spine. 'I'll think about it. Call me back in half an hour. I'll give you my answer then.'

Dr Fulton and Devon watched me hang up.

'I'm to call back in half an hour.' I shrugged. 'She'll let me know then.'

'If you're planning on helping that bitch, you're going to have a major problem with me,' Devon said, glaring at me, her arms crossed.

'Right now, I'm only worried about helping us. She picked her partners. Right now she may not like her options, but she's going to have to deal with the situation on her own.'

Devon nodded and some of the heat went out of her. She walked over and put her arm around me.

I tried to think of how many ways Marta could double-cross us. When I got to ten, I quit counting.

'Take a look, tell me what you think,' Dr Fulton said, holding out the phony book.

He had scuffed and nicked the binding, using a scalpel and diamond paper, so that it looked exactly the same as the original. The coffee mixture that he had experimented with worked perfectly to reproduce the stains on the inside, and the way he had copied Marta's writing was uncanny, down to the smudges and crossed-out corrections. He had carefully dog-eared the pages where it was appropriate and had dirtied and aged the whole thing, using a weak solution of acid mixed with fireplace soot.

'You're right,' I said, handing it back to him. 'Even Marta won't be able to tell the difference.'

He beamed with pride. 'Not quite the same as creating a "Monet," but not a bad piece of work, if I do say so myself.'

He set the book down on his desk, then sat in his chair and fooled with his pipe.

At quarter to one, I called Marta back.

'I can't guarantee you that Tanaka won't be there, but Nakamura has agreed to see you at the Seventy-second Street house. He said to be there promptly at eleven tomorrow morning. I told him that you had something important to say and asked him not to tell Tanaka you're coming. That's the best I can do for you.' She hesitated. 'You owe me now, Adrian. If it comes down to it, I'll expect you to remember.'

'You can bet on it, Marta. I remember everything. You might want to make yourself scarce tomorrow.'

'Is that some kind of threat?'

'Take it however you want.'

'I can handle myself – you're the one with problems, Adrian.'

She waited a moment, then hung up the phone without saying goodbye.

Turning, I told Devon, 'It's on. Nakamura's expecting us at eleven in the morning.'

The news seemed to surprise her, as if she had expected Nakamura to refuse my request to see him. She looked away for a moment, then faced me. 'Okay,' she said. 'It's best that we get it over with.'

Dr Fulton looked at the two of us, his face lined and tired. He shook his head. 'I wish I could think of a better way.'

'If you do, tell me. I'm still open to suggestions,' I replied.

He shrugged. 'Well, at least this way I'll be able to return Aynsley Bishop's Monet sooner than I thought.'

'That's comforting.'

He laughed. 'Tanaka is going to be awfully disappointed – I think he took a shine to it.' He thought for a moment, drawing on his pipe, then frowned. 'Now I'm going to have to think up a damned good reason for charging Aynsley the exorbitant fee I quoted her.'

Somehow I had the feeling Dr Fulton didn't need to do anything of the sort.

'Let's get some rest,' Devon suggested, pulling me toward the door.

'Good idea,' I said, allowing her to lead me out of the room.

'This Nakamura is liable to be far worse than Tanaka,' Dr Fulton said, stopping us in our tracks.

We both turned.

He was holding his pipe, his face wreathed in an ominous fog of gray smoke. 'You must treat him like the most dangerous of animals.'

Devon and I looked at each other. He was preaching to the choir.

CHAPTER TWENTY-EIGHT

The steps hadn't been shoveled, and the snow that lay almost six inches deep on top of them had crusted over with ice in the twenty-four hours since the storm had ended. Devon and I held hands and carefully crabbed our way up. Stan answered the door of Tanaka's townhouse, dressed today in an all-black, secret-agent ensemble. Turtleneck, wool trousers, crepe-soled half-boots, and a black beret. He looked like a Japanese version of the man from U.N.C.L.E., the blond one. It worried me that I was getting used to his outlandish taste in clothes. I was seeing more of Stan than I thought was healthy.

Regarding us solemnly, he stood aside and motioned us in.

'Your coats,' he said, holding out his arms. No bows today.

His hard eyes flicked behind us as two men I had never seen before approached from the interior of the house.

I nodded to Devon, who was looking at Stan suspiciously, and we handed over our coats.

'We're going to have to search you,' Stan announced, tilting his head at the two men behind us.

With an economy of motion, they rather politely but efficiently patted us down. Finding nothing that resembled a weapon, they nodded at Stan. Devon glanced at me – it was at her insistence that I hadn't carried the gun. It was safely tucked away in Dr Fulton's guest room. Now I had guns stashed at Devon's apartment, and at Dr Fulton's, but was standing in the lions' den without so much as a penknife. You're here to sell, I reminded myself. Warming up, I flashed one of my best smiles at Stan. He showed me his teeth, but his eyes remained flat.

Satisfied that we offered little in the way of a physical threat, Stan led us into the grand reception room I had last entered with Steven on the night I found McHenry's body. The Gauguin hung as it had before over the same two chairs, only this time it was Devon who nodded appreciatively.

'Please sit,' Stan said, pointing at the two chairs. 'I'll announce you.' He seemed to have taken over Kotani's position, and aside from his predilection to dress absurdly, he brought a more formal style to the role of gangster-butler.

The two men who had searched us took up positions at either end of the room, standing with their backs to the walls. Stan retreated in the direction from which we had entered.

Devon sat stiffly; only her eyes moved as she contemplated the richness of Tanaka's house.

'You okay?' I asked for the two hundredth time since the day had started.

'Yeah,' she answered, her voice small. Her hands were clasped in her lap, her back was rigid.

'Relax, it's going to be fine,' I promised, not at all sure that I was right.

After we had waited a little more than twenty minutes, a tall, dapper man carrying a briefcase entered the room through a door that led toward the rear of the house. He looked a little like Fernando Llamas, with tan skin and swept-back salt-and-pepper hair. He was accompanied by two large, swarthy thugs, and addressed them in

Spanish as they crossed the Persian carpet. Scarcely glancing our way, the three of them seemed in high spirits as they loped through the room. As they passed, the two men posted to keep watch on us straightened and seemed to come to attention but remained silently on station. Devon looked at me, eyebrows raised.

'I don't know,' I told her. 'Maybe they're Colombians. They sure looked pleased with themselves.'

'What were they saying?'

'It was in Spanish, how would I know?'

She tugged at the sleeves of her sweater, then the cuff of her jeans. We were both wearing our new purchases from Saks. This was day three in the same clothes, and Devon was not pleased about it.

'Do you think Marta's here?' she asked.

'I warned her,' I answered. 'Why?'

'Just curious,' she said, reaching under the neck of her sweater and adjusting the strap of her bra. Then she stood to look closer at the Gauguin.

'Did Paul McHenry paint this?'

'No! Now will you please sit down and give me a chance to think.'

'Ease up, Adrian. You don't have to bite my head off.'

She sat back down and started fiddling with her earrings. I was beginning to think the whole thing was some kind of freaky déjà vu experience. Steven had been unable to sit still as we waited for Tanaka, and now Devon was acting the same way. My mouth suddenly felt dry. I wondered where Stan had gone. Would we be offered any tea?

We sat nervously waiting for another forty-five minutes. It was almost noon by the time Stan escorted us up to the second floor and showed us into a room I had never seen before.

It wasn't a large room, maybe twenty feet deep and twenty-five across, carpeted in a thick wall-to-wall Berber. Against one wall was a platform raised some six or seven inches above the floor. On the platform, which was carpeted like the rest of the room, stood two large upholstered armchairs separated by a low, round mahogany table, on top of which sat a carafe of water, two glasses, and a large crystal ashtray. Facing the platform were six smaller upholstered armchairs arranged in a semicircle. Stan directed us to sit in the two center chairs facing the platform and wait. The two men who had frisked us took up positions behind us against the wall. To our left, opposite the door, were four heavily draped windows, which I assumed looked out on Seventy-second Street. The strange room was cool and silent; a slight odor of stale cigarette smoke lingered in the air.

We sat waiting in that quiet room for what seemed like an eternity. Devon took my hand and held it tightly, but we spoke only in whispered fragments, uncomfortable with the two guards standing so close behind us. If keeping us waiting was a considered effort at throwing us off balance, it was working. I had a lump the size of a boulder in my chest.

Finally, without fanfare or ceremony, in walked a tiny little man who could have been anywhere from fifty years old to a hundred and fifty. He was the color of caramel, and although he wasn't heavily wrinkled, there was a translucent glow about his skin that made him look ancient but healthy. Devon and I both stood as he walked toward the platform. He wore a well-cut business suit and miniature oxfords that had been buffed to a bright sheen. He hopped up onto the platform and took a seat in one of the armchairs. Looking at us with a kindly smile, he cleared his throat and gestured for us to sit.

'What can I do for you today?' he asked in a melodious voice, his English precise but heavily accented. Without waiting for an answer, he removed a gold cigarette case from his coat pocket and took out an unfiltered cigarette. Lighting it with a matching gold lighter, he waved away the smoke and coughed. 'I hope my nasty habit doesn't offend you. It's not very popular these days, is it? But we older people must be allowed our pleasures. Don't you think?' he addressed Devon.

She nodded. 'Yes, if it makes you happy, you should smoke.'

He peered intently at her with his clear brown eyes, then looked at me. 'You haven't answered my question. What can I do for you?'

He wasn't at all what I had expected. He looked like a kindly old grandfather, who could be trusted with your children as well as your life savings. Maybe this wasn't going to be so difficult after all.

'Mr Nakamura,' I began, 'we're here to do business.'

He smiled. 'What kind of business would you like to do?'

'The kind of business that will save you much time and energy. Possibly it will save you a great deal of face.'

He looked vaguely curious but less than impressed by my opening. I continued.

'It has come to my attention that Mori Miyatomo is in possession of several paintings that I sold Mr Tanaka.'

At the mention of Miyatomo's name, Nakamura's eyes focused on mine. He sat forward and listened carefully.

'I don't think Mr Miyatomo knows that these paintings are forgeries.' I paused, but Nakamura didn't react.

'Mr Tanaka knew they were fakes when he purchased them from me – for a fraction of what originals would cost. But I doubt that he has shared this important information with Mr Miyatomo. I became worried when news of an impending investigation by Tokyo museum officials reached me. These museum people are looking at Miyatomo's collection. I wanted to help you forestall any potential embarrassment by making sure that such an investigation didn't catch you by surprise.'

'Me?' he asked.

'It's my understanding that these forgeries in Miyatomo's collection were a gift from you.'

He frowned. 'Continue.'

'Normally, I would have asked Mr Tanaka to pass this information along. However, due to circumstances beyond my control, Mr Tanaka has had my partner killed and no longer seems willing to deal in good faith with me. To the contrary, Mr Tanaka is trying to strongarm me. He's trying to extort from me a painting by Monet – a painting that is well beyond my reach.'

Nakamura sat back and took a deep drag from his cigarette. He looked from me to Devon and then back again. I had his attention now.

'A most interesting story. Your concern for me is touching. Am I correct in assuming you wish me to intervene with Tanaka-san on your behalf?'

'Yes, sir. If I am of service to you.'

He smiled broadly. 'Service to me? I'm curious about this service.'

'There are several ways that I could help you. First, I would need to know exactly what you have done with all of the forgeries. Then I could intervene on your behalf – help replace the fakes with originals. Keep the museum from making this problem public knowledge.'

His smile faded. 'Perhaps. Describe to me in detail this painting business which you say you conducted with Tanaka-san.' He crossed his ankles and squinted at me.

'I met him through a woman named Marta Batista. After she introduced us – about three years ago – he started buying the work my partner produced for him. There were fake Renoirs, Degas, Pissarros, and others. Mr Tanaka would tell us what artist he wanted, what subject, then we would create it. He always seemed very pleased with the results.'

'How did he pay you?' Nakamura asked.

'Usually by wire transfer. Twice in cash.'

'This incident beyond your control?'

'One of my partners, the artist, was murdered during a robbery. As a result, I was unable to deliver a painting Mr Tanaka had commissioned. I offered to return his money – but he wasn't interested.'

He nodded and took another drag. 'I'm sorry for the loss of your partner. Now, where did you deliver these paintings?'

'Here, in New York. Mr Tanaka arranged the shipping to Japan.'

His eyes narrowed. 'Did Tanaka-san ever discuss what he was doing with the artworks?'

'No, sir. But I've done a little research – there are others in the same position as Miyatomo.' I hoped like hell there were. 'These forgeries are a time bomb waiting to explode.'

Nakamura pursed his lips and looked down at the floor. Then abruptly he stood.

'Please wait, I'll be back shortly.'

He stubbed out the cigarette, addressed the guards in Japanese, then smiled at us and left the room.

As soon as he had gone, Devon dug her elbow into my ribs and whispered, 'Good job! What do you think?'

I shook my head. 'I don't know what to make of him. We got his attention, though.'

She grinned and shook her head. 'You could sell ice to the Arabs. I think he's going to help us.'

I looked hard at her. 'Eskimos. It's – ice to the Eskimos.'

'Whatever. You were very persuasive.'

Nakamura didn't keep us waiting long. Not ten minutes had passed before he walked back into the room followed by Tanaka and another man I had never seen before who carried with him a black leather briefcase. The room shrunk the second Tanaka entered. He swaggered over to the platform and sat down next to Nakamura, looking down at me with his nose slightly wrinkled, as if he smelled something sour.

The third man, younger than both Tanaka and Nakamura, took a seat at the end of the semicircle to my right, and crossed his legs at the knee. He seemed to regard our little assembly with disdain. A slight pinching together of his eyebrows, a pursing of his moist lips. He had the pear shape and wet protruding eyes of a desk-bound bureaucrat, a functionary who lived by numbers and statistics. His eyes glinted with self-righteous malice, as though someone had put him in charge of the gas chambers and he damned well meant to do the job as efficiently as possible. He deferred to Nakamura, however, with a humility bordering on obsequiousness. As vicious and dangerous as Tanaka had proven himself to be, this ass-kisser, with his fish eyes and briefcase, seemed infinitely more poisonous.

'I believe you know Mr Sellars – have you met Miss Berenson?' Nakamura addressed Tanaka, who nodded. 'Mr Sellars has come to offer me his help. In return, he wants me to intervene with you on his behalf. It seems he thinks you are treating him unfairly.'

Tanaka smiled at his boss, his face and demeanor relaxed. Then, in Japanese, he spoke at some length and waved in my direction with the back of his hand as though he were shooing away an annoying pest. Nakamura listened impassively, nodding and smiling at his protégé. The longer Tanaka spoke, the harder it seemed for me to breathe. Devon clutched my elbow, and her fingers hurt as they dug in. Twice I started to interrupt but thought better of it as Tanaka continued.

When he finished, Nakamura pulled out his cigarettes and lit one. He sat back and puffed away, an old man simply enjoying his innocent vice, the proceedings seemingly forgotten. Tanaka smiled at the third man and poured himself some water from the carafe. A deep sense of dread took root in me, and suddenly I wished we hadn't come. What fools to think we'd be able to talk these hard men into letting us off the hook. But we hadn't really had a choice. I looked at Devon sitting next to me, pale but steady, and waited for Nakamura to say something.

He smiled at Tanaka, then leaned close to him and said something in Japanese. The grin on Tanaka's face faded. His eyes clouded and he started to say something, but Nakamura waved him to silence.

'Mr Sellars tells me that he sold you forgeries. That you knowingly bought them and paid him only a fraction of what originals would cost.' Nakamura spoke mildly.

Tanaka jumped to his feet. 'He's lying,' he shouted, pointing at me. 'He is nothing but a drug addict and a liar.' Then Tanaka seemed to realize who he was shouting at and sat back down. He continued in a more reasonable tone of voice. 'Surely you don't take the word of this *gai jin* over my own. If he sold us forgeries, it was without my knowledge.'

Nakamura pursed his lips and looked down at me. 'You have made some very serious allegations, Mr Sellars. I find the simple fact that you have had the audacity to come to me this way quite compelling.' He glanced at Tanaka, then back at me. 'But Tanaka-san has served me well for many years. He is a trusted and old friend. Why, as he asks, should I take your word over his?'

I stood to answer, but one of the men behind us stepped closer. Quickly, I sat back down. From his seat on the platform, Nakamura waved the guard off, then urged me to continue.

'Mr Nakamura, I can show you my business records, but they won't prove anything. I can show you the files of all the paintings I've sold to Mr Tanaka. Perhaps if you were to check his records of payment . . . but even those records could easily be manipulated.' Although I had rehearsed this in my head, it didn't sound very convincing. So I decided to change tacks. 'Certainly I didn't come here to prove that Mr Tanaka was a liar. It never dawned on me that he might have purchased forgeries without your knowledge. Certainly you didn't pay him for originals, did you? No – of course not.'

Nakamura's face darkened. Tanaka glared at me.

'Mr Nakamura, I came to you hoping to be of some help. The museum investigation is a fact. The paintings I sold Mr Tanaka were forgeries – that also is a fact. Mr Tanaka always knew he was buying fakes – if he told you otherwise, he was lying.'

At this, Tanaka leapt to his feet again, and growled something I couldn't understand. Nakamura motioned him back to his chair. Then he put out his cigarette and lit another.

'What you have told me today is most disturbing, Mr Sellars. But I'm afraid you haven't brought me any proof. I will certainly check into the paintings. If they are forgeries, you will have caused me quite a headache.' With this he shot a look at Tanaka that would have made a less hardened man tremble. 'But unless you can somehow convince me that my friend has done as you say, I'm going to have to hold you to blame.'

This was not going the way I had envisioned it. Whatever Nakamura really thought, he wasn't going to believe us over Tanaka unless we had compelling proof. Incontrovertible proof of Tanaka's deception. I glanced at Devon and nodded.

She spoke up for the first time. 'Mr Nakamura, what Adrian has told you is true. But there's more.' She opened her purse and the guard behind her moved in again.

This time Nakamura waved him away impatiently. Tanaka glared down at her, unsure what to expect.

'Please look at this, sir.' She stood and handed Nakamura the address book.

Tanaka's expression changed from open hostility to confused curiosity. He angled his neck to get a better look over Nakamura's shoulder, not seeming to recognize Marta's book.

Nakamura flipped through the book, then looked up. His lips parted as though he were about to speak, but he didn't. He opened the book again and went through it slowly, turning the pages one at a time. When he finished, his grandfatherly guise fell away and he suddenly looked like Attila the Hun.

'Where did you get this?' he demanded.

'From Marta Batista,' I answered.

'Did you show it to Chief Inspector Okuba when you were visiting him?'

Damn, he knew everything – almost. I nodded. 'Yes, Okuba saw it. Then he tried to take it from us. We left before he had the chance.'

Nakamura lifted the book and regarded it with a mixture of anger and disgust. He held it away from his body, gripped gingerly between his thumb and index finger as though the book might be infected with a dangerous contagious disease. He coughed and shook his head. Then he tossed it at Tanaka, who barely managed to catch it.

'Look at it, Tanaka-san. Read it carefully,' Nakamura spat. 'Then tell me some more of your lies.'

Tanaka flinched and looked down at the tiny man, confused. He still didn't grasp what was in the book. He started to say something, but Nakamura angrily waved him off, then began a tirade in Japanese. He waved his arms and stalked around the platform, raging like a rabid beast.

No more inscrutable Oriental attitude. Nakamura was blazing. What an incredible fucking spectacle. My heart was pounding somewhere south of my adenoids, but I couldn't have hoped for a better reaction. Devon's timing had been superb. Tanaka was going down, no doubt about it, and as scary as Nakamura was, I loved every second of it. I looked at Devon. Her mouth was clamped shut and her eyes were wide.

'Who else has seen this?' Nakamura directed this question to me.

'Only us,' I answered. 'But I've kept a copy of it . . .'

He glared fire and death at me. I didn't finish the threat. I forced myself to meet his baleful stare.

323

He barked orders in Japanese at the two guards, who then approached the platform. Then he turned and yelled at Tanaka for a full two minutes. His facial muscles contorted and spittle flew from his lips as he screamed in Japanese at his trusted old friend.

Tanaka's face blanched, but he stood silently and took it, head bowed. When Nakamura finished he gestured to one of the guards who took Tanaka by the elbow and escorted him from the room. Tanaka met my eye with a look of pure hatred as he was led past me. It was all I could do not to wink at him.

The man with the briefcase, who had yet to speak, stepped to Nakamura's side and whispered something unintelligible, then together they strode out of the room.

Devon and I were completely unnerved. Even the remaining guard, whose round face gave away nothing, stood a little stiffer than he had earlier.

We sat there for about fifteen minutes without saying a word. When my pulse had slowed as much as I believed it was going to, which wasn't a whole hell of a lot, I stood and walked to the windows. Devon followed. We huddled there and tried to figure out what to expect next.

'Good God, I've never seen anything like that,' Devon said, taking my hand.

Her fingers were cold. 'Some dinner conversation this is going to make. Although I doubt anybody will ever believe us.'

She smiled, then shook her head in wonder. 'Nakamura was so nice at first. Have you ever seen anyone change so fast?'

'No. That was in a class by itself.'

She looked at her watch. 'It's almost one o'clock. What do you think they're doing?'

'I hope they're torturing Tanaka. When they finish, I'd like to get the fuck out of here.'

Our guard had positioned himself by the door. He was the largest Japanese man I had ever seen, well over six feet tall. The hair on his cabbage-sized head was shaved to a rough stubble. He stood looking at the floor, but when I stepped closer, he lifted his gaze and unbuttoned his suit coat, revealing a semiautomatic held upside down in a shoulder holster. His eyes were as flat as Stan's, and he gestured to the chairs, seeming to indicate that we might be there for a while.

Two o'clock came and went. Then three. Devon and I were alternately terrified and bored. Sometimes both at once. Stan had poked his head in and allowed us each a trip to the bathroom, accompanied by the guard. But otherwise we saw or heard nothing more from anyone. When I asked Stan what was going on, he shrugged and rolled his eyes under the band of his beret.

'When you are needed, you'll be told,' he said, then left.

Not exactly comforting, but not too threatening either. Or so Devon and I rationalized.

At four-fifteen, things got seriously scary. The door to the room opened and Stan returned, followed by the guard who had escorted Tanaka out. The guard carried over his shoulder like a sack of concrete one very badly beaten Marta Batista. Unceremoniously, he dumped her on the floor just in front of the platform. Then he relieved Cabbage-head, who had been watching us for most of the afternoon, and took up the same position by the door.

Stunned, Devon and I looked at each other, then knelt to get a closer look at Marta. She made a gargling sound and opened her eyes, which were swollen but not entirely shut. Her face was a bruised mess, and she was bleeding profusely from several cuts. Someone had taken a razor to her lips – a wound pimps inflict on wayward whores. A cut that no plastic surgeon could put right. It was impossible to tell whether or not her injuries were life-threatening, but it was safe to say that no one would ever call her pretty again. She gave no sign of recognizing us.

'Oh, my God,' Devon moaned, backing away.

I looked up at the guard and shouted. 'What the hell is going on? I want to see Nakamura. Now!'

He blinked at me like I was out of my mind, but said nothing.

I walked over to where he stood. He tensed but made nothing resembling a threatening move. I wanted out now!

'Get Nakamura!' I shouted at him again, this time close enough to smell the lime aftershave he used.

No response.

Reaching past him, I started to open the door. I'm not sure what happened, but he moved faster than I would have thought possible, and I was lying on my back, the wind knocked out of me.

Devon hurried over and tried to help me up as I gasped for breath. I knelt on all fours until I could see straight, then stumbled over and collapsed into one of the chairs. She sat down next to me and leaned close.

'Adrian! Talk to me. Please . . .' her voice wavered. She struggled to keep from losing it.

'I'm all right,' I wheezed. 'I'll be fine.'

She looked around the room like a caged animal. Her eyes were wild, and her hands were flitting around like a couple of hummingbirds.

A raw mixture of anger and fear welled up inside me

as I watched Devon come unglued. Where had I gotten the idea that Nakamura was going to deal with us in some honorable fashion? That I would be able to smile and talk my way out of this insanity? That there was such a thing as honor among these thieves? What a laugh. After all that had happened, I still hadn't gotten it through my head that I couldn't think like Tanaka and Nakamura. Despair crashed down on me, squeezing my heart. I tried to suck in more air, but I couldn't get enough. Then Marta groaned. I looked at all the blood on her face, and I remembered how the gun had jumped in my hand when I shot Kotani. If I got the chance again, I knew I wouldn't hesitate. God help whoever got in my way.

Devon pressed closer.

'We're okay,' I told her, as soothingly as I could. 'Nobody's hurt us. It was my fault, I shouldn't have tried to get past him.'

She nodded and took a deep breath. I reached over and stroked her hair. Her eyes filled, but she didn't cry. Then she leaned against me and pressed her face into my shoulder, trembling violently.

Marta groaned again, this time louder, then she mumbled something in Spanish. Her words were distorted by her ruined mouth.

Devon lifted her head from my shoulder and looked down at her with a mixture of fear and pity.

'I've got to try and help her,' she said, standing and peeling off her sweater.

She stepped to Marta's side and knelt, laying her sweater over Marta's shoulders. The carpet was stained with blood, but the actual bleeding seemed to have slowed.

I took off my sweater, then my long sleeved T-shirt

and gave the shirt to Devon. As I was pulling the sweater back on, she asked me to hand her the carafe of water.

The guard stoically manned his position as if nothing untoward had happened. He gave no indication that he cared or that he even noticed as I mounted the platform and retrieved the water. I handed Devon the carafe and winced as she wet the T-shirt and dabbed at Marta's face. It looked useless, but it was better than doing nothing. Marta let out a stifled scream when the shirt brushed her slashed lips, and looked up frantically. I still didn't think she recognized who she was with, or for that matter where she was.

Devon pulled herself together as she cared for Marta. Somehow being needed had diminished or at least refocused her fear. The color returned to her face, and she seemed steady enough when the door opened and the man who had accompanied Nakamura walked back in, still carrying his briefcase. Stan followed on his heels, and the two of them stood for a moment just inside the door. I checked my watch – it was just after five o'clock.

The man with the briefcase walked over to the semicircle of chairs and sat down. He looked at Marta and shook his head.

'So unnecessary,' he mumbled. 'Such a foolish girl.'

Stan stood behind the man's chair and said nothing. His eyes barely stopped as they passed over Marta and swept the room.

'My name is Tenzo,' the man said, placing his briefcase on the floor beside his feet. 'I represent Mr Nakamura in certain of his American dealings.'

'I thought that position was filled by Tanaka.' I directed this at Stan.

Tenzo seemed not to mind. 'Perhaps,' he answered

328

for Stan. 'In any case, we seem to find ourselves in a bit of an awkward situation. You have something we want. Unfortunately, it has come to our attention that our friend, Inspector Okuba, also has his heart set on acquiring Miss Batista's memoir, although I suppose a copy would serve his purposes just as well as the original.' He paused to be sure I understood him, then continued. 'I'm sure you realize by now that we can't let that happen.'

'Let us go, and you will never hear from us or see us again,' I promised.

Tenzo laughed, a pleasant musical sound. 'I'm sure of it, Mr Sellars. Nothing would please me more than sending you and Miss Berenson on your way and closing the door on this little fiasco. Why, even the forgeries no longer seem worth quibbling over, although we would like to know what happened to Kotani-san and his assistant, Ito. However, there is another little fly in the ointment, as they say in some of your old movies.'

Marta gurgled and kicked out one of her legs. Devon tried to soothe her, stroking her arm and whispering softly in her ear. Tenzo watched, then shook his head again.

'Such a shame. Now where was I? Oh, yes, letting you go. As I said, nothing would make me happier. But what are we to do about Okuba? I'm afraid we'll have to deal with that situation before we can even consider letting you and Devon go.'

'Okay, Tenzo. What do you suggest?'

He picked up his briefcase and set it on his lap. Unsnapping the clasps, he opened it and pulled out a thick file.

'Chief Inspector Hiro Okuba has made us his business. We think he foolishly believes that his future with the NPA depends upon his ability to penetrate our organization.' Tenzo laughed at the thought. Then shaking his head, he continued. 'If Okuba only knew how many of his superiors are on our payroll, he might relax a little bit. But some zealous young men can't seem to learn. Therefore, we have made Inspector Okuba *our* business. We've built quite a file on him, going all the way back to his childhood.'

Tenzo removed a typewritten report from the file he was holding and made a show of studying it for a moment. 'We've analyzed his previous actions and come up with what we consider to be a very accurate and detailed psychological profile of Okuba.'

I looked over to see if Devon was following this. She caught my eye and nodded, then patted at Marta's forehead.

I was starting to hate this Tenzo. 'I'm sure it's all very impressive.' I held my arms up, surrendering. 'I'm moved, Tenzo. You can tell that, can't you?'

He smiled benignly. 'Frankly, your opinion means nothing to me. Besides, you look too grim to be impressed, Mr Sellars. But I suppose that's to be expected. As I was saying, our brief on Okuba leads us to believe that he has not in all likelihood told anyone about Miss Batista's book. No, we believe that he would keep such information to himself until he could use the book to his best advantage. He's not the type to willingly share his successes. If we simply let you go, he would do anything, I repeat *anything*, to get his hands on that book. You would not be able to deny him, Mr Sellars. And that leaves us in a quandary.' He wrinkled his nose as though a disagreeable smell had just entered the room. 'We could eliminate you. But if you really have a copy stashed away somewhere safe . . .' He shrugged theatrically. 'Well, that wouldn't very well solve our problem, would it?'

'Quit dancing around, Tenzo. What do you want me to do?'

'We, Mr Sellars. Not I. We would like you to set up a meeting with Okuba at your office to discuss the terms under which you will hand him Miss Batista's book. You will be accompanied by Stan – and Oda. He was the larger of your two guards. We anticipate that Okuba will come alone, confident that he will be able to handle you. When he arrives, Oda and Stan will simply eliminate our mutual problem. Then perhaps we can negotiate a suitable conclusion to *our* business.' He returned the report to his file, then began to replace the file in his briefcase but hesitated before snapping the clasps. 'Oh, there is one other thing. Miss Berenson is doing such a nice job nursing Miss Batista – we'd like for her to stay with us while you deal with Okuba.'

He stood with the briefcase and walked toward the door.

'That would be clean, wouldn't it? I lure him to my gallery – you kill him and pin it on me. What if I say no, Tenzo?'

Stopping just short of the door, he turned and glanced at Marta, then Devon. 'Don't you think the loss of one pretty face is enough for one day?'

Devon gasped.

Tenzo pointed at me with his precious briefcase. 'You'll do as we ask, Mr Sellars. You really don't have any options. No one threatens Nakamura-san. No matter what kind of leverage they may *think* they have.' He smiled coldly. 'Stan will bring you a telephone and Okuba's private number. Set the meeting for eight o'clock tonight. The sooner we resolve this, the better for all concerned.'

With that, he and Stan walked out, closing the door behind them.

Devon huddled on the edge of the platform, her chin resting on her knees. She looked down at Marta who lay quietly, eyes closed, either unconscious or in shock. I stood on the other side of the platform watching the guard, who seemed made of stone.

'I don't want to leave you here,' I said.

'Tenzo was right, you don't have a choice. I don't want them to do *that* to me.' She inclined her head toward Marta. 'You have to do as he says.'

Stepping to her side, I sat down next to her and put my arm around her.

'Once Okuba is out of the way, they'll use the same leverage to make me go and get them our copy of Marta's book. Then they can do anything they want to us.'

She nodded but didn't reply.

'Do you understand what I'm saying?'

'I'm terrified, Adrian. I don't want you to leave me here alone.' Her breath caught in her throat and she sobbed. 'But if you don't do what they ask – God only knows what they'll do in order to force you.'

I put my arms around her. There had to be a way out of this. Measuring the distance to the door, I glanced at the guard, but he had heard every word we'd said and as though he could read my mind, he loosened the automatic in his shoulder holster and widened his stance.

I turned back to Devon. 'Even if I do what they say, we have no reason to believe they'll keep their word and let us go.'

She looked up at me, wiping her eyes on the sleeve of

her shirt. 'Go. Do whatever you have to. I'll do my best to keep it together.' She hesitated, then whispered, 'It's auction night, isn't it?'

'Jesus, you're right. I forgot all about it.'

'Be careful – Oda or Stan might freak at the crowd.'

I nodded, trying to imagine their reaction to the circus they were about to witness. 'I might be able to lose them, get help,' I said softly, one eye on the guard.

She nodded, then started to cry again. 'I'm scared, Adrian.'

'Me too. But I don't think they'll do anything to us. Not yet. Not as long as they believe I have a copy of that book. Do what they tell you till I get back – I'll get us out of this, Devon.' I hoped my words sounded better to her than they did to me.

Suddenly she forced a smile. 'Don't get carried away and bid too much on anything.'

I smiled back at her. 'Not a chance. You hang tough. I'll be back as soon as I can.'

At that moment Marta cried out but didn't open her eyes. Our smiles faded. Devon grimaced, her face reflecting the horror she must have felt. But she didn't turn away. She picked up the damp T-shirt by her side and wiped Marta's forehead, whispering, 'It'll be okay. Just rest, Marta, everything will be okay.'

Stan cleared his throat.

I'd been so intent on watching Devon try and soothe Marta, I hadn't heard him enter. He held a cordless phone in one hand and a slip of paper in the other. Tenzo stood watching from the door.

'Call Okuba,' Stan said, pushing the phone at me.

He watched me dial. I prayed as hard as I ever had that Okuba would be out, but he answered on the third ring.

333

'Hiro, it's Adrian.'

'Where are you?'

'That's why I'm calling. We need to talk.'

'You're goddamned right we need to talk. I'm about an inch away from calling in the FBI – having them put out a warrant for you and Devon.'

Tenzo had been right: Okuba was keeping what he knew to himself. The greedy fool. Now it was likely to cost him everything. It was one thing to hear Tenzo talk about setting him up, but my stomach clenched at the reality that Okuba probably wouldn't be alive in a very few hours. Stan watched every breath I took. A drop of sweat ran down my nose and dripped onto the phone.

'Adrian, you still there?'

'Yeah, I'm here, Okuba.'

'Well, what do you want to do? You want to come to my office?'

'No, that wouldn't be a good idea.' Stan pointed to his watch and gestured to me to hurry up. 'Meet me at my gallery. Eight o'clock tonight. You know where it is?'

'I'll find it, Adrian. Will you have the book with you?'

'Yeah, Okuba. I'll have the book.'

When I handed Stan the phone, he turned and joined Tenzo, closing the door behind them.

Half an hour later they came back with Oda to get me. I made a last-ditch effort to forestall the inevitable.

'Tenzo, I'm sorry, but I don't have my keys to the gallery.'

His face darkened. 'Do not trifle with me.'

'I'm serious. I don't have the keys.'

He glared at me, then addressed Stan in Japanese. Stan shrugged and nodded.

'In that case we will break in. Stan is quite adept at such enterprises. With you there to turn off the alarm, it will be simple. Now, let's go. We have a schedule to keep.'

'Give me a minute with Devon, okay?'

Tenzo nodded, and the three of them stepped out of the room. If they did so to give us some privacy, it didn't make a lot of sense as the other guard stayed put, just inside the door.

Stepping to Devon's side, I folded my arms around her. 'Stay as loose as you can.' I spoke softly. 'I'll be back in a little while, and I want to find you in one piece.'

She nodded. 'The crowd,' she whispered in my ear. 'Be careful, but if you get the chance, don't hesitate.'

Tenzo poked his head in the door. 'We must leave now.'

She looked up at me, her face wet, her lower lip quivering. 'I love you, Adrian.'

Then I was striding down the hall between Oda and Stan, the smell of Devon's hair in my nostrils, my cheek damp with her tears. I paid close attention to the layout as we walked down the stairs, through the first floor of the house and then the kitchen to the garage. Stan fished a ring of keys out of his pocket and used one of them to unlock the garage door, which opened onto Seventy-second Street. I looked out into the dark; the sidewalk was empty. No cavalry about to swoop down and rescue us. Oda pushed me toward the car. After we had backed out onto the street, he carefully relocked the garage door, then jumped into the back seat next to me.

Stan drove what I assumed to be Tanaka's Mercedes sedan. I sat in the back between Oda and Tenzo. The car smelled of well-cared-for leather and some kind of lavender aftershave that Tenzo had used far too liberally. The windows were darkly tinted; little could be seen

335

from the interior as we turned right on what I assumed to be Park Avenue and sped toward the Delmonico.

'Aren't we a little early?' I asked Tenzo.

He grunted something I couldn't understand. I looked closely at him and realized how tense he was. His jaw was working, and his body stiffened every time the car hit a bump. The vein near his temple throbbed and a faint sheen of sweat moistened his forehead and upper lip.

'I'm surprised you came along,' I told him. 'You don't seem the type.'

He looked down his nose at me. 'What do you mean by that?'

'Nothing. It's just that you seem like an inside man. Not the type to get his hands dirty on a job like this.'

His right eyelid twitched. The tic was barely visible in the dim light of the car, but it was definitely a twitch.

'Seriously, Tenzo, why are you here?'

He didn't deign to answer me. I tapped him on the knee and asked again.

He pulled away from me, crowding the door.

'What's the matter, did Nakamura make you come?' A little school yard taunt had crept into my voice. 'What happened to his dear old friend, Tanaka-san?'

I saw Stan glance at us noncommittally in the rear-view mirror.

'Come on, Tenzo, talk to me. Where's Tanaka? What's going to happen to him?'

He pulled a handkerchief from his breast pocket and mopped his brow. Then he mumbled something in Japanese to Oda, who elbowed me in the ribs hard enough to remind me of what I had eaten for breakfast.

We rode the rest of the way in silence, while I rubbed my side.

CHAPTER TWENTY-NINE

The Delmonico was lit up like a cruise ship. A huge and divergent crowd had gathered together for one reason: to witness or participate in one of the last great public spectacles. It was auction night. The richest auction of the year. Christie's semiannual sale of Impressionist and modern master paintings. Young men with hundred-dollar haircuts dressed in dusty colored suits and over-sized coats, stood on the sidewalk talking with their dates, half of the would-be actresses and models in New York City. Older men in conservative dark suits disembarked from limousines, smoking cigars, their trophy wives in tow. As we joined the flow of foot traffic and drew closer, I recognized an elderly Italian scholar of noble descent, whose collection of Renoir nudes was internationally renowned. He was chatting amiably with a young American filmmaker, whose graphic on-screen depictions of bondage and sado-sexual violence had earned him enough money to buy the old man's collection twice over. They weren't the only odd couple standing on Park Avenue. The sidewalk was awash with disparate social groups, pumped respectively on scotch, cocaine, and the smell of money. It was a strange mix of old wealth and new culture. The seriously rich rubbing shoulders with the seriously ambitious.

After we had parked the car on Fifty-eighth Street, I walked, wedged between Stan and Oda, around the mound of snow and ice that had been scraped from the sidewalks onto the curb and waited with them by the corner of the Delmonico. I couldn't help laughing out loud. Tenzo had picked the worst night of the year to plan an ambush here. Oda placed a heavy hand on my shoulder as the crowd eddied around us.

It was a hell of a show. Especially if you'd never seen it before. Tenzo's face was a caricature of indecision as his eyes flicked back and forth over the crowd. The real players were almost indistinguishable from the wannabes, except to the pros, who could sniff them out blind-folded. They streamed in and out of the building in clots of three and four, waving at each other as they passed, using both the main entrance and the separate entrance that Christie's maintained. The greetings they called to one another practically crackled in the frosted air with the sound of fresh currency about to be exchanged for old oil paintings.

Policemen, mounted and on foot, directed traffic and provided security. Klieg lights washed the night, lending a cinematic flair to the evening.

The scene inside the Delmonico would be just as crowded and tumultuous as the gathering outside. Once the auction had concluded, an orgy of private buying and selling would take place in the galleries that occupied the building. More than one dealer would come close to banking 'fuck you' money on this night of nights. All of this free enterprise would be followed by a celebration of monumental proportions. The best liquors and the most expensive foods would be consumed in huge quantities. And more than a few back-room assignations would help to work off the hormonal surge, the hard-on that big money changing hands tends to incite.

Tenzo mopped his brow and muttered to himself. Oda stared at a blonde whose dress did little to protect her from the elements, but his grip on my shoulder tightened as I began to edge away. If I was going to lose my escort, it would have to be inside.

Deep down, I felt the pull of it all, almost tidal in its power. We should have been part of this annual rite of winter. I glanced at Tenzo, who seemed undecided as to how best to proceed, and tasted the bitterness of the bile that churned in my stomach. Steven and I had planned to give a party tonight, but the world had turned ugly, and parties were for people with real lives. People who went to work and then went home and had dinner, or went to the movies. People who saw their children every day. People who believed the world was basically a good place. I had never felt more separated from *real* people in my life. The wind suddenly seemed colder than it actually was. I hoped they were leaving Devon alone.

Several camera crews had set up their equipment in front of the building, and the reporters were aggressively shoving microphones at anyone who looked wealthy or even vaguely artsy. Tenzo continued to gape at the unexpected crowd, clearly unnerved by the lights and cameras as well as the uniformed officers. Stan and Oda seemed unmoved.

'What is this?' he finally asked me.

'Auction night, Tenzo – I didn't know – it slipped my mind. I'm as surprised as you. Maybe we better leave.'

He turned, a look of incredulity souring his features. 'How could you forget something like this?' His voice was shrill.

Before I could answer, the camera crews, trailing yards of cable, surged past us toward the far corner of Fifty-ninth Street. Falling all over each other, they looked like a flock of drunken pigeons following the leader. John McEnroe was emerging from a limo that had just pulled to the corner. How they knew to approach that particular limo in a crowd of similar cars was a great mystery. McEnroe swatted his way through the reporters glaring and brandishing not his namesake Dunlop, but a stack of auction catalogs – the weapon of choice in the new game he was trying to play.

Oda smiled and said something to Stan, who looked up but didn't seem in the least interested. As McEnroe passed not more than twenty feet away, Oda beamed at him. If Tenzo hadn't growled something in Japanese, I think Oda might have asked for the retired tennis star's autograph. It was the only sign of animation I ever saw in Oda. I hadn't realized McEnroe was that popular in Japan.

I looked away from Oda's adulation of the aging boy wonder and searched the crowd for familiar faces. I was hoping to see Bernie Liebovitz ogling the parade. Mary Lumpkin walked past but didn't see me. No sign of Bernie. The last two weeks had been such a nightmare, so terrifyingly surreal, that I felt more than a little disoriented to find out that the rest of the world was rolling right along, business as usual. I shivered, wearing only a sweater and jeans, and tried to put Oda's bulk between me and the wind. Stan stood beside me, and the three of us waited in the shadows at the corner of Fifty-ninth and Park for Tenzo to make up his mind.

He studied the crowd for a while, then turned back to us. He looked naked without his briefcase.

'I don't have to remind you of what's at stake here, do I?' he asked me.

I thought of Devon wiping the blood from Marta's face and shook my head.

'Good. We're going through with this. You stay close to Oda, Adrian. One word, one stupid move, and you will regret the results for the rest of your life – however short that might be.' He reached into his coat pocket and removed a microcassette recorder. 'Listen to this.'

He pressed the play button, and Caitlin's voice, high and squeaky, came out of the tiny speaker: 'Daddy, I'm leaving this message to tell you I want us to go to the beach at Christmas. Happy Thanksgiving. Call me soon. This is Caitlin. Akka Bakka Beecha.'

I lunged and snatched the recorder from Tenzo's soft hand. Oda immediately grabbed my arm and twisted it painfully behind my back, maneuvering us around the corner of the building as he did so. Stan stepped to his side, effectively shielding us from anyone who might have seen.

'Bastard,' I spat. 'Go near her and I'll kill you. Plain and simple, you oily fuck, touch her and I will find you and kill you.'

Tenzo shook his head, then slapped me hard across the cheek with the back of his hand.

Oda tightened his grip. My eyes watered.

A policeman mounted on horseback, part of the crowd-control unit, rounded the corner and trotted past us with barely a glance. Stan carefully blocked his view.

Tenzo waited until he was gone, then spoke. 'Pull yourself together, Adrian.' He moistened his lips with the tip of his tongue. 'Your little girl is safe and sound at home with her mother. And that's where she'll stay – as long as you don't try anything stupid. I believe their address is two-forty-two Landing Way, Arlington. Isn't it?'

I willed death to strike him down on the spot.

'Yes.' He smiled. 'I can see by the look in your eye that it is.' He reached out and plucked the recorder from my hand. 'This message was on the machine at your apartment. A bit rude of us to have taken it, but you do see the point, don't you? Of course you do. So, be a good

341

boy and follow my instructions.' He lifted his free hand and took hold of my ear, then gave it a good twist. It hurt like hell. 'Adrian, don't ever threaten me again. Do we understand each other?' He slipped the recorder back into his pocket, then put his hands on his wide hips, waiting for my reply.

Oda wrenched my arm higher.

'Yes,' I grunted.

'Good. Now, let's go.' He gestured to Oda, who released me.

Flexing my shoulder, flanked by Stan and Oda, I followed Tenzo into the Delmonico.

We made our way through the crowded lobby, then had to wait to board an elevator. I recognized a number of faces, some of whom waved or called out a greeting. Several looked enviously at my company, assuming I was escorting Japanese clients to the auction. I noticed several people drop their eyes to my casual attire, then look up, an unspoken question on their faces. If they had been players, they would have known that the right Japanese clients gave an art dealer the status to dress as he pleased. Unfortunately, these were not the right Japanese clients.

The eighth floor was quiet. The only other art dealer who occupied space on the floor was open but not yet crowded. His gallery was to the left as you got off the elevator, mine was to the right. I led the way to the glass doors that I had been so proud of, then stood aside to let Stan do whatever he planned to do in order to break in. He got down on one knee and examined the locks. They were the most expensive dead bolts money could buy. If you lost a key, you had to order a replacement from the manufacturer. The locks were advertised as too complicated for the average locksmith to handle. Stan smiled at

Tenzo, and said something about flimsy American hardware. Tenzo laughed, and we all watched as Stan produced a small set of tools from his coat pocket. He fumbled with the lock picks for about ten seconds, then pushed open the door. So much for truth in advertising.

'Turn on all the lights,' Tenzo ordered, after I had disarmed the burglar-alarm system. 'I want everything to look natural.'

I did as he asked. Then he instructed me to walk him through the place. Stan and Oda followed on our heels. Stan took it all in, pointing and commenting to Oda in Japanese at several of the paintings we passed. The whole world's an art critic. I glared at him, but he ignored me. Satisfied that he had seen enough, Tenzo motioned us into my office, where Oda propelled me into a chair. So far there hadn't been a glimmer of a hope of getting free of these thugs. Desperately, I tried to think of another option, but Oda never left my side.

I sat listening as Stan and Tenzo planned the ambush. Powerless to stop them, I focused on their words – hoping to spot a flaw in their plan, some loophole, a way out. They lowered their voices, but I heard them anyway. A man was about to be murdered in cold blood, and I had led him to the slaughterhouse. They discussed at length who would cover the front and who would act as backup. Tenzo seemed to think that Oda should be the point man, but Stan, instead of acting like the toady he had always seemed to be, argued vehemently to take the position himself. I watched from the chair Oda had shoved me into, wondering why they cared.

Finally convinced, Tenzo ordered Oda to take up a position just inside my office. The door would be left slightly ajar, leaving enough of an opening for Oda to observe the action and join in if necessary. Stan would hide just inside the viewing room, ready to take Okuba down after he walked into the trap. I was ordered to sit at Devon's desk, just inside the front doors, and wait for Okuba. When he arrived I was to lock the doors behind him and lead him into the main gallery. Stan would make the first move. I was warned to get out of the way when the action started. I promised that I would. Tenzo planned to hide in the back room until the dirty work was over, although that's not how he described it.

'In case you're harboring any thoughts of fleeing, Adrian, Oda will have a gun trained on your back at all times. And I have this –' Tenzo pulled the recorder out of his coat pocket and dangled it in front of me.

I nodded, swallowing hard.

Oda and Stan pulled silenced automatics from their coats and checked their clips. Satisfied, they conferred briefly, then took up their respective positions. I wobbled to Devon's desk and sat down. My knees were shaking and my heart was full of dread. But they had Devon, and they knew where my daughter lived. I didn't see any way out. Tenzo disappeared into the storage room. According to my watch, it was almost seventhirty.

The wait was interminable.

At seven-forty-five, a noisy group got off the elevator and headed, thank God, for the neighboring gallery. I breathed a sigh of relief. Then the door swung open and of all people in the world, Oscar Fedder pranced in. A nasty smile turned up the corners of his thin lips.

'Good evening, Adrian. You look surprised to see me.'

'Oscar, you've got to leave,' I spluttered.

'Leave? I have no intentions of leaving without my money, or a painting that approximates what you owe

344

me. I've been chasing you for weeks. Thought you could avoid me, didn't you?'

He walked to where I sat. I heard the viewing room door creak.

'Oscar, you're making a big mistake. Please leave, now!'

He looked at me through those thick glasses of his and widened his smile. 'Afraid I might embarrass you on your big night?' He laughed and stepped around me into the gallery. 'Well, that's exactly what I intend to do. I told you not to screw around with me. I'm a hard man.' He turned his back on me and walked farther into the gallery.

'Oscar, please – you don't know what you're doing.'

He turned back toward me. 'Oh, I think I know exactly what I'm doing, Adrian. I'm about to ruin you. And I think I'm going to enjoy every second of it.'

Over Fedder's shoulder, I saw Stan come out of the viewing room and approach him soundlessly from behind. Tenzo and Oda remained hidden.

'I warned you,' I said, wincing.

Fedder snorted. 'Save your warnings for someone who needs them.'

He turned back toward the gallery and found himself nose to nose with Stan, who held his automatic level with Fedder's belly button.

'What!?' he whirled back toward me. 'What is this?'

Stan grabbed him by the shoulder and spun him back around.

I was getting dizzy.

'Shut your mouth and do what I tell you,' Stan ordered.

Fedder's mouth opened and closed but no sound came out.

'Did you hear me?' Stan repeated.

'Do – do – you know who I am?' Fedder mumbled, regaining his voice. 'You're making the mistake of your life. I – uh – I insist that you put that gun away and explain what's going on here.'

Stan looked at me in disbelief, then pivoted and punched Fedder smack on the nose with his fist.

Fedder's glasses flew across the floor, and he went down hard on his well-padded ass, bleeding from both nostrils. Stan grabbed him by the collar and hauled him to his feet. Ignoring Fedder's bleating, he punched him again, this time in the stomach, I guess to insure his co-operation. Fedder looked sufficiently subdued to me. He was blubbering, and a large wet stain appeared at the crotch of his otherwise immaculate gray flannels. His nose was bloody and already beginning to swell.

At that moment, Tenzo burst out of the back room. He looked at his watch, then barked an order at Oda, who stepped out of my office and grabbed Fedder by the arm. I knew how that felt.

'Don't kill me,' Fedder whined. 'Please, don't kill me.' He started to sob.

Oda grimaced in disgust, looked at Tenzo, who nodded, then hammered the butt of his gun down on Fedder's skull, silencing him for the time being. Then Oda dragged his unconscious body into my office.

I have to admit to mixed feelings about the whole thing, but for the most part I had enjoyed the show.

'Resume your positions,' Tenzo commanded. 'It's almost eight o'clock.'

The novelty of watching Oscar Fedder take a beating wore off quickly. Time crawled by. The minutes dragged on, until I finally had to take off my watch and

346

put it in my pocket to keep from staring at it. I was starting to believe that Okuba was going to stand me up when he approached, looking wary. He stood for a minute framed in the doorway and surveyed what he could see of the gallery behind me. I kept both hands visible on the desk. The last thing I wanted was for him to pull out a weapon, thinking I might be a threat.

'Adrian,' he nodded.

'Hello, Okuba,' I replied, hoping that the trembling in my voice didn't sound as loud to him as it did to me.

He stepped in and casually perched on the corner of Devon's desk. My heart was thumping so hard that I was sure he could hear it.

'Are you ready to get real?' he asked, sounding like he'd been watching 'The Mod Squad.'

I looked at him, unable to answer, my throat all but closed. What the hell was Stan doing? Was I supposed to duck? What if I was in the line of fire? These questions went unanswered, because at that moment the door to the viewing room crashed open.

Okuba jumped up and spun to look behind me.

Stan was moving toward us fast. '*Ki o Tsukete! Okuba-san, it's an ambush!*' he yelled.

'*Kagami!?*' Okuba asked, moving away from the desk and drawing a revolver from his waistband.

'Down! Get down!' Stan screamed, halfway to the desk.

I hit the floor and tried to crawl under Devon's desk, which, being made of glass, offered little in the way of protection but seemed better than nothing.

The rest unfolded in slow motion.

Stan continued toward us, yelling at the top of his lungs, pistol drawn. Okuba looked around, but there was nothing offering even the slightest cover.

The door to my office opened, Oda's profile filling it. Then an orange flash and a popping noise as he fired. The first slug hit Stan with a loud smack, high on the left shoulder, spinning him like a top before he crashed to the floor and skidded to a stop not ten feet from where I lay under the glass desk.

Okuba backed toward the entrance, firing at Oda, but his shots went wide, splintering the door frame of my office.

Oda fired again, in rapid succession. The first bullet caught Okuba in the neck, flinging him back against the gallery doors. Three more shots hit him in the chest before he fell. I think he was dead before he hit the floor.

I looked back into the gallery.

Oda crouched and slowly approached Stan, who lay where he had fallen, eyes closed, either dead or unconscious.

The smell of burned gunpowder and cordite filled the air.

The door to the back room opened, and Tenzo peeked around it. He shouted something at Oda, who ignored him. Tenzo called out to him again, but still he didn't answer, concentrating, instead, all of his attention on Stan.

Oda drew closer, the gun extended.

Tenzo, seemingly offended by Oda's lack of respect, charged out of the back room demanding a reply. He bounced around Oda and stood in front of him, his face beet-red, his eyes bulging. Blocking Oda's line of sight to Stan, he poked a finger at the big man's chest and started to jabber in outraged Japanese.

I tried to crawl further under the desk, but it was too small.

Seeming to sense his moment, Stan rolled over with a

groan, gaining a clear line of fire. He shot once, hitting Oda smack in the center of his forehead.

Oda's mouth formed a surprised ring, his eyes widened, and his gun slipped from his fingers. Blood welled, then began to stream from the hole in his head down his shocked face. He stood, unseeing, for another second or two, then dropped to the floor as though his skeleton had turned to jelly.

Tenzo's jaw dropped to his knees. He turned and looked at Stan, whom I think he assumed was dead, and started to say something. But Stan didn't allow him to finish. He shot Tenzo as cleanly as he had shot Oda, once through the head.

I was too stunned to speak or move. Too scared to piss in my pants. All of the weapons had been equipped with silencers, even Okuba's, but they had sounded loud enough in my ears to be heard in the Bronx. I expected the police to swarm in at any second. But nothing happened. Minutes passed, but the only sound was Stan's labored breathing.

I knew I couldn't stay under Devon's desk forever, although a significant part of me wanted to. Reluctantly, I crawled out and approached Stan.

He regarded me through eyes half shut with pain. He was bleeding badly from his shoulder. The bullet seemed to have entered through his left shoulder blade, then exited under his collarbone. I couldn't tell if his wound was mortal or not. Moving as quickly as I could, I stripped off Oda's coat, struggling to roll him over in order to get at it, then draped it over Stan.

'Pressure,' he gasped. 'Got to stop the bleeding. Put pressure on the wound – both sides.'

His face was the color of ash, as I lifted his shoulder enough to wrap Oda's coat over it and press from both sides. He grunted, and the air whistled from between his teeth, but he didn't cry out. I held him like that for about ten minutes. Then he whispered something I didn't understand.

'He's dead? Okuba?' he repeated.

I nodded.

He closed his eyes. 'Karma. He was an asshole – but they shouldn't have killed him.'

'No,' I agreed.

'Hurry . . .' he mumbled something else unintelligible.

'What?' I asked, softly, worried that he was dying.

'The lights.' He opened his eyes. 'You've got to move Okuba and turn out the lights before anyone else comes. Otherwise, all hell will break loose, and you'll never get Devon out.'

I looked at him, confused.

'The lights,' he insisted. 'Turn them out.'

Standing, I walked to where Okuba lay in an expanding pool of blood. I grabbed him by the wrists and pulled his body into the gallery, where he couldn't be seen from the door. There didn't seem to be much that I could do about all of the blood. So I locked the doors and turned out the lights. Then I returned to Stan's side.

He looked up at me in the dim light and nodded.

'Why?' I asked. 'Why did you do this?'

He coughed, then smiled. More of a grimace than a smile, but still it heartened me to see it.

'I'm NPA,' he whispered. 'I worked with Okuba.'

My eyes must have bugged. No wonder he always seemed to stand out – what a perfect disguise. He was so obvious, so goddamned scary, I hadn't even considered this possibility.

'Fooled you, huh?' The corners of his mouth twitched as he tried to smile again.

I nodded. 'You scared the living shit out of me.'

'Good.' He coughed, and a weak groan escaped him. 'Wanted to warn Okuba, but Tenzo was always there.'

I looked around at the carnage. 'What now?' I asked. 'What do I do about Devon?'

'Help me up. We'll go and get her.' His voice was a whisper.

'Stan, you're not going anywhere except to a hospital.'

'It's not as bad as it looks. Just a lot of blood.' He took a deep breath. 'My name is Hideo Kagami. I hate the name Stan.'

He pulled himself up to a sitting position without my help. But the jacket I had wrapped around his shoulder fell away, and I could see that the bleeding had started again. I pressed the jacket against both sides of his wound and managed to staunch the flow. But no matter what Hideo said, he wasn't going anywhere.

'Lie still. It'll keep bleeding this way if you move.'

He did as I asked.

'You're going to have to get her yourself,' he admitted after a few moments. 'Take the keys out of my pocket. You've got to be quick and decisive. There's no other way. Get paper and a pen. I'll show you how to get in.'

'I think I should call the police.'

He frowned in disgust. 'I am the police. Call anyone else and Devon will die. Do you think that New York's finest are going to go charging into that house because you tell them to? By the time you explain this' – he looked at the bodies sprawled around the gallery – 'Nakamura will know all about what's happened here. He'll be long gone and your friend will he dead.'

The speech took too much out of him. His eyes unfocused, and his head lolled to the side. His breathing became fast and shallow.

'Hideo,' I shook him gently. 'Tell me what to do.'

He took a deeper breath and with some difficulty focused on me. Then he smiled, his face damp and waxy.

'Paper. Get paper.'

Kneeling over him I quickly sketched out a crude map of the house, based on what I had seen. He filled in the gaps, dictating as I drew.

'Take my keys – go in through the garage. Guard in kitchen – kill him.'

I blinked. Easy enough for him to say.

He stared up at me.

Frowning, I nodded. 'Is there an alarm?'

His eyes widened. 'Sorry – not thinking clearly. A key pad outside the . . . the . . .' He was suddenly racked by a spasm, then a series of choking coughs. When the coughing subsided, he rested a moment, then continued. 'The . . . kitchen door. Use the barrel key . . . disarm it, otherwise a buzzer – when you go in. Light flashes green – it's off.'

'Got it.' I repeated his instructions just to be sure, hoping he hadn't left out any other little details.

'Can you find the meeting room? Where you left Devon.'

'Yeah, I can find it.'

'Go there. Use the back stairs – past kitchen.'

I pointed on the map to where I thought he meant. He nodded.

'Another guard – just inside the door. Won't be expecting you.'

Was I supposed to kill him too?

352

'Get Devon – get out. Don't waste time. Use my keys – leave through front door.'

'Will there be other guards?' I asked. The plan sounded a little too simple.

'Not that you need to worry about. All watching Tanaka – at the back of the house – tatami room. Stay clear – get in and out.' He coughed again, this time more violently, and his eyes rolled slowly back into his head.

Gently, I reached into his pocket and removed the keys. Then I picked up his gun and slipped it into the waistband of my jeans.

'The silver one,' he whispered.

I looked at him confused.

'The key – silver. It will open garage and front door. Don't fuck around. If you shoot – kill. Take the extra clip –' His voice was very low, barely audible.

I made him as comfortable as I could. Then I called 911 from the phone on Devon's desk and asked for an ambulance. I explained that shots had been fired and gave the address, then hung up without identifying myself.

'Thanks,' Hideo whispered.

'Hang in there, help will be here soon,' I said, but his eyes were closed and I couldn't tell if he heard me.

Stepping to where Tenzo lay, I stooped and fished the recorder from his coat. I removed the tape of Caitlin and stuffed it into my hip pocket. Then I dropped the recorder onto Tenzo's chest and hurried out. I left the door unlocked behind me and hoped the ambulance got to Hideo before it was too late.

The elevator stopped almost as soon as I hit the button. I rode it all the way to the lobby alone. Surprised at such good fortune, I hoped it was an omen.

No such luck. The doors slid open on the crowded

lobby, and the first face I saw was that of Shelby Lewis, Fedder's assistant. I had conveniently forgotten him.

'Adrian, have you seen Oscar?' she asked.

I looked at her, trying to think of a reasonable answer.

Then she looked at me closer and her face blanched. 'Oh no – no, you didn't,' she moaned.

'Shelby, what are you saying?'

She covered her mouth, a look of horror in her eyes, and pointed at my hands.

I looked down. They were red with Hideo's blood.

'It's not what you think,' I started to say. But she opened her mouth to scream.

I grabbed her by the wrist and pulled her onto the elevator with me. She whimpered but was too scared to fight me.

'Sit,' I ordered, pointing to the back corner. She did. Then I punched the button for the twentieth floor and stepped off just as the doors shut.

The lobby was mobbed with people who either didn't have tickets to the main event or had had enough of the auction room and preferred the noise and energy of the party crowd. I was halfway to the front door, having pushed my way through a sea of beautiful miniskirted women, with their Bulgari knock-offs and their Armani-clad, sharp-eyed men, when I saw Detective Carstairs enter and start toward me. He caught my eye and waved over the heads of the people swirling between us. His lips moved as he called to me, but his voice was lost in the buzz of the crowd.

'What now?' I shouted in his direction.

There was no way I could explain the blood on my hands without telling him what had happened upstairs. Hideo had been right, Carstairs wasn't going to send troops charging into Tanaka's house unless I did some fast talking. And Devon didn't have that kind of time; I had to get clear of him.

Turning, I hurried back the way I had come and used the employee exit. I ran across the loading dock and into the driveway that opened onto Fifty-ninth Street. The iron gate was closed. I tugged at the padlock that secured it, but the lock was tight. The gate itself was more than twelve feet high and topped with concertina wire. Climbing it was out of the question. Gulping air, I stood there for a moment, then backtracked across the loading dock. This time I ran past the Delmonico's employee exit and entered the door that led into the Christie's portion of the building.

Just as I pulled it open, Carstairs came onto the far end of the dock.

'Stop! Adrian, I need to speak with –'

I slammed the door shut behind me, then hastily wedged a chair that had been sitting against the wall under the knob. What the hell was Carstairs doing anyway? It seemed an odd time to ask more questions about McHenry.

I was in a long hall that led to a flight of stairs and a service elevator, which both led up to the Christie's staging room. I'd picked up or delivered paintings there on numerous occasions. The staging room was a fancy name for the storage area directly behind the auction room. Whatever was to be sold – furniture, comic books, rugs, or paintings – was stacked in the staging room, then fed one at a time through a curtain to the auctioneer.

Twenty feet in from the dock, the hall angled sharply to the right. As I ran hell-bent around the turn, I collided with a squirrely-looking, uniformed rent-a-cop and sent him sprawling.

'Hey! What the heck are you doin'?' he asked as he picked himself up. He was short and skinny, with a red face. He had a mousy, limp moustache under a blade of a nose, and pale, squinty eyes.

'Sorry. On my way to the auction. I'm in a hurry,' I said, stepping back.

'Well, you just wait a minute. No one can use this entrance without proper authorization.' He drew himself up to his full five and a half feet and hitched his pants a little higher. 'I'm goin' to have to check on this.'

It must have been his chair that had been sitting just inside the door. I put my hands behind my back, so that he wouldn't notice Okuba's blood, and started to talk, 'Now listen, Officer –' I was interrupted by a loud banging.

Carstairs was bellowing through the closed door. 'Stop! Goddamnit – open up,' he shouted, continuing the kind of door-hammering only a cop knew how to deliver. His voice was muffled, but his anger was clear enough. 'I'll fucking nail you, Sellars.'

The rent-a-cop stared around me, down the hall. Carstairs was shouting and making enough noise to startle the dead. I might have talked my way past the guard, but not now. So I sucker-punched him. A crunching shot to the jaw that dropped him to the floor in a bony pile of skinny arms and legs. He never knew what hit him, but my hand felt like it was on fire. I took the stairs two at a time, rubbing my knuckles, then slowed as I entered the staging room.

I knew two of the four porters, who looked up in surprise as I hurried in.

'I have two million – five – that's two and a half – in the rear of the room – standing. The bid is against the telephone bidder . . .' The clipped cadence of the auctioneer's voice could be heard through the curtain that separated the staging room from the actual auction room. 'Two-five. Going once. Going twice.'

'Hey, man, you can't be back here,' Amos, one of the porters, whispered to me.

'I know,' I told him. 'I'm just going through – this way.'

I turned and pointed to the end of the curtain through which we could all hear the auctioneer rap his gavel and call, 'At two-five – third, last, and final call. Do I hear any advance?'

As I slipped through the curtain into the auction room, I could hear someone coming up the stairs like a freight train. I didn't wait around to confirm whether or not it was Carstairs.

On the other side of the curtain, the auction room was set up with more than six hundred chairs arranged auditorium-style, facing a podium on a stage at the front of the room where the auctioneer stood. There was a wide center aisle between the rows of chairs, and standing room to the sides and back. Along the wall opposite where I stood were television cameras and a roped-off press area, filled with reporters and photographers. There wasn't space for another body. The room was packed, well beyond standing room only.

All eyes were on the auctioneer, who dominated the room by virtue of the numbers he was calling in his British accent.

'Sold! Two million-five – to the gentleman in the back of the room.'

Heads turned to try and spot the lucky bidder – anyone who could spend millions on a wall decoration was worth at least a quick look. I noticed Dominick Pastore sitting toward the front of the room with an elderly couple. Mary Lumpkin was seated farther back, between a famous French actress and a minor member of the British royal family who was known mostly for his furniture designs. Jack Nicholson sat in an aisle seat, wearing his shades. The audience whispered and turned the pages of their catalogs, as if they were reading the libretto of a strangely foreign but wonderful opera, while the porters brought out the next lot.

I found myself next to the girls manning the telephones. There were six or seven of them, standing in a narrow aisle on one side of the enormous room, connected to bidders from around the world. One of the telephone girls was speaking Arabic, another Japanese, a third German. As I wedged past them, they all glared at me in a language anyone would understand. I worked my way through the standing spectators and bidders packed like sardines along the side wall, until I made it to the back of the room.

'The next lot – number two-twenty in your catalogs – a lovely, small Picasso. What am I bid? Three? All right. I have three million dollars to start it. Who will say four?'

Looking back over my shoulder, I saw Carstairs standing beside the curtain, talking into a small radio, looking right at me. I stumbled along the back wall, pushing my way through the crowd.

'Five million two. At five-two – the bid is on the phone. Against the room. I have five-two . . .'

Glancing back again, I saw that Carstairs was making his way past the telephone girls, a determined look on his face. I stumbled and nearly fell over someone's feet. Cursing under my breath, I regained my balance, then turned and found myself looking up at Anthony Connatser.

'Jesus Christ, Adrian. What the hell are you doing?'

'At five million seven. The bid is now at five-seven – in the room –'

I grabbed Anthony by the collar, and standing on my toes, I spoke into his ear. 'I'm in trouble. Do you remember Devon?'

'Of course I do.' He looked down at me, then a frown creased his mouth as he noticed my bloody hands.

'Going once . . . twice . . .'

'Anthony, she's in danger – I have to get to her. There's a man following me. He's trying to stop me. Please, get in his way.'

I pointed to Carstairs, who had almost reached the back of the room. Anthony looked in the direction I pointed, and his frown deepened. I stumbled past him, over someone's toes.

'Go for it, Adrian. I'll try and delay him,' he whispered after me.

Surprised, I turned to thank him, but he was already angling toward Carstairs. Why he was willing to help was a mystery to me, but I didn't stop to think about it. I wove in and out of the crowd, dodging my way to the door.

'Six million now – I have six million – for the Picasso – now on the phone – against the room.'

Somehow I made it out of the main auction room and into the slightly less crowded side gallery. Those without the clout to obtain main-room tickets were watching the auction on closed-circuit monitors. As I was making my way through the pack milling at the back of the room, I saw two cops stop just inside the door that led to the front of the building. One of them spoke into a microphone clipped to his collar, while the other cop scanned the room.

I stopped where I stood, then held my hands, which

were still red with Hideo's blood, over my head and started screaming. 'Help me! Oh, my God – help!' I shouted at the top of my lungs. 'She's been stabbed – stop him – he's got a knife. Help – he's going to kill her!'

There was a momentary silence. Then I shoved a man standing near me into the back of another man, who knocked over a woman. She screamed as though she had actually been stabbed – and all hell broke loose. People jumped up from their seats. Men and women hurried toward the doors in a flurry of fur, silk, and pearls – pressing toward the exit in a surge of fear. The panic quickly spread into the main auction room. The auctioneer called out from the podium for calm, but nobody listened. The cops were drawn into the mêlée, shouting into their microphones, pushed along at the front of the exodus. I joined the panicked crowd flooding toward the exit.

In the pandemonium that followed, I managed to slip away. I hurried to where we had parked Tanaka's Mercedes, the keys ready in my hand. The silver one winked in the glare of the street lamps. The blood on my hands had dried into a sticky mess. I tried to wipe them on the leather seat, but it didn't help.

CHAPTER THIRTY

The silver key didn't fit the lock. I pushed harder, then turned it over and tried again. But no matter what I did, the key refused to slide home. Damn it, what the hell was I supposed to do now, knock? I rubbed my hands together and went over it carefully in my mind. The silver key, I was absolutely sure Hideo had specified the silver key. I examined the garage door to make sure there wasn't another lock.

There weren't many pedestrians on Seventy-second Street, but it didn't seem wise to stand out here indefinitely, fiddling with the lock on Tanaka's door. The Mercedes was double-parked half a block away. I tried to remember whether or not I had seen an automatic garage opener clipped to the visor. I went through the keys again, slowly, one by one, but none of them fit. I was getting desperate when I noticed that there was another door, a servants' entrance, set in the side of the building just to the left of the large garage.

Snow and ice were piled up against the lower part of the door – it obviously hadn't been used since the storm. I kicked a path through the frozen mound and tried the silver key again. This time it slid in noiselessly and turned with the slightest pressure. A faint click and I was in.

The servants' door opened into Tanaka's three-car garage, which I had already passed through once before this evening. But Oda had hustled me into the car so quickly that I hadn't had a chance to look around. It was empty now, but even in the dark it seemed cavernous, much larger than when the Mercedes had been parked in the middle bay. A slight odor of gasoline hung in the damp and musty air. I didn't look for the light switch; instead I crept slowly toward an illuminated crack under the door I knew led into the kitchen.

The alarm keypad was at eye level, to the right of the door. A small red light pulsed on and off, indicating that it was armed. I fumbled with the key ring, feeling for the barrel key. Somehow the ring slipped from my fingers, and the keys hit the concrete floor with a loud jangle that echoed through the empty garage. I dropped my hand to the pistol in my waistband and froze, holding my breath. An eternity passed. Nothing moved, no one came charging out of the kitchen. I started to breathe again. Kneeling, I felt around on the floor for the keys, but they didn't seem to be where I had dropped them. A rustling sound off to my left startled me. I froze again, this time on all fours, cold sweat dripping down between my shoulder blades. Listening, I faced the direction the sound had come from, but whatever had made the noise was quiet now. Probably just a rat, I told myself. Scrambling around on my knees, I finally found the lost key ring and breathed a sigh of relief. Standing, I inserted the barrel key and turned it until the light flashed green, then paused in case anyone inside noticed that I had disarmed the system.

Nothing. Drawing Hideo's gun, I checked to be sure that there was a round in the chamber, then hesitated again. The only man I had ever shot had been threatening me. Was I supposed to just walk in blasting away? I took a deep breath, tightened my grip on the gun, then slowly turned the door handle and pushed it open.

The kitchen was brightly lit with fluorescent tubes that reflected off the stainless steel fixtures, practically blinding me after the darkness of the garage. Blinking, I stood there for a moment, the gun heavy in my hand, unwieldy with the weight of the silencer. Nothing moved; I was alone. No guard in sight. The only noise was the hum of the restaurant-sized refrigerator.

The house was almost too quiet as I made my way down a long hall and then up the flight of back stairs that Hideo had described.

The second floor was even quieter than the first. All of the lights were on. It was eerie, creeping along inside Tanaka's house. Nothing stirred as I passed the open doors of what I took to be guest rooms. The beds were all neatly made, and the rooms themselves looked spotless, almost too perfect. Every few steps the hardwood floor of the hall creaked under my weight. My hand tightened around the gun, the checkering of the grip rough on my palm. There had to be someone standing guard. If they couldn't hear my footfalls, they could certainly hear the drumming of my heart.

As quietly as I could. I made my way down the hall, then around a corner until I finally stood outside the closed meeting room. I put my ear against the smooth wood of the door and listened but heard nothing.

'They won't be expecting you this soon,' Hideo had said. His words echoed loudly in my memory. He better have been right.

I pushed the door open and walked in like I owned the place, the gun extended in front of me.

The sickening stink of burned flesh almost overwhelmed me as I stepped into the room. I pivoted and swept the corners with the gun, trying not to gag. But with the exception of Marta's huddled form lying next to the platform, the room was empty. The nauseating stench seemed to come from an antique bronze brazier, set at the edge of the platform nearest to her. I pulled the door shut and stepped to where she lay on her side.

Kneeling, I put the gun down beside her head and rolled her onto her back.

Her eyes opened, and she let out a hoarse cry. 'Noooo!' and raised her hands as though to fend me off.

My breath caught in my throat. Marta's hands, two charred and clawlike appendages, reached for my face. I stumbled back. The skin, what was left of it, hung in shreds from what had been her slender fingers. Some of the bone was exposed, hideously blackened. Most of the flesh of both hands, almost to the wrist, looked as if it had been seared over an open flame. The skin of her arms was blistered to the elbow. Greasy, black soot stained her shoulders and face. The smell was worse now that I knew what had burned.

The brazier contained ashes and a few fragments of the remains of her book, identifiable only by the red leather scraps of what had been the cover. A can of lighter fluid and a small pile of kindling sat next to a pack of matches on the table between the two chairs. Beyond horrified, I tried to imagine how it had gone down.

I pictured the guard forcing Marta's hands over the brazier as Nakamura, or one of his henchmen, poured lighter fluid over them. I could see it as clearly as if I'd been there. Hear the scrape of the match as it was lit and then tossed into the brazier, which held the book and kindling, already soaked with the flammable liquid. I shook my head to dispel the image of the flames eating into her flesh, and wondered how anyone could do such a thing.

A pitiful whimpering sound originated in the back of Marta's throat and sent chills up my spine. I left off speculating and wiped my mouth on the back of my hand, then knelt beside her.

'Marta, can you understand me?'

Her eyes looked past me. Madness lit them from within. I wasn't sure there was anything left of the Marta I had known.

I gripped her shoulder and shook her gently. 'If you can hear me, I need you to tell me.'

She snarled then, tossing her head back and forth. Most of the cuts on her face had crusted over, but the slash in her lower lip split open and oozed a red stream.

The floor of the hall creaked. Someone was coming. I picked up the gun and crawled to the far end of the semicircle of chairs facing the platform. Crouched there, I braced the gun on the arm of the chair, the door filling the sights, and waited.

Marta cried out again, sounding like an injured child.

The door opened, and the guard who earlier had alternated watching us with Oda stepped into the room, his face buried in a newspaper. He walked to the chair nearest the door and sat. I could smell his lime aftershave mingling with the stench of Marta's burned flesh. He sat there reading, oblivious to her pain, unaware of my presence.

My blood ran cold. I stood and pointed the gun at his head. Hideo had said, shoot to kill. But I didn't know where Devon was.

He must have sensed the motion; he lowered the paper and looked up at me. His mouth opened in surprise.

'Not a fucking word,' I said.

He nodded and raised his hands, the newspaper falling to the floor.

'Stand,' I ordered.

He did, looking down at Marta as though worried she might somehow dirty his Italian loafers.

His expression was the final straw. I squeezed the trigger and shot him just below his left elbow. The force of the slug knocked him around and practically took his arm off. He grunted loudly as he fell back over his chair. He lay face up on the floor, clutching his left elbow with his right hand, mouth open ready to scream.

I was bent over him in less than a second, the muzzle of the silencer pressed hard against his forehead.

'Quietly! Where are they? Where's Devon?'

He shook his head slowly back and forth as if he didn't know.

I pulled the gun back. The muzzle had left a red ring on the skin of his brow.

I whispered the question again.

'Please, I don't know.' He was shaking, his face a pale shade of green.

It looked like he was about to go into shock. I wanted answers before he did. I pressed the gun against his good shoulder, right up against the bony part, and squeezed the trigger again. He shrieked as the bullet shattered the joint, but I smothered his cry with my free hand. He struggled against me, then passed out.

He didn't represent much of a threat any longer, but I removed the gun from his shoulder holster anyway and tossed it over by the windows. I stepped onto the platform and picked up the lighter fluid and matches, then returned to his side and nudged him, not too gently, with my foot. It took a few minutes, but his eyes fluttered open and he looked up at me in terror. Slowly, I poured a stream of the flammable liquid into his hair and up and down his body, soaking his suit. Then I pocketed the can.

'Please,' he begged, his voice a feathery whisper. 'Don't.'

'What's the matter? Not so much fun from that point of view, is it?'

I lit one of the matches.

'Downstairs. They're downstairs in the tatami room,' he gasped.

I held the flame closer.

'How many?'

'Four, maybe five,' he choked. 'Please.' His eyes were glued to the match.

'Is Nakamura with them?'

'No. I think he left the house for a meeting.'

This surprised me. 'Tanaka? Devon?'

He nodded, his eyes never wavering from the flame.

I glared at him as the match burned down. I longed to toss it onto his suit, to make a human torch out of this piece of shit. Judging from Marta's hands it would be poetic justice. But he was luckier than she had been. I didn't much like the role of judge, jury, and executioner. He'd told me what I wanted to know; I didn't have the stomach to punish him further. I'd leave that to whatever God he believed in, or the police, whoever got him first. Turning away, I blew out the flame, then tossed the extinguished match at him.

He let out a high-pitched wail, then a kind of keening noise.

Ignoring him, I bent and slid one arm under Marta's knees and one arm under her neck, then gently lifted her like a baby. She opened her eyes but didn't resist me. I carried her down the front stairs and laid her carefully down on the floor by the front door.

'Wait quietly,' I told her, not knowing if she understood. 'I'm going to get us all out of here.'

She managed to crawl into a corner, then she closed her eyes and curled up into a fetal position.

I left her like that and went to find Devon. Halfway across the reception room, I heard a door slam behind me. It seemed to come from somewhere down the hall that led to Tanaka's dance studio. I hesitated, wondering if I should take the time to check it out, or go straight to the tatami room, which was in the opposite direction. If there were two or three guards with Tanaka and Devon, the last thing I needed was an unexpected visitor while I confronted them. I decided to take a look down the hall.

The door to the dance studio was open, but nobody was home. I hadn't seen a dark room since I'd been here. All of the bright lights made prowling around the enormous house a truly bizzare experience. Somehow it would have seemed more natural to do this sort of thing in the dark.

A toilet flushed in the bathroom down the hall. I ducked into the studio and pulled the door partway shut. Following Oda's example, I left myself a clear view of the bathroom door through the crack.

Running water, then silence.

Sweat dripped into my eyes.

The bathroom door opened, but no one came out. The water ran again, then stopped.

I held my breath, the gun shaking ever so slightly in my hand.

The water went on again.

I couldn't stand the waiting any longer. Jerking open the door, I stepped into the hallway, then charged like a deranged rhino into the bathroom, gun first, nearly giving the Filipino maid heart failure and myself a good knock on the head when I slipped on the wet floor and went down at her feet.

She dropped her mop and fell to her knees, jabbering away in Filipino or whatever it was she spoke.

Scrambling up, I tried to get her to quiet down. 'Please, I'm not going to hurt you.'

She bowed low, her forehead on the wet marble floor, her rear end pointed skyward, talking even faster and louder.

I pulled her up by the elbow. 'Shhh!' In her white uniform she looked even younger than she had in her kimono.

She recognized me and stopped her yammering. Eyes narrowing, her hand against her mouth, she regarded me curiously.

'Do you understand English?'

She nodded.

'I'm not here to hurt you. My friend – I'm here to get my friend. Is she in the tatami room?'

'Yes,' she answered softly in her heavily accented English. 'With Tanaka and the guards.'

'Nakamura?'

'He gone. Just guards, woman, and Tanaka.'

'How many?'

'Three guards. All have guns.'

I nodded. 'Have you been in there lately?'

She looked at me, confused.

'Have you been in the tatami room tonight?' I spoke slowly.

'Yes. For tea. I bring tea.'

I asked her to describe where everyone was located. As far as she knew, there were only the three guards. Tanaka was at the far end of the room, watched by two of them. Devon was seated in the center of the room, the third guard near her at all times.

'Will they want more tea?'

'Soon,' she answered, looking at me with her almond-shaped black eyes.

Her face was pale, her skin marred only by a purplish bruise on her left cheek. How often had Tanaka beaten her? I wondered what circumstances kept her in his employ.

She continued to stare at me.

'You want I go in with more tea – you follow?'

Surprised at her offer, I nodded.

'Follow now, to kitchen.'

She put down her mop and stood, then led the way back to Tanaka's kitchen.

Once there, she put a kettle of water on to boil and set a tray with ceramic cups and a teapot. She spooned powdered green tea into the pot, looked up at me, then hawked and spit on top of it. She softly spoke an imprecation in her own language over the pot as she added the boiling water. Then as a final touch, she opened a drawer and pulled out a twelve-inch butcher's knife, which she laid on the tray and covered with a fine white linen napkin. Domestic help was clearly not what it once was.

She looked at me, her eyes glinting hard in the bright fluorescent light. 'They treat me like animal – like whore. You help me get home to Manila – I help you with guards.'

I nodded. 'I'll help you any way I can.'

She held my eyes for a moment longer, then turned back to her tray.

'You follow. Wait outside till hear noise. Okay?' Eyebrows raised, she pointed significantly at my gun, then picked up the tray and walked out of the kitchen.

I followed her through the reception room and down a narrow hall that led to the back of the house.

Crouching, I waited in the small room where Steven and I had changed from our street shoes into slippers before entering the tatami room to meet with Tanaka. It was the same night that I had found Paul's body. It seemed like it had happened a century ago.

The murmur of men's voices speaking Japanese was audible through the shoji screens.

The maid crouched next to me. She had set down the tray and was bowing and whispering a prayer. Her eyes were screwed shut. She couldn't have been more than nineteen.

I tried to picture the placement of the guards relative to where Devon was supposed to be in the center of the room. I had to take them down, get her out, then get a clear shot at Tanaka.

Abruptly the maid stood and picked up the tray. She used her foot to slide open the shoji screen. As she entered and slid the screen shut behind her, I waited off to the side where no one inside the room could see me. Then I took up a prone position, the gun in front of me, just outside the screen.

Inside the room one of the guards made a loud comment as the maid walked in. A sexual reference that by his tone alone I would have understood in any language. The other guards laughed gruffly.

I wondered what they'd think of the long blade hidden on her tray.

It bothered me that I hadn't heard Devon's voice. But there was nothing I could do about it now. I had to trust what the maid and the upstairs guard had told me and hope she was in there, in one piece. I gritted my teeth and waited.

It didn't take long. The tray crashed to the floor, and one of the guards suddenly bellowed in anger.

Noiselessly, I slid the door open about a foot and poked the muzzle of the gun in. The maid was standing at the far end of the room, her young face a mask of rigid anger. She held one of the men who had been guarding Tanaka by the hair, that wicked blade pressed hard against his throat.

'Now!' she screamed. 'Shoot now!'

The other guard at that end of the room stood facing her, looking uncertain.

Tanaka sat naked to the waist, smiling as the maid cursed and began shouting something in her native tongue.

Devon and her guard stood in the middle of the room, their backs to me, watching the drama unfold beside Tanaka. Devon's guard slowly reached behind him and eased an automatic from a holster at the small of his back. He thumbed the safety to the off position and began to raise his weapon.

My shot hit him in the center of the back.

The bullet caught him between the shoulder blades and slammed him facedown in Tanaka's direction. As he fell, his gun flew out of his hand and skidded across the straw tatami, coming to rest a few feet away from Tanaka's left foot.

Tanaka and the guard next to him swiveled their heads in my direction. Then nobody moved. Even the maid and her captive stared in surprise. Devon screamed, an ear-piercing cry of fear and anger.

Before anyone could respond, I was on my feet and inside the room.

Tanaka grinned up at me. His torso was covered with intricately drawn tattoos, inked in red and green, black, yellow, even purple. He was sweating, and the sheen of his skin reflected the bright lights in the ceiling and made the dragons and samurai, maidens, Gods, and warhorses intertwined in complicated patterns across his chest, arms, and back writhe and seem to come alive with each breath he took.

'Well, well, the junkie has returned. Where's the rest of the cavalry?' he asked, his voice sarcastic and mocking.

'Devon, turn around and come to me,' I instructed.

She pivoted and stepped toward me.

'Adrian,' she cried in relief.

She stumbled closer, somehow stepping between Tanaka and me.

He moved quickly, scooping up the fallen guard's gun and rolling to the side. Before I could react, he shot the guard who had been standing next to him, dropping him to the floor with a neat hole the size of a dime, drilled just under his chin.

The maid shouted something in Filipino, then buried the knife to the hilt in the throat of her prisoner.

'Move!' I screamed at Devon.

She did, slowly at first, then quicker as she got closer. I managed to squeeze off two rounds in Tanaka's general direction, but I don't think I hit him. Then Devon was beside me, and we dove back through the paper screen.

Tanaka fired several times in our direction, but the bullets crashed harmlessly through the tattered shoji screens, digging divots into the wall well over our heads. Crouching low, we scrambled out of the little room. First I had to get Devon out – then I would have to end this thing with Tanaka. Otherwise, it would simply start all over again.

The maid screamed. Another shot. And sudden silence. Then I was pulling Devon down the hall toward the front of the house as fast as we could go.

We made it into the reception room, running as fast as we could toward the front of the house. Devon was breathing hard. We didn't speak. Everything was moving at the speed of light. The adrenaline had tweaked my system into overdrive. I had slowed a little to try and dig the keys out of my pocket without stopping when a bullet whistled by my ear and smashed into the frame of the Gauguin, knocking it from the wall.

Devon yelped, then stumbled and fell, knocking over a table and a large crystal vase of sunflowers.

Pivoting, I saw Tanaka poke his head around the corner of the hall we had just passed through. I raised the pistol and fired, missing his face by inches, plaster shattering near his head. He ducked back and I pulled Devon to her feet. I fired once more in Tanaka's direction, hoping the bullet would punch through the wall and take him down. The slide of the gun locked back with a jolt. The clip was empty.

The two of us backed out of the reception room and stumbled toward the front door. I tossed the keys to Devon and dug frantically in my pocket for the extra clip I had taken from Hideo. I came up with the can of lighter fluid and tossed it away. Finally I got my fingers wrapped around the fresh clip, stripped the empty out of the gun, and slapped the new load home. I could hear Devon cursing as she fumbled with the keys.

'The silver one,' I shouted, raising the gun to fire again.

'Got it,' she called, opening the door.

Then a freight train hit me in the right side, knocking the wind out of my lungs and throwing me back against the door frame. The gun was still in my hand, but I couldn't lift my arm. I looked up in surprise as Tanaka entered the entrance hall, smiling wickedly, his gun pointed at my chest.

'Stop!' Devon screamed.

But he kept on coming.

I stood there, holding my side. Numbness was spreading down my right leg and up through my torso. Blood, warm and wet, soaked my shirt. I couldn't move. Cold air circulated against my back, blowing, I supposed, through the open door. I wanted to tell Devon to run, but I couldn't get enough air into my lungs to make any noise at all. I tried again to raise my pistol, but my arm wouldn't move. I might as well have been clutching a lump of coal.

'This would have been much more fun if you'd delivered the Monet first,' Tanaka said, stopping some five feet away from me. He shook his head. 'It's too late now.'

He raised the gun and aimed it at my head.

It wasn't fair. We'd come so close. It shouldn't have to end this way. I mouthed the word *no* and tried to raise my hands.

He grinned and said, 'Yes.'

His knuckle whitened on the trigger.

Then, from nowhere, Marta appeared. She stumbled toward Tanaka, howling like a banshee.

Startled, Tanaka's hand jerked and the shot went wide, stirring the air by my ear.

Marta fell on him, shrieking and waving her charred claws at his eyes.

Tanaka grimaced and turned to push her off.

Devon grabbed the back of my sweater, then jerked me through the door. We crashed backward out into the night, tumbling down the icy steps. My gun slipped from my hand, clattering uselessly to the sidewalk near where we landed in a heap.

'Get up,' she screamed, trying to pull me to my feet. 'Up, we have to move.'

But I was too tired. It was all I could do to stay awake.

We heard a shot from inside the house.

Devon screamed and pulled frantically at me.

I tried harder. With her help, I made it to my knees. Then I just couldn't move any farther.

Tanaka appeared at the top of the steps. Slowly he brought the gun up.

'Nooo!' Devon screamed again.

Desperately, I tried to lift my arm and push her behind me, but she had already moved to my left, scrambling away.

I braced for the impact, praying it wouldn't hurt.

Shots, a popping noise, not as loud as I would have thought. But I felt nothing.

Looking up, confused, I watched as Tanaka staggered back and stared past me, his eyes wide. He tried to bring the gun up higher, but more shots spit from a silenced gun and something plucked at the tattoos on his chest. The pistol fell from his hand, and he slowly collapsed at the top of the steps.

The night became quiet. Devon fell to her knees on the sidewalk beside where I lay.

'Stay with me, Adrian. Please stay with me.' She was crying.

'I'm not going away,' I whispered, wondering why she thought I might.

It seemed like hours passed with me lying on that sidewalk looking up at Devon. In a funny way it was kind of peaceful. My side didn't hurt, but I was cold. Clouds hung low in the sky, reflecting the lights of the city. I drifted for a while then Detective Carstairs was leaning over me, saying something to Devon about Dr Fulton.

She nodded but seemed not to be listening. He leaned closer and gently pried my gun away from her.

Her mouth was moving, but I couldn't hear what she was saying.

'What?' I asked, but they seemed not to hear me.

It made no sense. I tried to listen, to concentrate, but instead found myself drifting again.

'Where's Dr Fulton?' I tried to ask Devon.

But the words wouldn't come out. Nothing seemed right. The concrete thickened around me, as if I were sinking into it. I struggled to keep my head from going under. It was hard to breathe, and then there were sirens.

CHAPTER THIRTY-ONE

It was on the third day after the showdown. That's how I thought of it now, as the showdown, although I never referred to it that way out loud. Not even to Devon. On the third day of my hospital stay, Detective Carstairs sat down with his notepad and began to question me in earnest.

'You're a lucky man, Sellars,' he said, pulling a chair close to the bed. He smelled like stale cigarettes. 'That Devon is something else. Where do you think she learned to shoot?'

The nurse had catheterized me minutes before he had arrived. It hurt and I wasn't feeling all that lucky, but I couldn't help smiling at the thought of Devon, blazing away like Annie Oakley at the bad guys.

'Dr Fulton, he's something else, too,' he continued, even though I hadn't answered. 'Hell, when he threatened to call the mayor, I decided to take a ride and check things out for myself. I didn't believe him. Not at all. At least not until he convinced me that he had the mayor's private number. He does, you know?'

'Does what?' I asked. I'd been only partially listening to him ramble on. It wasn't because I didn't feel grateful. I was. If Detective Carstairs hadn't shown up when he did, I probably would have bled to death. But at that moment I hurt too badly to properly thank him.

'He really does have the mayor's private number. Imagine, I get a call from an old man I've never heard of, who tells me that he's worried about two friends that might or might not be in trouble at a mansion on

Seventy-second Street, owned by Japanese hoodlums. That's what he called them, Japanese hoodlums. When he threw out your name, I began to listen, but I still didn't take him seriously.' He shook his head. 'The mayor's private number, who'd have thought it?'

'Why were you at the Delmonico?' I asked, confused.

'I've been watching you since you moved in with Devon. McHenry's studio wasn't right. He was into more than restorations – but I didn't know what. Figured you were his partner. I was pretty sure you didn't do him, but thought keeping an eye on you might lead me to whoever did. I gave you plenty of rope – hoped his killers might make a play for you if you were dirty. Guess I got sloppy. Lost you during the snowstorm – then Dr Fulton called. When I took a drive by the house on Seventy-second, I saw the big guy push you into a Mercedes. I should have made a move then, but I didn't know what was going down, so I stayed close. I waited in front of the Delmonico, but when you didn't come out, I decided to find you. That's when you came off the elevator in such a hurry.'

I nodded, beginning to understand. I wasn't a suspect. I was the fucking bait.

'That was some move you pulled at the auction. Hell, you're practically a legend at Christie's. I'd imagine they have "shoot on sight" posters of you displayed. You messed up the biggest auction of the year.' He laughed.

'What took you so long to get back to Tanaka's house?' I asked, slightly less than amused.

'You did. If you hadn't started a damned riot, I might have been able to help you a little sooner. As it turned out, you're lucky I got there at all.'

'Well, I'm glad you showed up in time.' The understatement of the year. The man deserved my eternal gratitude, and here I was acting cranky. 'I'm sorry if I sound like an asshole. I'm a little sore.'

'I understand,' he said, a smile lighting his hound-dog features. 'You two did all right without me.'

He pulled out a cigarette, then felt in his pocket for matches or a lighter. He came up empty-handed, seemed to realize where he was, and shrugged as he mouthed the unlit smoke.

'Nasty habit. Tell me, how did it go down?'

'I'm not exactly sure. Devon pulled me out of the door backward – we fell down the steps – then I was looking up the barrel of that gun and praying. That's all I really remember.'

'The muzzle seems kind of big from that angle, doesn't it?'

'It looked like the entrance to the fucking Holland Tunnel.'

He laughed, then cocked his head to one side and opened his notepad.

'I've talked at length to Hideo Kagami. If he hadn't confirmed what Devon and Dr Fulton told me, I'd find this whole story a little hard to believe. You mind clearing up a few details for me?'

'No. Go ahead,' I offered, trying to scratch a spot on my back.

His questions were fairly simple, mostly regarding the timing of the events that led up to Steven Ballard's murder and the showdown. The cigarette bobbed up and down between his lips as he wrote.

When he had finished with his questions, I asked about Hideo.

'That is one tough mother. Balls like a fucking tiger. Doctors all say he should have bled to death. Guess it wasn't his time.' Carstairs shook his head in admiration.

'He'll be fine. On his way back to Japan soon, I'd imagine.'

'What about the Filipino maid?'

He shrugged. 'Not so lucky.'

'Could you get me an address for Hideo?'

He looked at me curiously.

'I want to write him – you know, say thanks and all.'

'Sure,' he nodded. 'I'll get his address for you.'

He returned to the hospital twice in the days that followed, asking me to fill in this detail or that. Apparently the Japanese authorities wanted a copy of his report but weren't interested in interviewing me themselves. I asked him if he thought we were safe now.

He scratched his nose. 'Nakamura's American operations are wiped out. You can bet our friend Hideo will be all over him in Japan. With his troubles, I'd guess you're pretty far down on old Nakamura's list of things to do.' He stood and started for the door, then stopped and added, 'But now that you mention it, you probably ought to stay away from raw fish for a while. Might want to avoid karaoke bars too.'

I thought he'd choke to death, he was laughing so hard when he left.

After his third visit, he handed me a sheet of paper with a Tokyo address on it, then put away his notebook.

'We need to talk about McHenry.'

I looked up at him. 'Have you caught his killer yet?'

He frowned. 'No – not yet.' He pulled at his long nose for a second. 'I'm not interested in what the two of you were up to. But there's a connection – we lifted prints from Devon's apartment after the burglary and got a match on the prints we lifted at McHenry's loft.'

'What!?'

Nodding, he went on. 'One of the two you tangled with killed McHenry. He'll do it again, you know. Whoever he is, he enjoys his work. He's got an aptitude for it. Have you told me everything about that break-in?'

I lay there stunned for a moment, then found my voice.

'Marta Batista,' I croaked. 'She sent them to Devon's apartment. Shit ... why would she want McHenry dead? It doesn't make sense – and now it's too fucking late to find out.'

Carstairs studied me.

'Was she trying to get to me? Even then?' I asked.

He looked down at me, shook his head and pulled out his pad again.

'I don't know, Adrian. Tell me what *you* know.'

He started writing as I described where Marta had lived and the gang kids who hung around the building. I gave him all of the details I could remember. He listened and wrote, then asked me to repeat everything a second time.

'I'll check into it,' he said, finally putting his notes away. 'Maybe it's not too late to catch them.'

After he left, I lay there trying to think it through. But nothing made sense. The more I thought about it, the angrier I got. But it was over – there was nothing more I could do, so I tried to let it go.

That night the nightmares started. Most of them involved Tenzo and Caitlin, even though I knew he was dead. She would be standing somewhere I didn't recognize, with Tenzo holding her arm, or patting her blond head with his soft pink hands. Neither of them ever said anything. Nothing terrible actually happened in the dreams, but the threat, the sense of menace I felt, was so intense that I usually woke up sweating and reaching for the phone to make sure Caitlin was safe, regardless of the hour.

After the second midnight conversation with Marilyn, she promised to have Caitlin call me every evening to say good night. It was a promise she actually kept.

Devon's parents had flown in from Europe. Apparently they weren't very happy about her involvement in what had happened. Between visiting me several times a day and handling them, she had her plate full.

She was sitting on the edge of the bed one morning, working a crossword puzzle, when I realized that I couldn't imagine life without her. I didn't say anything; words, for the first time in my life, seemed completely inadequate. I'm not sure how other men handle it when the light goes on, so I tried to remember what Cary Grant had done in the movies. I ended up staring pitifully at her all afternoon, unable to imitate Grant worth a damn. I got the feeling she already knew how I felt anyway.

I spent a lot of time sleeping. One afternoon after I'd been in the hospital for over a week, I woke in the dimly lit room, aware of a presence at the foot of the bed. It was Devon, wearing a raincoat.

'I've been acting like everything is fine, but it's not. I've been so worried about you – so scared,' she said, sounding sad.

'I'll be fine. I promise.' I looked up at her and started to choke up. 'I don't think I've said this yet – but thanks, Devon. You saved my life.'

Her face turned pink. 'You don't need to thank me. Just get better.'

I nodded. There was more to say, but I was on uncharted waters. I didn't want to blow it this time. Finally I just spit it out. 'Will you go to the beach with Caitlin

and me over Christmas? And maybe next Christmas –
and the one after that?'

Her eyes filled. 'Yes – I think I'd like that.' She
stepped to the side of the bed, bent, and put her arms
around me.

I kissed her and held her as tight as I could. We stayed
like that for a long time.

Dr Fulton visited on a daily basis too, which surprised
me. As cantankerous as ever, he did a lot to lift my spirits. Twice he brought cookies that Sophie had baked for
me.

'I've made arrangements through Otani to buy back
the forgeries,' he announced a few days before I was due
to be released. 'Had to sell a few shares of GM, but I
can't wait to see those paintings in person.'

'You'll be impressed.'

'I'd better be. Otani held me up pretty good. You'd
think there was a big market for fake art.'

I didn't know whether to laugh or cry.

'Damned highway robbery,' he muttered, settling
into his chair as though he intended to stay for a
while.

'Ask Devon if you want some good financial advice –
she'll help you make back whatever the paintings cost
you,' I told him.

'Oh, we've already talked about it.' He leaned closer
to my pillow and lowered his voice. 'She gave me a great
tip on some chemical company in Arkansas. Bought a
thousand shares.'

While we were talking, a strange little man in a cheap
suit and clip-on tie walked into the room.

'Mr Adrian Sellars?' he asked.

I nodded.

He removed a thick document from a cheap vinyl

briefcase, dropped it onto the bed, then turned and walked out of the room.

'What is it?' Dr Fulton asked, after I'd had a chance to look it over.

'It's a lawsuit. Oscar Fedder is suing me.'

'What in the world for?'

'I owe him money, but that's not all. He's claiming, and I quote here: "damages resulting from physical and emotional harm brought about as a result of the defendant forcibly and against the plaintiff's will, detaining the plaintiff in the defendant's place of business, and subjecting plaintiff to a brutal physical beating." ' I lowered the papers and shook my head. 'As if the whole thing was my idea. I warned him, but Fedder wouldn't listen.'

Dr Fulton laughed. 'Never have thought much of Oscar Fedder. It might've been worth it, just to watch him get his ass whupped.'

I laughed with him, even though it hurt my side. I didn't want to think about how much money I owed my various creditors. If this was an indication of what was to come, I wasn't going to be in business much longer. To hell with it, I thought, tossing the lawsuit onto the floor. Duncan Marshall could handle the Oscar Fedders of the world.

Dr Fulton got up to leave, then looked at me, a mysterious twinkle in his eye. 'I'll be back tomorrow. I want to show you something,' he said, somewhat cryptically.

'Do you still have the phony address book?'

'Yes,' he nodded.

'Nakamura got away. Eventually he's going to get around to evening the score. Caitlin . . . none of us will be safe. I want Hideo Kagami to have the book. Maybe he can nail the old bastard first. Would you see that it gets to him, safely? Right away – without a return address.' I handed him the slip of paper Carstairs had given me.

'I'll see to it.' He started out of the room, then hesitated and turned back. 'You know something, Adrian? I'm actually growing quite fond of you. You're the first art dealer I've ever felt that way about.'

Two days later the doctors released me.

The evening before I was to go home, Dr Fulton arrived, carrying a portfolio case. Without an explanation, he set the case on a chair and withdrew a small, ancient-looking leather folio, which he placed in front of me on the tray table.

'Have you ever heard of the Vinchenzino Folio?' he asked.

'No,' I replied.

He frowned.

'In 1494 Albrecht Dürer traveled to Italy to study the work of Mantegna,' he began, wasting no time in rectifying the situation. 'Dürer copied everything he could find of the master's work before returning to Nuremberg the following spring. While he was in Italy, he was taken in by a Florentine family named Vinchenzino. Before leaving he presented the family with a collection of twenty-five drawings he had made of Florentine life. This collection passed down through successive generations of Vinchenzinos until the turn of the nineteenth century, when it disappeared without a trace. Today it would be worth millions.'

I nodded, trying to pay attention.

Dr Fulton continued anyway. 'Before the collection vanished, it was written about and well described but never photographed. As a student, I wrote several papers about Dürer's Florentine drawings. Over the years I even tried my hand at producing some sketches that would give scholars an idea of what they might have looked like – although I never actually showed them to anyone.'

'Uhh, Dr Fulton –' I interrupted, beginning to suspect where this conversation was going.

'Now, it's not that I'd want to see these placed on the market as originals. No, I wouldn't want any claims to be made. But I would like for you to look at them. Tell me how you think they might be received by the *experts.*'

I knew how he felt about art experts, so I tried to head him off. 'Dr Fulton –'

'Don't misunderstand me, Adrian. I wouldn't actually let them be sold. Never. Under no circumstances. You know me better than that.'

'Do you realize –' I tried again, but he refused to be interrupted.

'It's just that I'm curious to see what the experts would say.' He went on as though I hadn't spoken. 'Paul fooled them easily enough. I want to know how good my drawings really are. Now, please, take a look.'

I started to open the stained and frayed kidskin folio, then thought better of it. 'Dr Fulton, I don't think it's a very good idea.'

'Nonsense, boy. A look isn't going to harm anyone.'

I glanced under the blanket at the bandages wrapped around my middle, then up at Dr Fulton, who stood at the foot of the bed, rubbing his hands together in nervous anticipation.

'I'm not so sure.'

'Just a quick look, Adrian. Then we'll have some fun with these damned experts.'

Fifteen days after the showdown I stood with Devon on the loading dock of the city morgue. It was the first stop

I made after leaving the hospital. Steven had been there long enough. We watched as the casket holding his body was placed in the back of an unmarked white van for the long drive to his parents' home upstate. He was going to be buried in the family plot.

Devon was quiet as the rear doors of the van slammed shut and the engine started.

'Let's go,' I said, taking her arm as the van pulled away.

My entire body hurt as we slowly made our way down the loading dock steps and walked out onto the sidewalk to catch a cab. Indian summer had made a late visit, and the day was almost balmy. Devon put on sunglasses, then held my cane while I fished a pair out of my pocket. She was meeting her mother for lunch. Duncan Marshall was expecting me at his office to plan the demise of Sellars and Ballard. It hadn't taken long for news of Fedder's lawsuit to become public knowledge. Soon all of my other creditors would be filing their own suits. There wasn't enough money or art to go around. I wasn't happy about the prospect of losing it all, but it didn't bother me nearly as much as I would have expected. Devon watched me limp along, the sun reflecting off the lenses of her shades. I couldn't help smiling at her.

She finally attracted a cab and held the door open for me to enter first. But the sky was so blue, and the sun so warm, that I really didn't want to spend the afternoon in a lawyer's office discussing various bankruptcy options.

'Why don't you go ahead. I think I want to walk a little.'

Devon smiled at me. 'You sure?'

'Yeah. I'm sure.'

'Six o'clock then. Be home by six, my father wants to take us to dinner before their flight.'

I promised to be there, then watched as her cab pulled into traffic.

I walked – actually hobbled – a few blocks, until I found an empty bench and sat like an old man watching the traffic go by. My side hurt like hell after I'd been on my feet all morning, but I had no intention of filling the prescription for Demerol I had in my pocket. Each pull, every little ache and pain, was proof positive that I was alive. And that was glorious, especially on a day like this. I didn't intend to ever dull that feeling again.

Closing my eyes, I tilted my head toward the sun. My face grew warm. New York swirled past me, but the noise of the buses and trucks, the sounds of a distant jackhammer, even the shouts and conversations of the pedestrians on the sidewalk around me faded and slipped away. I imagined Devon and me watching Caitlin on the beach. A warm breeze blowing onshore fluttered the umbrella over our heads and lifted whitecaps on the choppy blue sea. Caitlin was laughing, digging in the sand, wearing a pink and green bikini.

•

EPILOGUE

The granite steps leading up to the High Court in Tokyo were slick with the late spring rain. The winter had been colder than usual. The pain in Hideo Kagami's shoulder had seemed to intensify with every shift in the icy wind as he recovered from his wounds at a small clinic just outside of the city. But he was back home, and the pleasure of being back in Japan after so long made even the fierce cold bearable. He took the steps slowly.

A group of reporters were gathered by the massive front doors, waiting to hear the charges as one of Japan's most powerful gangsters was about to be indicted for a laundry list of criminal activity. None of them noticed Kagami as he passed slowly in front of them and entered the hall of the High Court. He had been undercover for so long now that anonymity had become almost second nature to him. Today he was dressed conservatively, his hair short, his suit neither too cheap nor too expensive. He was middle of the road, indistinguishable from millions of his countrymen who worked office jobs for the companies that made up the large trading *keiretsu*.

He passed through the metal detectors, then waited with a group of other curious court-watchers for the next elevator. Several of those waiting with him were members of one criminal syndicate or another. They stood out from the other spectators, identifiable by their flashy suits and wraparound sunglasses – their permed hair, two-tone shoes and too loud voices. Kagami smiled to himself and thought about his days as Stan.

Sometimes he missed the freedom that Stan had enjoyed in America. Then he shook himself out of his reverie and entered the elevator with the others. Freedom was, after all, just an illusion, no more a reality than any of the other joys or hardships encountered in this life. Karma, it was all about karma.

By the time he slipped into an aisle seat at the back of the crowded courtroom, the three judges had already taken their seats on the dais and the court had been called to order.

'Your Honor, the defendant, Noburo Nakamura, is charged with crimes ranging from extortion and tax evasion to drug and weapon charges.' The prosecutor stood as he delivered the formal indictment against Nakamura.

Nakamura sat at the defendant's table whispering with his lawyers, the best money could buy, as the prosecutor listed charge after charge. From time to time, he would turn and wave to one associate or another, as the seats directly behind him filled with a supporting cast of other gangsters and family members. He looked relaxed, not at all troubled by the crimes he was charged with.

Hideo Kagami shook his head and smiled in spite of himself. The old man thought he would beat the charges. Expected to get off because he was owed too many favors by too many powerful men to ever stand trial.

Karma, Hideo thought. Things are the way they are.

He listened closely as the prosecutor finished reading the indictment. Nakamura's lawyer stood and asked to address the court. Now things would get interesting.

'These charges are ridiculous,' Nakamura's lawyer began. 'Unsubstantiated rumor and innuendo. It's a classic case of governmental abuse. My client respectfully asks that you dismiss these charges immediately.'

The prosecutor was on his feet. 'Your Honor, this is out of line. The defendant hasn't even entered a plea. There are no grounds to ask for a dismissal.'

The head judge briefly conferred with the two associate justices while the two opposing lawyers stood waiting for him to say something. Then the head judge cleared his throat and addressed the prosecutor. 'Do you have substantial proof of the charges you have brought against Mr Nakamura?'

The prosecutor smiled. 'Your Honor, the charges are in order. As the trial progresses I will offer ample proof of the defendant's guilt.'

Kagami stifled his own smile. The judge, who was probably bought and paid for, was in for a surprise. So was Nakamura.

'Your Honor, my client is a well-known philanthropist. His charitable acts are numerous, and he has never in his life been charged with a crime. These fictions, created by the prosecution, are beyond absurd. I ask that the court take into consideration the age and record of my client, and demand that the court hear this so-called evidence before formalizing any charges against Mr Nakamura.' The defense lawyer smiled at the judge, then looked portentously at the prosecutor.

Kagami sat forward in his seat. This was usually the time when these cases fell apart. The lead witness, having been threatened or worse, forgot his story or recanted. Any additional witnesses would follow suit, forcing the judge to dismiss the charges. Today, Kagami was confident that things were going to unfold differently.

The prosecutor reached into his briefcase and

withdrew a small, battered red leather address book. 'Your Honor, I would like to call the State's first witness – if the court is ready to proceed?'

The head judge nodded. 'You may proceed.'

There was a stirring at the back of the courtroom as a uniformed deputy pushed the slight form of a woman down the aisle in a wheelchair. A blanket was draped over her lap, and white bandages covered the stumps of her arms where her hands should have been. As she passed by Kagami, she looked over and caught his eye, then twisted her crooked lips into an ever-so-slight smile. But it never touched the bleakness in her frigid eyes. Kagami shivered involuntarily as she was pushed toward the witness stand.

'The State calls Marta Batista.'